KW-222-025

THE SPECIAL COUNTER-INTELLIGENCE BUREAU

THE SOUTHERN STAR

THE SPECIAL COUNTER-INTELLIGENCE BUREAU

THE SOUTHERN STAR

STEPHEN HUGH DODGSON

ATHENA PRESS
LONDON

The Special Counter-intelligence Bureau:
The Southern Star
Copyright © Stephen Hugh Dodgson 2009

All Rights Reserved

No part of this book may be reproduced in any form
by photocopying or by any electronic or mechanical means,
including information storage or retrieval systems,
without permission in writing from both the copyright
owner and the publisher of this book.

ISBN 978 1 84748 462 8

First published 2009 by
ATHENA PRESS
Queen's House, 2 Holly Road
Twickenham TW1 4EG
United Kingdom

Printed for Athena Press

I dedicate this book to my wife, Maria. My inspiration, without whose help and support this project would never have seen the light of day.

Thank you, my darling.

January 2008

CONTENTS

IT NEVER RAINS

It was still the early hours of the morning and the sun had not yet risen when the secure wagon, known in those days as a paddy wagon, pulled up at the rear entrance of the Western Canadian Bank. This was the largest and strongest bank on the west coast of Canada. The reason for such an unusual occurrence was the transportation of the largest and most valuable clear diamond in the world, the 'Southern Star'. Its owner had been the Earl of Monmouth; he had just passed away and it had been left to his distant cousin – Queen Victoria, his only living relative. It had been given its peculiar name because it had first seen the light of day in a mine in Natal. Now it was about to begin its arduous and dangerous journey back to Britain. It was the first time that this particularly precious stone had seen the light of day in many a year.

Once the wagon had drawn to a halt, the guard leapt down to the road and, banging with his fist upon the side, indicated to his colleague inside to open the door. As his colleague opened it, the guard stepped over towards the rear entrance of the bank, and again he banged upon the door with his fist. The door opened almost immediately and a face peered around it.

'Secure wagon,' the guard announced.

The door was opened and the guard stepped into the bank, where he was met by the sight of several clerks scurrying to and from the front entrance, carrying heavy wooden boxes.

These boxes contained in total three thousand pounds, a sum transferred once a year from the west coast of Canada by train and paid into the Governor General's treasury. This shipment consisted of cash made up from paid taxes and various bank customers' payments. The timing of the transfer was carefully chosen in advance, as at this early hour few people or none were to be found wandering about in the street until the station was reached. Still, little was left to chance; although the station was barely three blocks away, armed security guards had been placed strategically upon the roofs of each corner building, giving each man a clear view of the street below. The departure time of the particular train was also brought forward to coincide with the delivery of the valuable goods and to avoid leaving them standing at the station.

The clerk who had initially opened the door to the guard now brought forward a supervisor, who was carrying a smaller box. This he handed over to the guard, who accepted it, turned and left, returning to the secure wagon. There he placed the box with his colleague inside, who then closed the door behind him; the guard returned to his position by the driver before the wagon pulled away from the curb.

At precisely the same time a similar wagon drew away from the bank at the front; both were heading to the station. The one carrying the money travelled down the main street, while the one carrying the stone followed an adjacent route by back lanes. Once at the station, both were driven into the covered section of the goods yard, to be loaded into the specially designed and secured caboose. This was to be guarded by three armed members of the railway company. Security was helped by the fact that the caboose was to be totally isolated from the rest of the train – there was no internal or external corridor and only two small windows, both in the roof. Generally the cash was carried in one Chubb safe, but today a second safe, built to the same specifications, had been placed next to the original to carry the precious stone. Each was to be locked by three separate keys, all held within the caboose by the man in charge of security – a Mr Tindale. As soon as the money and the diamond were loaded, the caboose doors were shut, locked and bolted from the inside. Once done, the signal was given and amidst much noise and steam the locomotive hauled the caboose into position at the end of the station platform, so it backed onto the train itself. All the passengers had boarded earlier, and the platform now deserted except for two or three armed security men skulking within the shadows. The train pulled out of the station amidst a cloud of steam and smoke, and to the serenade of screaming and screeching wheels. The journey from west to east would take a week and the train would travel through some of the most impressive scenery in the world. After three days it left Calgary and the Rocky Mountains behind as it set off for the plains of central Canada.

Being the height of Canadian summer, the temperature began to rise, especially within the caboose. Most of the time the three occupants sat and played cards among themselves or read. Each one was a trusted railway company employee. Mr Thomas Tindale, as the senior employee, was in charge; he was to be assisted by Mr Alfie Fox and Mr Donald Munro. They were normally employed as railway guards and together could muster thirty-one years of experience.

Each one was a respectably married, God-fearing man; although, Alfie Fox's wife had been suffering from reoccurring nightmares. In them her husband would be held down at the waist by some force or weight, and a black silhouette of a cowboy type of character would stand over him. What happened next she could not say, for she always awoke at that point, soaked in sweat. Not matter how hard Alfie tried to calm her, the nightmare did not go away.

To try to cool their caboose down, Donald, being the tallest of the three, had opened both windows, creating a nice breeze. The train now trundled across the plain; as it passed a lake it began to veer to the left in a wide circle as it aimed for a narrow pass among some rocks. The engine driver, looking lazily ahead, noticed some tree trunks lying across the track and instinctively began to slow, blowing the train's whistle as he did so.

Thomas looked up, concerned. 'We are slowing down,' he remarked.

'This is not a normal stop, is it?' questioned Donald.

All three men stood up and listened intently, trying to work out what was wrong.

'Can you hear anything, Tom?' asked Alfie.

Thomas shook his head as he listened for the least bit of noise.

Donald stood by the wall, now fingering his revolver nervously. Each man was armed not only with a revolver but also with the Winchester repeating rifle.

The train came to a stop and soon the men could hear the driver and the guard shouting at each other.

'What's the problem?' asked the guard.

'Fallen timbers,' replied the driver.

As the trees had not been laid across the track in straight lines but laid across haphazardly, no one suspected anything untoward. The fireman climbed down from the train and had walked to the front of the engine. The sight that he beheld stopped him dead in his tracks, for there in front of him, sat upon a rocky knoll, was a tall, thin unshaven man; he was pointing a gun straight at the fireman.

'What can you see up there?' shouted the engine driver.

The fireman did not respond and remained rooted to the spot; he could not take his eyes off the gunman stood in front of him.

'What can you see, goddamn it?' shouted the engine driver again. His impatience got the better of him and he climbed down and was joined by the approaching guard.

As the guard walked past the caboose, he stepped up to the doors.

'Are you all right in there? Do not worry – there are just some fallen timbers to clear away!' he shouted through the door.

Just then a shot rang out from the front of the train. The guard and engine driver instinctively spun round to see what it was, although subconsciously they both knew. As they looked to their front they saw the body of the fireman fly backwards. Then a loud 'Whoop!' was shouted by several voices from the trees and several shots were fired at the train. The engine driver spun and fell, shot in the arm, as several riders now came into view. The man who had shot the fireman stepped from around the front of the train.

'Well, howdy, gentlemen! Ah'm sorry for the delay; yet, if you just pass over the money, ah shall let you be on yer way,' he greeted the two men jovially in a southern American drawl.

'Who the hell are you?' demanded the guard; he had rushed forward to assist his driver and now stood up to face this newcomer.

'Ah think we ought to teach this man some manners, don't you, Ted,' declared one of the mounted men; they had come to a halt next to the train and dismounted. Ted glanced up and, having flicked his head as some sort of signal, four of the men clambered aboard the first carriage.

Laughing loudly, they ordered everyone to remain seated and then began to take personal possessions, bags, watches, jewellery and rings. One passenger refused to hand over his watch to a well-tanned, almost swarthy fellow, who just sneered in return; he did not say a word but raised his revolver and shot the man at almost point-blank range.

'There now, do you think he feels better for that?' he shouted at the terrified passengers.

His companion looked about him. 'Just hand over your possessions and we will leave you alone,' he advised.

While this was going on, Ted had now pulled the guard over to stand in front of the caboose door.

'Tell the men inside to open up please,' he instructed the guard.

'No – no, I won't do that, neither would I expect them to open it,' replied the guard defiantly.

One of the men now knocked the guard to his knees and Ted withdrew his revolver from his holster and held it to the guard's head.

'Now, I am being very polite, but please ask, or I'll blow your head off,' he warned calmly as he cocked the gun.

The guard swallowed hard, he was beginning to sweat and shake uncontrollably. 'Open the door,' he stammered.

There was no reply. Inside, the three men had taken up positions behind the furniture and Donald glanced at Thomas nervously; the palms of his hands were wet and clammy.

Ted, now still holding the gun to the guard's head, now spoke up. 'My name is Ted Skerrat; you may or may not have heard of me. However, I am about to count to three, if you do not open the door by then I will shoot the guard.'

He paused. Still no sound came from the caboose; all that broke the silence were the excited shouts and hoots of the four gangsters on board the train and the whimpering and screaming of some of the women. 'One...' he began to count loudly. 'Two... Three...' There was still no sound from the caboose.

Without glancing to his left he squeezed the trigger and shot the guard through the head. Quickly replacing his revolver he turned to his two companions. 'OK boys, let's blow it.'

They ran forward excitedly with two canvas bags holding sticks of dynamite.

Donald turned to Thomas. 'You don't think they shot him, do you?' he asked nervously. He too began to shake and it was taking all his strength to control his bowels.

'Damn, we're trapped like rats in a barrel!' cursed Alfie; he had placed himself to one side behind a chair while Thomas and Donald were hiding behind the table.

Ted lit the fuse and the three men dashed to some rocks where they hid for cover. The engine driver instinctively began to run to the front of his engine, but then, realising that his three companions were still inside the caboose, he turned.

'Watch out – they are—' his shout of warning was cut short by a single shot from one of Ted's fellows in crime. Before he could be congratulated, though, the whole ground shook and there was a great roar. The caboose rocked and jolted, and shards of timber were blown into the caboose itself. Donald was killed outright when a large shard flew into his chest knocking him backwards. Another shard struck Alfie in the shoulder; as he lay helpless on his side the top safe, now shaken loose, toppled over and landed on his legs, pinning him to the floor. Even Thomas had been cut by flying wood; he was totally disorientated and stood up, trying to clear his mind. The three men stepped into the caboose; they shot Thomas repeatedly where he stood. He was dead before he hit the floor. Alfie struggled to try to reach his gun, which had been thrown clear as he fell; he could not see much until a black silhouette stepped against the bright sunlight. Ted did not say a word; he merely looked down on the prostrate Alfie.

'Oh God, oh God,' was all Alfie could say, as the realisation of his fate now hit him.

Ted shot Alfie three times, then looked at him, uninterested.

'Holy Jesus, look at this, Ted!' cried one of his colleagues. He had checked Thomas and had found the three keys which in turn opened the first safe.

The second man looked up. 'What is it, Abe?' he asked.

'Just come and look at this?'

Ted stepped over to the safe Abe was peering into. There sat the biggest diamond he had ever seen. He began to laugh, slowly at first, his voice rising to a hysterical pitch. 'We've struck it rich, boys!' he declared as he reached out and took hold of the stone.

They all began to laugh and dance. Abe opened the second safe, and there sat all of the money. 'Boy, the Colonel is going to love us, eh, Ted?' he said not glancing over his shoulder.

Ted stopped laughing immediately and, grabbing hold of Abe violently, he pinned him back against what was left of the table.

'The Colonel is not to know of the stone, all right,' he warned through gritted teeth.

'Yeah, yeah – sure, Ted, if you say.' Abe spoke slowly, carefully; he knew Ted Skerrat of old – as cool as ice but as dangerous as a scorpion.

The second man hurried over to the horses. There he fumbled around with the saddlebags, then returned to the caboose with all seven. He and Abe began to stuff all the money into these. Ted wrapped the Southern Star into his handkerchief then slipped it into his pocket. He jumped down from the caboose and began to walk slowly along the length of the train. He still could hear Joe and the Irishman, Danny, aboard the railway carriage, shouting at the passengers. Joe was ordering them to place all their valuables into a bag. He was also helping himself to those valuables that the passengers had not given up, such as earrings, necklaces, rings, pocket watches and even cigarette cases. Danny followed Joe along the carriage, though he was silent and contented himself with taking those valuables the passengers had already given up.

Ted thumped on the side of the carriage. 'OK, Joe, Danny, let's go.' Without waiting for a reply he marched towards the next carriage. Again he could hear the two men shouting, cursing and threatening the passengers into giving up their valuables. This time Ted simply pulled his gun from its holster and fired once into the air. By the time he had re-holstered his gun, the four men were hurrying towards their horses, where Abe and his comrade were waiting.

'Let's mount up,' ordered Ted. Soon they galloped off, firing their pistols in the air and whooping and shouting as they rode off, their job done.

The area about the train was now silent except for the rhythmic hissing of the engine as steam escaped from its boiler. At first the passengers were either too shocked or simply too frightened to move from their carriages. Nevertheless, soon two or three men ventured outside and clambered to the ground. There they found the bodies of the railway staff – the guard and driver next to the engine and caboose, the three men lying inside what remained of the caboose, then finally the fireman at the front of the engine. Still uncertain as to what to do, they wandered about or sat down upon the ground, stunned. Women and what children were upon the train wept.

'What shall we do?' asked one man.

'Where shall we go?' asked another.

'It would be best to wait here for help to arrive. The authorities will miss the train this evening and should be here by morning,' advised a third.

So they waited for help to arrive.

Meanwhile Ted Skerrat and his men rode as if the devil himself were chasing them. They realised too that the authorities would miss the train from the next settlement that evening and, with the aid of telegraphy, it would not take long for them to realise that the train had left its last destination and would soon be overdue. So they wanted to put as much distance between themselves and the railway as possible before then. They were making for the Canada–United States border via a well-known pass called Pine River Valley, which ran due north to south between Saskatchewan in Canada and Montana in the United States. But first they had to get clear of the area. Paradise Valley was still some distance away. Ted rode his gang hard until well after dark. Then and only then did he stop to rest. His men lit a fire and they all settled down around it to count their spoils.

'Do not forget that only what was taken from the passengers is ours, men. The money belongs to the Colonel and he knows how much to expect,' Ted warned them.

Abe and his companion sat, waiting expectantly to hear about what else had been found. Ted noticed them watching him, and he smiled to himself; of all the people who had seen what was also found it had to be Abe – probably the worst person in the world at keeping secrets.

'Also, we found this upon the train, gentlemen.' Ted produced the wrapped handkerchief; he slowly and deliberately began to unfold the cloth. 'Now, I know the Colonel is not expecting this.' He held up the diamond, which sparkled, illuminated by the fire roaring and crackling in front of the gang.

The men sat stunned, wide-eyed in astonishment.

'Here,' Ted passed the diamond on to the next man. 'You can feel what it's like to be rich, boys,' and with that he began to laugh loudly.

The diamond was slowly passed around the fire, each man in turn taking great care to study it like an expert; of course they were nothing of the sort, but who was going to tell them that in their hour of success? Eventually, the stone came back to Ted, who wrapped it up once more in his handkerchief and placed it back in his pocket.

'Now boys, the Colonel knows nothing of the diamond. So ah reckons it's ours. So there's no need to tell him.' Ted looked long and hard at Abe. 'All right, Abe?' he asked.

'Sure, Ted! You knows me – ah'm not one for telling,' responded Abe defensively.

The others began to snigger. Ted glanced up slightly, allowing the glint in his eyes to be discerned just beneath the brim of his hat. 'Now looky here, if anyone breathes a whisper to anybody outside this group, before I have managed to get our money's worth for this stone... then woe betide him.' He looked menacingly around the group. 'Do I make myself clear, boys?'

They all nodded and grunted their approval.

'You better had be telling the truth, Mr O'Brien. Otherwise you will be joining your ancestors,' threatened the smaller of the two men that Paddy had led into a building. It stood opposite the impressive government buildings in Montreal; it was now close to the Governor General's appointed time of arrival. The men who Paddy now led into the opposite building were Métis assassins;

things had still not calmed down since the 1870 rebellion, and this was to be their moment of glory. Sandy stood inconspicuously upon the stone steps; he had observed Paddy leading the two men in to the building and had nodded to him in acknowledgement.

'Up here,' declared Paddy as he began to ascend the stairs; he did not turn around to see if they were still following – he knew that they would be.

Charlotte peered carefully around the door frame at the base of the stairs. She quickly disappeared again to check her revolver and a new wrist gun that all four of the team had been issued with before this assignment. It was to be worn on either wrist, held one round and, when cocked, would fire on the impulse of the wrist muscle as it was raised, in the event that the wearer had to raise his or her hands. She still retained her throwing knives, which that she carried in a belt around her waist.

The Métis were of half-French, half-Indian ancestry. They had resisted British rule and had continually moved west ahead of the advancing British empire. By 1870, with the incorporation of Rupert's Land and the North-West Territories, they had nowhere else to go. Rising briefly in rebellion against the British and led by Louis Riel, they had brutally executed a political opponent of Riel's called Thomas Scott. In spite of this, before the British turned up, they had fled west into Saskatchewan. Alas, even this became part of the Dominion of Canada by 1878. Coupled with economic hardships this led to further turbulence in 1885, and were again put down, this time after some actions were fought. Their leader, Riel, was captured by the British and executed in the November.

Feelings were still running high and so it was that Will and his team Storm Force Alpha found themselves in an uneasy Canada. After the government received warnings of an assassination plot they had called upon Lord Porter to send a team to protect the Governor General.

After contact was made with the assassins, Will and his team had devised a plan with which to trap all of them. Sandy was to protect the Governor General when he was to turn up and act as personal bodyguard. Charlotte was to wait at the base of the stairs to make sure no one was following Paddy and the first two assassins. After leaving them in the room, opposite the theatre steps, Paddy was to retrace his own steps back down to the street; there he was check and make certain there was no one else lurking nearby. He was then to return to the room along with Charlotte. Will was waiting in the very next room for his moment. He was to offer them the opportunity to surrender, before eliminating them.

Will was in actual fact sitting at a desk in the very next room. He heard Paddy open the door. Will himself had left the interconnecting door open. It sounded as if all three men walked into the room.

'This better not be a trick, Fenian,' the taller man threatened.

'Look, Jean, we have a good view from here,' the second smaller man stated as he walked over to the window. He knelt down before he reached it so as not to be seen from the street below.

'All right, Fenian, you have completed your part. Go, we do not want some squealing Irish pig giving us away,' the first man now stated to Paddy.

Will heard the slamming of the door and assumed that Paddy had gone. Without saying a word, he stepped up to the doorway and was able to watch through the gap between door and frame, as the two men set themselves up at the window. He cocked his own wrist gun which was worn on his left wrist, leaving his right hand free to throw his knife. This he now slipped into his hand, the blade and handle hidden by his jacket sleeve.

Charlotte watched Paddy descend the stairway; he looked across at her and smiled before heading out into the street. There in the beautiful summer sunshine, he glanced about him. The street was now beginning to fill up with people and the North-West Mounted Police, better known as the Mounties. Paddy then looked across at Sandy and, by touching his forehead, he gave the signal that all was now in place. Sandy had observed this and, realising that the Governor General was now not far away, he loosened his jacket and felt for one of his revolvers. As always he was carrying two, one under each arm.

Satisfied that there were no further Métis assassins, Paddy turned and hurried back into the building. As he hurried past her,

Charlotte stepped out from her hiding place and followed him up the stairs.

Meanwhile, Will, observing that the two French-Indians were becoming a little excited, stepped into the room. At first he was not noticed, so he cleared his throat to get their attention.

'Good morning, gentlemen. I'm afraid your game is up and I must insist upon your surrender,' he said calmly.

The two men spun round, shock and horror written across their faces.

'That Irish pig double-crossed us!' exclaimed the taller one of the two and he began to raise his rifle from under his coat.

Will was not willing to give him – or anybody else for that matter – two chances. He raised his hands as if to surrender, causing both gunmen to hesitate. That was all that was required; the wrist gun fired, killing the first man and throwing him backwards over his companion. He, trying to struggle to his feet, looked as if he too was trying to raise his rifle. This left Will with no option but to throw his knife into him, killing the man instantly. After pausing slightly, Will stepped over to the two dead men just as the room door was kicked open and Paddy and Charlotte's arms appeared outstretched into the room, revolvers in hand.

'Nice little toy, that.' Will smiled as he checked his wrist. 'At least it works.' He glanced at his two companions.

'Decided to go out in a blaze of glory, eh?' remarked Paddy as he too walked over to the two men. He looked down upon the taller one of the two. 'Well, if you hadn't shot him, I certainly would have,' he sneered.

'Paddy, that is most unlike you!' cried Charlotte.

'He has been really goading me over the past couple of days,' replied Paddy, as he re-holstered his revolver.

Will glanced down through the window to where Sandy stood. He was looking up, hoping to see his comrades. Will waved down and Sandy smiled one of those boyish smiles of his in return.

'Come on, let's get out of here and go home,' declared Will as he retrieved his knife from its victim and they all left the room.

It was now a year since they had followed Von Klugge's gang across Europe and dealt it a fatal blow in Montenegro. Will had taken Madeleine home with him and had introduced her to Rosie, his lovely young daughter. Thankfully, the pair had instantly got on well together – so much so, that he had been able to set up home with Madeleine and she now looked after Rosie. This also had the blessing of his parents and after this assignment they were to be wed. Of course Paddy, Charlotte and Sandy were to be there, as well as Hannah and Lord Porter – in fact Paddy was to be best man, and Charlotte was to be chief bridesmaid, while Lord Porter was to have the honour of giving Madeleine away.

Paddy had returned to Ireland and had taken Charlotte with him. Together they had toured around the countryside; from Charlotte's point of view she had never enjoyed herself so much. As for Sandy, he had returned home to Tyneside; as always, all he had said about it was that 'it was good to get a break'. Charlotte still had feelings towards Sandy, although he had as yet not responded nor said anything. She thought he might have been on the verge of saying something once or twice when she caught him looking at her, but as yet he had been most silent on the matter. Paddy had offered to prompt him, but Charlotte had asked him not to – much to Paddy's chagrin.

After returning to Drumloch from leave they had been quite busy, not only on other cases but also because training was an ever-present task and they also had to take their turn at security duties around the castle. Archie had observed Charlotte training her team colleagues in the art of t'ai chi ch'uan, better known today as kung fu. Charlotte was also well acquainted with ju-jitsu and, following an investigation of the oriental arts by Lord Porter, he approved of a training program with which to train all present and future agents in ju-jitsu. He further instructed Charlotte to train Archie in the use of the many weapons that could be used and, more importantly, the philosophy behind the weaponry. Charlotte had been taught in the art of fighting by Buddhist monks from Tibet; they in turn used the philosophy of the ninja, especially within the art of ju-jitsu passed down by each sensei through time.

Thanks to Lord Porter's – and to a certain extent Archie's – foresight, this meant merely adapting present training techniques as opposed to starting from scratch. For instance, Charlotte had had the importance of stealth, subterfuge, disguise, patience and trickery impressed upon her at every given moment by her trainers in Tibet. This she was at pains to pass on to Lord Porter and Archie. Lock picks, small crowbars, ropes, grappling irons and collapsing ladders were introduced, as well as new weaponry which sometimes Charlotte advised upon accepting, such as a hollow staff in which a sword which contained; this was now carried by all agents. This, she insisted, was to remain blunt, so that the blade could be grasped and the handle used as a hook for pulling the user up walls. Alternatively the blade could be placed into the ground and the handle used as a step; a cord attached to the handle allowed the sword to be lifted once the operative was in place. Weighted chains for entangling opponents' legs when thrown was another new weapon. A hollow sheath which held the dagger could be converted into a blowpipe for discharging pepper or chilli dust into pursers eyes. It could also be used as a snorkel for hiding or moving underwater and Charlotte taught her colleagues as well as Archie how to use it when hiding under soil or leaves. She also showed them how to use a Jo stick or heavy club.

But the two items that created the greatest excitement within the organisation were the shuriken, or throwing stars, that Charlotte soon showed she was a past master in the use of, although, she still preferred her throwing daggers and the shuko, or 'tiger claws'. These fitted over both hands and feet and enabled the operative to climb not only trees and wooden walls but also stone walls; they could also be used as a close combat weapon. Finally Charlotte introduced the nonchaku, small heavy rods connected together by a short chain. Regrettably, not everyone could actually get to grips with these and, many bruised eyes and lumps and bumps later, it was decided that only Charlotte should use them. Along with abseil training and other weapons of a much more modern era – such as the wrist gun and the tripwire connected to a bundle of dynamite placed around a detonator – these had kept all the agents rather busy.

Acquaintances had been improved upon, as had friendships. Charlotte got on well with all the other female members – especially Elizabeth, who was becoming very close to Charles. She was also becoming very close to Hannah and they had returned to Hannah's for the Christmas of 1890. Although this ranked as certainly one of the best Christmases in Charlotte's memory, it was slightly dampened by the fact that Sandy still had not said anything to her regarding his feelings. This had been noticed by Hannah one evening while they sat by the fire relaxing.

'Penny for your thoughts?' Hannah had asked her.

Charlotte smiled coyly. 'Oh, you would not want to know,' she had replied sheepishly.

'It's Sandy, isn't it?' Hannah had asked.

'Is it that obvious?' Charlotte had asked.

'You do think a lot of him, don't you. Remember – he is an ex-seaman,' Hannah had teased.

'Oh, what is wrong with me? Getting myself all flummoxed over a man who has not declared any feelings towards me whatsoever. Gosh! At one time I didn't wish to be with any man at all,' Charlotte had cried as she shook her head in mock pity.

Hannah smiled a loving caring smile, like that of an elder sister reassuring had her sibling. 'Maybe you should say something, Charlotte,' she advised tenderly.

'What! A lady cannot do that – I mean, what will he think of me?' Charlotte had cried in response.

This had made Hannah laugh. 'There you go again, worrying yourself over what he thinks.'

Now, in jubilant mood they returned to their hotel to pack their bags and return to 'dear old Blighty', as Will jested. He sent off a telegram and together the four friends sat in the lounge to relax.

'Well then, what are your plans this time, Paddy?' asked Will.

'Oh, I shall return to Ireland – there are plenty of places for me to return to,' he replied dreamily.

'What do you plan, Sandy?' asked Charlotte. She turned and smiled at him.

'I honestly do not know. I may go for a complete break up in the Scottish Highlands,' he replied.

Paddy sighed loudly and shook his head, while Will just smiled and was silent.

'Have you anything planned?' Paddy asked Charlotte at length.

'No, nothing,' she hinted, more in hope than in anything else, but again it was to no avail. It appeared to go straight over Sandy's head.

'Anyone for another drink?' he asked as he finished his and stood up.

Things were regrettably going to alter their plans, however. For Hannah had not only received their telegram instructing her of their success in foiling the attempted assassination, but she had also received a second from the British agent installed in the US border region who was instructed in turn to intercept the Ted Skerrat Gang.

Hannah was standing by the telegraphy machine that evening when the two messages arrived. She read them with interest and then took them to Lord Porter, whom she found at his desk.

'You should read these, my lord. It appears that the Ted Skerrat Gang have slipped the net and got through to the United States,' she reported as she handed him the first slip of paper.

'Hmm, that's most unfortunate.' He sat thoughtfully, then placed the piece of paper down upon the desk and began to tap lightly with his right hand, still thinking. 'Who have we got out there at the moment?' he asked Hannah after a pause.

Hannah quickly checked the report sheet in front of her. 'Only Storm Force Alpha, my lord, and they have just finished their present assignment guarding the Governor General,' she replied.

'Hmmm… were they successful?' he asked at length.

'Of course, my lord,' she replied.

This was not intended as arrogant; the organisation had been successful to date every time and none more so than Storm Force Alpha.

Lord Porter rubbed his chin. 'William Price – he is about to be wed, is he not?' he questioned.

'He is, as soon as he returns,' Hannah responded.

Lord Porter sat in thought again. He glanced to his left, then, tapping the desk with his right index finger, he breathed a deep sigh. 'Well, sadly, it will just have to wait a bit longer, I'm afraid. Storm Force Alpha will have to deal with the problem, Hannah. Instruct them as to what to do.'

With a sad heart she returned to the telegraphy room and sent the two replies off.

Before Sandy had a chance to return with the drinks, a young bellboy entered the lounge that was occupied by Will, Paddy and Charlotte.

'Excuse me, Mr Price, telegram for you.' He held out a silver tray.

Will took it and left the boy a tip. 'Why, thank you, sir,' he replied politely, touching his cap with his hand. He spun on his heel and hurried from the room with a large smile.

Will looked at the telegram with suspicion.

'Well, aren't you going to open it and put us out of our misery?' enquired Paddy.

Jolted, Will opened the telegram. 'It's from Hannah,' he remarked, surprised.

'That was quick,' responded Charlotte, as Sandy returned and placed the drinks upon the table.

Will's face dropped with disappointment.

'What is the problem, Will?' asked Sandy now sitting down.

'We been given a new assignment,' declared Will quietly.

'Really? Wow!' exclaimed Charlotte.

'Are you sure? That can't be right, man,' argued Paddy.

'I am afraid it is. We are to travel to Jamestown and meet a Sergeant Hackett of the North-West Mounted Police. There, we are to help in retrieving not only a stolen amount of cash but also the "Southern Star" diamond.'

Sandy whistled. 'That's the largest diamond in the world, isn't it?' he asked.

'I believe so,' responded Charlotte.

Then the realisation began to set in.

'Oh, Will,' groaned Charlotte, 'your wedding! What are you to do?'

He shrugged his shoulders. 'There is nothing I can do, really.

I'm sure if Hannah and Lord Porter could have sent someone else they would have done,' he replied.

'You never know – Madeleine has time now to find a better suitor,' mocked Sandy.

'Like who? I'm here as well,' joked Paddy.

'Hey, that's a thing. I hope Hannah informs her of the delay,' remarked Will.

'The course of true love never runs smooth,' smiled Sandy.

'Listen who's talking,' responded Paddy, as they now stood up.

'I read it in a book once,' quipped Sandy in response.

'Obviously you never read any further!' declared Paddy.

Sandy looked puzzled but said nothing.

'Right, I'm going to sort this out. I suggest we all have an early evening and get a good start in the morning,' announced Will, and he headed over to the reception desk.

Sure enough, they were all up bright and early the next morning as they headed for the railway station.

'Where is this Jamestown?' asked Sandy.

'It's in… let me see. Ah yes, it's in the north-west provinces,' answered Will, as he struggled with a map. 'It's down on the border,' he added.

'Something tells me this ain't going to be as straightforward as it sounds,' groaned Paddy.

'That's why they are sending us,' smiled Will.

They clambered aboard their train and found their compartment, into which they settled down.

Charlotte chose her favourite seat – next to the window and facing the way the train was travelling. This time Sandy sat opposite her, while Will and Paddy sat by the compartment door. Soon the train was pulling away from the station and they were travelling further west in the morning sun.

'How long is this going to take us?' asked Paddy as he sat down.

'Four days, I think,' replied Will as he checked the tickets. 'Yes, four days, three nights.'

'So we have sleeping berths, then,' responded Sandy, glancing up from his news-sheet.

'Of course, nothing but the best for the boys,' stated Paddy.

'And the girls,' reminded Charlotte.

At that point Will pulled out the telegram from his inside jacket pocket.

'Let's see just what happened then, shall we?' he announced.

Sandy looked up from his news-sheet again. 'Ah, I have just read the report here.' He smiled as he pointed to a column on the sheet.

'Let's see how close the press can get, then, shall we,' replied Will. 'It appears that a train carrying both the Southern Star and a large amount of cash was travelling from the west coast for Montreal... but this was about a week ago now.' Will looked up, puzzled.

'Yes, it took that long for the alarm to be raised and for the security forces to go in and bring all the passengers out,' responded Sandy, 'at least according to this.' He tapped his news-sheet with a finger.

'The train was then stopped by a barrier of trees lain across the tracks at a place called Lynx Pass. When the train stopped a well-known gang, known as the Ted Skerrat Gang, pounced; they shot the guards and the engine staff. They robbed each and every passenger, shooting one in cold blood, finally making off with the money... and the diamond,' Will finished.

'So we have to retrieve the diamond?' questioned Paddy.

'And the money, as well as bring the perpetrators to justice, this time,' added Will.

'Oh, what a pity! That takes all the fun out of it,' mocked Sandy.

'Hannah was most insistent this time. It appears that relations between Canada and the United States have not been very good so far and we should be very careful about leaving bodies lying around, as it could begin a major diplomatic incident,' explained Will.

'But they won't know we are there anyhow,' argued Paddy.

'Precisely – we have to keep it that way,' Will warned.

'So what do you suggest we do to get the diamond back, then?' asked Charlotte.

Everyone fell silent, deep within their own thoughts.

'We need to locate this gang's hideout first,' said Sandy.

'Ha! Just what do you intend to do if they don't stop until they reach Texas?' challenged Paddy.

'There is not a lot we can do. They have the money and the diamond; we want them back,' argued Sandy.

'So you're suggesting we just ride into their own territory, hold them all at gunpoint and bring them all out again?' asked Charlotte.

'Nice idea, but it will take some doing. How many are there in the gang?' asked Paddy.

'Seven,' replied Will.

'So, capturing them will take some doing,' responded Paddy.

'Yes – I just can't see them giving themselves up, somehow, can you?' asked Sandy.

Again they all fell silent.

AN UNEASY FEELING

It was now the morning of the second day. Ted had roused his fellow gang members and as they sat about the fire drinking their coffee they discussed the previous day's robbery.

'What are we to do now, Ted?' asked the dark-skinned Joe. His real name was Gianluigi Bonetti; having become involved in crime in his native Italy through his connections with the powerful Mafia, he had escaped the clutches of the local police forces to flee to New York. Yet his dreams of becoming rich while having to do very little were soon to be disappointed. For, like every other migrant that arrived in America at that time, he had found that the streets were not paved with gold after all. Already averse to hard work, it did not take long for Gianluigi to slip once more into a life of petty crime.

Then, one evening as he was robbing a small corner shop, the owner tried to hit him with a cosh. Aroused, Gianluigi did not think twice about pulling out his knife and stabbing the owner several times. To avoid the police, he this time decided to go west, into the frontier lands of the Midwest. He quickly got himself a job as a cow hand and one night he and his friends rode into town to spend their hard-earned wages on women and whiskey – both great vices of Gianluigi. This particular night, though, was to be different, as it was to be disturbed by the now infamous Ted Skerrat Gang, sick and fed up of hard work and blisters, robbing the local bank. Gianluigi literally jumped upon his horse and rode after the gang. Many of the locals thought he had gone to get the money back; they could not have been further from the truth. He thought of nothing but himself and merely wished to join the gang, to become a very useful member in time.

'We carry on towards Pinewood Falls, as if nothing had happened, boys,' replied Ted. He glanced across at Abe McCabe, who nervously nodded in agreement. Ted didn't mind Abe, but he did have a tendency to talk freely, especially once he had had one or two drinks. They had met many years ago; both natives of Missouri, they had grown up fast, as their fathers had been killed when they were young owing to the Civil War. Ted had since then always held a grudge against the damned Yankees, while Abe drifted into petty crime through necessity. Along with his younger brother, Joshua, Abe had teamed up with Ted, initially to rob mines, small hardware stores and the like. Nevertheless, their reputation became such that they ended up having to move from Missouri and Kentucky, where Ted earned a fearful reputation for brutality. Rather than run to Texas, where Ted realised everyone would have expected them to go, they travelled north-west, along the Mississippi.

It was here that they met the Pisco Kid, the youngest member of the gang, who was undoubtedly the quickest draw, but had initially had a reputation based upon one successful shoot-out and having become a failed card shark. For this he had shot his opponent, so he too was on the run. He was an impulsive character who felt he had to live up to his reputation. He was generally bad tempered and not averse to killing in cold blood. After he joined the gang they moved into bank robberies and stagecoach hold-ups. This was when they met Danny Flynn, an Irish immigrant who worked shotgun for the Wells Fargo stagecoach company.

It was while performing his duty that Danny met the gang. His bravery and stubbornness, carrying on even after everyone else lay dead and he had run out of ammunition, had impressed Ted. Danny had been a bare-knuckle fighter, not only in his native Ireland but also in New York. A man of few words but intense loyalty, Danny was counted along with Abe by Ted as one of his most loyal members.

The gang was soon increased to six with the inclusion of Gianluigi, whom the gang simply called Joe. He too was very excitable and Ted became very aware of the importance of not teaming him up with the youthful Pisco Kid, for fear of letting things get out of hand. Needless to say, two such characters did not always see eye to eye and the older members – usually Danny

– were forever pulling the two apart, especially when it came to gaining the affections of a certain Alice Winters, a young girl who lived and worked with Ted's girl, Texas Rose.

The final gang member was a French Canadian by the name of Pierre Cambierre – known as Frenchy – a man on the run from the British authorities for his participation in the 1885 Métis rebellion. He too had proven to be a useful member of the gang and his knowledge had allowed them not only to hole up on the Canadian side of the border to avoid detection by US marshals, their deputies and the US army, but also to attack and burn various farmsteads and prospectors or Indian settlements north of the border. This in turn made them well-known to the North-West Mounted Police, who had vowed to capture them and bring them to trial.

'What about the diamond?' asked a concerned Joshua.

'What about it?' replied Ted.

'Well, how do we get rid of it and how will we get our share?' he asked innocently.

'What are you worrying about, Josh?' Ted stood up and narrowed his eyes.

'Nothin', Ted, he don't mean nothin', he's just a boy,' remarked Abe, seeking to calm the situation down. Of all the members he knew Ted the best and he knew you did not question this man – not without expecting trouble, anyway.

Ted glanced at Abe, then looked back at Josh. 'It would be wise to have a word with your younger brother, Abe – teach him some manners,' growled Ted, as he flung the remains of his coffee over the fire and walked towards his horse. 'Come on, let's move out,' he ordered; the rest followed, leaving Danny and Joe to put out the fire.

Their progress was now much slower; they were entering the mountainous regions of the borders and Ted felt they had put enough distance between themselves and the train robbery. They could now afford to take their time, and he did not wish to be held up with accidents such as horses becoming stone-bruised or anything like that, so he was quite prepared just to walk his horse south. However, he had deliberately aimed for narrow passes and shallow streams that Pierre now led them through. The reasons for this were twofold: firstly, Ted did not wish to leave any tracks behind him for the authorities to follow; and secondly, it did make the going easier. It also allowed for a variety in the daily diet of beans and beef jerky, as Pierre and Danny showed off their fishing skills, catching trout for lunch while the rest of the gang set up camp. Ted sat by the bank watching the water, then removed his boots and placed his feet into the cool water.

'How long do you reckon it'll take us to get back, Ted?' asked the Pisco Kid.

'Oh, about three, maybe four days,' he replied lazily.

'Once you handed everyone's share out, will that be the end of the gang?' he then asked.

Ted looked up; he had not thought of that. 'Well, that would be up to each individual. Ah had not thought of it quite rightly,' he admitted.

'What will you do with your share, Ted?' The Kid sat down next to Ted on the bank.

Ted blew out his cheeks. 'Ah really don't know. Ah have always promised Rosie ah'd take her to San Francisco,' he replied quietly. 'What of your plans, Pisco?'

'Oh, I don't know – invest it in a ranch, have plenty of cattle. Get married, raise a family,' the Kid replied.

'Alice?' asked Ted.

The Kid looked at him thoughtfully. 'Maybe, maybe no – only she will know the answer to that.'

'And what about Joe?' asked Ted.

'Joe! He's just an Italian scum belly. He don't know any better,' scowled the Kid.

'Yez two want to get together and sort out your differences. Neither of yer want to let this get out of hand,' warned Ted.

'That's up to him. Ah'll deal with him!' sneered the Kid.

'Maybe so and no doubt he will say the same of you. But remember in Pinewood Falls there ain't just me to deal with but the Colonel as well. He don't want the place littered with unnecessary dead bodies, now, do he?'

'Why not? They'll not be his men,' replied the Kid defiantly.

'No, but they will attract the authorities and that is what he does not wish for.'

'Huh… if it weren't for us, he would not have half his wealth.' The Kid scowled once more.

Ted began to replace his boots. 'That's maybe the case, but at present we need him to keep the authorities from our door. Just remember that,' he warned as he walked away.

He moved over to the campfire, where Joe had begun to cook the fish and Joshua and Abe were busy sorting out the bags with all the valuables in.

'What do you reckon, boys?' asked Ted as he settled down beside the two brothers.

'Ah reckon we'll make a tidy sum out of that lot,' smiled Abe.

'Good enough to retire on maybe?' joked Ted.

'Y'never know, Ted, yer just never know,' laughed Abe.

'*Would* you retire?' asked Joshua, concerned.

Ted looked at him. 'Yeah, of course ah would, if ah made enough,' he replied.

'Would you?' Joe now asked Joshua.

Joshua glanced at his brother and looked distinctly uncomfortable. 'Well, I don't rightly know,' he replied.

'Hell, I'd be off to Mexico,' announced Joe. 'Find myself some pretty little señorita and raise a family. Plenty bambinos running all over the place.' He waved his hand in an example gesture.

'That's if yer've got it in yer,' growled the Kid as he joined the rest by the fire.

'Why, yer jumped-up no good…' Joe reached for his gun, but was easily beaten to the draw by the Kid.

'Go on, yer Italian yellow-belly, draw!' the Kid mocked him.

Ted stood up and, drawing his own gun, warned, 'Put 'em away, boys. Whoever fires the first shot will be dead with the second.'

Joe placed his gun back into its holster as he mumbled and cursed under his breath. The Kid glanced at Ted and, showing his immaturity through laughter, he re-holstered his gun, then sat down next to Danny.

'Now ah'm getting a bit sick of this immature argy-bargy, boys. Sort yerselves out or ah will do it for yer,' Ted threatened both Joe and the Kid.

The rest of the meal was spent in silence, after which they

began their slow ride back south towards their eventual destination.

They were not the only ones breaking camp that morning, for not too far away a group of four riders were also getting themselves ready to ride. Murdoch McLeod was the leader, a big broad tall man with a great mop of ginger hair and a beard so thick that almost all you could see was his nose from under his hat. His booming voice was as big as his frame, and he was not a particularly clean man – many years spent in the mountains accounted for that. He was now the owner of the ranch in Paradise Valley and had lived there now for some seventeen years. He had been placed there by the British government as an agent to keep watch on the then-volatile border area with the United States for any further incursion by the Fenian Brotherhood movement and the unsettled Métis people. An ex-army sergeant from the Black Watch regiment, he had served under a certain Captain Porter during the Egyptian campaign.

McLeod was known affectionately as 'Mad Dog' by his friends and cow hands because of his violent temper. However, he was very loyal and supportive of his staff, and it was widely known that if you were desperate for work all you had to do was knock on McLeod's door and he would give it to you. The three men who rode with him that day were all in debt to him for that very reason.

There were two Indians – now dressed as cow hands, but Mad Dog still allowed them to follow their own customs. They had come to him one winter's evening two years ago, after having escaped from their reservation and had been told by their own chief that if they made it to Canada (the land of the red shirts), they would be given work and sanctuary. Who had informed the chief, McLeod never found out; still just as puzzling was who had directed them to his door once they had arrived in Canada. On that subject they remained tight-lipped. Black Eagle, the elder of the two, wore an eagle's feather in his hat; the second one was Two Crows. Both had quickly become bilingual and loyal workers.

Just as loyal was the fourth member of the party, another Irish immigrant by the name of Liam Flanagan. He had arrived in this part of the world as a member of the Fenian Brotherhood and had been involved with the forces under the command of Colonel O'Neil. Once in Canada and, realising that this invasion was not in the least going to assist the freeing of Ireland but was just an excuse to cause Britain bother, he deserted. Wanted by both sides, he hid in the hills until driven by starvation, exposure and fever he struggled down towards the Paradise Ranch. His intention was to rob the kitchen of some supplies, but, as he approached the kitchen door he collapsed and passed out.

Liam was found by one of Murdoch's house staff, which consisted of an Indian by the name of Brown Buffalo and his wife, Starlight. It was she who had found Liam flat out cold at the back, and with the help of a couple of cow hands she had carried him indoors. Murdoch ordered them to lay him in his own bed; however, when Liam came round Murdoch was waiting for him. He questioned Liam as to where had he come from, what he was up to and of course who he was. Liam, never one to shy away from the truth, told Murdoch everything and expected to be handed over to the authorities. However, to his surprise Murdoch accepted Liam's story and offered him a position at the ranch. Liam took it and proved to be Murdoch's most loyal employee. He had almost become his shadow, for in Liam's own words, 'Murdoch has saved me, so now I wish to be on hand to repay the debt if need be!'

As time wore on, Murdoch's employees became accustomed to these scouting parties that he did often on the spur of the moment. They quickly came to accept that Murdoch was the eyes and ears locally of the North-West Mounted Police; they did not realise that he was also very much the eyes and ears of the British government. To help shroud the real truth, several Mounties stopped at the ranch as they were passing through from time to time. This all the cow hands had come to accept as part and parcel of Paradise Valley.

For this particular scouting mission, it appeared that Murdoch had only found out about it the previous afternoon, but it was important enough to mount up and ride out almost immediately. Murdoch had indeed just received the telegram the previous afternoon. He was informed that it was most likely the Ted

Skerrat Gang, which the authorities knew to be in the area; he was easily able to deduce where they were going, having actually seen them himself in Pinewood Falls and having spoken to Ted on more than one occasion. For Murdoch often rode into town – Pinewood Falls was the nearest settlement to the ranch – to collect supplies and foodstuffs. The only thing he was unsure about was which pass they would take to cross back into the United States. There were three that could be taken; the most easterly, and the one that Murdoch suspected, was Paradise Valley Pass. The next one going west was Pine River Pass – a more direct route – and finally the hardest and most westerly was Indian Creek Pass.

He had deduced that they would use Paradise Valley Pass, as no one would expect them to use that. So after leaving their ranch they had simply rode up the valley. Black Eagle had at first ridden on ahead as scout. Murdoch often used the two Indians as scouts, for as he said, 'That's what they grew up doing, so let them do it.' They rode on well into the night, but sadly to no avail. They struck camp and waited until first light. Now, as Murdoch sat upon his horse, he was approached by Liam.

'Do yer still tink they will come this way?' he asked.

'Ahh… To be honest, we should have seen them by now, but we will carry on up this valley for another two hours or so, then we'll cut across towards the Pine River,' explained Murdoch through a mouthful of chewing tobacco.

Two Crows then led his horse away from the camp, while Murdoch and Liam waited for Black Eagle to collect his things together. Once ready, they followed Two Crows. The valley was well wooded with steep sides and screes, and visibility was very poor; still, Murdoch knew his two Indians and knew that if anybody was to ride into the valley now, they would pinpoint them.

After moving north slowly for two hours, they still had not uncovered a thing, so Murdoch reluctantly ordered his small team to ride west over to Pine River Pass. This was not easy, for the valley sides were not only steep but quite high also. They ate jerky as they rode rather than waste time setting up camp. The going became slow, hard and painful, and eventually they had to dismount from their horses and lead them up towards the very peak of the valley. Murdoch was very much aware that they needed to be off the crest by nightfall, as the temperature at these heights could, and generally did, fall to almost freezing. This was the domain of the lynx, the eagle and the mountain goat and, well aware of the point, each man made sure his gun lay loose within its holster, in case of emergency.

It was late afternoon by the time Murdoch and his team had reached the heights and glanced down into Pine River Valley. The sun had lost much of its heat by this time – which was just as well, for it had been hard, warm work ascending the crest. They had left the treeline behind some time earlier so had not had any cover and were not likely to find any for some time yet.

'Once we reach the treeline, we'll make camp for tonight,' ordered Murdoch.

The others simply nodded; there was no need to waste valuable energy by talking and they trusted their leader enough not to question him or grumble. Even if they had felt aggrieved they would probably refrain from complaining, as it would only bring down the wrath of Mad Dog upon them – a fate they were not willing to risk.

Frenchy led the gang along a narrow cleft just above the water's edge; the going was just as slow down at the bottom of the valley as it was at the top. Neither group realised it, but they were actually homing in on the same direction.

'When can we break for camp, Ted?' asked the Pisco Kid.

'When Frenchy finds somewhere suitable,' came his reply.

They were all becoming tired, as the euphoria and adrenalin began to die away. Concentration was the hardest thing for them to maintain and when Joshua was knocked from his horse into the river by a low branch being swept back by Joe, it brought a cursory warning from Ted and not a few sniggers from the others. With that in mind, Frenchy soon found a small meadow in which to pitch camp; they shortly had a fire going and were cooking.

'Ah want to try to make that old abandoned prospectors' settlement by nightfall, boys,' announced Ted.

'Whut, Valley?' questioned Joe.

'Yep, that's the only one hereabouts ah know of,' smirked Ted.

'How far's that, Pierre?' asked Abe.

'Six, mebbe seven hours from here.' Frenchy looked up as he lit a cigar from a burning twig.

'Seven bloody hours!' cursed the Kid.

'Do you have any objections, kid?' challenged Ted.

The Kid glanced at him but said nothing; he simply toed the soft meadow grass, while one or two others began to snigger at his discomfort.

'Now then, ah reckon that if we make Valley this evening, we could be in Pinewood Falls by tomorrow nightfall,' announced Ted.

One or two of the gang began to shout and whoop. Ted quickly raised his hand. 'Shush, you bloody idiots – d'yer want to bring the redcoats down upon us?' he asked angrily.

'Aw, come on, Ted, we left 'em all behind us – they don't know where we are,' argued Abe.

'How many times do ah have to tell yer? Never take anything for granted,' warned Ted.

They all fell silent and their attention was drawn towards the fire and the cooking pot.

Frenchy had sat slightly apart from the rest of the gang upon a boulder overlooking the river. He ate his beans and sat his cup of steaming coffee on the ground next to him. The Kid joined him.

'All right, Frenchy?' the Kid asked.

Frenchy turned and looked at the Kid slowly and almost contemptuously; he did not care much for this stuck-up little brat. He believed a good smacking would do him the world of good, but for the time being he was willing to put up with him. 'Yes, I am fine,' he replied.

'Ahh… this is a wonderful country is it not,' the Kid remarked, looking down at the stream.

'*Oui*,' Frenchy replied nodding slowly; he waited for the sarcasm.

'Do you think this could be the next state?' asked the Kid.

'*Non*,' replied Frenchy.

'Pity you French didn't kick out the redcoats like we did. You could always call upon us red-blooded Yankees to kick their butts,' the Kid announced with a snigger.

Frenchy looked at him and stood up. He turned and walked over towards the campfire. 'Come, we go soon,' he remarked to Ted.

Ted nodded. 'OK, boys, mealtime's over. Let's mount up,' he ordered.

They quickly broke camp and rode out, at the same pace as before – which basically was walking.

From now on they were to follow the riverbank as best they could; again the going was slow and tedious. The light was fading fast on the valley floor; the trees had sheltered them well from the midday heat, but as the light began to fade so the temperature began to drop. Ted was well aware that once the light began to go it would soon be dark and dangerous for the horses, so he reluctantly called a halt before they reached the abandoned town of Valley.

'We'll make camp here, boys,' he remarked as they reached yet another grassy meadow.

They all dismounted and set about starting a fire.

'Ah think we should set watch tonight,' he announced.

'Why, do you think we're in danger?' asked Abe.

'Only from yerselves,' Ted replied. 'No, it'd be wise to guard 'gainst mountain cats, ah reckon,' he said rubbing his hands.

'How far from Valley are we?' asked the Kid.

'We will ride through it tomorrow morning. There's no hurry,' assured Ted.

'Secure the horses down by the river, boys,' instructed Danny, as he led his horse to the water's edge.

The rest followed and soon they were all settling down around the fire.

Murdoch and his men were also just about to set up camp. They had eventually reached the treeline, and Murdoch had taken them a little further down the valley side before setting up camp, to get a little more cover.

'Right, we'll rest up here. Tomorrow we should reach the riverbank and we'll check that old prospectors' place, Valley,' he announced.

The others looked and nodded. Black Eagle was cooking something he had caught earlier that day and, although tired and stiff from the hard day's going, they were all in good spirits.

'Black Eagle, ye can take point tomorrow. Liam, Two Crows, keep yer eyes and ears open. We must remain as silent as possible – we cannae be too far away from our quarry now,' McLeod announced.

'What is it we're lookin' for, Mad Dog?' asked Liam.

'The Ted Skerrat Gang – we have it on good authority that they were behind that train hold-up. If it was them then they'll be heading down this way towards Pinewood Falls. If we do spot 'em, then we can take it as definite that it was them all right.' He glanced about the little group.

'And if we do find them… Are we to challenge them?' Liam went on.

'If ah think it safe to do so, yes. But if ah think any of 'em may slip the net, then we simply follow 'em. We know where they're goin', and time is on our side in this instance.' Murdoch broke into one of his guttural laughs, then spat out his tobacco and lit a pipe. As he lay down upon his blanket he began to hum 'Ye'll take the high road' to himself contentedly.

Liam too laid back and listened while watching the sky. Two Crows and Black Eagle settled down under two trees, resting their backs against them. They often slept this way when in the saddle, dozing in the sitting position as they rested their rifles upon their knees, close to their horses.

The night passed uneventfully and both sets of riders broke camp at first light, little realising that they were both targeting the same abandoned settlement. But, while Black Eagle rode as scout for Murdoch's group, Ted now led his own group of riders with no scout as such. They were not expecting to see anybody, although Ted still gave instructions to ride quietly. Black Eagle led Murdoch's group downhill along a path to the back of the settlement, riding carefully and slowly, while Ted rode in to the settlement from the riverbank. Black Eagle, being sharp-eyed, spotted Ted's group first. He stopped where he was and gave the startled cry of a crow, Murdoch's preferred warning cry.

Murdoch and his men immediately stopped and they scoured the abandoned village.

'There, over there!' pointed Liam.

Murdoch followed the direction of his arm and spotted the group of riders.

Ted too had stopped; he instinctively half-raised his arm as he tried to listen.

'It's only a crow,' mused the Kid as he rode past.

As if to prove the point a bird flew from the trees slightly to the front and left of the group. Ted spurred his horse on again, but more cautiously, instinctively resting his right hand upon the handle of his gun.

By now Murdoch, Liam and Two Crows had joined Black Eagle and together they watched Ted's men ride through the settlement.

'Let's take 'em now!' urged Liam, becoming excited.

'No, they could bolt all over like a flock of hens,' warned Murdoch, although he realised that this was probably the last real chance of stopping them before Pinewood Falls, their destination.

'But the plain opens from now on, Mad Dog,' argued a disappointed Liam.

'There's still the gorge just above the steppe,' explained Murdoch, despite knowing that it was a bit of a long shot. For Ted's group now had the easier ride, while Murdoch would have to detour back through the trees and well back from the river if they were not to be seen.

'But if we hit 'em now—' persisted Liam.

'Look laddie, if we'd had been in position then we could have sprung the trap, but we're no' in position. Therefore, it's better this way,' Murdoch justified, trying to hold his temper. He realised that he could not afford to allow anybody to spring the trap, for it would jeopardise his identity in the future.

Liam, realising that he was close to upsetting Mad Dog, changed tack. 'D'yer think we can get to the gorge in time?' he asked.

'We will just have to wait and see,' replied Murdoch, not

taking his eyes off Ted and his gang, who were now two-thirds of the way through the settlement.

Ted had ridden through deliberately slowly, as he also knew this was the best spot for an ambush, but luckily there appeared to be no one else around. Abe rode up to Ted's side.

'You ever get the feeling you're being watched?' he said glancing around nervously.

'Like now, you mean,' replied Ted with a smile.

'Yep, this place gives me the creeps,' declared Abe; he too now nervously fingered his gun.

Soon they were leaving the run-down settlement behind them, although Ted for some reason couldn't help but keep checking over his shoulder.

'Do you think they saw something?' Liam nervously asked Murdoch.

'No, they saw nothing, they would have bolted by now. But they sure as hell can feel something,' murmured Murdoch.

Ted then spurred his horse to the front.

'We shall ride solid now till we reach Pinewood, boys, no slackin',' he warned, as he broke his horse into a trot. He wanted to put as much space between himself and that godforsaken place as quickly as he could. He could not remember the last time he had the jitters like that, but he did not want them again.

Once they had begun to disappear across the meadow away from them, Murdoch urged his horse forward.

'Come on boys, if we're to keep up with 'em, we mus' hurry onwards,' he warned.

The others followed, but it was soon apparent that they were beginning to lose ground on Ted Skerrat's gang. They could not possibly hope to ride anywhere near as fast as Ted's men were now riding, since they were spooked.

'Let us break on to the meadows and chase 'em, boss,' urged Liam as he became concerned.

Yet Murdoch surprisingly was not so worried, 'Let 'em go, we will get them later. When they least expect it,' he advised.

'But how?' asked a stunned Liam.

'Ahh, that's for me to know, laddie,' replied Murdoch.

He carried on as before. Even Black Eagle had at first shown a little concern as their quarry appeared to slip from their grasp, only for Murdoch to calm him down, as he assured him that all was not lost. To Liam and the two Indians, it appeared as if Murdoch was more than happy with the present outcome.

'Are the Mounties going to arrest them in Pinewood Falls then, boss?' asked Liam almost incredulous.

'Naw lad, they don't have jurisdiction down there. Although we may have something else up our sleeves,' Murdoch assured him.

'Oh, like what?' Liam asked.

'Ye'll see, my lad. Ye'll see,' Murdoch replied jovially.

They carried on following, now at a safe distance of course, but to all intents and purposes Murdoch had no intention now of actually stopping them. They continued onwards towards Pine River gorge. Regrettably, they were too late to trap Ted Skerrat and his gang and as Murdoch sat above the gorge he could see his quarry head towards the ford at Pinewood Falls. After a short pause in which he appeared to be in deep thought, he turned his horse and headed back towards Paradise Ranch. The others followed him in silence wondering what his next move would be.

In fact Murdoch already knew what he was going to do and that was to telegraph Military Intelligence back in Britain. This was now a lot easier than it had been in the past, as the system employed used various strategically placed warships sat across the Atlantic to relay the message to Britain. Therefore, it would only take a few hours to reach HQ. They in turn would then telegraph Hannah at Drumloch and it was this very message that she received at the same time as Will's confirmation of the outcome of his mission. She and Lord Porter, as we have seen, would then organise a team to go out and meet Murdoch at Paradise. She, as we have already mentioned, would give the telegram to Lord Porter, who reluctantly chose Storm Force Alpha, as they were already there and had indeed just foiled an assassination attempt upon the Governor General. So it was not long before an answering telegram would be winging its way back across the

Atlantic. This of course was the one which arrived in Will's lap as the team relaxed that evening, having succeeded in their duty.

Ted had deliberately not led his men through the gorge, but rode over it below the Lion's escarpment, which was a natural rock shelf which gave a beautiful panoramic view of the plains as they fanned out south below Buffalo's Mount and the main settlement of Pinewood Falls.

'There she be, boys – home! Let's get ourselves a well-earned drink. But remember, no loose talking,' Ted warned menacingly.

One or two of the gang galloped forward, whooping and cheering as they raced towards the ford. They then charged across, making a lot of noise and certainly telling all the townsfolk they had arrived. As they left the river on the near bank, the Kid pulled his gun from its holster and began to fire into the air. This was taken up by Joe, not wishing to be left behind, and then Joshua. The various townsfolk hurried to the front of their shops and dwellings. The sheriff and his deputy came running out of the jail, opposite stood the only saloon in town, Texas Rose's, she hurried to the balcony on the first floor with one or two of her girls. Bert the barman stepped out on to the porch.

Two men who were stood outside the hardware store and dressed in uniform grey glanced at each other. They mounted their horses and then glanced across the street at the sheriff. He was called Calvin Redford and was the only man in town strong enough to be able to stand up to Ted Skerrat. Lamentably, he was also aware that to keep the peace he had to bow to the Colonel, and these men in grey were just two of his Dixie riders. He glanced back at them and nodded; they then turned their horses and trotted out of town.

'Ned, get ma Winchester, will yer?' he turned to his young deputy, Ned Parker.

Ned turned and literally ran into the jailhouse, returning in a matter of seconds, by which time Calvin had now stepped out into the middle of the street. The Kid rode right up to him and stopped in front of the sheriff. If it was to antagonise him then it failed miserably, for Calvin just looked past the Kid to Ted, who was now just entering the town.

'Howdy, Sheriff. Boy have we missed you! It's good to see you.' The Kid grinned from the saddle.

'Howdy, boy,' was all Calvin had to say. He was waiting for Ted to ride up.

'Well, howdy, Sheriff – and a mighty fine day it is too,' greeted Ted, as he rode up to the saloon and immediately dismounted.

Calvin walked over to him slowly. 'Good fishin' trip, boys?' he asked.

Ted always called these jaunts 'fishing trips'. Calvin knew this; he was of course well aware what they really were. Yet he was under instruction from the Colonel to leave well alone unless they brought trouble back with them.

Ted strode confidently up to the sheriff. 'Yep, certainly were,' he replied as he glanced about his gang. 'And ah reckon ah should buy all you good folk a drink, now come on.' He slapped the sheriff across the back of the shoulder and led him towards the bar. As they stepped up to the bar, a young woman dressed in a black dress hurried down the stairs.

'Ted, Ted! Oh, Ted, ah've missed yer!' She ran across the bar and threw herself at him.

He caught her in mid air and, as she threw her arms about his neck, she then showered him in kisses.

'Whoa there, pretty angel. Why hell, let a man get a drink,' he remarked cheerfully.

'It's good to see yer,' declared Rosie as she eased her grip around his neck.

'Well, let's drink on that, then yer can take me upstairs, woman, and show me just how much yer missed me,' he announced, amid much laughter and back slapping.

As they laughed and joked inside the saloon, two of Ted's men remained outside; this was the Kid and Joshua. As they secured their horses the Kid noticed an old buck wagon parked over at the general hardware store.

'Hey, ain't that luscious Lucy's wagon?' pointed the Kid.

'Ah guess so,' replied Joshua.

'Come on, let's have a little fun,' urged the Kid as he led Joshua across the street towards the wagon.

Lucy Wightman was a young woman who now lived alone at

Indian Creek, an old prospectors' settlement just a few miles north of Pinewood Falls. She had moved there as a young girl with her parents. Her father had worked a claim there for many years; unhappily, scarlet fever ravaged the settlement, taking both her parents and many of the prospectors. Those that did not die soon moved on all, except Lucy, who remained alone. She would often drive her wagon into town for her supplies and on a Friday night, when she would get herself drunk. People often wondered how or where she got her means of support from. Some said her father had left her a large legacy, others that she obtained it in less favourable ways. Either way as she became the source of curiosity she also fell victim to the townsfolk's scorn and cruel jibes. She had at first tried hard to keep up her feminine appearance, and some that could remember said that she was quite a pretty girl. Unfortunately, owing to both necessity and through lack of self-confidence and belief, her appearance began to go downhill, until she looked no better than a bag lady. Her hair was unkempt and straggly, she looked unwashed and her clothing, which was very masculine, was moth-eaten.

It was not uncommon for her to be beaten and pushed around just for laughs on a Friday evening by various bored youths and drunks, and this only added to her sorrowful, lonely, miserable and unhappy existence. On this occasion she did not see the two men creep up behind her until it was too late.

'Hello, Lucy!' shouted the Kid into her ear.

This of course startled the poor girl and she jumped, dropping her basket full of vegetables upon the ground.

'Oh Lucy, look what you've done! Come on, let's help yer,' offered the Kid, as he then ran about stamping upon what vegetables he could see.

Lucy ran about after him, this way and that until she was tripped up by Joshua. She fell full length into the mud; the two men simply burst into loud laughter.

'What have yer done now, Lucy!' cried the Kid, and he kicked a potato she was just about to grab across the street.

'Leave her alone, yer've had yer fun,' interrupted the voice of Calvin.

The two men stopped and half turned to face the sheriff. He

was watching both of them his arms folded. The two immediately burst into laughter again.

'Now go and join the rest of yer friends in the bar, leave the girl alone,' he remarked.

'Ahh, she's not worth the effort anyhow,' cursed the Kid and, as he turned, he deliberately kicked up mud into her face. They then both walked over to the bar, still laughing loudly at their antics.

Lucy picked herself up and, still crouching in front of the sheriff, she hurried to the wagon and clambering aboard drove off, nervously glancing over her shoulder as she did so. Calvin watched her leave. Then, turning himself, he strolled back to the jailhouse. Yep, now that Ted and his gang were back, it will be business as usual again, he thought to himself as he sighed heavily.

MAD DOG MCLEOD

At long last the train pulled into Jamestown railway station.

'Gawd, I feel as if I've been on here all my life,' moaned Paddy.

'Then maybe we should be awarded medals, for having to bravely put with you for that long,' smirked Will.

'Carry on like that, sunshine, and you will not be around to collect it,' Paddy threatened.

Having clambered down from the train they glanced about the platform.

'There you are – there's our man over there.' Will flicked his head over towards the exit, where three men stood in bright red coats.

'That'll be Sergeant Hackett, I'm thinking,' announced Paddy as they strode towards the exit.

Having handed their tickets in to the ticket inspector on the gate, Will walked confidently over towards the sergeant. He noticed them looking towards him; a look of expectancy fell across his face. However, just to be sure, Will spoke first.

'Sergeant Hackett?' he asked.

'Yes,' came the reply. The sergeant now stood, raising himself up to his full height and placing his hands upon his hips.

'Ah, good. Allow me to introduce myself – I am Will Price and these are my colleagues, Miss Charlotte Nicholson, Sean O'Brien and Sandy McBride.'

'Well, howdy,' smiled the sergeant, pushing his brimmed hat back upon his head. 'No one said anything about a woman,' he commented, albeit agreeably.

'Do not worry yourself, Sergeant. Charlotte here is as good as anyone in unarmed combat,' assured Will.

'On that I can't rightly comment, though it is not me you will have to convince.' He smiled again. 'Anyhow, I'm forgetting my manners – this here is Constable Adams and Constable Courtney,' he introduced his two colleagues.

He then turned and led them towards some horses tied to a rail at the front of the station. 'I've taken the liberty of having the horses brought up to the station. I was not sure if you would wish to ride out immediately or freshen up first,' stated the sergeant.

'How far have we to ride, sergeant?' asked Will.

'Oh, about two days,' he replied.

Will half turned to look at Charlotte; she was still dressed in feminine clothing. She nodded gently then turned to the sergeant.

'Is there anywhere that I may change, sergeant?' she asked.

'Yes ma'am – if you would care to follow me down this street to the hotel, I am sure they will allow you to change in there.' He gestured with his arm.

'Well, let's go then; once I've changed into more appropriate attire the sooner we can ride out of here,' she remarked.

Together they strolled down the street, each now leading their horse, bringing many a curious glance from the local inhabitants, until they arrived at the hotel.

'Here, Charlotte. Here's your bag,' Sandy stepped forward and handed over her bag. She thanked him and was led by the sergeant into the hotel foyer.

Sergeant Hackett quickly returned and joined Will on the front porch.

'So what is this Murdoch McLeod like?' asked Will.

Hackett smiled. 'Well, I would like to be present when Miss Nicholson walks in, that's for sure.' He paused and glanced back at the hotel.

'Do you think that will be a problem?' asked Will.

'Naw, not if she is as good as you say. Mad Dog is a hard taskmaster though; you will find his personality as large as his frame. Comes from a military background – as yet, we have not witnessed a softer side to him,' Hackett warned.

'Such as?' enquired Will.

'Well, hell, he hasn't seen a bar of soap for years, I reckon,' smiled Hackett. 'Oh, don't get me wrong, he is a fine host; he works hard and plays hard, but he does not believe in washing too often. He reckons that the more muck you have the more waterproof you are. We often stay over at the Paradise Ranch when we are patrolling this neck of the woods. I know Mad Dog very well,' explained Hackett.

'Is he Canadian, American or what?' Will asked.

'Oh, he is Scottish – ex-army, I believe. Although he has been here now for nigh on twenty years. He settled at Paradise just after the Fenian rebellion.'

'So how does he feel regarding the Irish?' asked Paddy.

'You see, that is one aspect about Mad Dog that I do like,' Hackett began. 'He's not fussed what nationality, religion, colour or creed you happen to be; he has this happy knack of seeing you for the person you actually are, of seeing within. If you accept him for what he is, then he will accept *you*. He does not suffer fools lightly and he may give you all a hard reception to test your mettle.'

Hackett had just finished his sentence when Charlotte re-emerged from the hotel. She was now dressed in the clothes of a young man, which she found more manageable for riding.

'Thank you for waiting,' she smiled as she readjusted the belt containing her throwing daggers. After passing her bag, which now contained her dress, to Sandy, she mounted her horse.

'Pleasure, ma'am,' responded Hackett as the others mounted their horses.

They followed the road for a few miles, then struck out across country.

'We leave the road here; we're aiming for those mountains over yonder,' pointed Hackett.

'Do you think we will reach them tonight?' asked Will.

'Yep, we'll set up camp at the base tonight, then cross them tomorrow,' Hackett replied.

They rode along at a comfortable pace, taking in the beautiful scenery around them. Charlotte rode alongside Courtney, who kept glancing at her surreptitiously.

'It's all right, you can talk to me if you wish,' she said eventually.

'I am sorry, miss – to see a very attractive young lady like yourself riding out here... well, it doesn't always happen.' He flicked his head to one side.

'Carry on, young sir; flattery will get you everywhere,' she teased him.

His face flushed and he dropped his eyes. This reminded Charlotte of another fellow not so far away and she glanced over her shoulder to smile at Sandy who, as always when riding, brought up the rear.

As the day finally began to disappear they crested a small hill. Ahead of them still lay the Rocky Mountains; nonetheless, this was as far as they were going tonight. Sergeant Hackett led them to a small flat area where large boulders appeared to create a defensive ring.

'This will do us for tonight – we'll pitch camp here,' he announced as he dismounted.

Courtney and Adams did likewise, and so too did the four companions. Soon a fire was going and Sergeant Hackett was cooking some beans and coffee.

'You're not a bad cook, for a bloke,' commented Charlotte as she ate a plate of beans.

'Ha! When you have had to look after yourself for as long as I have, miss, you tend to become a half-decent cook,' he smiled.

'So then, Sergeant… what brought you out here?' asked Sandy.

Sergeant Hackett looked at him, surprised.

'Oh, you will get used to our Sandy here. May not say much, but takes it all in,' smiled Paddy.

'So you picked up on my dialect, did you?' responded Hackett.

'Yes, is it Yorkshire?' questioned Sandy.

Hackett hung his head and gave a short laugh; then, shaking his head he glanced once more at Sandy. 'Yeah, it is – Wakefield, to be precise. I joined the army to escape the cotton mills. I then volunteered for the North-West Mounted Police for the adventure and luckily have not looked back since. But there's not many who pick me up for my dialect these days,' he replied.

'And what of you, young sir?' Charlotte turned to ask Courtney.

'Oh, I am Canadian, ma'am. But I came looking for the adventure all the same,' he replied.

'And I suppose the same reasons drove you here also, Mr Adams,' remarked Will.

'Sure did; although I'm English I just wanted to taste the life of adventure. To ride around this lovely country, to feel free, not meet a soul for days.' He shook his head. 'I just couldn't resist it.'

'So what of you four?' Sergeant Hackett asked them.

'Well, we all were invited to join this organisation – the Special Counter Intelligence Bureau – just over a year ago,' explained Will. 'I myself am ex-army – the Sherwood Foresters. Sandy here is ex-navy, while Paddy was a farm foreman and was used by the army as a scout,' he went on.

'And you, miss, what did you do?' Hackett asked, as he turned to face Charlotte.

'Me, I fought for a living, Sergeant,' she replied sternly.

He smiled. 'You? But there are no marks on yer. You are surely the prettiest fighter I have ever set eyes upon,' he mocked.

'Oh, believe her. That angelic face hides a multitude of sins,' responded Paddy.

'Forgive me, miss, I did not wish to jest lightly. You certainly do not look like a fighter. But to work within such an organisation I know you must be good,' apologised the sergeant.

'Apology accepted,' smiled Charlotte.

They all rested by the fire. Paddy collected some flexible branches from the trees nearby, then he and Sandy began to construct three shelters. This was done by sticking one end of the branch firmly into the ground then bending it over in an arc. A second branch was tied to the central point of the arc and bent so that it ran back to the ground forming a tripod; the frame was then covered in leaves and thick undergrowth to create a simple shelter. Sergeant Hackett looked on, bemused, although he recommended that for safety against curious wildlife they should remain within the light of the fire, while the three Mounties kept watch.

It was a peaceful night; the warmth of the fire kept the night chill at bay and they were all up by first light. The four agents began to prepare themselves in case of trouble. This brought curious glances from their escorts, especially as they began to arm themselves with their specialist weapons. The three Mounties viewed them with smiles.

'What are these?' asked Sergeant Hackett as he took Sandy's

revolver. 'Peashooters – and this...' He looked scornfully at Sandy's rifle.

'They are my tools of the trade. They suit me fine,' replied Sandy indignantly.

Sergeant Hackett shook his head, and glanced at Paddy's sawn-off shotgun, his 'Macootcha', then at the throwing stars. 'When we arrive at Mad Dog's we will issue you lot with Winchester rifles,' he declared.

'I myself wouldn't mind looking at one of those. As far as my colleagues are concerned they are quite happy with what they've got,' responded Will.

'If we have a good day today, we should reach Paradise by tonight,' announced Sergeant Hackett as they broke camp and rode off.

'So, Sergeant, how are you so sure this crime was perpetrated by the Skerrat Gang?' asked Will as he rode alongside the sergeant.

'For starters, we had the descriptions of the train passengers. Then Mad Dog managed to track them back towards Pinewood Falls,' he explained.

'Why did Mad Dog allow them to escape?' Will enquired.

'Oh, I'm not privy to everything Mad Dog does, but there must have been a reason for it. He's as cunning as a fox, is Mad Dog,' answered Hackett.

'So you know quite a bit about this gang?' Will went on.

'Yep, they've been raiding across the border for a few months now. It's a matter of trying to be in the right place at the right time. Obviously we can't just ride over the border to arrest them, so we have to wait for them to come to us.'

'That's why we came then,' stated Will, nodding.

'Precisely – if we can just flush them out.' Hackett clenched his fist.

The density of trees increased steadily as the day wore on. It was becoming quite dark when they crested one more hill and looked down into yet another wooded valley. Although hidden partly behind a large rocky crest which had a deep defile cut into it, the agents could perceive a large glade a few miles further on, in the centre of which stood what appeared to be a large ranch.

Several lights twinkled away from the windows; it looked a very welcoming sight.

'Well, lady and gentlemen, that is Paradise Ranch – home to one Murdoch McLeod – and this is Paradise Valley,' announced Sergeant Hackett as he surveyed the scene.

'You can understand how it got its name,' commented Will, admiringly.

'Oh yeah, it's beautiful, don't you think?' smiled Hackett. He spurred his horse on and down the valley towards the ranch.

'Will they be expecting us?' asked Charlotte.

'More than likely; Murdoch's scouts have probably been watching us all afternoon,' replied Hackett.

'Why so sure?' Will quizzed.

'Because he uses Indian scouts. Apart from anything else they are very loyal,' said Hackett.

As they arrived at the entrance gate a young cow hand stood to one side; he was holding a rifle.

'Howdy – folks,' he greeted the group as they rode up.

'Howdy, is Murdoch expecting us?' asked Hackett.

'Yep, yer'd best take the guests up to the boss's house now,' the cow hand responded.

'Who was it this time – Black Eagle?' asked Hackett.

'Yep, picked yer up this afternoon,' came the reply.

'Argh – one of these days I'm gonna surprise *him*,' laughed Hackett and rode past the young cow hand. The sergeant led them up to the large house that stood apart from the rest of the ranch.

They drew their horses up either side of the large porch steps and approached the door. There Sergeant Hackett knocked loudly upon the door; it was quickly answered by a small retiring Indian.

'Good evening, Buff. I believe Murdoch is expecting us,' announced Hackett.

The Indian said nothing but opened the door wide, bowed and gestured with his arm for them all to enter.

They walked into a large hallway and were immediately greeted with very poorly sung verse of 'Ye'll tek the high road an' ah'll tek the low road', which appeared to be coming from the sitting room.

'Well, well, I do believe we are about to witness a special occasion,' smiled Hackett as he led the four companions into the room.

They were greeted with the view of a very large man sat in a small bathtub in front of a roaring fire, with soap bubbles all over. 'Buff, hurry up with me hot water, man. Buff? *Buff*! Godforsaken bloody Indian, where the hell—' he shouted and cursed as he rubbed his back with a back scrubber.

Charlotte sniggered and instinctively placed her hand over her mouth.

The large man in the bath spun round surprised. 'What the hell's this? Can a man no' have peace an' decency within his own home? he cried, trying rather pathetically to hide himself. 'Hackett, mek yersel' useful an' ge' me that towel.' He pointed to a filthy piece of cloth hanging over a chair just out of arm's reach.

Hackett stepped forward and gave him the towel so that he could firstly wipe away the soap from his eyes, then cover his waist.

The big man now stood up. 'Are these the agents we've been expecting?' he asked.

'Yep, they most certainly are,' replied Hackett, then half turned to the four companions. 'This, my friends, is Murdoch McLeod,' he introduced the large man. 'Now, Murdoch, this is Will Price, Sean O'Brien—'

'Irish, eh! Another bloody one,' cursed Murdoch.

'You have a problem with the Irish?' questioned Paddy.

'No, luckily – it is just there are so bloody many of you here I'm surprised there are still some at home,' Murdoch replied sarcastically. He took a gulp of whiskey from a glass.

Hackett continued. 'Sandy McBride and Miss Charlotte Nicholson.'

Murdoch immediately spat the drink from his mouth. 'A bloody woman, *here*?' He looked horrified.

'Thank you for the compliment, kind sir,' responded Charlotte.

'An' just what the hell do you do? Yer not the cantoniere, are ye?' he asked.

'What on earth is a cantoniere?' Charlotte asked curiously.

'It was a woman who carried brandy in the front line for the troops,' answered Sandy.

'I'll give him sodding brandy!' she cursed in anger.

'Well, at least yer a feisty little devil,' he answered; his nostrils flared and his eyes widened in both anger and embarrassment. 'Now then, if yer don't mind, ah'd like to get dressed, so that ah can tak to yez a bit dignified, like,' he explained in a gentler tone. 'Buff? *Buff!*' he hollered.

The little Indian was actually next to Will. 'Yes?' he nodded.

This paused the great Murdoch and he cleared his throat. 'Show our guests to the guest rooms, where they should have gone in the first place.' He gestured with his thick arm.

Buff now herded the guests into an adjacent room, then went back to attend to Murdoch, who could still be heard shouting and cursing as he dried himself and got ready.

'That, my friends, is Murdoch – Mad Dog to his friends,' Hackett smiled.

'More like a whirlin' dervish,' sighed Paddy heavily.

'Does he always have to shout and bawl like that?' asked Charlotte.

'Actually, we've caught him in a good mood. It's the first bath I've actually seen him take since I've known him.' Hackett shook his head.

'Second, actually, and my mood is fast changing,' announced Murdoch as he filled the doorway. They could not distinguish his facial features as they were hidden beneath a thick mop of ginger hair or behind a thick matted beard. He stepped into the room slowly and deliberately, and Charlotte couldn't help but notice how huge he was.

'Well, I asked for assistance from this newly organised deadly Bureau and they send me you lot. Working within the corridors of power certainly have made Porter soft,' Murdoch said disparagingly.

'Hang on a minute – there is nothing wrong with Lord Porter – and further, how can you pass judgement upon someone you have never met?' challenged Will.

'*Lord* Porter!' exclaimed Murdoch. '*Lord* now, is it? Well, ah knew him as Captain Porter. He was ma company captain in

Egypt, when we served in the Black Watch together.' He paused for a moment. 'We certainly choked among the same muck. Ah've every right to judge him; ah've known him a lot longer than ye, laddie,' Murdoch growled. 'As it happens, he was the best officer ah ever served with – showed me how to lead men; a real fire-eater, he was,' he added, his voice falling to a softer tone. He strolled over to a large drinks cabinet and opened it. 'Anyone wish to partake?' he asked.

Everyone accepted except Sandy and Charlotte, who both settled for water.

'What's the matter with you, nancy boy or something? The girl ah can understand…' Murdoch sneered at Sandy.

Sandy sat silently, waiting until Murdoch had finished. 'Drinking does not prove how hard you are, it merely shows how stupid you can become,' he replied calmly.

Murdoch growled and clenched his fists by his sides. 'A comedian, eh?' he murmured.

Sandy did not respond and simply took a sip from his water.

Murdoch returned to the drinks cabinet and poured the others their drinks, after which he grabbed a whiskey bottle and sat down clutching it.

'So what is it you know about this case?' he asked as he took a swig from the bottle.

'That we have been assigned to recover the Southern Star diamond as well as the cash that the Ted Skerrat Gang stole from the train,' began Sandy.

'The Ted Skerrat Gang have been raiding across the border of late and are both wanted here and in the US,' added Will.

'They are holed up at a place called Pinewood Falls, which is just across the border in Montana,' said Paddy.

'To which you yourself appear to have tracked them too, but, alas, failed to intercept them before they got there,' said Charlotte.

Murdoch looked long and hard at her, then placed the bottle down upon the table slowly but deliberately, not taking his eyes off Charlotte. 'Right then, it appears you need to know my role in all of this. Ah, too, am an agent for the government. Ah act as Sergeant Hackett's eyes and ears in this region. Nobody else knows of this, not even my staff. If ah had intercepted this gang and they had blown my cover, then maybe – just maybe – it would have destroyed all we've done here over the past twenty years. That was a risk ah could not take, especially as the US government do not know that this gang are now in possession of this diamond,' he explained.

'Hang on a minute... are you saying that no one knew of the diamond being on the train?' asked Will incredulous.

'That's right, no one did.' Murdoch shook his head. 'All Ted Skerrat was after was the money; they found the diamond quite by accident. If the US government finds out about the diamond... why, they will come down so hard upon them, the poor devils won't know what's hit them. Worse still, the Americans cannot be counted upon to return the diamond either,' he added.

'We are not on the best of terms, are we,' remarked Sandy.

'No, diplomatically we are not,' Murdoch agreed.

'Unhappily, we cannot just ride over the border to arrest these reprobates,' added Sergeant Hackett.

'So we brought in yourselves and tomorrow we will devise a plan with which to trap our quarry,' smiled Murdoch.

'And retrieve the goods,' added Will.

'Don't even *contemplate* returning without the goods,' warned Murdoch menacingly.

'Oh, don't worry – we haven't failed yet and have no intention of doing so this time; it is just the perpetrators we may fail to bring back with us,' smiled Paddy.

'One thing ah hate is these half-a-jobs,' snarled Murdoch.

Sandy stood up at that point. 'I'm off to my bed. I will see you all in the morning.' He turned and left.

Murdoch pulled a face as he left the room.

'Actually, I think it best if we all retired,' Will said as he and Charlotte stood up.

'Ahh, right, hang on a minute. The men are to be quartered in the same building as my cow hands. But the young lady here I was not expecting, so she will have to stay here in my house.' He paused and looked at Charlotte. 'As my honoured guest,' he smiled.

'I do hope the bedding is cleaner than your clothing,' she remarked coldly.

'Eh, what? Am ah to be insulted in ma own home?' he cried, offended.

'Will you be all right, Charlotte?' asked Will quietly.

'Of course she will – ah may be a few things but dishonourable, never. She will be quite safe under ma roof,' Murdoch proudly announced.

Will glanced at Sergeant Hackett.

'Is that right?' asked Paddy.

'Yep, that's one thing – if Murdoch gives his word, it will be honoured,' he remarked as he stepped outside.

'Just shout, angel, if you need help,' Paddy whispered as he passed her.

'I'll be fine,' she smiled at him.

The front door was closed, then Murdoch went back to the guest's room.

'Buff? *Buff!*' he again shouted.

'Yeh, yeh,' came the reply from the little Indian.

'Go fetch your wife, we need to set a up a room for Miss…' Murdoch looked at Charlotte and raised his eyebrows.

'Charlotte, just call me Charlotte,' she remarked.

'For Charlotte here – and make it comfortable!' he barked loudly, although the poor man was actually stood next to him.

'Will do, sir,' replied the Indian and with that he bowed and hurried off, soon to return with a slightly younger lady, possibly in her thirties.

'Ah, good. Miss, er, Charlotte, this is Buff's wife, Starlight,' introduced Murdoch.

'Pleased to meet you – that's a lovely name,' responded Charlotte.

Starlight bowed and smiled, then began to lead Charlotte away to another room.

'Well, ah'll tek ma leave, miss. Goodnight,' Murdoch said.

Charlotte turned and smiled. 'Goodnight,' she said, then she disappeared after Starlight.

Murdoch stood watching where Charlotte had been for some little time; a pang in his heart brought him back to reality. 'Agh, women – naught but trouble.' He shook his head. 'Buff? *Buff!*' he shouted again.

Again the Indian hurried up to him. 'Yeh?' He bowed his head.

'Ah need anether drink – fetch me ma bottle,' ordered Murdoch as he sat by the roaring fire and stared into it, lost in his own world.

Starlight led Charlotte into a back room, which looked very snug and comfortable.

'Thank you, Starlight. May I ask you a couple of questions?' Charlotte asked.

'Yes, miss,' replied Starlight, bowing her head.

'Well, for starters, you do not have to bow, and my name is Charlotte,' she said, and led Starlight into her room.

'Yes, miss, thank you,' responded Starlight.

'What is this Murdoch actually like and why does your husband put up with all that shouting?' questioned Charlotte.

'He nice man, really; bark is worse than bite. We work for him because he give us somewhere to live.' She shrugged her shoulders and smiled.

'Really? How? Why?' Charlotte became inquisitive.

Starlight looked a little sad. 'After battle of Wounded Knee, we managed to hide from soldiers and escaped to Moon Land. The cold was terrible and I began to weaken further. Our ancestors were not ready for us and so they carried us to safe place. There we were discovered by Murdoch's men and brought here. He look after us and at first we feared him almost as much as soldiers. But rather than send us back to them, he kept us here, so we work for him,' she explained. 'Is room all right for you?' she asked.

'Yes, fine, Starlight, thank you. Goodnight,' Charlotte smiled.

'Goodnight, Miss Charlotte,' called Starlight as she left the room.

The next morning Charlotte decided to go for a quick stroll around the immediate area that was enclosed about the main house. As she rounded the cow hands' accommodation she was not surprised to find Sandy sat alone upon a pile of logs overlooking the splendid wooded valley below them.

'Stunning, isn't it?' she remarked as she sat next to him.

'Good morning, Charlotte – yes it is,' he replied, not taking his eyes off the splendid scenery.

'Penny for your thoughts – do they involve a woman?' teased Charlotte.

Sandy smiled. 'Sadly, no. I was thinking of how best to get the gang with the diamond north of the border, actually,' he said.

'Did you have a good night?' she asked him. She was desperately trying to get some sort of conversation going. The more time she spent with Sandy the more she felt for him, and she was certain that he felt the same in return, but for some reason he just would not broach the subject.

'Fine thanks – and yours? I do hope Murdoch did not offend you in any way,' he responded.

'No, his manners were impeccable. I am actually beginning to like this man,' she smiled.

'I am surprised at that, Charlotte. I took him for just a tub of lard that likes to throw his weight about,' growled Sandy.

Charlotte's heart sank a little. 'You may find below his hardened exterior that he actually has a heart of gold,' she explained. 'He's not a little dissimilar to yourself, Sandy,' she went on, standing up and continuing with her stroll.

Sandy remained seated and watched her walk away. If only he could drum up the confidence to tell her how he felt. What on earth was he afraid of? he wondered. Frustrated, he turned his attention back to the wooded valley.

Soon Paddy joined him and sat down beside him upon the logs.

'Top o' the morning to yer, young sir, and how are you this fine morning?' he greeted Sandy.

Sandy smiled – if anyone could cheer you up it was Paddy. 'Hello, Paddy… not so fine actually,' he replied, despondent.

'Oh, and why's that then?' Paddy asked.

'Well, I cannot come up with a viable plan to get both the gang and the diamond north of the border, and secondly, I cannot bring myself to tell Charlotte just how I feel for her. I want to tell her, but for some reason I just clam up. Why?' pleaded Sandy.

'Maybe you're afraid of rejection – have you thought o' that now?' asked Paddy pointedly.

Sandy looked thoughtful, and looked at Paddy. 'No, I have not. But I am twenty-five years of age, so why should that bother me now?' he asked puzzled.

'Maybe because you have never felt this strongly before about anybody. You have said yourself in the past that you prefer to remain aloof, keep everyone at arm's length. You don't allow anyone in and yet, whether you like it or not, you are fighting over yourself whether to allow Charlotte in or keep her at your door,' Paddy explained.

'Maybe you're right, Paddy. I will give it some thought and try to gain the confidence with which to tell her how I feel. I won't do it while we are on this case, though,' Sandy replied.

'Fair enough, but just remember, as an old lady once told me, "it never came to stay but only came to pass",' warned Paddy.

'Oh? And what is that supposed to mean?' asked Sandy.

'Even someone as patient as Charlotte will not wait around for ever.' And with that Paddy stood up and began to stroll back to the house.

Sandy sat for a short while then followed. He was having great difficulty coming to terms with all this emotion inside of him. He reached the front porch at the same time as Charlotte; as always, he stepped back to allow her to ascend the stairs first.

'After you,' he gestured.

'Thank you, Sandy.' She smiled but her reply was not as warm and soft as usual.

Maybe Paddy's right, he thought and sighed.

They wandered into the guest room, where Sergeant Hackett, Constables Courtney and Adams, Will, Paddy and Murdoch were all waiting for them.

'Ah, good – now that we are all here, let us begin,' announced Murdoch.

'The Canadian authorities wish not only for the return of the money and diamond but also the criminals responsible for the crime,' began Sergeant Hackett.

'Before we begin to put together some kind of plan, ah have a small confession to mek, 'pon a small matter which ye all probably do not know anything about,' began Murdoch.

Paddy sighed heavily and folded his arms. 'Something tells me this is going to make things a lot more complicated than they may at first have appeared,' he groaned.

'It's no' that bad,' assured Murdoch. 'On the other hand, we are about to send ye into a foreign country, where ye will not only come across that country's authority, such as the sheriff, deputy and, if yer unlucky, even army, but also a group of law enforcers known as the Dixie riders,' he went on.

'All right – what is it we need to know?' asked Will.

Murdoch stood up. 'Pinewood Falls sits on the very eastern edge of Greendale County, which is in itself within the area known as Montana. Although not yet formed as a state, it is still governed by the US.'

'Gawd, this just gets better and better,' moaned Paddy.

Murdoch looked at him disapprovingly. 'After the Civil War, in the 1860s, some Confederate soldiers opted to settle in this area rather than go back to their home states. They were put here not only to colonise but also to police this wild frontier area. So they quickly formed themselves into a type of militia known as the Dixie riders and were led by Colonel Cody.

'At first it was a great success; they broke up the Fenian training camps within their area and kept the Métis peoples under check.

'But sorry to say, as is usually the case, once those were achieved, rather than wind down their operations they began a program of ethnic cleansing, as it were. At one time there were thirty to forty ranches within Greendale – today there are ten, all owned by ex-leaders of the Dixie riders. It was also a very busy place, especially within the border passes for prospectors. They've all now been driven away. At one time Indians would traverse the region in their annual tribal movements north. We don't see that any more, after the Battle of Wounded Knee – or massacre, I should say – the Dixie riders stop any Indians from entering the county and send them back to the army post at Harper's Crossing over in the south of the county. We have been hearing of off-hand executions, shootings and general beatings of any unwanted people within the county.' Murdoch paused and glanced about the group. 'That, my friend, also includes the Irish – you either have to be descended from a family living in the region before 1864 or from someone of Confederate stock. Until, that is, Ted Skerrat and his gang appeared. Now, they do not interfere with the Dixie riders' authority and it appears they actually have to abide by their regulations, but it is known for them to ride abroad to do various tasks for the Colonel. We believe the train robbery was one of them.

'The Colonel is a wily old fox; he is an actual ex-Confederate army colonel and ah believe he is now nearing his sixtieth birthday. Do not be misled by his white hair, ice blue eyes and soft calm features. This man is ruthless – he would kill ye on a point that most of us would simply dismiss, so be very careful,' Murdoch paused once more.

'So basically, he employs the Ted Skerrat Gang to do work very similar to what we do for the government?' questioned Will.

'Yeah, precisely,' nodded Murdoch.

'Just out of curiosity, how many Dixie riders are there?' asked Sandy.

'Oh, most of them are broken down into small detachments and are posted all over the county – a bit like the North-West Mounted Police are for the Canadians. Most are always kept at his own ranch, known as Jefferson's Ranch, just south of Richmond. All told I would say there is probably about sixty of them,' Murdoch estimated.

'So we are looking at a small army, then,' retorted Sandy, a little dismayed.

'How many are kept at these towns?' asked Paddy.

'It depends upon the size of the town and where it is; for instance, there are five at Pinewood Falls, ten at Richmond, five again at Eagle's Pass – which is to the north of the county – but only three at Harper's Crossing. Don't forget each town has its own sheriff and deputy as well; all now fall under the Colonel's will.' Murdoch took a swig from yet another whiskey bottle.

'So instead of looking at seven men at Pinewood Falls we are now looking at fourteen at least,' declared Sandy.

'Yep, just about,' replied Murdoch as he quickly nodded his head. 'Oh, one last thing: if the Colonel is to form a posse, he will usually raise it from his own ranch hands, but he has been known to use other ranch hands too.'

'This is getting better and better,' announced Will dryly.

'What are these Dixie riders used for?' asked Charlotte.

'They are used generally to guard the local banks and

telegraphy office, but also as couriers to keep the Colonel informed of whatever is happening around his county,' explained Murdoch.

'Is there anything else we need to know?' asked Paddy.

'No, ah don't think so; ye know that we cannae rely upon the US army for assistance,' Murdoch replied indifferently.

'Just one more thing – how big is this county?' asked Sandy.

Murdoch looked at him puzzled, then shrugged his shoulder. 'About forty miles wide at the widest point which is the eastern border along the Pine River, and sixty miles long at its longest point, which is marked by the Canadian border,' he replied.

'So then, to the plan... Has anybody got any ideas?' asked Sergeant Hackett.

'We need to antagonise this Ted Skerrat Gang into chasing us north,' mused Will.

'Very good, but how?' asked Murdoch.

'Could we not steal the diamond, then have them chase us? We could maybe ambush them somewhere,' suggested Sandy, shrugging his shoulders.

'Right, but would that not mean staking out the town for a period of time?' remarked Murdoch.

'And where would you intend to ambush the gang?' questioned Sergeant Hackett.

'There's that defile just down the road there,' retorted Paddy; he thrust his thumb over his shoulder.

'Devil's Cut, ye mean,' retorted Murdoch and he huffed at the thought. 'If ye could draw them on that far, there's also an old abandoned prospectors' settlement just south of the border in Pine River Valley called Valley. Me an' some of ma men could possibly ambush them there,' he added thoughtfully.

'*We* could do that,' responded Will.

'Any more ideas?' asked Murdoch as he glanced about the group.

'Remember, these are ruthless men – if anything goes wrong while they are chasing you, they will simply gun you down,' replied Sergeant Hackett.

'Perks of the job, isn't it?' shrugged Sandy.

They all sniggered.

'Anyway, ah need to go into Pinewood Falls tomorrow, so if ye wish ah can take two of yer in with me – give ye yer first taste of the town,' suggested Murdoch.

'I'll go,' answered Sandy immediately.

'Are ye sure ye can handle it, nancy boy?' mocked Murdoch.

'I'll go along too,' replied Paddy.

'Well, don't say too much – I've told yer how they feel about the Irish,' warned Murdoch.

'Murdoch, what access points are there to Pinewood Falls from Canada?' asked Sandy.

'There are three routes from here. The first is rather flat and brings ye out behind Buffalo Mount, which is the route we shall take tomorrow. The second follows Pine River and leads through the gorge created by the meeting of the river and the west side of Buffalo Mount, which is the one that leads to Valley. The third and most difficult route is down Indian Creek; it is very narrow and not much used at all. It also takes a lot longer,' explained Murdoch.

'So, it is this Colonel Cody who is actually the mastermind behind this gang,' mused Will, as he sat forward and placed his hands together in front of his face in mock prayer.

'That's right,' replied Sergeant Hackett.

'So, what are we to do with him?' Sandy enquired.

'At present that's to be a more long-term operation,' responded Murdoch.

'Unless, of course, you can get him to ride back with this gang?' questioned Hackett.

'Ha! According to your information he knows nothing of the diamond, though,' replied Sandy.

'Yeah, that's true, and he is not likely to find out either,' sighed Murdoch. 'Next, Sergeant Hackett has been informing me that you intend to use peashooters against these guys?' he said, a question in his tone.

'We carry two Smith and Weston revolvers in shoulder holsters and also use Lee-Enfield rifles – except Paddy here, he carries a sawn-off shotgun,' explained Will.

'Well, out here we wear Colt revolvers on our hip and carry these,' he held up a rifle. 'A Winchester,' he explained. 'Now, if ye wish, ah can supply ye with one revolver and one Winchester each.'

'I'm sure we shall all take you up on your offer of revolvers, but on the other hand, I know both Sandy and Paddy are rather attached to their rifles,' replied Will.

'I would prefer to keep my handgun as well,' declared Charlotte.

'All right, that's three Colt revolvers and two Winchester rifles,' announced Murdoch.

'Ah'll have those ready for ye by dinnertime. For ye two going into town tomorrow, we shall have to dress ye all appropriately – we shall have those ready for ye too.'

He stood up, cut a piece of chewing tobacco and slipped it into his mouth, then reached for another bottle of whiskey. The meeting was clearly at an end, and therefore the four companions all stood up to leave.

'Where are ye lot off to?' asked Murdoch.

'Prepare for tomorrow, have a walk – you know, live a life,' responded Sandy.

'Ah well, if ye don't want a drink,' mumbled Murdoch, as he took another swig from his bottle.

The four companions did not see him again until dinner. Murdoch sat at the end of the table and, in a drunken stupor, he slurped and burped his way through the meal. It became so bad that all four companions stopped eating their own meals and, placing down their knives and forks, they just watched Murdoch.

'What the hell are yer lot gawkin' at noo?' he challenged through a mouthful of food.

The four companions silently looked at each other and stood up.

'Can a man no' eat his meal in his own house ane mare!' cried Murdoch as he thumped the table, bits of food flying in all directions.

'It is not what you are doing, Mr McLeod, but the way in which you are conducting yourself. To be honest, I do not think it does you justice,' replied Charlotte.

'What do yer mean, lassie?' growled Murdoch. He began to clench his fists in anger.

'Look at you – you are a miserable, filthy, uncouth drunkard, sir,' she retorted.

Murdoch sat and looked at her open-mouthed, stunned into silence. 'Am ah no' in ma own house?' he eventually asked.

'You are, luckily for you. I have come across better-mannered beggars in the road than you, Mr McLeod,' Charlotte stated, then turned on her heel and left the table.

Will, Sandy and Paddy were as stunned as Murdoch; they just looked at each other.

'Well, do yer think ah should 'ave to put up wi' this?' questioned a now irate Murdoch.

The three glanced at him and left the table, with Murdoch glowering after them.

'Can a man no' do anything within 'is own castle without being insulted?' he growled, his temper continuing to rise.

Sergeant Hackett put his napkin down upon the table as he too left; he felt better to leave now than face the wrath building up within Murdoch.

'Buff? *Buff*!' he heard Murdoch shout. 'Fetch me anether bottle.'

Paddy caught up with Charlotte outside. She had walked as far as the gate, there she stopped and began to watch the valley.

'Well, that certainly put a flea in his bonnet,' he smiled.

Charlotte stood erect, arms folded. Tears fell down her cheeks, not out of pity or hurt but of temper. 'I'm sorry, Paddy, but all I could see in there was my father. I watched my mother put up with far too much over the years. It all became too much.' She shook her head.

'Never mind, angel. You've got to remember though that Murdoch is not your father. This is another chapter of your life, and Murdoch is a development of this area. He has grown this way to survive, whether we approve or not, and he will be here long after we have gone, too,' reasoned Paddy, as he slipped his arm around her shoulders.

She buried her head deep into his chest and began to cry in earnest.

'That's it, angel, let it all come out,' assured Paddy, and patted her arms.

'You must all think of me as some silly clod,' she said at length.

'No, we don't; we accept you as being a vital cog within the team. And one of us thinks a little more than that of you,' he hinted.

Charlotte smiled. 'Thank you, Paddy – likewise I think of you as the brother I never had,' she eventually whispered.

'Ah, but who said it was me?' Paddy raised his finger.

Charlotte smiled, but her eyes fell to the ground. 'Please do not tease.'

'Who said I was? I would never mock the strings of the heart. But a little birdie did tell me this morning that he would love to let you know how he feels, but as yet just cannot find the right words to express his feelings.' Paddy smiled, placed his finger under her chin and raised her face so she looked him in the eye. 'You really are a lovely person – not just looks but personality, too. Give him a little time and he will come round. Even if I have to kick his backside to do it.'

Charlotte broke into laughter. 'You know, Paddy, you are a fine fellow too and you are the best friend that I have ever had.' She kissed him on the cheek lightly.

'Well, I'll take that as a compliment, then,' smiled Paddy and they went for a stroll around the perimeter fence.

It had not gone unnoticed, as the rags at the windows of the house fell back.

'Miserable am ah? Filthy, ay? Uncouth?' Murdoch growled to himself as he took yet another swig from his bottle. 'What on earth am ah doin', allowin' mesel' to be insulted by a woman – an English woman at that,' he went on. He took another swig, then looked at the bottle thoughtfully. 'Agh!' he exclaimed, and threw the bottle against the wall.

Everyone was up bright and early the next morning. One of the cow hands had set up the buck wagon. Sandy and Paddy were preparing themselves for the journey. Paddy was to ride shotgun while Sandy would sit in the back.

Both Will and Charlotte walked over to join them. 'Take care and do not take any risks,' warned Will.

They both nodded in response.

Charlotte placed her hand upon Sandy's as he rested his arm against the sideboard. 'Take care, Sandy – no heroics,' she smiled.

He placed his hand tenderly upon hers and smiled back. He was about to open his mouth when Murdoch stepped out of the house.

'Good morning to ye all. Ah see yer all prepared and ready to be off.' He smiled broadly. Sergeant Hackett stood openmouthed, as did the two cow hands. Liam shook his head in disbelief. For once Mad Dog was neither drunk nor cursing and swearing.

'Mad Dog, is that you?' Liam stammered.

'Of course it's me, ye beggar,' replied Murdoch. He strolled past Charlotte. 'Good morning, sweet princess.' He bowed politely and, taking hold of her hand, he kissed it gently. Then, straightening, he rubbed his hands together. 'Right, let's be off then, shall we?' He clambered up on to the wagon, flicked the bridle and off they set.

Will just managed to call after them, 'Do whatever Murdoch tells you to do.'

They stood and watched the wagon move away. Charlotte walked down the road a little way as far as the gate.

In the wagon, Paddy turned to Murdoch.

'Well, then, how far is the town?' he asked.

'It will tek us a good few hours to get there. We'll be gone all day,' warned Murdoch.

'Ah well, not to worry. It's not as if we had anything else planned,' yawned Sandy.

'The young lassie – Miss Charlotte – are ye and her an item?' Murdoch asked Paddy.

'Me? No, we are just very good friends,' he replied.

'Oh… she is a very attractive young woman. She would mek any man proud,' Murdoch went on.

'Oh aye, she would that,' admitted Paddy.

'She's feisty, too; a lot of men prefer their womenfolk to be feisty,' nodded Murdoch.

Paddy smiled – he realised where this conversation was going to go. 'Given it's an asset round these parts,' he replied.

'Well, it is. Round here yer need a feisty woman at yer back; she would do well here if she could get the right decent man to protect her. Now I'm not saying that for mesel', ye mind, but ye never know what's around the corner.' Murdoch glanced sideways at Paddy, wondering if he'd got away with it.

Paddy showed no emotion and just watched the road ahead.

It was some time later and Sandy's back was beginning to ache, when they passed a rather large hill to their right.

'That's Buffalo Mount, which overlooks Pinewood Falls. Pine River and the gorge are on the other side of that hill. There is a crag at the top of the mount known as the veranda; it gives an ideal viewpoint overlooking the town. Ye could use that to stake the town out – ye would use a track going up from this side to reach the top,' suggested Murdoch.

'So no one would realise we were there?' Paddy asked, he looked over at the hill with interest.

'Precisely,' smiled Murdoch, chewing some chewing tobacco.

'Tell me, Murdoch, how long have we been in the United States?' asked Sandy, looking over Murdoch and Paddy's shoulders.

'Oh, about an hour,' Murdoch replied thoughtfully. 'Now look, ah'm going to go back to ma old ways – it is to protect me cover. Ah'm not a lunatic, all right, but call me "Mad Dog".' He glanced over his shoulder at Paddy and Sandy.

They returned his glance and both burst into laughter.

'What noo?' cried Murdoch.

'Well, it depends on your point of view,' replied Sandy.

Murdoch looked on contemptuously and, as he sat back to drive the wagon, he could be heard mumbling over his breath.

They were soon at the ford that led across the river; there was no one about except for one man on the far bank. He had dismounted and sat waiting upon a rock, his horse tied behind him. As the wagon drew closer the man stood up.

Paddy observed he was dressed all in grey. 'Dixie rider?' he asked in whispered tones.

'Yep,' Murdoch replied.

The man stopped them by raising his hand. 'Howdy, Mad Dog, who's the two new guys?' he asked casually.

'New cow hands, fresh from the old country,' replied Murdoch.

The man looked suspiciously at both Sandy and Paddy. 'Uh-huh.' He nodded.

'Yep, this is Sean an' this here is Sandy,' explained Murdoch as he spat some tobacco upon the ground.

'OK then, Mad Dog, you know the rules, best let them know,' said the man as he stepped back to let the wagon pass.

'Och, we're anly here tae store up; we'll be gone in a few hours,' raved Murdoch back.

He drove the wagon up the only real street in the town, and described places as they passed. 'That's the sheriff's office and opposite is the only saloon in town – Texas Rose's; that's Ted's girl and that's where the gang lives,' Murdoch explained quietly. He drew the wagon to a halt outside the hardware store. He and Paddy then jumped down while Sandy stayed with the wagon, dropped the back board and waited.

Sandy used the time to have a good look at the street. There were one or two cottages, a side street, then Texas Rose's, followed on both sides by a few stores and a bank just up from the saloon. He smiled to himself. I wonder what Will would make of that, he thought. One thing he did notice was the atmosphere, people were watching him and the feeling was one of suspicion and fear. Presently a middle-aged man strolled up to the wagon.

'Howdy,' he greeted Sandy – not in a friendly manner, but officiously.

'Hello,' replied Sandy; he smiled to ease the stranger's suspicion.

'Ah'm the town's sheriff. Whut brings yer to town, stranger?' he asked coldly.

'I've come in with Mad Dog; we are collecting stores and then returning to the farm,' Sandy explained.

The sheriff nodded his approval. 'Good, just as well, because if yer were to stay any longer, cowboy, we'd have to take those guns away.' He pointed to Sandy's Colt on his hip and the Winchester in the back of the wagon.

'Oh, all right, Sheriff, I'll remember that for next time,' Sandy replied.

Satisfied, the sheriff walked off with a grunt. Sandy sighed a little, then glanced at the hardware store. Where the hell are they, are they making the stuff? he wondered. Just then a very scruffily dressed woman came out of the store. She was struggling with a very heavy load, which she dropped before she reached her wagon which was parked immediately in front of Murdoch's. The package split open and vegetables and other foodstuffs rolled all over.

The crowds stepped forward and began to laugh at the woman's misfortune. Sandy noticed that she glanced about her nervously as she tried in vain to gather everything about her. Nobody went to her aid. Disgusted, Sandy jumped down from the wagon and landed next to her. Instinctively she shied away, hiding her face and trying desperately to make herself as small as possible.

'It's all right, I'm trying to help you,' he assured her and he gently held her arm.

She glanced at him from below matted hair and a dirty shawl. She was too stunned to say anything – was this another sick trick? She had not seen this stranger before, and had not received such help for a long time.

The crowd had fallen silent now as they stood and watched Sandy gather up the lady's goods and place them upon her wagon.

'There you go, miss; I think that's the lot,' he said as he placed the final items upon the back of the wagon.

However, before he turned around he heard a click in his ear and felt the cold end of a gun barrel against the side of his head.

'What the hell do yer think yer playin' at?' came a threatening voice.

Sandy straightened up slowly; he looked neither left nor right.

'I was simply helping this lady with her things,' he explained.

'Lady? *Lady!*' exclaimed the voice as it broke into a high-pitched snigger. 'Well, hell, that's luscious Lucy – she ain't no lady,' he threatened.

Sandy turned his head to face the voice, and came face to face with the Kid, who was sneering into his face. Sandy glanced past him and saw the lady cowering in fear in a doorway.

'Excuse me.' He stepped past the Kid and, holding out his hand, he helped the old lady to her feet. 'Come on, I'll help you to your wagon.' He began to lead her past the Kid – he couldn't take her round the front of the wagon because of the crowd.

'What the hell! Don't yer know who ah am – are yer deaf?' shouted the Kid and he cocked his gun.

'You fire that and it will be the last thing you do, Kid,' warned Calvin softly, as he stood behind the Kid with his gun squarely placed in his back.

As Sandy led the woman slowly to her wagon – for she appeared weak on her legs through sheer fear – the Kid lowered his gun.

'As God is my witness, Sheriff, if he crosses my path agin ah'll kill 'im,' the Kid growled. He turned and pushed his way back through the crowd towards the saloon.

Once the woman had sat down upon the wagon Sandy handed her the bridle.

'There you go, dear lady, safe journey.' Sandy smiled and began to walk away.

The crowd also began to disperse as the wagon drove off. Sandy did not look back, but the sheriff stepped in front of him.

'Stranger, I do not know who you are but ah'm telling yer, yer've now made one hell of an enemy. It's ill to go against the way people feel in these parts. Out here only the strongest survive; there is no room for the weak.'

Sandy looked at him. 'Where I'm from, Sheriff, the strongest help the weak. It makes bigger men of us.' He turned and walked back to the wagon.

Not long after Paddy and Mad Dog appeared and began to place the supplies upon the wagon. Sandy assisted in securing the goods to the back.

'Everything all right?' asked Murdoch.

'Fine – there is nothing more I need to see in this town,' Sandy replied and sat back down.

Murdoch turned the wagon around and drove back out of town the way they had come in.

The Kid stepped out onto the porch in front of the saloon and watched them leave. Sandy met his gaze and stared back in contempt. This annoyed the Kid all the more as he stood tensely and clenched his fists.

The return journey was uneventful and it was quite dark when they arrived back at Paradise Ranch. Brown Buffalo had kept supper back for them and Charlotte and Will waited up for them.

THE FIRST CRACKS

They ate supper and retired to the guest rooms.

'Well, what happened? What's the town like?' asked Will.

'There is nothing much to it really – one main street and one lesser street leading off to the west, creating a "T" as it were. The two largest buildings are the saloon known as "Texas Rose's".' Sandy paused.

Will raised his eyebrows at that and smiled.

'And then there's the bank,' Sandy went on. 'As you enter the town from the east, you cross a ford to begin with. The first buildings are small cottages, then you hit the stores and saloon. Incidentally, opposite the saloon is the jailhouse and just two stores up from the saloon sits the bank. It has an armed guard upon the roof. The main street appears to run in a line from south-east to north-west; the stores are on that street. The street that runs from it, goes in a south-westerly direction; there are only cottages upon this street,' Sandy paused again.

'The armed guard… is there only one?' asked Will.

'It appears—' Sandy began, and was interrupted.

'There is only one on the roof at any time. A second guard – possibly the relieving guard – sits within the bank itsel',' added Murdoch.

Sandy glanced at him; Murdoch indicated to him to carry on.

'Dixie riders?' asked Sandy.

'Yes,' replied Murdoch.

'So the bank falls within the Colonel's domain,' responded Paddy.

'Oh yes, quite so,' answered Murdoch.

'Are there many houses?' asked Charlotte.

'No, it is not a big town. We would term it a village really,' replied Sandy.

'Although ye did not see it, the church is the very last building on the street at the northerly most point, while the cemetery is just out of town along the residential street,' added Murdoch. 'But I'm very impressed, nancy boy, ye took a lot in.' He smiled and nodded his head.

'Do you have to belittle him all the time?' admonished Charlotte.

'Sorry? What? No, ah was just teasing,' apologised Murdoch as he tried to defend himself.

'Anyway gentlemen, I think it is time for us to retire; it has been a long day. Tomorrow we shall work out how best to watch this place,' announced Will. He turned and left the room, and was followed by Sandy and Paddy.

Charlotte and Murdoch remained in the room, both silent. Surprisingly Murdoch had neither reached for the whiskey bottle nor cut off any of his chewing tobacco; he was soon to surprise Charlotte all the more.

'Excuse me, little miss, but I'm a little parched – may I have a cup of your tea?' he asked very politely.

'Why, yes,' replied Charlotte and poured a cup out for him.

He smiled and very slowly raised the cup to his lips to drink from it. His expression of sweet contentment soon changed to one of horror; he immediately spat the tea out into the fire. 'Agh, woman, are ye tryin' to choke me?' he cried clutching his throat.

'Mr McLeod, you are very uncouth, sir! If you are to ask a lady for a cup of tea, at least have the decency to drink it and not spray it all over room,' scolded Charlotte.

'Och, ah thought it was proper tea! Wha' is it?' asked an exasperated Murdoch.

'It is camomile tea, Mr McLeod,' retorted Charlotte. She stood up, 'It is supposed to calm you down. Now, if you will excuse me, I must retire,' she declared and left Murdoch sat in the room alone.

Murdoch watched her leave. 'Keep yer temper, bonnie lad. Buff? *Buff*!' he shouted as he tried yet another sip of the tea.

'Yes, sir,' the Indian bowed as he entered the room.

'Get me a bath, and ma razor,' declared Murdoch.

The Indian stood open-mouthed. 'Your *bath*, sir?' he asked, incredulous.

'Yep – ye know what one looks like, don't ye?' challenged Murdoch in return.

The Indian bowed and hurried from the room.

'Ah'll show ye, Miss Charlotte and ah'll sweep ye off yer feet. I haven't lost my touch with the ladies yet, he thought as he admired his image in the mirror.

Will, Paddy and Sandy were stood by the perimeter fence to the ranch house when Charlotte joined them the next morning.

'Good morning, gentlemen,' she greeted them, smiling.

'Good morning, Charlotte,' they replied in unison.

'Is Murdoch about?' asked Will.

'I haven't seen him, why?' questioned Charlotte.

'It's time to start casing this town, we believe,' responded Sandy.

'Oh – are we all to go together?' she then asked.

'No… not at first anyway. We reckon it may be wiser to do it in pairs, on twelve-hour shifts,' explained Paddy.

'Twelve hours? That's a long time,' Charlotte observed.

'As Paddy and I know where to go, I reckon it is only fair that we do alternate watches. Will and I can manage the night watch, while you and Paddy, Charlotte, can manage the daylight hours,' suggested Sandy.

They all agreed.

'We shall change on the stroke of eight,' decided Will.

'Which means we ride at six from here,' added Paddy.

'When do you plan to start?' Charlotte asked.

'This evening; Sandy and I shall ride out at six,' declared Will.

'Do Murdoch and Sergeant Hackett know of this?' she asked.

'Not yet – I am just about to go and tell them,' responded Will and left for the house.

'I shall go and get my equipment ready for this evening; excuse me.' Sandy left.

Charlotte glanced nervously at Paddy and sighed. 'You know, just when I think I'm about to get some response out of Sandy, he puts up this brick wall again,' she moaned.

Paddy smiled. 'He is probably not wanting to cause any distractions for either of you while this case is ongoing,' he replied.

'I wonder sometimes if he really does care for me,' she retorted.

Paddy smiled again. 'Come on, angel. I shall take you for a little stroll.'

That same morning in Pinewood Falls, three of Ted's gang came out of the saloon and clambered upon their horses. The Kid led the way as he turned his horse north and began to trot out of town, followed by Joe and Joshua.

'Where we goin', Kid?' asked Joshua.

'For a bit o' fun,' sneered the Kid over his shoulder.

As the three riders headed towards Indian Creek, a lone figure stood at the saloon window, watching them.

'Where are they off to?' Ted asked Abe as he observed them ride away into the distance.

Abe looked up. 'Hmm? Oh them... gone for a ride, ah guess,' he replied indifferently.

'Hmm, ah don't want any problems regardin' their stupidity,' murmured Ted.

'Ah, they'll not be gone long,' replied Abe.

Ted just looked at him, but his attention was distracted by Rosie as she cuddled in closer to him.

'Oh, Ted, yer could take me out for a ride in the buggy, honey?' she suggested.

'Not today,' replied Ted as he prised her arms away from him.

'Oh, go on, Ted,' she repeated.

'Rosie, ah said no!' he stated sharply.

She looked forlorn and disappointed; but she knew Ted of old and she knew not to push her luck.

He began to ascend the stairs to the first floor, followed by Rosie. Ted could not get used to this waiting; he knew the Colonel would wish to see him soon but would wait until the dust about the robbery had cleared. In the meantime, Ted had to wait and make sure he did not lose the cash. He also had to keep an eye on Abe, for fear of him talking and blowing the lid about the diamond. It made him a little more edgy than usual.

Will found Sandy in his room, cleaning his revolver.

'Are you taking your Smith and Wesson?' Will asked.

'No. The Colt goes better with this attire, but I shall take my Lee-Enfield.' He held up two full magazines.

Will nodded. 'Good, I shall take my Colt plus the Winchester and my walking stick for good measure,' he smiled.

'Oh yes, you can't beat a bit of cold steel,' laughed Sandy as he raised his sword bayonet and shadow fenced.

'Should we take some hand grenades?' asked Will.

'Would not do any harm – take the satchel,' shrugged Sandy.

'It appears that Murdoch left with his cow hands this morning to do some perimeter fencing. I've told Sergeant Hackett of our plans,' Will explained.

Sandy nodded. 'Right then, this evening it is,' he smiled.

Lucy Wightman had just fed her two pigs and checked her small allotment. She lived alone now since her father passed away at the old prospectors' settlement in Indian Creek. As she closed the small gate to the pen behind her and stopped, she thought she had heard something. She listened intently... There it was again. Someone was coming up the track towards her cabin. It usually meant trouble, especially where horses were concerned. It would not be the first time a group of young men had rode out of town just to give her a rough time.

Lucy looked about her quickly; there was no time to pause. She opened the pen gate and shooed her animals out into the open, so that they could run away if threatened. Then, glancing about her nervously, she hurried over to the cabin, picked up her rifle then fled into the woods which stretched upwards and behind her residence.

The Kid halted his horse in front of her cabin. His fun had been curtailed the day before by that pestering stranger – now bored, he was gunning for more.

'Luscious Lucy, luscious Lucy,' he shouted teasingly. 'Look what we've brought for yer! Joshua wants ta give yer a kiss,' he mocked.

Joe began to laugh.

'No, ah don't! Ah wouldn't kiss that,' cried Joshua in his immature way.

They waited a short while for a response; of course there was none.

'Joshua, go an' get her out o' there,' cursed the Kid impatiently.

'What, why me? Ah might get something,' argued Joshua.

'Look, just go an' get her, or yer *will* catch something,' threatened the Kid.

Joshua looked at the Kid then at Joe; he sighed heavily before dismounting and storming into the cabin.

He soon reappeared. 'There's no one here, Pisco, she's gone,' he cried.

'Damn her!' cursed the Kid, he unholstered his gun. 'Let's look for her, she can't have gone far.' He clambered down from his horse and began to slam open shed and out house doors.

'Ah, forget her, Kid, let's ride on,' protested Joe.

'Ah damn well won't – she's not going to get the better of me. Ah'll teach her,' shouted the Kid.

'Hey, look what ah've found,' shouted Joshua, as he raised a flagon of whiskey.

The Kid stopped, then stormed over to where Joshua was standing and snatched the flagon from his hand, he began to drink the contents immediately.

'Hey, leave us some!' protested Joshua.

They soon found another flagon and together they became very drunk and disorderly.

'Ah know how to sort her out,' cursed the Kid, as he staggered into the cabin. There he lit a fire and, staggering outside once more, began to whoop and shout.

Lucy watched with horror as her home began to burn with what possessions she had. Tears welled up in her eyes; she could not do anything now, as they were so drunk and wild they would surely shoot her dead. Likewise she could not allow herself to cry out for fear of being discovered, so all she could do was sit where she was and wait until it was safe to come out. The three riders did not wait too long after that – having satisfied their small minds they clambered back upon their horses and rode off towards Pinewood Falls.

Murdoch had still not returned by six o'clock. Sergeant Hackett stood with the four companions at the front of the house.

'You know this will take time and will become very monotonous,' he warned.

'Yes, but we must gain some kind of picture as to how these operate and their habits before we strike,' replied Will.

'A Chinese man once said, "The first small step taken is one step closer to a thousand miles",' remarked Charlotte.

Sergeant Hackett nodded. 'That I do not doubt – just remember these are dangerous people. Take care.'

Charlotte stepped forward. 'Take care the pair of you.' She glanced at Sandy and smiled.

Will and Sandy then mounted up.

'See you in the morning,' said Will to Paddy and Charlotte as he spurred his horse forward.

'Charlotte,' called Sandy.

'Yes,' she replied, her heart leaped in anticipation.

'Look to Polaris; I shall be looking, too.' He smiled then turned his horse and rode away.

She sighed and shook her head. Look to Polaris? she thought, disappointed.

It was quite dark when the two riders reached the blind side of Buffalo Mount.

'Here we are,' announced Sandy as he turned his horse from the road and began to look for a small path or track. He soon found it. 'I think this is what we're looking for, Will,' he said and spurred his horse up the track. Sandy had become a little more proficient with horses since his initial training days at Drumloch Castle; he was now had been able to keep up with Will.

The two rode to the top of the mount; it was heavily tree-covered and with the ground thick with shrubs they found they had plenty of cover.

'This is brilliant!' exclaimed Will, 'They could be just ten yards away and miss us,' he went on.

Sandy nodded. They dismounted and they walked towards a bare patch of ground which had a rocky lip to the edge; this overlooked the town of Pinewood Falls.

'This must be the "veranda", that Murdoch informed us about,' said Sandy as he looked down Pine River Valley.

'Quite spectacular, isn't it,' said Will as he admired the view.

'Yes, but we appear to have overlooked one or two things,' said Sandy.

'Oh? What are they?' replied Will as he glanced at the town through his field glasses.

'Well, firstly, it won't affect *us* much, but it will Charlotte and Paddy,' Sandy looked at Will.

'Well, come on, what is the problem?' demanded Will.

'All right. Which way is this ledge facing?' Sandy asked.

'South.

'Right, now if they use field glasses, what is likely to happen?'

Will looked to the sky. 'Oh, hell,' he hissed.

'Yes – if the sun catches the lens in either field glass, they'll be seen for miles,' remarked Sandy.

'We must warn them to be careful,' suggested Will.

'Likewise, we cannot light a fire,' Sandy stated, looking a little disgruntled at his own words.

'Mind, this does not mean that we are going to cuddle up at night to keep warm,' mocked Will.

'More importantly, if we ride into town now and antagonise Ted Skerrat's gang into chasing us back across the border, what's the odds of them actually taking the diamond with them?' Sandy said pointedly.

Will looked at Sandy, dismayed. 'Damn, that's true,' he responded. 'So we will have to locate the diamond, then?' he went on.

'It would help,' answered Sandy as he sat with his back to the boulder.

It was eight when Murdoch returned. Although he still wore his thick matted buffalo coat, his hair had been cut and his beard neatly trimmed. Having dealt with his horse and the cow hands, he entered the ranch house and strolled straight into the guest rooms.

'Evening,' he said as he entered.

'Good evening,' both Charlotte and Paddy replied.

Sergeant Hackett almost choked on his drink – Murdoch was actually wearing clean smart clothing.

'Ha' ye eaten, dear little lady?' Murdoch asked Charlotte as he kissed the back of her hand.

'Well, er… no, we've been waiting for your return,' she replied, slightly taken aback.

'Well, then, if you give me a few moments, miss, ah shall be ready for dinner,' he apologised. Then, turning to Paddy and Sergeant Hackett. 'Excuse me, gentlemen, ah shall only be a moment.' He bowed and left the room.

The three companions sat in total silence; they glanced at each other.

'Yes, we are awake,' announced Paddy.

'Well, I don't know what has happened or what's been said, but I have never seen Murdoch like this before,' remarked Sergeant Hackett.

They were still debating this unusual turn of events twenty minutes later when Brown Buffalo stepped into the room and thumped a small dinner gong with his stick.

'Are you sure we are not dreaming?' stammered Sergeant Hackett.

Paddy simply shook his head. 'Dinner is served,' he said, and led Charlotte out of the room.

They were led to the dining room by Buff, where he opened the door and gestured to them to step inside. Still rather puzzled, Charlotte did so. She stopped and gasped, for before her stood the magnificent sight of a clean and freshly shaved Murdoch, dressed in his best army uniform. He smiled when he saw that his impression had given the effect that he had indeed wished for.

'Please, Miss Charlotte, if ye would care to sit here at ma right…' He then held out a hand to take Charlotte's and led her to her seat, which he pulled out for her; as she sat he pushed it in for her.

'Thank you, Murdoch,' she remarked.

Starlight had done the same with Paddy and he now sat opposite Charlotte while next to him sat Sergeant Hackett.

Murdoch, broadly smiling, sat down last.

'Murdoch, is this your birthday or something?' asked Hackett suspicious.

'No, I shall be honest. It was the scathin' attack by Charlotte here that made me think,' Murdoch explained. 'To be frank, ah think she is the prettiest, loveliest woman ah've ever met.' He tenderly placed his hand upon hers as he looked her in the eyes.

Charlotte coughed and cleared her throat; she smiled coyly. 'Mr McLeod, what is it you are trying to say?' she asked.

'Ah'm saying is there room in that lovely heart for a big oaf like me? Yer'd want fer nothin', lassie, and ah'd mek sure naebody would harm yer,' he confirmed.

Charlotte sat back, dumbstruck; she then caught Paddy's eye and it appeared to bring her out of her trance, so that she smiled, rather embarrassed. 'Mr Murdoch, after this operation we may never meet again – my path lies elsewhere,' she began to explain softly.

'Aye, it would if yer remain where yer are, but if yer left...?' he left the question unfinished.

She sat back and shook her head gently.

'Ah know it has come as a shock to ye, lassie. But give it some thought, that's all ah ask,' he finished sheepishly, as if only now realising the other two were in the same room.

They sat and finished a glorious meal; Murdoch proved to be the perfect host. As they finished eating he turned to Charlotte.

'Tea, miss?' he offered as he raised a teapot.

Paddy looked suspicious, while Charlotte smiled.

'Yes, thank you,' she replied, accepting a cup.

'No alcohol?' questioned Sergeant Hackett.

'No, but I'll get you a drink if you wish, Sergeant,' offered Murdoch. He made as if to stand.

'No, no, you are all right, I'll settle for tea,' replied Hackett.

Murdoch turned once more to Charlotte and as he removed a cloth from a bonbon dish he offered her a chocolate.

'Where on earth did you get those from?' asked Paddy.

'I've been saving them for a special occasion,' replied Murdoch.

Charlotte quickly retracted her hand. 'How long have you been saving them?' she quickly asked.

'What? Och, not long,' he replied. He took one himself and ate it. 'Look, they are all right,' he said, trying to convince the others.

Soon they retired to the guest rooms, where Murdoch again proved the perfect host as he gave anecdote after anecdote about his army career and the first few years at Paradise. Eventually the evening drew to a close; Charlotte and Paddy asked to be excused, as they were required to be up early.

'Goodnight, miss – ah do hope ye have had a pleasant evening?' asked Murdoch with a broad smile, holding her hand he kissed it gently.

'Thank you, Murdoch, I have had a wonderful evening,' she smiled in return.

'Please, do not forget to give ma offer some thought,' he implored once more as he looked at her seriously.

She returned his gaze and sighed heavily. 'Mr Murdoch, as I explained…'

'Please, miss, it is a genuine offer, and ye could do a lot worse,' he pleaded.

'All right, Murdoch, I will give it some thought,' she answered softly, then walked Paddy to the front door.

'Goodnight, angel.' Paddy glanced from her to the room they had just vacated.

She nodded as she bit her lower lip. 'Goodnight, Paddy,' she groaned.

'Well, how do you feel?' he asked.

'I don't know,' she replied thoughtfully. 'I'm in a bit of a turmoil at the moment.' She sighed and glanced back to the guest room.

'You need to give it some thought, angel; remember time is on your side and also remember I genuinely believe your heart lies elsewhere,' he said, then turned and walked away.

Charlotte watched him walk across the ground away from the house; she glanced at the guest rooms, then thought of Sandy for the first time that evening. She shook her head and retired to her room.

Charlotte and Paddy were mounted and about to ride out of Paradise when Murdoch called to them.

He strolled over to Charlotte. 'Here ye are, bonnie lassie, ah've had these picked for yer, to eat throughout the day.' He proffered a small basket up to Charlotte.

She looked under the cloth cover; there sat the shiniest apples she had ever seen. 'Thank you, Murdoch, they look ever so sweet.' She smiled and took hold of the basket.

'Aye, lassie, picked them mesel' frae ma own garden,' he replied proudly.

Charlotte smiled. 'See you later, Murdoch,' she said as she spurred her horse on.

'That ye will, wee lassie. That ye will,' Murdoch stated as he stood and watched the two riders disappear into the trees.

They had rode on a little way before Paddy turned to Charlotte. 'Well, what are you to do now?' he asked mockingly.

'I don't rightly know, Paddy. Here is a man I compared to my father, but he has proposed to me – almost – and yet there is Sandy. If I wait much longer for *him* I will grow old and frail,' she mused.

'It's not that long ago, Charlotte, that I seem to remember you wished to grow old alone,' declared Paddy pointedly.

'Yes I know, but after last night, Paddy – the way he looked at me, how he treated me...' She paused, then looked at her companion. 'I'm being silly but I must give it some thought.'

'Oh, that's something you will have to do, for he *will* want an answer,' warned Paddy.

Sandy and Will were standing by their horses when Charlotte and Paddy arrived at the veranda at Buffalo Mount. They warned them of the dangers of using field glasses recklessly and explained their own thoughts from the previous night.

'Right, we'll watch the town today, then ride back to Paradise at six. Tomorrow we will set off for Indian Creek and try to reach the town from that side,' suggested Paddy.

Sandy and Will both agreed, then, clambering upon their horses, they turned and rode off.

At first all was quiet but at about ten that morning Paddy noticed two riders approach the ford from the east. The sentry on the far bank also noticed them and rode off into town. This rider only rode as far as the sheriff's office; he quickly dismounted and rushed into the jailhouse.

'Sheriff, Sheriff,' a voice shouted excitedly.

'Yes, what is it?' asked Calvin; he had been out at the back of the jail.

'There's two riders crossing the ford,' the sentry stammered.

'Well, shouldn't you be challenging them?' Calvin asked.

'It's a US marshal and a deputy,' the man blurted out.

'Are you sure?' demanded Calvin.

The man nodded quickly.

Calvin turned. 'Right. Ned?' he shouted out to the back of the jail.

'Yes, Sheriff?' replied Ned as he stepped into the main office.

'Quickly go and inform Ted that there is a US marshal and deputy riding into town this very minute, yer hear?' instructed Calvin. 'You.' He turned on the unfortunate Dixie rider. 'Get out back and cut some wood, make yersel' useful.' He jabbed a thumb over his shoulder.

By now the two riders were walking their horses along the street; nobody paid particular heed to them and people went about their daily chores. At the same time Ned entered the saloon. He ran up to the bar.

'Where's Ted, where's Ted?' he asked the barman.

'Upstairs with Rosie – he don't wish to be disturbed, boy,' replied Abe, who was sat at a table close by playing cards.

'Well, somebody ought to tell him that there is a US marshal and deputy riding into town this very minute,' Ned replied excitedly pointing back out of the door.

Abe looked at Ned, aghast. 'Are you sure?' he cried.

Ned nodded.

'OK. Joshua, go and get Ted – oh, and yer better knock on the Kid, too,' Abe urged his brother. 'Joe, go and cover the back; Danny, you cover that window; I'll cover the door.' They all hurried about their tasks.

'Where's Frenchy?' asked Joe.

Abe looked around him. 'Oh, he's taken the barber's daughter out for the day in that buggy of theirs,' he said, remembering.

He and Danny peered out of the saloon across the street at the jailhouse, just as the two riders clambered off their horses.

'Howdy,' greeted Calvin, coming to the front door just as they were stepping on to the porch.

'Howdy, Sheriff,' replied the marshal. 'Ma name is Roscoe, US Marshal, an' this is ma deputy, Tom Marvin.'

'What brings you two to these parts, Marshal?' asked Calvin.

'We've been trackin' a no-good scoundrel by the name of Ted Skerrat and two brothers – Abe and Joshua McCabe – north from Missouri. We have reason to believe, Sheriff, that they may be hidin' in these here parts,' he replied.

Calvin appeared to think for a moment, then replied, 'Nope, can't say ah've heard the names. Might they be usin' an alias, Marshal?'

'It's possible, but they haven't done so as yet,' replied the marshal.

'Well, anyway, there's me forgettin' ma manners. Boys, come in, make yourselves at home,' Calvin invited. 'Coffee?' he offered them as they sat down, once inside the jailhouse.

'Thanks, wouldn't mind if a do, pardner,' responded the marshal.

'Have you been ridin' long, boys?' asked Calvin.

'Weeks – we picked up Ted's trail down in Missouri and we've doggedly stuck to it all this way,' boasted the marshal.

'Look boys, ah've just got to go send a message. I'll not be long – make yerselves at home.' Calvin walked towards the hardware store then quickly hurried down a side street that would bring him around to the back of the saloon. The Dixie rider out at the back had gone, too, not only to raise the alarm with his fellow riders but also to collect his own horse from the front of the jailhouse.

Paddy had been watching this scenario unfold before his eyes.

'Charlotte, come here, what do you make of this?' He gave her the field glasses.

'Is that the sheriff?' she quickly asked.

'Yes, there are two men in the jailhouse at present, but there has been a lot of activity of men coming and going; one even hurried into the saloon,' Paddy explained.

'Isn't that strange,' muttered Charlotte as they watched the sheriff hurry into the saloon from the rear.

'Ted, Ted!' called Calvin as he entered.

'Yes, Sheriff?' Ted replied calmly.

'There's a US marshal and a deputy sittin' in ma jailhouse askin' questions about yer,' he stammered.

'Where they from?' asked Ted.

'Missouri, ah believe,' replied Calvin.

'Well, boys, it would be a shame to let them ride all this way and not see us,' declared Ted.

'What are yer goin' to do?' asked Calvin.

'Give them a greetin',' replied Ted with a smile. 'Right, boys... Abe, Danny, watch the street. Wait until we are in position, then step out of this here saloon.' He looked at Abe.

'Sure, Ted,' Abe smiled back.

'Pisco, Josh, Joe – come with me now,' Ted ordered. He was just about to run out of the back of the hotel, when Calvin stopped him.

'What about Ned and me?' he asked.

Ted looked him, contemptuously up and down. 'You, Sheriff, wait here,' he ordered. 'Ah'm sick and tired of waitin' round here; ah'm goin' to sort these two out,' he declared and was gone.

They quickly retraced the sheriff's steps to the back of the jail; there they waited and listened intently.

'Pisco, wait here. When you hear me hollerin' for the marshal, go in through the back door,' ordered Ted.

The Kid smiled. 'Sure, Ted, sure thing.' He hooked his coat back and waited.

'No shootin', mind – not until yer hear me firin' ma pistol,' warned Ted.

'It'll be like takin' candy from a baby,' The Kid sneered in reply.

Ted led the others to the front of the jailhouse; he left Joshua to one side of the building and placed Joe on the other, while he himself stepped out to the middle of the street.

'Hmm,' murmured Paddy, watching as the gang got into position.

'What *are* they up to?' asked Charlotte. Neither could tear their eyes away from the scene now unfolding in the town below.

'I think we are about to witness Ted Skerrat in action,' warned Paddy.

'Hey, Marshal, you lookin' for me?' shouted Ted.

Inside the marshal and his deputy sat bolt upright.

Again Ted shouted. This time they hurried to the door unholstering their guns as they did so. As they reached the door they stopped, then the marshal stepped out on to the porch slowly.

'Howdy, Ted. We've come for yer and we aim to take yer back with us,' he warned.

Ted began to laugh. 'Ah'd like to see yer try, Marshal.'

Both reached for their guns and several shots rang out one after the other. The marshal fell forward dead, while his deputy staggered out of the doorway, then slowly crumpled to his knees on the porch and fell forward into the street, also dead.

From within the jail stepped the Pisco Kid, reloading his gun as he did so. The others, Ted included, began laughing loudly and slapping their thighs as they stepped closer to the two dead bodies.

'Poor sods, they stood no hope,' muttered Paddy.

Charlotte lowered her field glasses. 'That was cold-blooded murder,' she said quietly.

Calvin came running out of the saloon, closely followed by Rosie. Both ran to Ted, but Calvin ran to confront him, while Rosie ran to make sure he was all right.

'What the hell did yer do that for? Ah could 'ave got rid of 'im,' cried Calvin. 'Yer realise my neck is in a noose now?' he went on.

'Oh, shut up, Sheriff, will yer?' Ted shook his head. 'We'll clean up the mess.'

'But what about the Colonel? What are yer goin' to do when he finds out? Ah should arrest yer by rights,' protested Calvin.

'We'll see what the Colonel has to say when his couriers return,' Ted sneered as he glanced over his shoulders to two grey mounted men.

They both watched him without saying a word. Then, turning their horses, they rode off towards Richmond.

'What'll we do now, Ted?' asked a concerned Abe.

'Let me take them out,' urged the Kid.

'No, let 'em go about their business,' Ted glanced back at Calvin. 'Sheriff, if ah'd a let 'em go they would only have come back sooner or later,' he said, trying to justify his actions.

The sheriff now stood tall. 'You may find more than just the Colonel comin' after yer now,' he warned defiantly.

'Well, then yer can let me know when they do arrive, can't yer!' Ted sneered into Calvin's face as he walked past him back towards the saloon.

Rosie walked with him, linking her arm in his. 'Ah'll sooth yer aches, Ted,' she said.

The rest of the day was spent quietly. Charlotte and Paddy kept a close eye on all the happenings. There was not much in the way of conversation. Paddy was thinking of the events that day while Charlotte was deep in her own thoughts. When six o'clock arrived, Paddy touched Charlotte upon her shoulder.

'It's time to be going, angel,' he whispered.

She nodded silently and together they rode back towards Paradise. As they arrived at the ranch, Sandy and Will were waiting for them at the gate.

'Evening – everything all right?' greeted Sandy with one of his boyish smiles.

'No, not really,' replied Paddy.

'What happened?' asked a concerned Will.

Paddy explained the actions of that day. Sandy turned to Charlotte gently held her hand.

'Are you all right?' he asked softly.

She looked at him suspiciously. 'Have you been talking to anybody lately?' Her eyes narrowed.

'About?' he asked innocently.

Realising she had just put her foot in it, she closed her eyes and sighed heavily.

'I'm sorry, Charlotte.' Sandy's eyes fell; he let go of her hand and turned away to watch the trees.

'I'm sorry, Sandy.' It was now Charlotte's turn to apologise. 'I'm just not used to you being so attentive, that is all.' She smiled and placed her hand gently upon his arm.

He turned back and smiled. 'Maybe I should be more so in future,' he said quietly, almost whispering.

She was about to answer when Paddy interrupted.

'Excuse me, but I have a hole to fill and I'm rather hungry,' he stated as he dismounted from his horse.

Sandy assisted Charlotte in dismounting from her horse.

'Charlotte,' he began nervously, 'may I have a word with you, privately?' He had been pondering all day on how best to broach the subject of asking Charlotte's hand without sounding really silly.

She paused and looked not a little sad when he asked his question, which not only surprised him but worried him also. She placed her fingers gently to his mouth.

'Sandy, Murdoch has asked me to stay here with him,' she replied softly.

'Oh, I, er… well, I hope you'll both be happy.' He tried to sound positive but fell well short as he lowered his eyes in disappointment.

She placed her hand below his chin and raised his face to look at him. 'I have yet to give him an answer, I just require a few more days.' She smiled at him and looked gently into his eyes.

'No, honestly, I really do think you will be happy here.' He cleared his throat and rubbed his hands down his trouser sides.

'I was looking for Polaris last night.' She smiled in her attempt to reassure him.

He smiled in return, then, turning, he led her towards the front porch. His emotions were in turmoil. I've messed up again, because of being too cautious, he thought.

At about that time just to the south of Greendale County, a large mass of people had begun to gather, down by a shallow rocky riverbank. Once upon a time this would not have caused a stir, but now these were native Indians led by a warrior called Grey Wolf, a lieutenant of Geronimo. He had fought a guerrilla war against the white man for many years, until his people were weak with hunger and disease, and he eventually surrendered. However, although the white man may have taken their freedom, they could not gain the Indians' loyalty or souls.

Assigned to a reservation upon land the white man deemed useless for anything, especially growing food, their situation only became worse. So a meeting with the tribal elders was called, and at this meeting it was decided to move north. The British were known for their tolerance of the indigenous tribes and generally left them alone. Also, it had come to Grey Wolf's attention that if they moved north towards the settlement of Pinewood Falls, there was someone there who could guide them across the border and find them help and assistance. It was a long shot, especially with the old, infirm and the young. But Grey Wolf was a warrior of the old school, who saw his first duty being to protect the weak and needy of his tribe. If he was to try and escape the hell of this reservation, he was not going to leave anyone behind who would suffer any reprisal for his actions.

They gathered by the old riverbed at the northern boundary, there were no guards, as no one expected them to go anywhere; the authorities were correct in assuming that Grey Wolf was honourable enough not to leave the old and infirm behind – though neither did they expect him to take them with him.

Grey Wolf chose this moment deliberately; it was a clear night with a full moon. He was to take them up the old riverbed which at first led them away from their eventual destination. They would require as much light as possible and, because the going was expected to be slow and hard, they required as much time as possible before the authorities would raise the alarm the next morning. Further, the intention was to move solely at night and to rest by day; because of the nature of the group he was leading, Grey Wolf only intended to move ten miles per night. Despite all the difficulties, the arrogance of the authorities actually gave Grey Wolf and his people extra breathing space as they began to check all the routes they expected him to take; of course the old riverbed was not one of them.

The wise old warrior led his people along the riverbed all night; he planned to stay on this track for the night and then strike due north on the second night towards Sweet Water River, which was the southernmost boundary for Greendale County. He obviously wished to avoid any white settlements, for he realised that if any of the group were to be spotted then all their cover would be blown and they would be in deep trouble. So he threw ahead a screen of young warriors to act as scouts every evening; they were under strict instructions not to get involved in any fracas whatsoever, but to collect as much food as possible for the rest of the tribe. He also realised that his biggest problem would be to get across the Sweet Water River; this was going to be a problem, for he could not use the ferry at Harper's Crossing. Not only was it a large white settlement, but he knew that there was also a small army outpost there.

By lunchtime the following day the whole area was up in arms looking for them and because of the circuitous route he was taking they missed him and his people completely. In fact, they did not get round to checking the riverbed until the third day, by which time Grey Wolf was long gone. However, things were not going entirely to plan for Grey Wolf either, firstly because due to the high amount of old and infirm the tribe found it very difficult to achieve the ten miles he had hoped for each night. Secondly, the crossing at Sweet Water was more daunting than first envisaged and it was found necessary to build their own rafts just for the crossing. Although these were built in one night it meant that they were a day behind already. Finally, and possibly more tragically, the only person who appeared to know whom to contact at Pinewood was the one fatality at the Sweet Water River crossing, as he was washed away while trying to take the rope across the river. All Grey Wolf knew of the contact was the name White Feather.

To Will and Sandy's surprise they were led straight into the dining room by Brown Buffalo. There again the table was laid, again Murdoch stood proudly at the end dressed in his formal army evening attire. Starlight led them all to their seats and again Murdoch paid particular attention to Charlotte. Sandy and Will sat dumbstruck.

'No, you're not dreaming,' hissed Paddy across the table at Will, who was sat next to Charlotte. Murdoch had taken particular care to keep Sandy at the far end of the table.

'Well, boys, what d'yer make of Pinewood now?' Murdoch asked.

'We need to get closer to the town, so we intend to travel down Indian Creek tomorrow,' replied Will.

'Yes, Will and I believe that the best way to antagonise these fellows will be to locate and steal the diamond,' added Sandy.

Murdoch glanced from Sandy to Will and back again. 'An' just how d'yer intend to do that, may ah ask?' he responded.

'We are going to have to break into the saloon from the rear and retrieve it that way,' explained Sandy, a mischievous grin on his face.

'Just like that, eh?' replied Murdoch, shaking his head.

'This sort of thing is what we are best at,' responded Will.

'If, as planned, we do get them to chase us north across the border, we feel the best carrot would be the diamond,' remarked Sandy.

'These are not yer run of the mill natives. These are highly intelligent, dangerous, callous murderers,' argued Murdoch.

'Yes, we know,' replied Charlotte quietly.

'We will hopefully lead them here, to the Devil's Cut—' began Will.

'Naw, yer'll ne'er get that far,' interrupted Murdoch as he shook his head. 'Takin' the diamond is one thing, but to lead them all the way here is anether. Yer best bet is to lead them to Valley, ah'll wait fer yer there.'

Will glanced at each team member in turn. None spoke: Charlotte nodded her approval, Paddy opened his hands in answer while Sandy simply shrugged his shoulders. 'All right then, Murdoch. Valley it will be,' he replied.

It was now Murdoch's turn to sit silent; he looked from one to the other around his table. Then as if coming out of a trance, he laughed. 'Tomorrow is another day, and one thing is for sure. Something will happen sooner or later between the Colonel and Ted Skerrat.'

Will and Sandy sat up simultaneously and glanced about them.

'It may have already – Ted and his men gunned down a US marshal and his deputy today,' explained Paddy.

'Then time is now of the essence. It won't take long for the authorities to get involved,' warned Sergeant Hackett.

'Or the Colonel, for that matter,' added Murdoch. 'As the Indians say "two bears cannae share the same cave".'

Again Murdoch proved to be the perfect host as he chatted and joked; he was charming and jovial and fêted Charlotte as if she was a princess.

This Sandy did not miss. Unfortunately, sitting at the opposite corner of the table, there was not much he could do but watch.

He became quiet and remorseful and, for the first time, felt something he did not like, something which made him annoyed – jealousy had reared its ugly head. Finally he could take it no more and he stood awkwardly and excused himself from the table. The effect upon the group was quite profound, for until that moment everyone else had been happy. However, now they all fell quiet, especially Charlotte. Even with the skilful prodding of Murdoch, their spirits fell flat.

'Tomorrow, ah shall ride with ye as far as Pinewood Falls; we shall take the two Indian scouts, an' Liam, if he wishes to come along. Ah'll lead you all into Indian Creek an' travel down that way. Two Crows shall remain with you an' guide through Greendale,' declared Murdoch as they all stood to retire to their beds.

It took almost a day to ride from Pinewood Falls to Richmond, not counting the few miles extra towards Jefferson Farm. It was well into the early hours when the two Dixie riders from Pinewood rode up to the ranch entrance. They were stopped by two men at the gate.

'Whoa! Howdy, friend – what brings yer to these parts?' asked one of the men.

'Ah have some important news to give to Colonel Cody,' replied one of the riders.

'Well, friends, if yer will just tie yer horses up over by the canteen. Dusty here will go fetch 'im.' The man pointed with his Winchester rifle.

The riders nodded and both dismounted from their horses so as not to disturb anyone as they slept. As the man by the name of Dusty ran off, the two riders led their horses towards the canteen, where they tied them up next to a trough. Rather than enter the canteen they remained upon the porch. One lent against the supporting bar while the second yawned and sat down upon the step. They did not have to wait long as the Colonel came strolling over towards them.

'Well hello, Jake, what brings you up this way?' the Colonel asked.

'It's the Ted Skerrat Gang, Colonel,' the first rider said, standing straight.

'Oh? An' what have they been up to now?' the Colonel enquired.

'They've just shot a US marshal and his deputy, Colonel,' the rider replied in an officious manner.

'What!'

The rider repeated his words.

'An' jist where the hell was Calvin in all of this?' growled the Colonel.

'It appears he was tryin' to send the US officials on a wild goose chase, Colonel, but Ted paid him no heed,' said Jake.

'Right – they will pay heed of me. Go an' git three men, Jake. Ride back to Pinewood. Ah wants Ted and his fellow friends escorted back to here.' The Colonel placed his hand upon Jake's shoulder as he gave his orders.

'Yep, Colonel,' Jake replied and went to get three men.

'Yer don't have to set off till first light, so rest and freshen up yer horses, boys!' the Colonel shouted after Jake. When he turned around, the Colonel held up his thumb, which Jake returned in a gesture of acknowledgement.

THE PROSPECTOR'S DAUGHTER

By first light Jake and his four fellow Dixie riders rode out from Jefferson's Ranch. The Colonel in parting had instructed them to use force if necessary, but he wanted to see Ted back at the ranch as soon as possible to account for his actions. The Colonel was not best pleased – after all, the last thing he wanted was for the US authorities to start sniffing around and discovering exactly whose rule of law was actually being adhered to in these parts.

Jake was to follow the direct road back to Pinewood Falls; still, it would take him the best part of a day to reach even at a steady pace. He was a little apprehensive – this confrontation had been coming for some time now, after all. Jake realised that Ted himself was not the real danger, he was far too calculating to rush in headlong. No, it was the younger members of the gang, the two hotheads – Joe and the Kid and the easily led Joshua; they were the real dangers. They were far too unpredictable; he would require as many guns at his back as possible, so even before he had left the ranch his mind was set that his first port of call was to be the sheriff's office.

Charlotte too was up early that morning; her mind too was set. She got ready and dressed with a purpose that had been lacking of late. Enough of all this talk of Murdoch or Sandy; it had become too much of a distraction, she thought. She walked decisively into Murdoch's lounge, where he had just put on his gun belt and stood very erect and very smart.

'Good mornin', ma wee bonny lassie,' he greeted her with one of his broad smiles.

'Good morning, Murdoch,' she replied resolutely. 'Before we ride this morning, we need to talk.'

'Ah, do we now?' He rubbed his chin, as if already well aware of the contents of the conversation. 'Well, yer'd best sit down, wee lassie, don't stand on ceremony.' He gestured for her to sit with a broad wave of his arm.

'Thank you, but I'd best stand, Murdoch,' she replied. She stepped closer to him and placed her hands together in mock prayer in front of her face as if thinking of what to say next, but in truth she already knew what to say to Murdoch. 'Mr McLeod, I must thank you for your wonderful and generous offer. Yet I must decline it, as our paths lie elsewhere.'

Murdoch made as if to interrupt her, but she held up her hand to stop him.

'Please, Murdoch, allow me to finish. When I was living at the Buddhist monastery, they taught me that each of our lives are mapped out for us. Mine lies elsewhere, as I have explained. The timing is not right for me to be here… Maybe in another life…' she shrugged her shoulders.

'So yer wish to be wi' that nancy boy, eh?' exclaimed Murdoch, his voice raising.

'Maybe, maybe not. That is up to him to see the signs now,' replied Charlotte calmly. 'My road lies with my friends, Murdoch, come what may.' She pursed her lips as she finished. She realised the disappointment that Murdoch must be going through and the actual courage it had taken him at the beginning to offer her his hand; yet her mind was now made up.

'Under that rough, gruff exterior, Murdoch, you are very sensitive and caring. You will meet the right girl for you, in time.' She placed her hand upon his and looked him squarely in the eyes.

Murdoch huffed and his eyes dropped to his feet; he shuffled nervously. 'Aye, well, it's a great shame it's not yer, Charlotte. Ah would've treated yer like a princess. But ah thank ye for yer honesty and decency in lettin' me know yer answer, rather than keepin' me waiting,' he finally declared, proudly standing his full height. 'If ye change yer mind though, the offer still stands,' he added quickly with a wicked smile.

Charlotte smiled in return; she shook her head and turned to leave the room.

'Ah hope, whoever he is, he realises just how lucky he is!' called Murdoch after her.

She walked outside; the others were waiting for her. She placed her hat squarely upon her head and looked up at the sky. Although it was still early the sun had begun to rise.

'It's going to be a warm day,' sniffed Paddy.

'Well then, let's be off,' cried Murdoch as he followed Charlotte out of the house and jumped upon his horse.

They all rode out from Paradise Ranch. Charlotte was riding behind Murdoch and Will; she glanced back at the now disappearing ranch. Thoughts of Murdoch and Sandy briefly crossed her mind then she quickly dismissed them as she remembered Storm, her friend at the Tibetan monastery. She smiled to herself then, looking forward once more, she rode on. Sandy, following, was watching her, wrapped up in his own thoughts. By trying to be the gentleman, and through his fear of rejection, had he now gone and cooked his goose? he wondered. He deserved it; no one could be expected to wait for ever. He swallowed hard. As soon as possible he would have a word with Charlotte about his feelings for her.

By midday they were sitting upon the ridge which separated Pine River Creek from Indian Creek. The views were breathtaking – deep tree-lined valleys as far as the eye could see. There were no sounds other than the ones they were making. They were all resting, having just eaten. Will looked through the bag which contained the hand bombs, while Charlotte sat upon a large boulder looking east. Paddy walked over to her and gave her a cup of coffee.

'Thank you, Paddy.' She smiled as she took the mug.

'It's a grand old day, is it not?' he replied as he rested with his back to the boulder, taking in the same view.

'Yes, it is. It's moments like these when you feel glad to be alive,' she murmured as she sipped the coffee.

'Sandy has been very quiet… in fact, he has not said much at all,' remarked Paddy; he did not glance at Charlotte.

'That's up to Sandy, he is free to choose his own destiny.' Charlotte turned and smiled at Paddy. 'I've told Murdoch of my decision,' she went on.

'Did he take it well?' asked Paddy.

'Very.' She paused. 'Actually, I have grown to like the old bear.

However, I have allowed things to distract my attentions lately. It will not happen again,' she said soberly.

'It will all come out in the wash, Charlotte, you will see,' replied Paddy in a matter-of-fact manner; he threw away the dregs of his cup then walked away.

Soon they were on their way again. Owing to the rough terrain and steepness of the incline the going was slow, but eventually they reached the bottom of the valley. Murdoch then turned left and led them along a small narrow creek.

'This here is Indian Creek – it will lead us almost into Pinewood Falls,' he announced as he turned in his saddle to face those following.

The valley itself was quite narrow, with steep, tree-covered, rocky sides; the pace was again slow and deliberate. Then, somewhat unexpectedly, they entered a secluded grassy meadow. It all appeared peaceful and idyllic except for two badly charred and blackened buildings to their left. Two Crows, who appeared to be the only one who knew of this place, hurried forward, concerned, and the others followed. There to their surprise they came across the equally startled figure of a woman, whom Sandy immediately recognised as the old lady from Pinewood that he'd assisted. As she stood up, Two Crows leaped from the saddle and hurried to her side. He began to fuss over her and talk away excitedly in his own tongue.

'Slow down, Two Crows! I cannae understand yer when yer jabberin' away like that,' groaned Murdoch.

Sandy too had dismounted, but rather more slowly. The old lady was not paying Two Crows the slightest bit of attention; rather, her eyes were fixed rigidly upon Sandy, who returned her stare.

'It is all right, miss,' he began and raised his hand to calm her. She looked as if she would run any minute. 'We are not going to harm you. What happened here?' he asked slowly.

She did not answer, but stood rooted to the spot. Her eyes never left Sandy as he stepped closer and closer to her, until he was directly in front of the woman.

The others remained on their horses, fearing that if they made any attempt to dismount then she would bolt and run away.

'It is all right, miss. These are my friends,' explained Sandy, smiling. He noticed that although the lady showed no visual sign of answering or doing anything for that matter, tears were streaming down her face. He slowly reached out and took hold of her hands.

At last her eyes moved, falling to their hands.

'Charlotte,' Sandy called calmly but without looking, 'could you come here, please?' He did not remove his hands nor his eyes from the lady's face. Only now did he begin to question her actual age, for as he studied her more closely she looked younger than he first assumed.

Charlotte hurried over to Sandy and stood by his side, she glanced between Sandy and the lady as she awaited his next instruction.

'This is my friend, she is called Charlotte. She will look after you; if you can, tell her what has happened here,' he explained softly and calmly. He then placed the lady's hands in Charlotte's and, looking at Charlotte for the first time, he smiled sadly, then left them together.

Charlotte placed her arm around the lady and began to lead her away; as she turned she watched Sandy over her shoulder.

Sandy had now turned his attention to the burning remains of the building. He had noticed that the lady had been holding a stick in her hand, so he deduced that she might have been searching for something, prodding the smouldering ashes as she went.

Murdoch stepped over to Sandy. 'Two Crows says she is called Lucy,' Murdoch whispered. 'This was her home, and that, over there,' he pointed to the second smaller burning building, 'was her shed.' He looked about.

'Was this done deliberately or was it an accident?' asked Sandy, almost quietly.

'As yet we don't know. She did have some animals,' Murdoch explained. 'I've sent Liam and Black Eagle off to look for them.'

Sandy nodded. Paddy and Will had now joined them within the shell of the building and together they began to search the embers for anything of value that they may save.

Charlotte had led Lucy away to the water's edge, where they

now both sat. Charlotte was cleaning Lucy up and trying to calm her down also. The men were searching the building; there was not a lot to find. Sandy unearthed a silver picture frame, which contained a picture of two women. One was older than the other, but you could see that they were related. Paddy found a similar picture frame that held a picture of a proud-looking man. They were given to Two Crows, who handed them over to Lucy. He appeared to have taken this incident harder than she had. He came hurrying back to join the rest in the building.

'We need to find Peggy,' he said earnestly.

'Peggy?' cried Paddy.

'You mean there was someone else in here?' cried Sandy alarmed.

'No, she was my doll, my companion, my only friend,' replied Lucy quietly. She had followed Two Crows towards the house.

They all turned to face her, surprised.

'We'll try to find her,' responded Paddy, as he and Sandy began to search the ashes once more.

'Don't forget, gentlemen, we still have an operation to pull off here,' warned Will.

'That can wait for the time being,' replied Sandy sharply.

Will did not respond; nevertheless, he was surprised, as they all were, at Sandy's tone.

They eventually found Lucy's peg doll, which they tried to clean up before handing it back to her. By now Liam had begun a small campfire and although Lucy was still very apprehensive she had at least begun to talk to Charlotte, as she continued to watch Sandy with admiration in her eyes.

'So then, what are we to do with Miss Lucy here?' asked Murdoch, as they sat around the fire.

Lucy looked up, startled, her eyes darting from one to the other terrified.

'It's all right, Lucy, we do not mean you any harm – but you cannot stay out here any longer,' assured Charlotte.

'Has she told you what happened yet?' asked Will.

'No, I have not,' Lucy spoke up, clearing her throat.

'What happened, Lucy? You can tell us – you're among friends now,' Charlotte said calmly.

'Three members of that gang came yesterday and burned the place down because they couldn't find me,' she replied sadly.

'Which ones, do you know?' asked Paddy.

'The Kid was one – I think the others were Joe and Joshua.' She narrowed her eyes over the last name as if she was not too sure.

'The Kid... was that the one who was pushing you around when I met you?' questioned Sandy.

'He always does; he takes great pleasure in pushing me around. Sometimes he hits me, sometimes pistol-whips me, kicks me...' She shook her head.

'So what do the townsfolk do?' asked an astonished Charlotte.

'Nothin' – they're frightened. The only person to stand up to them was you.' She looked at Sandy.

Murdoch, who had during this conversation been talking to Two Crows in the shadows, now returned to the fireside. 'Well, that solves that mystery.' He looked at Lucy.

She looked back rather shyly.

'What mystery?' asked Will.

'Well, over the past few years, more and more Indians have been finding their way north into Paradise Valley... sanctuary,' explained Murdoch. 'This, despite the fact the Dixie riders tend either to shoot or return any native Indians they find upon the road. How these Indians came to know about us at Paradise Valley was proving to be a bit of a mystery – certainly to me it was.' He turned and smiled at Lucy. 'Still, Two Crows recognised you straightaway and he tells me that you are responsible for all these migrant Indians, Miss Lucy, or should I call yer "White Feather"?' He sat and watched Lucy.

She sighed heavily and looked to the ground. 'Yes, it was me. I knew you would help those who are destitute and in need of help. But I cannot stop now; since the massacre at Wounded Knee, I have become extremely busy and we must not turn those people back now,' she pleaded.

'What would happen if we *did* turn them back?' asked Will.

'Because of the authorities' greed and incompetence, the natives have been largely removed from their land and deposited in certain plots of land,' explained Murdoch. 'These places – or reservations, as they are called – tend to be in spots that the authorities or businesses find useless. Agriculture is poor, disease is rife and the overall economic situation becomes at best perilous – or collapses altogether.' He sat quietly, watching the flames of the fire dancing in the evening air.

'We have not come here to get involved with other countries' problems and we still have our own little problem to solve. One thing is for certain, though – we must not leave you here, Lucy,' announced Will.

'Yep, I agree. Lucy shall come back to Paradise with me,' declared Murdoch, thrusting a large thumb into his chest to emphasise the point.

'But what of the natives?' she pleaded.

'I shall leave Black Eagle and Liam here. They shall remain for another week. After that I'm afraid all this must cease; any more natives and my government will be telling me to return them. At present they are happy to turn a blind eye, as it were. Let's keep those north of the border safe, shall we?'

Lucy quickly glanced at Sandy, then her face fell. 'I guess you're right.' She held the two pictures out in front of her.

'Who are the pictures of?' quizzed Paddy.

'This one is of my mother and I; it was taken when I was fourteen. They were happy times. My mother was always cookin' something. The cabin always smelt of freshly baked bread.' Her face lit up and she smiled as she reminisced, then a dark shadow fell across her face once more. 'My mother passed away of the fever, shortly after this picture was taken.' She became sad once more. Then she held out the picture of the man. 'This was my father, Ben Wightman; he was a fine, proud man. A prospector for as long as I care to remember, he taught me to read and write and what was right and wrong in this world.' Again she fell silent as she thought of her beloved father. 'We lived peacefully here, mindin' our own business, until one day the Colonel comes a-gallopin' up the track there with his men and killed or moved most of the prospectors out o' here. They killed my father as he tried to stop them, then they burned the whole settlement down. I hid out o' the way and then later built ma own log cabin here.' Tears began to run freely down her cheeks once more. The group sat silent for some time, contemplating Lucy's tale.

'I learnt many years ago that what goes around comes around,' Charlotte said at length.

'I think this Colonel deserves a good kick in the pants,' stated Sandy.

Lucy smiled. 'I would dearly love to see that.'

Jake and his men had by now arrived at Pinewood Falls. It was becoming dark, which helped to cloak their arrival. He led his men up the street towards the main street, and just before they reached it he led them in behind the jailhouse.

'Now you all sit tight here while I see the sheriff,' Jake ordered, as he dismounted from his horse. He walked into the jailhouse via the back door.

'Well, hell! Howdy, Jake,' greeted the sheriff as he noticed Jake in the shadows.

Ned sat up and spun around, surprised. 'What the hell do yer want, Jake?' he questioned.

'Ah've just come from the Colonel, Sheriff. He wants to see Ted and the boys,' Jake stated.

'Oh – when?' asked Calvin.

'He will have to ride for Jefferson Ranch tomorrow morning, Sheriff,' Jake replied.

'So yer'll be wantin' me to tell 'em then, ah guess, Jake?' suggested Calvin.

'Nope, the Colonel wants me to tell 'em. Ah just want yer to back me and the boys up, Sheriff.'

'Yer not turnin' yella, are yer, Jake?' mocked Ned.

'Do yer want to tell 'em, Ned?' threatened Jake, turning on him.

'Sittin' here ain't getting the job done though, is it?' remarked Calvin; he stood up and began to put on his gun belt.

Ned also stood up and grabbed his hat.

'Yer'd best get yer boys,' Calvin gestured to Jake.

Jake nodded, and opened the back door. He waited a short while, then was followed in by three riders. Calvin stopped as he walked to the front door.

'Is there enough of us?' he said sardonically. He turned and walked through the doorway without waiting for a reply.

The six men now crossed the street towards the saloon. It was well lit up and, judging by the noise and commotion coming from within, very busy also. Calvin stepped up on to the front porch; next to him stood Jake.

'Do yer want to go in first, Jake, or shall I?' he asked as he rested his hands upon his belt buckle.

Jake glanced at the sheriff then back into the saloon, and swallowed hard. 'Nope, ah'll go in first.' And with that he stepped through the doors, to be followed by the rest.

Immediately the noise and gaiety stopped as all eyes fell upon the new arrivals.

Ted had been stood at the bar; he pushed his way through the throng to the front. 'What's the matter, boys?' he greeted them through gritted teeth.

'The Colonel wants to see yer, Ted,' replied Jake.

'Well, it didn't take yer long to tell him, did it, Jake?' growled Ted. 'Ah likes loyalty, ah hope the Colonel appreciates yer. Of course, one or two of the boys may not understand Jake, so ah'd watch yer back.'

'Are yer threatenin' Jake, Ted?' questioned Calvin.

'Me, Sheriff? Nah. Ah was just warnin' him, as a friend,' jested Ted with a sneer.

'Come on, yer've done what yer came for.' Calvin flicked his head.

They turned to leave. 'So when does the Colonel wish to see us, anyhow?' called Ted after them.

'The day after tomorrow, Ted,' Jake replied, looking over his shoulder.

'Then we'll ride tomorrow afternoon,' stated Ted. He stood and watched the six men leave.

'Hell Ted, are yer just goin' to stand there an' take that from that yella-bellied scumbag?' cursed the Kid as he stood next to Ted.

'Yer forgettin', Kid, we still need to see the Colonel anyhow,' he replied as he returned to the bar.

Slowly the noise and joviality began to return to the saloon.

Sandy was sat by the grassy bank, lazily throwing stones into the stream. The others were either sat by the fire or chatting among themselves. It had been decided to wait until first light before setting out again for Pinewood; the light which was just starting to come across the crest which led into Pine River. Sandy was angry and his jaw line stiffened as he thought of Ted Skerrat and his men.

'You're not lookin' too happy there, my wee friend,' Paddy observed as he sat down next to Sandy, slapping him across the back.

'I'm not, Paddy,' Sandy said determinedly.

'Well, I remember an old lady once telling me that it never came to stay, it only came to pass.' Paddy smiled. 'But I wish to talk to you as a friend. You see Charlotte over there?' he asked.

'Yes,' replied Sandy.

'Well, you'd best pull your finger out, my lad, if you still want her. She will not wait for ever.'

'I know – I aim to have a word when we're alone.'

'Good lad, good lad… but make it soon; the suspense is killin' us.' Paddy smiled as he slapped Sandy upon the shoulder once more and stood up.

Sandy sat and watched him walk over to the horses before he too followed. There he met Charlotte; together they readied their mounts for that morning.

'Charlotte, we need to talk,' he blurted, rather awkwardly.

She stopped and looked at him, rather scornfully. 'What about? Lucy?' she retorted.

Sandy stopped. 'What! What has Lucy got to do with it?' he asked, astounded.

By now, though, Charlotte had climbed upon her horse. She glanced down at Sandy. 'I've seen how she watches you and how concerned you were when we found her yesterday,' she replied dryly. Before Sandy could answer she spurred her horse and moved off.

Sandy bit his lip. 'Oh hell, but what has Lucy got to do with us?' he asked himself.

Before they rode away, Murdoch came over to them. 'I shall take Lucy here back to Paradise with me. Liam and Black Eagle will remain here for a couple of days, and Two Crows is to travel with you. He is a good scout, so take note of what he is telling you. Be careful – the Indians have a saying: "It is the bear yer don't see that gets yer".' He stood back and raised his hand as a gesture of farewell.

'We should not be any longer than four days. When we do come we shall ride up Pine River Valley to that abandoned settlement you told us about,' declared Will. 'If we are to be any later than that then we shall ride on to Paradise and rearrange a trap for our friends,' he added, as he spurred his horse onwards.

He was followed by the rest; Two Crows quickly rode ahead to act as guide. Lucy stood behind and to one side of Murdoch; she watched anxiously and admiringly after Sandy as always brought up the rear. Murdoch turned and walked past her.

'Now then, lassie. We must get yer home safe an' sound an' get some clean clothes fer yer. Dinna worry about yer new-found friends – once they're finished here they'll be off home an' tae new adventures, nae doubt,' he announced as he stopped by Lucy's side and looked over his shoulder to where the riders had been.

The going was a lot easier now; the incline was not as steep and the path had become a track wide enough for a wagon. They all rode in silence. Two Crows led the way, followed by Will and Charlotte together, then Paddy and Sandy. It was not long before they reached the edge of the trees. Ahead of them was flat scrub, then the edge of town, marked by the large church at the end of the main street.

'Right, we will leave our horses here, Two Crows!' called Will. Two Crows crept to his side. 'Wait here with the horses; we're going to see if we can creep around behind the town tonight and raid the saloon.'

Sandy slammed a round into the chamber of his rifle and looked at Will, who acknowledged the action with a nod. Sandy then set off along the riverbank, followed by Paddy, who had now loaded his sawn-off shotgun. Charlotte and Will watched the two creep along the bank then lay flat among the scrub in readiness to give covering fire if necessary. The riverbank was well overgrown at this point with grasses and willow, so it was not long before the two were out of sight.

Luckily, there was little chance of being seen from across the river either. They still crept along carefully, using hand signals rather than speaking. Paddy observed Sandy with interest – there was now a new determination about him, and he had been fairly quiet since the last night at Paradise, even by his standards. They eventually reached a sandy dyke behind the bank, and the pair of them settled in to take stock of the situation.

'That's the saloon, there.' Sandy nodded his head towards the next building along.

Paddy had a quick look over the bank side. Although the bank itself was overgrown there was some land which was flat and open between the bank and the saloon. 'Do yer wish to have a closer look?' he whispered.

Sandy nodded. 'Too bloody right, I do.'

They crept on a little further, until they were directly behind the building they wished to see. The whole back of the saloon area was open. There was a back door which obviously led to the rear of the bar area and a flight of steps leading up to the first floor. At the landing outside the door, it was possible to get on to the roof, from which it would be possible to sneak round to the room windows.

'Is there any need to go over there?' asked Paddy.

'No, I don't think so; we can see everything from here,' responded Sandy.

Just then the first floor door opened and a young, well-dressed lady and a young man stepped out. They hurried down the steps, happy and giggling together. Sandy and Paddy hid lower in the grass, and Sandy brought his rifle up to his chest in readiness if needed. The young couple, totally oblivious of the two men in the undergrowth, walked away along a path behind the bank. Sandy raised his rifle to his shoulder. They could hear snippets of conversation; the man at least sounded French.

Paddy watched Sandy with interest – this was a side to Sandy that he had not shown much of in the past. 'Are you all right, Sandy me lad?' he asked.

'Never better,' came Sandy's response, as he watched the disappearing couple. Once they had gone he returned his attention to the saloon and surrounding area.

Paddy waited patiently.

'Right, I've seen enough. Are you ready?' asked Sandy.

'Certainly am.'

'Good, then let's get back to the others,' Sandy turned and they crept back the way they had come.

Will sat listening intensely under the shade of a willow tree as Sandy gave his report.

'All right, we wait until darkness, then we will go in,' Will decided when he had heard everything. 'Now, who wants to be burglar?' he asked.

'I will,' replied Sandy.

'I'll go with him,' spoke up Paddy.

Will looked at Charlotte. 'All right with that?'

Charlotte nodded her approval.

'Fair enough. Charlotte, you cover the back door and I shall cover the street,' Will declared.

They sat and waited; from their position they could just make out the road to Richmond as it wound its way past the cemetery. By mid-afternoon Paddy noticed a large cloud of dust coming from that direction.

'Something's amiss,' he declared as he sprang up upon his hunkers.

Sandy quickly produced his field glasses and probed the horizon. 'Eleven riders – it looks as if the birds have flown,' he announced, then he handed the glasses to Two Crows.

'Yes, that is the gang and four Dixie riders,' he confirmed.

'So what now?' questioned Paddy as he glanced at Will.

'I say we still take a look around the saloon. The gang has most likely set off for Jefferson's Ranch. We can catch them there,' he suggested.

'Let us hope they have left the diamond behind them,' remarked Charlotte.

'Here's hoping,' smiled Sandy.

Meanwhile, as Grey Wolf and his tribesmen were struggling north, the US authorities had finally woken up to the fact that the Indians were in fact heading for Canada. So at long last they had begun to scour the area between the reservation and Sweet Water River. They did not believe that the Indians could cross the Sweet Water River without having to head towards Harper's Crossing, where an army post was placed upon alert. Of course they would be desperately disappointed, for Grey Wolf and all his followers had already crossed the Sweet Water and were heading slowly towards the border, their goal.

Nevertheless, they were finding the going hard. The weather was mild but the weaker members of the tribe were beginning to suffer from lack of food and decent cover for shelter. They were also struggling to maintain even eight miles each night. Grey Wolf was well aware that so far they had been extremely fortunate. They had avoided detection by both the army and any civilian searching parties; in fact, they had not seen a living soul since the initial breakout. But that could all change – it would be only a matter of time before the authorities realised that the obvious route lay north. This in turn would mean all passes to Canada would be guarded and the whole area just south of the border would be swamped by the army.

Once darkness had fallen, Will led his team along the riverbank towards the town of Pinewood Falls. Now that the gang had ridden out, their task was to find and recover the diamond. Again they operated in silence, only using hand signals, for fear of being detected. Once behind the saloon, Sandy and Paddy hurried across to the steps leading to the first floor. Charlotte and Will followed; Charlotte took up position covering both exits while Will slipped to the corner of the building. On seeing that, both Sandy and Paddy hurried up the steps swiftly and silently. A quick check to make sure no one had seen them at the top was followed by Paddy cupping his hands together and almost throwing Sandy on to the roof. Sandy turned and, after pulling Paddy up behind him, he hurried to the first set of windows. A quick check showed that there were five rooms along this side of the building. Sandy paused and glanced down at Will, who nodded and held up his thumb as an indication that everything was still all right.

'If you were Ted Skerrat, Paddy, which room would you have?' asked Sandy quietly.

'I'd take this one, to be sure,' Paddy replied, pointing to the nearest window.

'Yes, so would I,' said Sandy thoughtfully, as he glanced along the roof. Paddy was obviously thinking along the same lines as Sandy; if someone was to come crashing in through the front door, the nearest window offered Ted the best chance of escape into the darkness via the seclusion of the shadows at the rear of the buildings.

The windows were shut, so Sandy withdrew his sword bayonet and began to slip the blade up under the sash so as to cut the string attachment.

'What on earth are yer doing?' asked an incredulous Paddy.

'What the hell does it look like?' retorted Sandy as he struggled with the window.

'Come here,' sighed Paddy as he gently pushed Sandy to one side. He knelt down, placing his hands deliberately and strategically upon the lower sash; he pushed and shook it, then slid it up out of the way. 'There – if yer want to break in, simply open the window.'

'Right,' Sandy replied, astounded.

'Don't ask,' remarked Paddy as he noticed his friend's look of surprise. Sandy stepped into the window and swung himself into the bedroom.

Paddy followed and immediately crept over to the door. There he opened it ajar so as to view the passageway. There was quite a bit of noise and laughing and clapping coming from downstairs. Good, Paddy thought to himself, keep yourselves busy...

Sandy had crept to the bedside table; he quickly checked it over, then opening the drawers one by one, he quickly checked the contents by brushing the palm of his hand flat across each garment. He found nothing so he turned to the chest of drawers next to the bed, using the same technique; again it drew a blank.

'Shh,' whispered Paddy, as he watched a young lady come into view at the top of the stairs. She walked along towards him, then opened a door in front of him on the opposite side of the passageway. Both he and Sandy remained static for fear of creating any noise.

'Hey, Val, what the hell yer doin'? Come down here, will yer?' another woman shouted.

'Yeah, ah'm coming!' the lady shouted back and slammed the door behind her as she stepped back into the passage; she hurried away down the stairs without looking back.

'All right,' whispered Paddy.

Sandy began his searching once more, checking even under the mattress; unluckily it revealed nothing. 'Drawn a blank, I'm afraid,' he said to Paddy.

'Right, it will be the first room, then, on the street,' cursed Paddy as he rubbed his chin, realising his initial assumption had proven wrong for once.

'Come on!' urged Sandy as he slipped back through the window. He caught Will's eye and pointed to the first room. Will nodded and, holding up his thumb, he crept forward to the corner of the saloon and main street. Paddy had by now closed the window silently and together they edged along the side of the roof. They had to step very carefully, for the edging was very narrow, especially between the windows and the guttering. The guttering of course would not take Sandy's weight, let alone Paddy's. They also had to be careful not to be seen from the street now, and once move Paddy performed his opening trick for them to enter the room. Again Paddy took up position by the door, where he was now able to see down the stairs more clearly while Sandy searched the room. Once more the bedside and dressing tables drew blanks. Sandy stood up and scratching his head he glanced about the room.

'Now what's the matter?' asked a concerned Paddy.

'Aha! I know…' Sandy answered thoughtfully as he crept over to the wardrobe. He carefully opened the door and quickly felt the garments inside by running his hands down each side simultaneously. 'Here we are!' he exclaimed triumphantly as he withdrew a small velvet bag from a lady's dress. He quickly opened the bag and looked in.

'Well,' cried Paddy anxiously.

Sandy smiled and held out his hand flat. Upon it sat the biggest diamond Paddy had ever seen.

'Wow – no wonder they want it back!' Paddy said, astounded.

Sandy quickly put it back in its pouch then slipped through the window, closely followed by Paddy. Glancing about, Sandy held up a thumb for Will, to let him know that they had been successful. They then quickly but carefully crept back along the edge of the roof. Will too withdrew along the side street back towards the steps. They all hurried back to the riverbank where Charlotte was still covering them. After a quick check by Will and a nod of the head, they were all off again back along the bank to where Two Crows waited for them.

'Did you find the diamond, then?' asked a cheerful Will as they reached their camp.

'Yes, here it is,' Sandy handed over the velvet bag.

Will quickly opened it and whistled softly when he saw it. 'That could please a good few ladies of Nottingham.'

'Right then, leader, we have the stone – what now?' asked Paddy.

'We ride for Richmond,' announced Will. Turning to Two Crows. 'Lead the way, my friend,' he stated.

They quickly mounted up and, turning away from Pinewood Falls, they moved out. As it was dark the pace was slow, but they all felt that at long last they were beginning to get somewhere – they certainly had achieved the first part of the quest and that was something.

Regrettably, as they rode west, they failed to see two riders crossing the ford to the east of town. These two rode into Pinewood slowly and deliberately.

'Halt!' called the sentry from the bank. 'State yer business, stranger,' he challenged, stepping out from behind a rock.

The two men glanced at each other. 'Barney Greenway, and this 'ere is Black Bob,' replied the nearest rider. 'We're jist passin' through,' he went on.

'That so?' the sentry nodded slowly. 'Well, if yer wish to pass through town, yer'll have to report to the sheriff's office.' He turned and pointed towards the jailhouse with his rifle.

The two riders looked at each other and rode their horses on slowly without answering. The only distinguishing feature the sentry could make out about these fellows was that the one called Barney chewed a match or stick as he spoke. The other, Black Bob, just glowered at him from under the rim of his hat.

They arrived at the jailhouse.

'Wait 'ere, Bob, ah'll go an' see the sheriff,' said Barney as he dismounted. He stepped upon the porch and walked through the doorway. The first person he saw was Ned, sitting half-asleep at his desk.

'You the sheriff of these 'ere parts?' Barney asked a little surprised.

Outside, Black Bob remained in his saddle. He noticed a sentry watching him with interest from the roof of the bank and another unsavoury character peeping from behind a water barrel further up the street.

In the meantime, Ned had almost fallen off his seat when startled by this new stranger.

'No, he ain't – I am, mister.' Calvin stepped out from the shadows.

Barney readjusted his stance to face Calvin. 'My pardner and I were thinkin' of passin' through,' he began and jerked a thumb over his right shoulder.

'Whut's yer business here, boy?' Calvin challenged.

Barney hesitated, then sighed. 'All right, my pardner and I have been hired by both the Dakota Territory and the State of Missouri to apprehend Ted Skerrat and anyone riding with him, dead or alive.' To prove his word, Barney produced a slip of paper and placed it flat upon Calvin's desk.

As Calvin read it, Barney continued. 'Ah'm also to meet up with a US marshal by the name of Roscoe, who was headed this way with his deputy. Have yer seen them, Sheriff?'

Ned jumped with shock, which caused Barney to look at him askance.

'No, can't say I have, Mr Greenway. Now then, if yer wish to enjoy the hospitality of this town, yer'll have to hand in all yer weapons here. Don't worry, yer'll be safe; yer've just missed Ted and his gang. They rode west for Richmond this afternoon,' said Calvin.

Barney sighed, dejected. 'Can we git rooms at the saloon across the way there?' Again he jerked a thumb over his right shoulder.

'Yep, sure can, but I warn yer – be careful whut yer say, it's run by Ted's woman, Texas Rose,' declared Calvin as he began to collect Barney's guns.

Barney stepped back out into the street. 'Give 'em yer guns,

Bob, we'll stay at the saloon tonight. It appears we've just missed our quarry,' announced Barney as he withdrew his rifle.

'It looks as if they'd be gettin' warned 'bout us bein' here,' Black Bob flicked his head up the street towards the water barrel.

'Never mind, we'll get 'em sooner or later,' hissed Barney.

'Come on, ah'll take yer over to the saloon an' get yer rooms sorted.' The sheriff gestured as he led them both across the street and into the saloon.

'Evenin', Bert,' he called to the bartender.

'Evenin', Sheriff,' he greeted him back.

'Why hello, Sheriff, what can I do you for?' asked a rather flamboyantly dressed woman.

'Why hello, Rosie,' replied Calvin as he cleared his throat. 'These here two gentlemen are just passin' through an' require a room fer the night.' He gestured towards Barney and Bob with a wave of his arm.

She turned her attentions to the two tough-looking characters stood next to him. 'Why hello, boys,' she greeted them, as she began to rub her hand across Barney's chest and eye him up and down.

'This 'ere is Miss Rosie, boys,' introduced the sheriff.

'Why don't I show yer to yer rooms, boys, an' make sure yer comfortable?' she suggested as she began to lead Barney towards the stairs by both hands.

'Ah'd be obliged, ma'am, if yer jist showed us the rooms,' answered Barney, pulling his hand away and tipping his hat.

Rosie smiled. It wasn't often she was able to talk to men, Ted made sure of that. So with him out of the way and these two strangers just passing through, she was not going to pass up the opportunity of a little flirting. 'Sure thing, boys, but be sure to come down an' have a little drink with me an' ma friend there, Kate.' She flicked her head towards a young petite brunette who gave a dazzling smile as a response, with a wave.

Barney, also not a one for giving up the opportunity of gathering information, sniffed and glanced at Bob. His demeanour was as dark as ever. 'We'll see how we feel once we've freshened up, ma'am,' offered Barney with a smile.

THE CHASE BEGINS

Two groups of cowboys were sat by two separate campfires only a few yards apart. These were Ted's men and the Dixie riders; never easy bedfellows, they were not going to start sharing now. Ted and his men sat around one fire while Jake and his three companions sat around theirs. Apart from them being so close in proximity, a passing stranger would never have guessed that they were actually travelling together. Furtive glances were passed between the two groups occasionally, but that was all the contact they had with each other.

'Hey Ted, do yer remember that farmer yer shot down in Missouri that time when he wanted to teach yer a lesson?' asked Abe.

Ted sat staring at the dancing flames. 'Nope, ah daresay that ah don't,' he replied at length.

'Ah remember when that posse tried to take us in at Red River – boy, was that something,' stated Joe.

'It sure was,' replied an excited Joshua.

'How many did we get that day, boys?' Joe asked.

'Seven, maybe eight,' replied Abe.

'Naw, it were more like twelve,' boasted the Kid.

'Ha!' exclaimed Abe. 'Ah fair remember Danny here hittin' that one with that stick that tried to ride away. Fairly crushed his skull in.' He began to laugh, followed by the others.

Danny, never one for much talking, simply smiled.

Ted glanced up. 'Ah remember Danny shootin' that bounty hunter at almost point-blank range with that shotgun of his,' he said and joined in with the laughter.

'Threw him several feet it did,' added Joshua.

'Blew him away,' laughed the Kid, the rest following.

The gang then began to calm down.

'What are we to do once we've seen the Colonel?' asked Joe.

Ted glanced at him. 'What d'yer mean?' he snarled.

'Well, are we to carry on west or go south?'

'Ah don't know about you boys, but ah'm goin' back to Pinewood Falls,' replied Ted as he watched the fire once more.

'Don't yer think we've been there long enough now, Ted?' asked a concerned Abe.

'You lot can do as yer please. Yer not beholden to me. Once this is all settled with the Colonel, we can ride on back to Pinewood and divide up our spoils.'

'Yer like Rosie, don't yer, Ted?' asked the Kid.

'So, what's that to you?' retorted Ted as he narrowed his eyes; his hand slipped down his side and rested upon the butt of his gun.

'Hey, Ted, ah was only sayin',' explained the Kid.

'But what would happen if yer found her with someone else?' asked Joe.

'Ah'd kill 'em, kill 'em both. No one double-crosses me – ah couldn't care who they are,' snarled Ted.

Again the gang fell silent.

'Ah sure miss home cookin',' reminisced Abe; he flicked his head to the side as he spoke and sighed.

'And a comfy bed,' added Frenchy.

'Ha, yer'll always struggle with a comfy bed, especially as yer always in it with that Sally – is that what yer call her?' scoffed the Kid.

'What's it to you? And what of you and Alice?' Frenchy retaliated.

'Alice? Have yer been seein' her again behind ma back, yer slimy little scumbag?' cursed Joe, he stepped forward and grabbed the Kid by the lapels, lifting him off the ground and pushing him backwards.

A scuffle ensued between the two.

'Calm down the pair of yez, or neither of yer will be around to see bloody Alice,' warned Ted, as he stepped between them, holding a gun in his hand.

'Just remember, Kid, Alice is with *me*,' pointed Joe.

'Ah'll not tell yer agin,' warned Ted calmly as he looked hard at Joe.

'Come on, boys; let's get some shut-eye, we've still to get to Jefferson's Ranch tomorrow,' said Abe.

They all settled down, some by the fire; Joe lay down by the horses and Danny to lay down by some rocks. Soon the camp was quiet as they waited for first light.

In the meantime, Barney and Black Bob had settled down at a table in the bar area with Rosie and Kate. The girls were all smiles, which contrasted sharply with the hardened determined looks of the two strangers.

'So boys, what brings you out aways here?' asked Rosie.

'Just passin' through, kinda followin' Clark and Lewis, ah guess,' replied Barney.

'Clark and Lewis?' asked a surprised Kate.

'Well, we had nothing better to do,' mumbled Bob.

'What brought *you* here?' Barney asked Rosie.

'After the war a lot of ex-Confederate soldiers came out here to settle. My father was one of them. I took the name Texas from his home state,' explained Rosie.

'Yer've done well,' remarked Barney as he glanced around the bar.

'I was fortunate, shall we say,' she said dryly.

'Oh? How?' asked Barney.

'Well, my father being an ex-Johnny Reb, things worked out just swell; as Colonel Cody became more influential, the more privileges we received.' She shrugged her shoulders.

'Colonel Cody, who is he?' Barney took a swig from his glass.

'The local land baron. Yer won't see him without at least twenty guns at his back. He's also the local judge, jury and executioner round here.' She gave a loud cackle at Barney's expression.

'But what of the sheriff?' he asked.

'The sheriff? He's a spineless no-good coyote.' Rosie downed her drink in one, then poured herself yet another.

All this time Black Bob sat in the corner and skulked under his hat. He observed everything that went on and what was said but said nothing himself; he made no sound and showed no emotion.

'What's up with yer friend? Doesn't say much, does he?' Rosie then asked as she flicked her hand in Bob's direction.

'He's a quiet type,' smiled Barney.

'What about Ted? Rosie, yer ought to be careful,' declared a concerned Kate.

'Who is Ted?' Barney pressed.

Rosie looked at Kate scornfully then at Barney rather coyly, 'Ted Skerrat, he's been livin' here for the past few months,' she replied. She toyed with her glass.

'You and this Ted, are you partners or something?' Barney quizzed.

'Hell no! I made the mistake of making a play for him when he arrived; he's domineered me ever since,' Rosie complained with a sigh.

'Why don't yer just tell him it's over?' said Barney.

'Tell him, tell Ted? Yer can't do that, he'd kill me dead – he's already said so,' Rosie answered, taking another swig from her glass.

'So where is he now?' Barney leant forward on his elbows.

'What is this? Yer not a marshal or something, are yer?' It was now Rosie's turn to ask the questions.

Barney chuckled slightly. 'Hell naw, I just don't want to be shot at,' he smiled.

'Hmm.' Rosie flicked her head.

'Is he here?' Barney shrugged.

'Nope, he's gone to Jefferson's Ranch just outside Richmond.' Rosie finished yet another drink. She did not notice Barney and Bob look at each other.

The two men emptied their glasses then stood up. 'Well, yer'll have to excuse us ladies.' Barney began to ascend the stairs.

'Are yer not stopping,' Rosie asked startled.

'Naw, got to be up early, Rosie. Goodnight.' Barney doffed his hat and continued up the stairs.

Only Bert the bartender was up and about when Barney and Bob collected their things and left the saloon. After several hard days in the saddle, a horsehair bed – even rough ones like those – upstairs was a welcome luxury.

Barney paid Bert for the night, then followed Bob out of the door. They walked across the street to the jailhouse to collect their guns.

'Mornin', Sheriff,' greeted Barney as he walked in.

'Come for yer guns, ah guess,' responded Calvin as he yawned and scratched his shirt lazily. 'Ned, give the men their guns back.'

'Thank yer, Sheriff,' said Barney as he fastened his belt.

They were soon riding out of town, heading west towards Richmond.

'Well, Bob, thanks to Rosie we now know where to go,' remarked Barney.

'Yeah, but what do we face when we do catch them up?' remarked Bob.

'It's not Ted and the McCabe brothers ah'm worried about, it's this 'ere Colonel Cody. What's he like?' thought Barney aloud.

'Well, if necessary we'll resort to shootin', like always,' grunted Bob.

'I guess so,' remarked Barney as he glanced sideways at his partner.

At that point in time, Ted Skerrat and his gang were just mounting up.

'Remember boys, not a word of the stone and leave the news of our breaking up to me,' warned Ted quietly; he looked particularly at Abe.

'Sure thing, Ted,' Abe replied.

Jake and the other Dixie riders were waiting for them to appear, and as they did so, Jake half turned in the saddle.

'We'll cut across country at this point and head direct to Jefferson's Ranch.' He pointed in the general direction he wished them to travel.

'You lead the way, Jake, yer in charge,' mocked Ted sarcastically.

Jake threw a sharp glance at him as he spurred his horse on; the rest followed silently. As they rode along Joe came up to the Kid's side.

'How is Ted going to divide the value of the stone?' he asked quietly.

The Kid looked at him; he had not thought of that. 'Ted will have something in mind,' he replied.

'Yeah, but what? I intend to collect my share,' he warned.

The Kid turned to him and smiled. 'Well then, for once we agree, lover boy.'

Joe scowled back at him; he was becoming sick and tired of being at the wrong end of the Kid's sarcastic wit and of being made fun of. He held his horse back a little, allowing the Kid to ride ahead, not taking his eyes off him as he went. Danny came up to him.

'Ah dunno why yer pays him so much heed – take what he says wi' a pinch o' salt.' He smiled and flicked his head towards the Kid.

'One of these days ah'll teach him a lesson; ah'll kick him so hard…' Joe left the rest unfinished for Danny to complete in his own mind.

They rode across country direct towards Jefferson's Ranch; it was mid-afternoon when they reached their destination. Colonel Cody had seen them arrive and was waiting for them on his porch. Ted led his gang slowly over to him; they were still sat in the saddle.

The two most dominant characters in Greendale County smiled at each other.

'Well howdy, Ted,' greeted the pleasant, aging, smiling Colonel Cody; he held his arms out wide.

Ted sat and watched him. 'Howdy, Colonel,' he replied at length.

The Colonel stepped up to Ted. 'Ah hear you've done a bit o' shootin', Ted. Now why don't yer step into ma house an tell me all about it.' His pleasant smile remained as he gestured towards his front door. 'An' you boys, get yersel's over to the canteen an' have some bacon 'n' beans – Slim, Billy Joe, show them the way.'

As the others walked away, led by the two Dixie riders, Ted dismounted from his horse and followed the Colonel into the house. The door was closed behind him and two further men stood either side of Ted inside.

'Now what the hell do yer think yer were playin' at, shootin' a US marshal? Do yer think they'll just forget about him?' The Colonel had now turned to face Ted, his arms were moving about as he spoke. His pleasant smile had now disappeared, replaced by a grotesque, snarling grimace.

Ted stood calmly and stared back at his employer. 'If I hadn't done it then, he would only have come back,' he replied quietly.

'Yeah, but in the meantime we could've maybe arranged an accident,' growled the Colonel. 'But as yer didn't wait, yer now goin' to pull every bounty hunter this side of Missouri down on us.'

'It'll be some time afore they come lookin' again,' Ted retorted, more in hope than confidence.

The Colonel stopped and glared at him. 'The army is already preparing itself for to come into the county, maybe lookin' for Injuns – but it wouldn't take long before some loose-tongued idiot tells 'em of the marshal.' The Colonel now stood directly in front of Ted.

'Anyhow, ah still got all this money for yer, Colonel,' Ted raised a bulging carpet bag.

'This'll cost yer more than three grand, Ted,' warned the Colonel as he snatched the bag from Ted's hands. 'Now then, yer goin' to stop here until ah says otherwise. There's been some beds made up for yer an' fer the boys over in the dormitory; now go on, get yersel' something to eat.' The Colonel flicked his head and waved Ted away with his hand. The two men stood either side of Ted now turned to face him. He stood rigid and glanced slowly from right to left, then back at the Colonel; he nodded with a sneer, then turned and began to walk away.

'Remember, Ted, no trouble now, otherwise ah'll just have to hand yer over to the authorities,' warned the Colonel, in a calm and pleasant manner.

Ted left the house behind him and walked over to the canteen, where the rest of the gang were sat waiting for him.

'Well, Ted, is the Colonel happy with his haul?' asked Abe.

'Not exactly,' replied Ted. 'We're going to have to wait here, for the time bein' at least,' he said softly.

'What d'yer mean?' The Kid jumped forward.

'Just what ah said – we've to stay here until told otherwise,' growled Ted.

'Why, that no-good son of a—' cursed Joe.

'Calm yersel' down, boys. We'll ain't gonna here that long and besides, it'll mean our haul shall be quite safe.' Ted sat back and smiled. Nobody would think of checking Rosie's wardrobe while he was here. It also cheered the rest of the gang up as they felt the same. 'Yeah, we'll hole up here for a short while, then ride back to Pinewood,' remarked Ted.

'Did yer tell the Colonel of our future plans, Ted?' asked Abe.

'Nope, paid no mind to that, not until every one o' us is sure as to what we're about,' replied Ted as he began to eat.

At the same time the Colonel was instructing one of his riders. 'Now Slim, ah wants yer to escort Jake and three men back to Pinewood Falls, then ride south to Harper's Crossing. Just observe this army build-up; if they cross into Greendale ah wants to know. Now take ten men with yer; as for yer, Jake, keep an eye on this Calvin – ah wants him watched.' Slim and Jake nodded in response then glanced at each other.

'When do yer wish us to leave, Colonel?' asked Jake.

'Tomorrow, first light,' replied the Colonel as he turned away and slipped the contents of the bag into a large heavy metal safe.

It was late afternoon when Paddy and Two Crows arrived at a small river known as Beaver Creek. They rode over towards a small meadow, which was totally isolated and shrouded from the road and the far bank.

'This will do nicely.' Paddy smiled at Two Crows, who nodded in response and dismounted, while Paddy turned and waved to the others from the saddle. Soon they were all dismounted. Two Crows had begun a fire, while Charlotte had begun to cook – she hadn't been given the job because she was a woman, simply it was her turn. The others were just as capable of cooking as she.

They had been riding constantly since leaving Pinewood Falls behind them, so they were in desperate need of stretching their legs and caring for their horses. These were now being attended to by both Will and Sandy. Paddy had walked back towards the track and clambered up upon the highest rock, so that he could keep lookout for the time being. Satisfied that they had not been followed he soon returned to the camp, where he busied himself by building three shelters. These were built, as before, out of suitable branches and material.

Will began to hand out the hand bombs. 'I'll distribute these now, just in case,' he explained.

After eating, Paddy and Will settled down to rest. The sun was now low in the sky. Two Crows was resting against a tree. Sandy took a deep breath and stepped over to Charlotte. She was not looking and received a bit of a shock when he stood over her.

'Oh, Sandy – is everything all right?' she asked.

He reached out and held her two hands, pulling her gently to her feet. 'Come on, Charlotte; let's go down by the river. We need to talk,' he said determinedly.

She glanced at Paddy, mystified. He placed his hat further over his face but winked so that Sandy could not see.

'What on earth is the problem, Sandy?' Charlotte asked. The one thing she wished to hear he had not mentioned during the previous year, so what was he to say now?

He led her by the hand down towards the riverbank, sat her down upon an old tree log that lay there, then he began to pace backwards and forwards.

'Charlotte, there are a few things that need to be said, and the air between us needs to be cleared,' Sandy began nervously.

Charlotte sat upon the log, watching him intently as he paced back and forth. 'But what on earth's the matter, Sandy? Have I done something to upset you?' she asked.

'Sorry, what? Eh, no,' Sandy spluttered. 'And this does not involve Lucy,' he went on.

'Lucy!' exclaimed Charlotte, looking totally confused.

'No, there is nothing between us. Charlotte, as you are aware that we – I mean, I – er…' He began to rub his chin in earnest.

'Sandy, what on earth are you prattling on about?' Charlotte raised her hands in frustration.

Sandy stopped walking to and fro, and looked straight at Charlotte; he sighed heavily. 'It's no good, I just cannot think of any other way of putting it,' he eventually said sadly.

'Say *what*, Sandy?' Charlotte glanced sideways at him.

It was now dark and the first stars were beginning to sparkle as the moon put in its appearance. Sandy walked towards Charlotte, knelt down upon one knee and gently reached out for her hand. Charlotte found herself giving him her hand without realising.

'Charlotte, there is something I have to say... something I wish to ask you,' he began quietly. He raised his eyes so that he now looked her squarely into her own. He swallowed hard, then began in a clear yet soft tone; he spoke clearly and deliberately. 'Firstly, that you mean a great deal to me and that I love you dearly and secondly –' he again swallowed – 'Charlotte, would you do me the greatest honour a woman can give a man and give me your hand in marriage?' He paused, still watching her, waiting for her to start laughing or shouting at him and his silliness. 'There, I've said it now,' he mumbled and allowed his eyes to fall to his feet.

Charlotte gently reached forward and turned his face towards hers. She looked longingly into his eyes and smiled lovingly at him. 'Oh Sandy, I have admired and loved you since...' she paused and glanced at the trees as she shook her head slightly... 'since practically the first moment we met at Drumloch – do you remember – in the lounge where you were, as always, sat alone?' She stroked his fringe back caringly. 'Up to that moment, Sandy, if someone had said I would meet a man that would capture my heart as you did, then I would have laughed at them – but you did.' It was her turn to pause.

'How? What did I do?' Sandy questioned.

Charlotte smiled once more and held a finger to his lips; it was now her turn to glance away. 'You did nothing, you did not have to. You were just yourself. That was enough for me.' She glanced back at him. 'But...'

Sandy dropped her hands; he looked sad dejected. 'It's all right Charlotte, I understand – there's always a but.'

She looked at him in puzzlement, then began to laugh. 'I was going to ask why mention it now, after all this time?' She shrugged her shoulders.

'I was afraid,' replied Sandy.

'You? Afraid?' she looked at him suspiciously.

'Yes, I was – firstly of offending you, especially once I got to know of your past. Secondly, of rejection – I felt if I stuck my big grubby boot in it I would not get a second chance. Finally, thirdly, once Murdoch came on the scene I feared I would lose you for ever.' He smiled nervously at her.

Charlotte's eyes began to fill; she smiled at him and shook her head. 'Oh, you silly…' She left the rest unfinished as she hugged him.

'Would you like to borrow my handkerchief?' he offered as he watched her wipe away a tear or two.

'No,' she laughed, continuing to wipe the tears. 'These are tears of happiness. I was beginning to think you were not interested after all,' she admitted.

'Oh, Charlotte, like you I have been interested since we first met. For someone as beautiful as you to take an interest in a buffoon like me… Well, I did not know what to do.' He shrugged.

'Well, my answer to your proposal is yes,' she smiled.

Sandy smiled as he sat next to her upon the log.

'You can kiss me, I won't bite.' She closed her eyes and leant forward.

'What – I, er…' Sandy spluttered.

Again Charlotte smiled. 'Well, am I to wait for another year?' she asked.

Sandy sighed. 'Oh hell.' They fell into a loving embrace.

I could happily get used to all this kissing malarkey, thought Sandy.

They were just settling back to watch the stars together when they were disturbed by rustling coming towards them in the bushes. Sandy instinctively held up a finger for Charlotte to be quiet.

'That will be Paddy or Will, I'll wager,' cursed Sandy as he withdrew his gun, then leaped into the bushes.

He quickly fell upon a man, who tried to turn and run. In the confusion Sandy quickly brought him to the ground. 'All right Will, what is the—' He abruptly stopped speaking and stood up, pulling a young Indian boy to his feet. The Indian looked terrified, and Sandy realised that he had withdrawn his gun. He quickly replaced it into his holster; then, holding the Indian he led him back to the camp, where Charlotte and Two Crows were.

'Two Crows, can you please have a word with this young Indian fellow and find out what on earth he was doing hiding in the bushes?' asked Sandy, as he passed the Indian on to Two

Crows, who took him aside. By now both Paddy and Will were roused and standing around the young Indian. He by now was happily chatting away with Two Crows as if they were two long lost friends.

Presently, Two Crows led the young Indian back to the group. 'He from Blackfoot tribe, like me,' began Two Crows.

'His chief, Grey Wolf, is trying to lead the tribe to Indian Creek to meet White Feather and reach safety.' He paused. 'But they have found the going hard; the young and the old are beginning to suffer so they send out scouts to look for food, berries and suchlike. That is what he was doing when you leaped upon him, Mr Sandy.'

'What is his name?' asked Charlotte.

The two Indians again conversed in their own native tongue before Two Crows turned back to them. 'White Cloud.'

'Well, now, I suppose we may have something spare from last night,' offered Paddy.

Two Crows turned once more to the young Indian and explained to him what was being said. The youngster stepped to one side and began to call like a bird; suddenly the whole camp was alive with Indian warriors.

'How long have *they* been there?' asked Will, putting his hands on his hips.

'Since when Mr Sandy leaped upon the boy. Luckily their chief has strictly ordered them not to get involved in any fighting, or our friend Mr Sandy would now be dead,' stated Two Crows.

'At least I would have managed to tell Charlotte how I felt about her before I popped my clogs,' laughed Sandy.

'Well, that would have made her day, she'd been waiting long enough,' announced Paddy.

'What do you mean? More to the point, what do you know?' cried Sandy.

'Hell, Sandy, *everyone* knew except you, you clod! Many's the time we've been wanting to throttle you,' said Will.

'Aye, lass, it's about time. I told you that you would find Mr Right.' Paddy smiled as he gave her a friendly hug.

'Yes, it appears you were right again after all. Now I intend to look after him and keep hold of him,' she declared.

They laughed together then turned their attention back to the matter in hand and sorted out some provisions for the Indians, which Two Crows handed over to the leading warrior. He bowed and said something to Two Crows before turning and quickly disappearing back into the darkness with his fellow warriors and the young boy, who stopped and hesitated at the bushes; he turned and smiled, then with a wave he too was gone. The small group stood silent, watching the inky darkness.

'The warrior, he says that Grey Wolf and the Blackfoot will never forget this act of kindness from the white man,' explained Two Crows as he again settled down below the tree.

Will and Paddy also settled down once more.

'Don't stay up too late, you two!' shouted Paddy to Sandy and Charlotte.

They paid no attention to him as they returned to their log and watched the river run past and the stars in the sky. They sat upon the grass resting their backs against the log, and held each other in their arms.

'I shall never forget this moment,' said Charlotte softly, as she rested her head upon Sandy's shoulder.

Sandy smiled to himself; although he realised that they needed to discuss what to do next, for the time being he was willing just to enjoy his moment with Charlotte.

She awoke to find that Sandy had slipped his coat over her during the night. He sat upon the log watching the river run past.

'Good morning, sweet pea,' he greeted her as she stirred.

She smiled and stretched. 'Good morning, Sandy – where are the others?' she asked as she turned around.

'We're here, little angel,' replied Paddy.

'We are not going to leave you alone with this slow-witted numbskull,' teased Will.

Charlotte smiled shyly at Sandy as he brought her some cooked breakfast.

'Oh, look at that, Will! We never had breakfast in bed,' scoffed Paddy.

Sandy turned and smiled; he did not mind their jibes.

'I trust you slept well?' he asked Charlotte as he helped her to her feet.

'Yes, thank you,' she replied.

'Like a log,' sniggered Will. Paddy began to laugh.

'I am not going to live this down, am I?' asked Sandy softly to Charlotte.

'Would you want to forget?' laughed Paddy.

'Log it in the report, Paddy,' scoffed Will.

Sandy sighed heavily; Charlotte smiled and walked away behind some bushes to get freshened up.

'Which way do you think we should ride for, Jefferson's Ranch or Richmond?' asked Will, once they were all mounted.

'Well, I've just "twigged",' laughed Paddy; Will joined in.

'Oh, give it a rest, will you!' retorted Sandy, becoming tired of it.

'I remember Murdoch saying that these two – Ted and the Colonel – do not get on well. So I would ride for Richmond first to see if the gang is there,' stated Paddy.

Will nodded, then looked at Charlotte.

'Makes sense,' she replied.

Sandy nodded in assent.

'All right then, Two Crows, lead on to Richmond,' Will ordered and they set off once more.

That morning, as they had breakfasted, they had left further provisions behind for the Indians, allowing Two Crows to leave some sort of sign for their scouts. This he had done willingly; he himself had not eaten and Paddy was sceptical as to whether Two Crows had actually slept at the camp that previous night.

As they rode along, Charlotte fell back slightly so that she could ride alongside Sandy.

'Sandy,' she said.

'Yes, sweet pea,' he replied.

'When we're alone, you may call me Charlie – I would very much like that,' she announced, reaching out and holding his hand.

'Charlie... but why?' Sandy asked puzzled.

'It was my mother's pet name for me; no one has ever called me it since,' she explained.

'Then, Charlie, I would be honoured to call you by that name.' Sandy squeezed her hand gently and, looking into her eyes, he gave her one of his boyish smiles.

Paddy turned to Will and mockingly rolled his eyes. 'Gawd listen to all this slaver!' he joked.

Barney and Bob were also stirring themselves not so many miles away. They had been camped higher among the rocks and they too were deliberating as to whether to ride for Richmond or Jefferson's Ranch.

'What d'yer reckon on, Barney?' Bob grunted.

Barney sniffed the air. 'Ah reckon we should ride for this ranch and check the place out. Yer know, the usual thing: the layout, how many guns, that kind o' thing.'

'Yeah, ah guess so,' replied Bob.

'After all, that's where this Rosie reckons they're headed,' added Barney.

'But can she be trusted?'

'Well, we won't know that till we get there,' Barney replied.

They too mounted up and rode west that morning, but Will and the Storm Force team were heading for Richmond, while Barney and Bob were now heading for Jefferson's Ranch.

'We'll stick to a steady pace; we should be there by nightfall,' explained Barney.

Bob merely grunted in response and followed his companion.

The area the two parties were now traversing was interspersed with large rocky outcrops running in a general north–south direction. There were large forested areas and between each rocky outcrop there were grassy plains or steep gulleys or creeks. To the north – or the parties' right – the trees became denser and the rocky areas more frequent; to their left, or the south, there was more of the same but with fewer rocky outcrops. In fact, just north of Harper's Crossing there was a large swampy plain, known as Buffalo Valley. Undulating hill country finished the scene.

Slim and Jake were also in the saddle by this time; they rode out from Jefferson's Ranch and headed east towards Beaver Creek and eventually Pinewood Falls. Sadly, the route they took was in direct line with the approach of Will and his companions. Neither party knew of this and both were oblivious to the other until it was almost too late. In fact, Will was discussing the timetable at that time.

'Remember, I was working on us being away only four days. So tonight we will quickly case this town of Richmond and then head off towards Jefferson's Ranch to regain the money,' he announced.

'That would work out just fine,' replied Paddy.

It was then that Two Crows came hurrying back on his horse. 'Dixie riders, they come, they come this way.' He pointed excitedly in the direction of the riders.

'All right, Two Crows. Come on, let's get out of the way,' ordered Will and led them up behind a rocky outcrop. Behind this, both Sandy and Paddy dismounted and clambered on top of the rock. Sandy had his rifle ready, while Paddy cocked his Macootcha.

It wasn't long before Slim rode past with fourteen riders heading towards Beaver Creek, oblivious to the four agents sat close by.

'That was close – they must have been almost upon us!' gasped Will.

Sandy and Paddy waited for a few moments then clambered back down.

'Let's ride on,' ordered Will.

'What about Grey Wolf and his people?' asked Two Crows.

'I'm sorry, Two Crows, we cannot afford to become embroiled in local issues now. We must press on,' declared Will sternly.

'If they are in such a state as they say, they won't stand much of a chance,' stated Paddy.

'It would make our timetable very tight if we were to go back now. But it could also work to our advantage,' counselled Sandy.

'How?' asked Will.

'We'd have the cover of darkness,' explained Sandy.

'But it could also blow our cover,' pointed out Will.

'We could still raid the ranch and be gone before they notice,' argued Charlotte.

'We will most probably live to regret this, but come on,'

ordered Will as he turned his horse and led them back the way they had just come.

Slim was leading the riders towards Beaver Creek when he suddenly held up his hand to stop the following riders.

'What's up, Slim?' asked Jake.

'Do you see what ah see?' Slim pointed to a wisp of smoke spiralling upwards towards the sky.

'Ah sure does – who d'yer think it is, Slim?'

'Ah don't knows, but ah'm sure as hell goin' to find out,' warned Slim. 'We'll ride over to the rock over there. Blue, yer can see from there who it is and what they're up to.' He led them forward more cautiously now.

As they reached the boulders and rocks, Blue dismounted and climbed up towards the vantage point mentioned by Slim.

'Well, what d'yer see?' called Slim as he became impatient.

'Looks like Injuns, Slim, there on the far bank,' hissed Blue.

'Is there many?' Slim asked.

'Yeah, a whole tribe by the looks of it,' Blue affirmed.

'What'll we do now, Slim?' asked Jake.

Slim looked at him almost contemptuously. 'Yer know the Colonel's orders – all Injuns are to be rounded up and returned to Harper's Crossing,' he replied.

'But what about Pinewood Falls and the sheriff?' protested Jake.

'They'll just have to wait,' snarled Slim. 'Now listen, Jake, you take seven men downstream and round up the Injuns from that direction. Ah'll travel to this ford here and start from this end. Remember, we don't want to startle them – the more we round up the better,' warned Slim.

With that the group parted. Jake went downstream with seven men; they were screened from the Indians by a line of rocks and trees. Slim crossed just upstream of the Indian camp.

Shortly after crossing Beaver Creek, Slim ordered his men to dismount and began to creep through the thick undergrowth towards the Indians. They had got to within fifty yards when a loud yell gave away their positions. This was quickly followed by the first shot.

'Who fired that?' shouted Slim, annoyed, as shots began to zip through the branches and leaves around him.

Two warriors came running at him through the bushes. Slim fired his gun instinctively at the first Indian, who fell dead; the second leaped forward onto Slim. The pair fell to the ground, another shot rang out and the Indian fell over, dead. One of Slim's men pulled the Indian off him.

'Hell, Slim, ah thought yer were a gonner.' He smiled down at him.

The whole area was now full of screaming and shouting women and children, all running to and fro totally confused. At this point Jake added to the confusion by charging into the camp, still mounted. Grey Wolf and a small band of warriors began to organise some stiff resistance as they tried to fight a covering withdrawal. Grey Wolf pulled down a rider and beat him to death with his tomahawk. Another rider was killed as he rode past, the warrior who killed him was then shot by someone from the bushes.

'We got 'em, boys! Let's press home our attack!' shouted Slim. As he stood up, the man next to him was flung forward violently. He had obviously been shot, but from behind – and the Indians were in front of them. Who was shooting at them from this angle? Slim wondered.

Jake and the survivors who had ridden into the middle of the Indian camp now joined Slim and his men. Another rider suddenly fell dead from his horse.

'Hell, Slim, they've got round behind us!' cried one of his men.

'Let's get back to our horses,' called Slim; he began to slip away through the undergrowth, followed by his men.

One of them stepped right in front of Paddy.

'Well, good afternoon,' Paddy greeted him before firing one barrel of his shotgun into the man's chest. It threw him backwards and he lay dead where he landed.

Slim, Jake and the others all made it back to their horses and, quickly mounting, they rode off.

'They was bounty hunters, Slim,' cried one of the men.

'Yellow-bellied Injun lovers!' cursed another.

To help calm the Indians down and prevent them mistaking Will and his companions for attackers, Two Crows led them forward into the Indian camp.

Women and children sat cowering behind bushes or trees. Some were shocked, some hurt, some regrettably lay dead. Grey Wolf quickly dispatched several warriors to collect up as many of those that had fled as possible. Time was now short, and they would have to make for Indian Creek tonight with all possible haste. When Grey Wolf spotted Two Crows he stepped forward and greeted him as a long lost brother.

'This is Grey Wolf, the tribal chief,' introduced Two Crows. Grey Wolf was a small man with grey hair; he looked of mature age but lean and fit nonetheless.

'Good afternoon,' they greeted him in unison.

Grey Wolf looked at them thoughtfully. 'Once again, you have proven to be true friends to your Indian brothers. We will not forget your acts of kindness and help,' he nodded.

'Where are you going?' asked Charlotte.

'We are heading for Indian Creek and the mountains – we shall be safe there. We are to meet with White Feather, who will protect us with the help of the redcoat.' He spoke with authority and purpose.

'Two Crows, this White Feather... is that not Lucy?' asked a puzzled Sandy.

He nodded. 'Yes, it is,' he replied.

'Then, Grey Wolf must actually look for Black Eagle,' retorted Charlotte.

Grey Wolf perked up a little at that name as if he recognised it.

'Grey Wolf, White Feather is not at Indian Creek; you must look for Black Eagle – he will be there for three more nights,' warned Will.

Grey Wolf nodded in response, then turned as if to leave. 'The spirits of our ancestors shall ride with you to protect you on your journey,' he said looking forwards the forest. 'Now I must round up my people and make for the mountains.' He leaped into the bushes and, followed by his warriors, was gone, leaving Charlotte, Will, Sandy, Paddy and Two Crows behind at the camp they had stood at only that morning. If it had not been for the dead bodies lying around, they might have thought it was all a dream.

'Is everyone all right?' checked Will.

They all answered in the affirmative.

'Then, let's move out – we've some catching up to do,'
declared Will. For the second time that day, they rode west for
Richmond.

ONWARDS AND WESTWARDS

It was dusk when Barney and Black Bob arrived near to Jefferson's Ranch, they had found a small outcrop where they could climb and get a clear view across the plain towards the ranch, which lay to the west of them still. The outcrop itself formed a small bowl with high steep sides and one small exit. The inside was large enough to set up camp but the horses required to be tied up under the trees just outside. This offered shelter from the wind and security from being spotted from the ranch. Barney quickly checked the ranch over through a set of field glasses. By the time he had finished with his preliminary search, Bob had a small fire going.

'Well, what d'yer reckon?' Bob asked when Barney rejoined him by the fire.

'There's a large body of men there; on the gate there are two sentries, as well as at least one sentry at the front porch. Most tend to wear grey garments, but I have seen one or two wearing brown and/or black. Ah'm assuming that these people are members of Ted's gang,' explained Barney.

'And Ted hisself?' asked Bob.

Barney shook his head. 'Ah didn't see him. But those not wearing grey appear to be housed in the far dormitory.'

'So, what d'yer reckon then?' Bob questioned.

'Ah think we'll keep this place under observation for the time being. You can do first watch.' Barney tossed the field glasses to Bob, who finished his coffee, then scaled the rock to the vantage point. Barney settled down to get some rest.

It was quite dark by the time Slim and his men returned. They almost galloped in, which caused some consternation both inside and outside the ranch.

'Hey, Barney, come and look at this,' called Bob, as soon as he saw them riding into view.

Barney responded immediately and scaled the rock to be by Bob's side in seconds. 'What's the problem?' he asked as he took the field glasses from his companion.

'Look over there – riders, at least a dozen of them – and they're riding hard,' Bob said pointing.

'I guess so,' murmured Barney as he watched them thoughtfully. One or two of the riders looked hurt, he thought.

Inside the ranch compound, men now hurried around. Then the Colonel appeared.

'What the hell yer doin' back here, Slim?' he growled menacingly.

Slim dismounted quickly. 'We came across those Injuns the army is lookin' for, so followin' your orders we began to round them up, but then became ambushed ourselves by bounty hunters,' he explained.

'How many men did yer lose?' asked the Colonel softly.

'Three, Colonel,' Slim replied.

'An' yer sure these here were bounty hunters?' The Colonel had slipped his arm around Slim's shoulders and he looked him straight in the eyes.

'Positive, Colonel,' Slim replied nervously.

'Did yer kill any Injuns?' the Colonel asked.

'Yeah, we got a few,' Slim smiled and nodded quickly.

'And these here bounty hunters, did yer get any o' them?' The Colonel smiled.

'No, ah don't think so,' Slim shook his head. 'It was all so confusin' – ah was just trying to get the men out of the ambush,' he pleaded.

The Colonel nodded silently and then passed Slim on to someone else, who led him away. 'OK, boys, we'll mount up. Billy Joe, leave Slim here in charge of five men. Now get me Ted.' With that he turned and stormed back into the house.

The ranch compound quickly became a hive of activity, as everyone hurried around preparing their mounts. Ted was found and led towards the ranch house.

'Come in, Ted,' greeted the Colonel.

'What's the matter, Colonel?' asked Ted casually.

'It appears that some of my men found the Injuns this after-noon and as they were dealin' with 'em, they in turn were jumped by a party o' bounty hunters,' answered the Colonel.

'A party!' exclaimed Ted surprised.

'Yeah. Yer see, Ted, yer gotta think yer actions through. A lot o' men will come lookin' for yer with a price on yer head. So ah suggest yer ride west towards Eagle's Pass; there's an old prospectors' mine there, where yer can hole up until the dust settles,' ordered the Colonel. Ted knew that if the Colonel suggested something he really meant that you *had* to do it.

'Would they not have come to collect on them there Injuns, Colonel?' asked Ted.

'Naw, there's more money in huntin' for you, boy,' retorted the Colonel.

'And what of you?'

'Ah'm goin' to do some bounty huntin' of ma own,' he said slightly cryptically as he removed an ivory-handled pistol from a writing desk.

It wasn't often the Colonel wore his pistol, but on the few occasions that he did, men knew he meant business.

'So, when d'yer wish us too ride?' asked Ted.

'Immediately,' came the reply.

Ted stood and paused a moment, then nodded as he turned and left.

Barney was watching the door when Ted exited the house. He put down his field glasses for a moment in disbelief then held them to his eyes once more. That was Ted Skerrat, he thought.

'Bingo,' he whispered to Bob, who was still lying by his side.

'Have we found him?' asked Bob.

'Yep, sure have,' smiled Barney.

'Are we goin' to go in and get them?'

'Ah guess so,' replied Barney.

They both fell silent as they watched with interest the com-motion going on within the ranch compound.

'What d'yer think they're doin', Barney?' asked Bob presently.

'Ah'd say they're about to ride,' Barney replied through gritted teeth.

'All o' them?'

'It looks like.'

Then, to Barney's surprise, a small group of riders rode out from the ranch and headed due west. He observed their progress through his field glasses.

'Damn,' he cursed.

'What's the matter?'

'Our bird has just flown the nest.'

'Where's he gone?'

'Ah dunno, but he's a-headed west. Come on, we'll follow.' Barney jumped up and descended the rock, closely followed by Bob. Soon they were riding out themselves, but Barney realised that he would have to give the ranch a wide berth, so they at first headed east for a few miles before turning south, hoping to pick up Ted's trail the next day.

Shortly the Colonel led most of his men eastwards towards Beaver Creek. He left Slim and five men behind as security for the ranch. Colonel Cody cut a fine figure as he rode in his full Confederate uniform, complete with rank insignia. They were to ride direct for Beaver Creek, thus missing out Richmond and, luckily for them, Will and his Storm Force team, who had just arrived at the outskirts of Richmond.

'Well, we're here – what now?' asked Paddy.

'Why don't Will and I ride up to the saloon as two bounty hunters and simply ask for Ted?' suggested Sandy.

The others looked at him, surprised.

'Do you not think that's a bit risky?' questioned Charlotte.

'Probably, but we don't exactly have much time now, do we?' said Sandy pointedly.

'All right Sandy, but *I'll* do the asking,' warned Will. 'Any shooting, get out of here quick,' he advised Paddy and Charlotte. He glanced back at Sandy. 'Firstly though, I think we should wear our wrist guns, don't you?'

Sandy nodded and together they began to slip on their new equipment. Sandy wore his upon his right wrist, unlike Will, who wore it on his left. Will always preferred to keep his right hand free for his throwing knife.

'Sandy!' Charlotte called as she hurried after him.

He stopped as she rode alongside him; she placed her arm around him and kissed him passionately upon the lips. 'Take care,' she urged.

'Wow!' he groaned.

'Just as well I'll be doing the talking, then,' commented Will sarcastically.

They rode up to the saloon and dismounted outside. Carefully they stepped up on to the porch and slowly entered the bar. As soon as they entered all joviality and music stopped; all eyes fell upon the two strangers.

Will and Sandy slowly glanced about them, then stepped over to the bar.

'Well, howdy boys, what can I get yer?' asked a pleasant-looking bartender.

Will looked at him. 'You can tell me the whereabouts of Ted Skerrat and his gang,' he smiled.

'Ted Skerrat?' asked the bartender, looking surprised.

'That's right,' replied Sandy.

'I... I don't know... as far as I know he's generally found down at Pinewood Falls,' the bartender replied with a nervous laugh.

'Now that's funny, they told me I would find him here,' answered Will, as he picked up an empty whiskey glass; he looked into it and blew out some dust.

'Ha, maybe one of these gentlemen could tell yer where to find him,' stated the bartender, still nervous.

The man next to Sandy grunted, then turned his back.

Sandy turned slowly and looked at his back. 'And what's your problem, sir?' he asked threateningly.

'Huh, ah wouldn't help no John Bull,' he grunted.

'We may have our faults, sir, but we may be made of sterner stuff than you give us credit for,' threatened Sandy.

'Why, you—' the man turned back around and reached for his gun at the same time. He did not get far, for as he turned back, Sandy simply jabbed two fingers into his eyes as hard as he could. The man fell to the floor screaming and holding his face.

'Is there anyone else who would like a piece of me?' growled Sandy as he stood clear of the bar and looked slowly around the saloon.

'They've gone to Jefferson's Ranch; yer'll find them there,' a woman said.

'Thank you, ma'am.' Will doffed his hat; then, patting Sandy on the shoulder, he walked out of the saloon. Sandy followed slowly, walking backwards so as not to turn his back. As they stepped outside they quickly mounted up and turning rode out of town.

Those nearest to the screaming man ran to his aid; one or two others ran to the door to see where the two strangers had gone.

'What on earth did you do that for?' asked an angry Will.

'It got your answer quickly, didn't it?' responded an equally maddened Sandy.

'It could have caused a lot of trouble,' muttered Will.

'I've got no respect for these people – they're just bullying scum,' sneered Sandy.

Will looked surprised. 'Sandy, this is not like you; you're becoming too involved. Keep your mind on the task in hand,' he ordered, then rode off past Sandy, leaving him and Charlotte together.

'What did you do?' asked a concerned Charlotte.

Sandy sighed heavily. He watched Will ride on ahead, then he rubbed his chin. 'He's right,' he mumbled, then reached out and squeezed Charlotte's hand briefly. 'Come on,' he said as he spurred his own horse on ahead.

Two Crows led them towards Jefferson's Ranch. It was the early hours when he halted and dismounted from his horse. He now spoke in whispers.

'The ranch is over there, not far.' He pointed in the direction where the ranch lay.

'Right,' whispered Will, and withdrew his gun. 'Two Crows, stay here with the horses. Any shooting, get out of the way quick.' Two Crows nodded in response.

'It's all on foot from here. Sandy, bring your rifle. We shall see if there are any sentries,' declared Will as he led them towards the perimeter fence.

'Shh, did yer hear that, Gus?' asked one of the sentries.

His companion stepped over to him. 'Hear what?'

They both stood listening to the quiet rustle of the occasional gust of wind. 'Ah thought ah heard horses,' the first man said in a hoarse voice.

'Argh, yer just gettin' tetchy; next yer'll be hearin' Injuns,' mocked Gus.

By now Sandy and Paddy had climbed quietly over the fence; they had seen the two sentries on the gate and the lone sentry on the door. Will indicated that he wished them to head over to the side windows; they noted that there were no patrolling sentries. Once they reached the house they quickly checked it over. It all appeared to be in darkness and quite empty. The windows were all sash windows, so Paddy was able to twist the frame ever so gently to drop the top half of the window. They then all clambered in. Any instructions or orders were still being passed by hand signal; not a word was being said. As they quickly passed from room to room searching the house, Will left Sandy at the back of the hallway to watch the front door. His rifle and handgun were cocked and ready, and he also withdrew his sword bayonet.

Charlotte was ordered to watch the back door, in case anybody came through, while Paddy and Will crept into the lounge. Here they found what they were looking for: set into the far wall was a large steel safe.

'I bet that is our target,' Paddy flicked his head towards it.

'Can you crack a safe?' asked Will looking a little concerned.

'Ah, don't concern yourself, ah'll have this crib cracked in no time,' smiled the big Irishman.

Will smiled. 'I am not even going there.' He shook his head slowly.

As Paddy settled down in front of the safe, putting his ear to it and turning the disc, Will glanced about the room; he knelt with his revolver at the ready.

Only the staccato clicking of the disc broke the silence, then in next to no time Paddy sat back and tried the large handle. It opened first time. He looked at Will and winked as he gave a broad smile.

'Now then, is that not something?' he whispered.

Will, though, was more interested in what was inside the safe. 'Let's look for our money, shall we?' he suggested.

They quickly found and bagged the three thousand pounds.

'What about the rest?' questioned Paddy as he held up two handfuls of dollars.

'That is clearly nothing to do with us. You know as well as I do it stays here,' sighed Will.

'Oh well, you can only ask,' sighed Paddy, closing the door as quietly as possible.

They then waited to see if what appeared to be a loud bang had alerted the sentries; it had not, so they began to creep back, collecting Charlotte and Sandy along the way.

'My, that was quick,' whispered Sandy as they dropped down from the window.

They crept around the back of the house, and looked across the vast expanse of cleared earth towards the first of two dormitories. Unbeknownst to Will and his team, the first dormitory had been the one used by Ted Skerrat and his men.

'We have to get from here to there without being seen or heard,' said Will.

Sandy had a quick look. 'Well, sorry to say, we can be seen from both the front porch and the gate by whoever may be over there,' he said.

They searched in vain for some way of getting across the empty square of dirt to the first dormitory.

'We are just going to have to walk over to it,' said Will at length.

'All right, I'll cover you.' Sandy flicked his head as he brought his rifle to his shoulder and peered around the corner of the house. Will took a deep breath. 'Go,' Sandy whispered hoarsely.

Will began to creep across the open stretch of ground. Charlotte followed a few steps further back, then finally came Paddy. All appeared to go well; Will made it across without being seen and Charlotte was about to when one of the sentries on the gate looked up.

'Hey, Gus – who the hell are they?' He reached for his gun and pointed towards Charlotte and Paddy. It was the last thing he ever did, for as a shot rang out he was flung backwards. Sandy quickly reloaded his rifle and fired another shot off almost immediately. Gus also fell dead, a neat hole drilled through his forehead.

Phew, that was a close one, thought Sandy as he looked for the sentry on the porch; the man had reacted quickly and had fired off two quick shots at Paddy as he ran across the open square. Luckily they were fired randomly and were nowhere near their target. Sandy took careful aim and fired off one more shot; the third sentry fell backwards off the steps and lay still upon the ground. Paddy in turn took two hand bombs from his belt; removing the pins with his mouth, he flung them into the open area to try to cause a little confusion.

Now, though, Slim and the other two men had begun to react and were firing at Sandy, who was kneeling by the corner of the house. Sandy flung himself forward on to the ground and behind the raised porch. Will and Charlotte, realising that this was all the resistance they were likely to receive, now crept along the back of the two dormitories until they were level with where they assumed the three riders to be firing from. Paddy remained at the front of the first dormitory and fired along the building; this was largely ineffective but gave the defenders the false impression that the attackers were still at the front of the buildings. He also rolled a third hand bomb along the porch, which exploded before it reached the doorway that Slim and his companions were shooting from; nevertheless it caused them to take cover. Sandy too was now returning fire, which further kept the attention of the defenders.

Again Will resorted to silent hand signals as he carefully and quietly opened the back door to the second dormitory. He and Charlotte crept inside; all was dark, and the occasional ricocheting bullet from Sandy made it extremely dangerous. Then Will accidentally stood upon a creaking floorboard. All three defenders turned around. Charlotte and Will both fired two shots simultaneously and two of the defenders fell backwards, dead; one of them crashed out through the doorway.

'Don't shoot, don't shoot!' cried Slim, as he raised his hands.

'Drop the gun,' ordered Will, calmly.

Slim did as he was told slowly, then knelt; Charlotte stepped forward and kicked the gun away.

'Where is Ted Skerrat?' asked Will.

'He ain't here, he ain't here!' Slim cried, still on his knees with his hands raised.

'I know that, you clod, but where *is* he?' Will asked again menacingly.

Paddy and Sandy had now turned up; Paddy stepped in through the door.

'Lie on the floor, face down,' ordered Paddy.

Again Slim did as he was told; as he lay down Paddy tied his hands behind his back. Next he placed his knee into the small of Slim's back, grabbed his hair and pulled his head back violently. He cocked his gun in Slim's ear and placed the barrel next to his temple. 'Now then, sunshine, I shall only ask this once: where is Ted Skerrat? You have three seconds.' Paddy spoke calmly and clearly.

Slim began to sweat profusely; he desperately tried to persuade the agents of his lack of knowledge. Still Paddy counted slowly and deliberately, 'One… two…'

'All right, all right,' Slim pleaded. He swallowed hard. 'They've gone to Eagle's Pass.' He coughed and swallowed.

'Why there?' Paddy tightened his grip upon Slim's hair.

This made Slim choke a little. 'There's an old prospectors' mine there.'

'Now there's a good fellow. That wasn't so hard, was it?' said Paddy in a cheery fashion. He then pushed Slim's head forward, banging his face off the floor, bursting his nose and making it bleed.

A bag was roughly placed over Slim's head and his feet were trussed up to his hands, so that he could neither see nor move.

Will then flicked his head to everyone indicating that the time was right to leave. They returned to Two Crows, who was waiting with the horses.

'Thank you, Two Crows. Do you know the way to Eagle's Pass?' Will asked. Two Crows nodded.

'That will make us late, mind, Will,' warned Paddy.

'If we are to return on time, we should start heading back now,' added Charlotte.

'We not only have the diamond but we also retrieved the money,' stated Sandy.

They all sat in the saddle, quietly contemplating their next move.

'So what is it to be?' asked Will at length.

'I'm for catching these bullies,' said Sandy determinedly.

'Paddy?' asked Will.

Paddy nodded. 'I'm for going onwards.'

'Charlotte?'

'I'm all for completing our task,' she said in response.

'Good, then let's put as much distance between this place and us as we can, shall we?' urged Will as he spurred his horse onwards. 'Two Crows, lead on.'

Colonel Cody halted his men just short of Beaver Creek.

'We shall camp here for the night,' he ordered. 'We will see more at first light.'

'Are we to follow the Injuns, Colonel?' asked Blue.

'Naw, that's an army matter. Let 'em earn their pay. They'll be headed north now, anyway. Nope, ah'm more interested in these here bounty hunters. They're the ones that will cause the most danger,' he explained. Because the Colonel had managed gain control of everything of importance within the county of Greendale, he did not care for the idea of having various groups of bounty hunters and detective agencies such as the Pinkerton Agency running amok within his boundaries. As always, his response to any problem of this sort was to devise a way of eliminating it permanently. That night as he lay under the stars that is what he put his mind to: how to end the latest incursion by bounty hunters.

The following morning, they arose early and travelled the short distance to Beaver Creek. It did not take long to find the Indian camp.

'Well, they're not going to be hard to find, are they?' the Colonel remarked. 'Especially if they keep leaving dead bodies around like this.' He sat back in his saddle and sniffed the morning air. He then slowly rode across to the camp itself, and dismounted; he paid particular attention to the fire. It had been the one started by Two Crows, then used again by the Indians. 'Yep, this was used by Injuns all right,' he said almost to himself. 'Jake,' he called.

'Yeah,' replied Jake as he stepped forward.

'Now then, boy. Show me where these bounty hunters came from,' he ordered as he patted Jake on the shoulder and pushed him onwards.

'Over this way, Colonel,' offered Jake as he led him towards the trees and rocks.

'Did yer see any of them?' the Colonel smiled.

'They came from nowhere, Colonel, we didn't stand a chance,' began Jake.

'Aha… and how many were there?' the Colonel went on.

'Ah don't rightly know – possibly three or four.'

'And how many of you were there?'

'Fourteen, but we were now fighting on two sides,' Jake tried to explain.

'Ha ha – did nobody think of checking the area out first?'

'Hell, Colonel, we saw these Injuns and just wanted to get in among them!' laughed Jake.

'Is that right,' the Colonel nodded. He had now withdrawn his revolver and without saying anything further he raised his gun and shot Jake dead.

'Right boys, let that be a lesson to yer all. Watch yer flanks and never attack an enemy without first checking the area,' he warned.

He walked back to his horse and mounted. 'Blue, take three men; yer now to replace Jake at Pinewood Falls. Billy Joe, ride for Harper's Crossing – ah want to know as soon as the army ride north.' He led his men back towards Richmond.

Grey Wolf had by now decided to rest his people. He was aware that they were not far short of their target of Indian Creek; in spite of this, he had pushed them hard throughout the night, as the previous night's experience had been a very close call indeed – he did not expect them to be able to fight off any more unwanted attention as a group. So, realising all this and hoping for a bit of luck, he dispatched six of his best scouts, to see if they could find some way of reaching Indian Creek in daylight. If there was a way, he was determined to go for it and to make a dash for freedom. Camp was quickly set up, but unlike previous days when optimism was rising and detection by the authorities had not materialised, this time there was a sombre quietness. It was true some people were so tired they just slept, and the old and ill did not have much strength left either, but there was still a distinct feeling of concern about the place. After discussing his concerns and plans with the tribal elders, Grey Wolf decided to rest himself. His scouts had still not returned by sunrise; nevertheless, he was not destined to rest for long, as two of his scouts returned with important news.

Four of them had discovered an old dry narrow stream bed which appeared to run in an easterly direction; it was not far to the north of the camp. Two scouts had carried on along the bed while two had waited; when the first two failed to return they retired back to their camp to inform Grey Wolf. He immediately called a council for all to attend; he had decided in his own mind to go for it.

'I have called you here to this council to give you the news that our ancestors have smiled upon us today. We have found an old stream bed just to the north of here which, with their help, may lead us to our destination. We shall all assist each other. Warriors shall help the old, women shall help the infirm and children shall help their younger brothers and sisters. Together we shall achieve our destiny.'

At the end of his short speech, all the tribe could muster was a quiet groan. He then turned to his two scouts. 'You will lead us along this bed; you are our eyes and ears. With that goes much responsibility – beware,' he warned. The two warriors glanced at each other then bowed briefly to Grey Wolf before turning and taking up their positions. Soon the tribe was on the move again in one last effort to reach safety. Grey Wolf knew that they could not take much more; his people's future rested on the events of today.

Barney and Black Bob had also decided to ride by night and rest up by day. They were not worried about keeping up with Ted Skerrat, as they had a general idea of where he was going. They had found his tracks through the night and felt confident that they would catch him soon enough. So after a warm breakfast and a coffee or two they settled back for rest. Barney, however, was awoken mid-morning by Bob kicking him gently.

'Wha... what is it, Bob?' he asked, struggling to find his bearings.

'Come an' look at this,' replied Bob as he gestured back towards the road.

Two Crows was still leading Will and his team along the road; they too had found Ted's tracks and, worryingly, two other sets had joined later. Will had decided not to rest at present but to keep going if possible, still aware that they needed to put as much distance between themselves and the Colonel as possible. But now Two Crows, after dismounting and checking the tracks, pointed towards some rocks in the near distance.

'These two tracks now go south, they no longer follow Ted Skerrat,' he announced.

'So it looks as if we're the only ones on to them at present,' responded Will.

'That we know of – there will be others sooner or later,' warned Paddy.

'Yes, so we've got to get hold of Ted and his merry band before they do,' added Charlotte.

Two Crows had now remounted. 'Lead on,' ordered Will and they all set off again.

Barney and Bob sat watching them from their observation point.

'Bounty hunters?' asked Bob.

'I very much doubt it, especially as they are using an Indian scout,' replied Barney, deep in thought. 'Naw, ah don't think they're bounty hunters, but ah'm not sure who the hell they *are*,' he admitted rubbing his chin.

'Whoever they are, they're after the same quarry as us,' declared Bob as he watched them ride off.

'Ah don't think it's no Sunday school outing, that's for sure.' He glanced at Bob. 'We will have to make sure we find Ted first, that's all. There will no doubt be more coming along,' warned Barney as he returned to the fire and poured himself a fresh mug of coffee.

It was not till lunchtime that Will and his companions finally halted.

'Ohh,' groaned Sandy as he stretched himself.

'What is the matter with you?' sniggered Paddy, as Sandy began to walk around rather stiffly.

'I've got aches and pains where I didn't think I had anything to ache,' moaned Sandy.

The others sniggered.

'I wouldn't get too comfortable, Sandy. I plan to ride again after a short rest,' warned Will as he smiled.

'Ohh, this is just a terrible nightmare,' groaned Sandy; he then noticed a small stream and limped over to it.

'Now what are you going to do?' asked a giggling Charlotte.

'It's all right for you lot, you must have backsides like elephant skin, not like my delicate, soft, tender skin,' he joked. He now reached the stream and, to everyone's surprise, stepped into the water up to his shins, then sat down.

'What the devil?' Will shook his head.

They all burst into laughter at the sight of Sandy sitting in this stream up to his waist with a silly grin of relief wrapped across his face.

'Ahh, that's better,' he sighed. 'Look at all this steam,' he called as he glanced about him.

'Would you like to partake in lunch?' Paddy laughed as he offered Sandy a plate.

'You will have to bring it here; I can't just interrupt my medication,' Sandy smiled.

'Hey, what did your last servant die of?' cried Paddy.

'Well, it wasn't overwork, that's for sure,' laughed Sandy in return.

Charlotte passed him a plate while he was still sat in the water; she shook her head as they giggled at him.

Meanwhile, Grey Wolf and his people had now reached Indian Creek. They had eventually come across it; that morning had been difficult and slow. The two warriors sent on ahead that morning had been met as they headed back towards the camp a little earlier. They too had found the junction of the two streams and had turned left – or north – and had walked for some two or three miles. There they had found the actual creek they were seeking. The news of the discovery had had an invigorating experience upon the tribe and many had renewed their efforts. Still, it remained no easier and on they struggled. The going was slow and, although they tried to remain quiet, every scrape or crash appeared to be tenfold louder than normal. Finally they arrived at the remains of Lucy's cabin.

Grey Wolf looked about him as his people sank to the ground, some out of tiredness, some out of despair. As they all sat upon the green meadow wondering what to do next, a shot rang out, then a shout. But it was not a shout to be afraid of – this was in their native tongue. Grey Wolf turned to where the sound had come from; there, stood upon the rock in cowboy attire, was Black Eagle. He smiled a warm welcoming smile, then jumped down from the rock. He approached Grey Wolf, then knelt in front of his once great chief.

'Oh great chief, Grey Wolf,' Black Eagle began. 'I am the son of Running Bear. My name is Black Eagle and I would be honoured to escort you and your own to safety and White Feather.'

Grey Wolf stepped forward and assisted the young man to his feet, 'You know of White Feather? Then take me too him.'

Just then Liam appeared; the Indians immediately went into defensive mode with guns, knives and tomahawks at the ready, but Black Eagle stepped in front of them.

'Wait!' he cried, raising his hand. 'This is my friend – he is with me.'

The Indian warriors reluctantly dropped their weapons.

'Black Eagle, we must rest and eat. How far must we travel until we are safe?' asked the chief.

'You are safe now, my chief, but it is two day's walk to where I need to take you. Rest and eat now; we will set out once you are refreshed,' advised Black Eagle.

Murdoch stepped into his house; he had been busy all morning branding cattle; now he felt parched for a cup of tea. That in itself was a minor miracle. It had only been since Charlotte had been around that he had finally got round to dealing with his heavy drinking. He still had the occasional whiskey at night and still enjoyed his chewing tobacco, but the drinking was certainly not at the level it had once been and the chewing tobacco now was taken only when in the saddle. The house smelt of roses and he could hear the pleasant singing and humming of Lucy as she went about tidying up. Yep, I could get used to having a lassie about the house, he thought, as he leant back against his sideboard in the hallway.

He was still stood there listening when Lucy appeared; she stopped abruptly when she saw Murdoch.

'It's all right, lassie, ah was just enjoying that beautiful wee tune ye were humming,' he smiled.

Her eyes dropped as she stepped back into the kitchen.

It was then that Murdoch realised that the floor had been polished and there he was stood in his boots. 'Ah, well, I, er...' He smiled to himself and shrugged as he gingerly began to remove his boots. He followed her into the kitchen and was hit by the most beautiful aroma.

'What's that?' He sniffed.

'Oh – I thought – that is, I—' Lucy struggled to explain.

'It smells absolutely lovely. What on earth is it, lassie?' Murdoch again asked.

'Bread,' she replied softly, embarrassed.

Murdoch picked up on that straightaway. 'So, lassie, ye come inta ma house, and in just two days – *two days*, mind yer – yer makin' yersel' right at home, cookin' and creatin' these lovely smells and polishing the floor an' things! Ma house smells like some sort o' garden, so it does.' He stopped and glowered at her.

Lucy, thinking she was being chastised, slunk away.

'An' long may it continue! Ah could easily get used to all this fine livin' and havin' a woman's touch about the house,' he explained with a broad smile.

'Did Starlight not do anything for yer?' Lucy timidly asked, turning.

Murdoch hesitated and coughed slightly before answering. 'She most probably *would* have if only ah would have let her. But alas, it took a young lady from England an' yersel' to get me head out of a bottle an' back into reality, lassie.'

Just then Starlight came into the kitchen; as soon as she saw Murdoch and Lucy together she stopped and made as if to leave. 'So sorry, so sorry,' she apologised.

'Ah, Starlight, the very person,' called Murdoch. 'Now then, as ah've got the two of yez together, ah want yez to make up a list of cleanin' things that we can purchase next time ah goes to town,' he explained. 'An' Starlight, where is Buff?'

'Chopping firewood, Mr McLeod.' She curtsied instinctively, in fact she was not too sure what to do – it was the most Murdoch had ever said to her.

'Right – ah must go an' find him.' Murdoch walked purposefully out of the house, only to stand on a large splinter; this made him leap about on one foot, and he began to shout and moan, but stopped himself short of swearing.

Since seeing Lucy and what was left of her little cabin, it had got Murdoch thinking just how badly he had treated his own two house servants. He was so now determined to change all that. After all, had not his own mother been a chamber maid when she had met his father. 'Buff? *Buff!*' he shouted from the porch.

'Yes, Mr McLeod?' replied Buff as he appeared quickly from around the corner of the house.

'Ah, there yer are. Good, now then... Ah've been thinking. How about yer and yer lovely wife havin' yer own home, say over there?' Murdoch smiled as he pointed to a peaceful part of the ranch compound.

Buff's face fell. 'I'm so sorry have we offended yer somehow, Mr McLeod,' he said sorrowfully.

'Eh? No, no, it's no' that. Yer'll still be workin' for me an ah'll organise some sort o' salary for yer an' yer good wife. It's just yer own cabin out o' the way, like.' Murdoch smiled. 'An' stop callin' me Mr McLeod; ma name is Murdoch,' he declared as he stood to his full height.

Brown Buffalo looked at him, dumbfounded; he just blinked occasionally.

Murdoch looked at him, still waiting for an appreciative response. But poor Buff couldn't believe what he had just heard. 'Well, go on, Buff, go an' tell yer wife yer good news,' urged Murdoch.

Two cow hands who happened to be near stood open-mouthed as they heard Murdoch's proposal. 'An' what are yer two sorry-lookin' numbskulls gawkin' at?' Murdoch challenged.

It appeared to bring them out of their lethargy and, shaking their heads, they walked on.

Murdoch then turned to go back indoors. 'Ah still ha' na had ma tea,' he moaned.

Back inside the house Buff and Starlight were chatting away excitedly in their native tongue. Lucy stood by the large table kneading more bread dough; she smiled a lovely peaceful smile at Murdoch as he stepped into the kitchen once more.

'That was a lovely gesture, Mr McLeod,' she praised him.

'Ahh, well, for a while ah had just about forgot about friendship and havin' company about the house.' He paused and sighed as he looked at the freshly baked bread sitting upon the windowsill. 'But that was then; this is now.' He perked up. 'Now then, where's ma cup o' tea, lassie?' he demanded as he sat down at the table.

WANTED

The Colonel rode into Richmond, to find the whole town in total consternation. The sheriff stood upon his porch as the Colonel rode up to him.

'Howdy, Hank, what's doin'?' the Colonel asked.

'Ah was about to ask yer the same thing, Colonel,' replied the sheriff.

'Oh? And why is that?'

'Have yer been to yer ranch lately?' the sheriff asked.

'Ah was not there last night – why?' The Colonel became suspicious.

'Ah think yer'd best step inside,' advised Hank as he entered the jailhouse.

The Colonel glanced at Casey who sat next to him; then, giving him his reins, he dismounted and followed the sheriff. Yet he was stopped in his tracks when confronted with the sight inside, for there sat in the far corner was Slim, holding a plaster to his nose, which was obviously broken, and nursing two splendid black eyes.

'What the hell hit yer?' asked a surprised Colonel.

'A sack was tied over my head, Colonel, and my face was bounced off the ground,' explained Slim.

The Colonel glanced at the sheriff, who nodded and held up the offending sack. He sighed, 'OK, Slim, what happened?' he asked.

'Well,' Slim swallowed hard. 'There was a lot o' shootin' goin' on in the compound, so me Benny an' Fannon ran to the dormitory door. There we found the two gate sentries dead, an' the shootin' was comin' from the corner of yer house, Colonel,' he began.

'Was there many?'

'Ah think that there were four, Colonel.'

'All right, go on.'

'Well, Davey then bought it, an' they began to creep down the back of the dormitories without us knowing,' Slim went on.

'Then what?' The Colonel began to walk around Slim slowly.

'Well, two o' them came in through the back door, an' shot Benny an' Fannon. Ah couldn't do anything else, Colonel,' pleaded Slim. 'Ah had to surrender.' He began to shake and sob.

'Why did yer have to surrender, Slim?' questioned the Colonel.

' 'Cause they had me cold, Colonel. They tied me up an' put a sack over my head.'

'Did they ask you any questions?'

'Yeah, they were askin' about Ted an' his boys.'

'So what did yer say?'

'Ah had to tell 'em, Colonel. They would've killed me if ah hadn't,' protested a nervous Slim.

'OK, Slim, calm down, calm down.' The Colonel patted Slim upon the shoulder to reassure him. 'Sheriff, raise a posse an' head south towards Harper's Crossing, just in case they've gone that aways to give us the slip. It's a murder case now, boys – there'll be a hangin' to be done,' he declared loudly.

'Where do yer think they've gone, Colonel?' asked Hank.

'They'll have gone west, eventually, so that's where ah'll be a-headin'. Ah'll first have to ride over to the ranch, though – see what damage has been done. Yer'll be lookin' for four riders, ah guess,' the Colonel replied. 'Come on, Slim, we'll take yer back to the ranch.' He walked out of the sheriff's office.

'When d'yer want us to ride, Colonel?' asked Hank.

'Tomorrow morning,' he ordered over his shoulder. Then he rode out of town with his men and Slim.

It was not far from Richmond to Jefferson's Ranch and they soon arrived at the house. 'Collect what yer need, boys, we may be gone for a few days,' warned the Colonel as he stepped into his house. He hurried into his lounge where the safe was. Everything looked all right so he knelt and opened the safe. 'Damn!' he cursed and punched the safe door. 'They've got my money,' he growled. 'Josey!' he called.

'Yeah, Colonel,' replied a man who had stepped into the room.

'Go get me Slim,' he ordered through gritted teeth.

Soon the unfortunate Slim was hauled into the Colonel's room by Jasey and Casey.

'Ah, Slim,' the Colonel greeted him, as his men pushed Slim to the floor in front of the Colonel.

'What – what's wrong, Colonel?' replied Slim in a weak and nervous voice.

The Colonel casually waved his hand towards the safe. 'Slim what d'yer see?' he asked.

'A safe with money.'

'Quite correct – but what is missing?'

Slim studied the contents of the safe as best he could. 'I-I don't know, Colonel.' Slim shrugged.

'D'yer see a carpet bag in there, Slim?' taunted the Colonel.

'Naw, Colonel, ah don't.'

The Colonel stepped towards the safe, and bent forward to look inside. 'Funny that, neither do I… Yet ah'm sure a left one there the day before.' He turned back towards Slim.

'They… They must've took it,' stammered Slim.

'Did yer see them with it?'

'Naw, but… but…'

'But what?' The Colonel quickly drew his gun and shot Slim through the heart; his body was flung backwards into the hall. 'Incompetence, total incompetence,' muttered the Colonel. He glanced at Josey. 'Get that body out o' here, before it bleeds all over the place.'

The two men turned and carried the dead body of Slim out of the house. Just then Vince stepped into the room. 'Colonel, when d'yer wish to ride?' he asked.

'They've taken the train haul, Vince,' murmured the Colonel as he stared into the safe.

'We'll get it back, Colonel, yer'll see,' assured Vince.

'Too right we will! Now tell the boys, one hundred bucks to the one who gets it back,' the Colonel announced, as he closed the safe door.

'Ah will, Colonel – now that's mighty generous of yer.'

The Colonel glanced at him and grunted. 'OK, if all is ready we shall ride now; come on!' he ordered as he stormed out of the house.

Outside, his men were either sat on their horses or readying their saddle packs.

'Is everyone ready to ride?' he called as he reached his horse.

'We certainly are, Colonel,' came a voice.

'OK, we ride west, boys. We'll bring those responsible for the shootin' of our boys and have 'em hang,' threatened the Colonel as he mounted his horse and led them all out of the compound.

Ted Skerrat stood up; he with his other gang members had been sat by the fire eating lunch.

'We must ride on,' he warned as he looked west.

'Yer not getting touchy, are yer, Ted?' asked Abe.

Ted turned sharply and snarled at his tormenter. 'Don't push it, Abe. If we are being chased by bounty hunter's an' the like, then I wish to remain alive to enjoy the spoils ah've gained.'

'How far d'yer intend to ride west, Ted?' asked the Kid.

'As far as it takes,' came the reply.

'But Ted, the further we go the more distance between us an our treasure,' argued Joe.

'That's right, so if they are chasin' us the less chance they have of getting' their mitts upon the diamond,' explained Ted with a smile.

'But Ted, what if someone else steals it?' asked Joshua.

'Like who?' Ted turned upon him.

'Well, ah dunno, Ted, but anybody could take it, ah guess,' pleaded Joshua.

'An' just who knows about it bar us?' asked Ted, pushing his face into Joshua's.

'Ah dunno Ted, ah just thought—' Joshua was becoming frightened and upset.

'Well, keep those thoughts to yersel',' threatened Ted. He looked about the group. 'Has anyone else got anything to say on the matter?'

'Just one thing, Ted,' began Danny. 'When d'yer intend to turn back towards Pinewood Falls?'

'Like ah said, when I consider the time's right, an' not before,' he replied. Again he paused and glanced about the group. 'Now come on, it's time we moved out,' he ordered.

They hurried about, readying their horses and putting out the campfire.

'Where is it we're headed, Ted?' asked Joe.

'We're headed for an old prospectors' mine up in Eagle's Pass, beyond Fort Bastion.' Ted flicked his head in the direction he was talking about.

'Eagle's Pass!' exclaimed Frenchy.

Ted scowled at him. 'Are yer goin' deaf?' he challenged.

'Naw, but Eagle's Pass? That's miles away,' argued Frenchy.

'Both the Colonel and I feel we'll be safe there,' explained Ted.

'Oh, the *Colonel* does, does he?' asked the Kid.

'OK, Kid, now what's the problem?' Ted was becoming tired of all this pettiness.

'Has it not struck yer that the Colonel may want us out o' the way.'

'Hey, Kid, yer a genius, a bloody genius,' mocked Ted. 'Of course he wants us out o' the way. So he can deal with any bounty hunter's hisself,' Ted shook his head. He then spurred his horse onwards and led his men towards Prospect Pass.

By now Will and the team were also preparing to ride. Sandy was still wet from sitting in the stream.

'Yer want to be careful, yer'll get chapped,' warned Paddy.

'Are you feeling a little more comfortable?' asked a still smiling Charlotte.

'Oh yes, though no doubt they will be sore again shortly,' replied Sandy, as he cast a dark glance at Will.

'What's that for?' protested Will.

'You are a slave-driver, sir,' teased Sandy.

'Here, I just want to get back to Madeleine,' declared Will and without waiting for a reply he spurred his horse on.

'Whose idea was it to give up a life upon the ocean wave?' muttered Sandy almost to himself, as he followed the others.

'Two Crows, how far do you think we'll get today?' asked Will as he rode alongside the now smiling Indian scout.

'We shall reach Prospect Pass by nightfall, I'm a-thinking.' the Indian replied.

'Oh God, is it far?' groaned Sandy at the back of the group.

'Come on, you wounded soldier, you,' laughed Paddy, as he slapped Sandy across the back.

'You just don't care,' moaned Sandy.

They rode on at a fairly steady pace, although Two Crows was always careful not to tire or blow the horses. Also, he and Paddy regularly took turns in acting as scout. Paddy did this to give Two Crows a rest and also to keep his hand in. They had been riding for about two hours when they came across Ted's last campfire; it was hidden behind some rocks a short distance from the road and it was Paddy who noticed it. He was acting as scout when he suddenly halted and scrutinised the ground. Will and Two Crows halted immediately, then Charlotte and Sandy pulled up too.

'What is it, Paddy?' asked Will as he sat in the saddle looking around him.

'The tracks here leave the road,' Paddy called back; he looked at the rocks where the tracks led to. 'They appear to go over to those rocks there.' He flicked his head towards the rocks and everyone now focused on them.

'All right, I'll have a look – cover me, Sandy,' ordered Will as he walked his horse towards the rocks. As he reached them he dismounted, withdrawing the Winchester from its saddle holster. He crept onwards until he was behind the rocks; there he found the smouldering remains of the campfire.

'It's all right,' he called. 'It's just an old camp. Two Crows, come here,' he ordered.

They all rode forward, Two Crows at the front; he dismounted to have a look at whatever Will was shouting him for. Knelling down, he ran the palm of his hand only a fraction above the smouldering embers, he checked the fire.

'Two, possibly three hours old,' he stated as he looked at Will, then glanced about the camp. 'Do not move,' he told Will. The Indian then checked the grass around the fire, as Paddy peered around the rock.

'Six, maybe seven men here,' he declared, then stood up and

hurried around to the other side of the rock towards some trees and shrubs.

Paddy watched him with interest. 'He makes it look so simple, doesn't he?' he finally remarked in admiration.

Two Crows, though, did not pay him any heed; he soon hurried back to the group. 'Seven horses – this is our gang,' he stated happily.

'Good, so Ted's about two hours ahead of us,' remarked Will as he glanced west.

'How long to Prospect Pass, Two Crows?' asked Sandy.

Will was jolted out of his thoughts. 'Why, are you sore again?'

'No, just out of curiosity really. It doesn't appear that this gang are moving with any conviction, as we're now only two hours behind them. If it's going to take three, possibly four hours to reach this pass, we may just find them there, as by then it will be nightfall,' explained Sandy.

'Good point,' observed Paddy.

'We shall arrive in two hours' time,' replied the Indian scout confidently.

Grey Wolf approached Black Eagle. 'Now, Black Eagle, son of Running Bear... now is the time to save my people and your brothers; they have rested long enough. You say it will take us two days, then let us begin.' Grey Wolf spoke deliberately and nodded slowly once he had finished.

Black Eagle had knelt throughout the whole speech; now he stood.

'Grey Wolf, my chief, I shall be honoured to lead my friends and brothers to Paradise.' He waved his arm in the direction to which they had to travel.

Liam had agreed to wait behind at Indian Creek, just in case their friends reappeared. They moved at the speed of the slowest person and, with the going all uphill, it became painfully slow. Black Eagle now walked; he had offered his horse to two old and infirm characters. To add to the difficulties of the walk, darkness came very quickly as soon as the sun fell behind the crest of the western side of the valley. Because of the slow speed as they climbed higher, the sun had sunk well below the western horizon.

'Who is it you are waiting for?' Grey Wolf asked Black Eagle.

'Four friends – they are not from here; their chief is the Great White Squaw' (a complimentary reference regarding Queen Victoria) 'from across the big water. A fellow Indian, Two Crows, rode with them,' replied Black Eagle.

'Ah, yes, we met them earlier,' said Grey Wolf thoughtfully.

'Are they all right?' asked Black Eagle hopefully.

'They saved us from the grey riders at Beaver Creek and left us food. They rode west – why, are you expecting them?'

'Yes we are, sometime tomorrow, we hope. They are trying to capture the Great Grey Chief, Cody. But come, you must tell my boss of this news, when you meet him tomorrow,' Black Eagle.

'Is that White Feather?' questioned Grey Wolf.

Black Eagle shook his head and smiled, for like himself, many years earlier, Grey Wolf too had assumed this White Feather character to be a man. Nothing could be further from the truth – White Feather was actually a woman.

'Tell me, Black Eagle, what is this White Feather like? What tribe does he belong to? Is he courageous, powerful and sympathetic to our ways?' asked Grey Wolf.

'My chief, firstly White Feather is a squaw, and furthermore she is a white man's squaw,' began Black Eagle.

'What's this? What is this talk with the double tongue?' cried Grey Wolf, at that several warriors leaped forward, tomahawks in hand.

Black Eagle instinctively stepped back but, remaining calm, began to explain. 'White Feather is very helpful towards our people; she too has suffered at the hand of the white man's greed. She used to pass the fugitives along to a great white warrior known as "Mad Dog", my leader. He would allow us to settle upon his land and live as free peoples.'

'Do they work together, to defy the white man's authority?' asked Grey Wolf.

Black Eagle smiled. 'No, my chief, white squaws can be as deceptive as our own. Still he will not turn anyone away. He may be fearsome, but he is as wise and therefore a great warrior,' he explained admiringly.

'Good, so then we may talk as equals at the table.' Grey Wolf smiled thoughtfully.

They struggled onwards and upwards, painfully slowly.

Hank stepped out of the sheriff's office and into the street, fastening his gun belt to his waist. Sat before him were at least fifteen men; all except for his deputy were volunteers.

'OK men, we shall ride south, towards Harper's Crossing. We are looking for four men riding together, or they may have split up into pairs. Ah wants them all alive so as to see them hang for the wilful murder of the four men at Jefferson's Ranch. The Colonel has set off west – he thinks he'll get them all, but let's see if we can make a difference and show him, eh, boys?' He then clambered upon his horse and led them out of town towards Harper's Crossing.

Hank had been sheriff of Richmond for three years, before that he had been the town's deputy. He was, unusually for the county, a local with no Confederate connections at all. He was not an admirer of the Dixie riders, whom he believed were acting in a most disrespectful and presumptuous manner as time went on. They needed to be brought into line, to respect the law of the county.

Hank, nevertheless, realised only too well that the Colonel would not give up his authority lightly – yet he required the riders to uphold this authority. Hank also realised that one day, sooner or later, the proper authorities would turn up and relieve the Colonel of the duties of his self-styled protectorate. All of those that were guilty of supporting the Colonel and his Dixie riders would also fall. Hank knew that if he wished to retain his position he would have to disassociate himself from the Colonel, the man who placed him in this position in the first place. He reckoned that the best way of doing this without being caught out was to be seen to be giving the community of Richmond some self-respect and a self-belief that they could manage alone without their protector. Yes, Hank was guilty of carrying out the Colonel's wishes in the past and of sometimes causing harm to innocent people, but he had only been carrying out orders, after all. Sadly, he had convinced himself of his innocence of all wrong-doing; now he needed to convince those citizens of Richmond.

Two Crows and Will finally arrived at the summit of Prospect Pass. It had been a steep climb to this point that they now stood upon – Will reckoned on at least a mile, but the ground either side still climbed higher to form two large high peaks with bare steep rocky and crag-faced sides. Will ignored the higher ground and rode over to the beginning of the descent on the other side of the pass. Two Crows rode with him, and as they looked down into the next valley the Indian pointed to an imaginary point off in the distance.

'Fort Bastion,' he announced.

By now Paddy, Charlotte and Sandy had joined them.

'Beautiful view,' admired Charlotte.

'Yes, it is a pity we cannot enjoy it in daylight,' Will replied.

'Are we to set up camp here?' asked Paddy.

'Yes, we shall,' replied Will as he dismounted.

'When will we arrive at Fort Bastion?' asked Paddy.

'Tomorrow afternoon, late on,' replied Two Crows.

Paddy nodded in response.

A fire was quickly lit and water brewed so as to make a cup of tea.

'People back home, would never believe this,' remarked Sandy.

'Believe what?' asked Will.

'Well, here we are sitting in the middle of the wild west, trying to brew tea,' he smiled.

'What do you mean, *trying*?' retorted Charlotte as she poured out a cup for herself and Paddy.

'Thank you,' declared Paddy as he took the mug of steaming tea.

'Do you think the Colonel is on to us?' asked Charlotte.

Sandy looked up at the sky and sighed. 'As sure as God made little green apples.' He smiled at her.

'How far behind us do you think they could be?' Will asked.

'That's the big question,' replied Paddy.

'I know if someone stole *my* money and I wanted it back

badly, I'd be riding hell for leather to get it back,' stated Sandy.

'The other question is, are we catching Ted and his gang?' asked Paddy.

'We will find that out tomorrow,' remarked Will.

'So just how do you intend to find it out, then?' asked Charlotte.

'Paddy and I shall ride into town and simply ask,' smiled Will as he turned to face her. 'You and Sandy can wait outside of town to make sure we ourselves are not being followed, then join us on the far side of town.'

Charlotte sighed loudly and pursed her lips in annoyance. Sandy glanced at her and smiled. 'We will have our turn at some fun yet.' He reached across and squeezed her hand.

She glanced at him and smiled, but it did not hide her disappointment nor her sadness.

Ted Skerrat and his men were at that point in time riding into Fort Bastion.

'We shall not stay long here, we shall only get some provisions,' stated Ted.

'What!' exclaimed the Kid.

'D'yer have a problem with that, Kid?' threatened Ted. His tolerance of the Kid was beginning to wear thin, for the Kid had complained all the while since leaving camp at lunchtime. It was now a foregone conclusion and readily accepted that the gang would break up on arrival back at Pinewood Falls, and that the Kid, Danny and Abe and Joshua McCabe would ride west to the sea. Ted was hoping to remain in Pinewood for the time being at least, Joe was even thinking of settling there, and Frenchy was thinking of taking Sally north back to his home country. But first they had to weather this storm and put up with the inconvenience.

'Ah'm darn sick of all this running, Ted,' complained the Kid.

'So what d'yer intend to do about it then?' growled Ted.

'And ah'm darn sick of yer complaining, Kid. Yer've done nothing but moan since we left camp,' stated Joe.

'An' what is it to yer, yer thieving, lying yella-bellied spic,' threatened the Kid.

'Yer want to be careful, Kid – one of these days I might just decide to take a potshot at yer myself,' warned Joe.

The Kid just glared at him.

'Yer two better shut up, or neither of yez will be around to do anything,' warned Ted. He did not like this idea of running any more than the next man, but what the Colonel said actually made sense.

Fort Bastion was a small settlement; it consisted of a hardware store, a saloon, a small church, a blacksmith's, a sheriff's office, a telegraphy office and several cabins. They rode up to the hardware store and dismounted. Ted looked about him as he stepped up on to the porch.

'Abe, go get our provisions; Danny, give him a hand, will yer,' ordered Ted.

'OK, Ted, but where are yer goin'?' asked Abe.

'Ah'm goin' to have a whiskey, d'yer mind,' he retorted.

'Ah'm all for that,' stated the Kid cheerily, as he followed Ted over to the bar.

Joshua followed but Frenchy stayed by the horses and watched the locals going about their own business. Fort Bastion being a bit of a frontier town, nobody paid them much attention.

'Howdy, boys,' greeted the bartender as Ted and the Kid, followed by Joshua, wandered into the bar.

'Howdy,' replied Ted; he paused and glanced about him. It was just like any other frontier bar – full of trappers, travellers, prospectors and carpetbaggers.

'What can ah get yer fellas?' asked the bartender in a cheerful manner.

'Whiskey,' replied the Kid.

'Where're yer fellas headin'? Are yer plannin' on stayin' long?' the bartender asked.

'The old prospectors' mine and no,' answered Joshua.

Ted sighed heavily and glowered at him, He should have known better than to tell the McCabes, he thought.

Three glasses of whiskey were quickly placed upon the bar; Ted studied his glass for a short while, while the Kid and Joshua drank theirs straight off.

'Another, bartender,' demanded the Kid.

'Hey, don't drink too much of that, Kid,' warned Ted.

'Are yer me mother or something?' the Kid responded sharply.

Ted placed his untouched drink back down on the bar. 'If yer think ah'm goin' to carry yer all over this godforsaken country, yer've got another think comin', Kid,' he replied through gritted teeth, then turned and walked out of the bar.

Joshua gingerly placed his empty glass upon the bar. 'Yer want to be careful, Kid. Ted don't like it when folk push him too far,' he warned.

'Would yer like another, mister?' asked the bartender, as he tried to pick the atmosphere up once more in the bar.

'Nar thanks, ah'd best be goin'.' Joshua turned and hurried out after Ted.

The Kid finished his drink then, glancing at the bartender, he too turned and left. The others were already mounted when he walked into the street and over to his horse. Without waiting or saying a word, Ted rode out of town for the old mine. Ted was deep in thought when Abe rode up alongside him.

'Are yer all right, Ted?' he asked concerned.

Ted turned to face him slowly. 'Yep, shouldn't ah be?' he challenged.

'Sorry, Ted, but yer don't appear to be yersel',' Abe tried to explain.

Ted did not reply; he was arguing within his own mind about whether he should turn back to Pinewood Falls or just wait as the Colonel had ordered.

Will and his team were now settling down for the night. They had decided to keep a lookout just in case the Colonel came up behind them unexpectedly; nonetheless, the sentry wasn't posted until after eating dinner and therefore missed two riders climbing higher than they. These were Barney and Black Bob, who had been following Storm Force all day. They did not light a fire for fear of being discovered, especially once they had noticed the sentry. Sandy was to do the first watch, then Charlotte, but as expected they ended up doing the two together. This intrigued Barney as he watched from the shelter of some rocks above them. He had never known bounty hunters to take their woman on a chase with them.

'Perhaps they're not bounty hunters after all,' suggested Bob.

'Nar, they've got to be – what else could they be? They're armed to the teeth,' argued Barney.

Charlotte involuntarily shivered where she sat.

'Are you all right, Charlie?' asked Sandy.

'I don't know – there is something out there,' she replied without looking away from the distant rocks about them.

'Have you seen something?' he asked as he crept to her side.

'No, it's just a feeling.' She shuddered again involuntarily.

'Don't worry, Charlie, I'll look after you,' Sandy smiled.

'Ha, I've managed all right on my own so far, but thank you for the offer,' she smiled in return.

Sandy began to laugh at that. 'Ah, yes, you would probably do better yourself, sure enough.'

They sat together quietly in thought. Charlotte was sat slightly behind Sandy and above him. She watched him; he sat with his back to a rock, a piece of grass hanging out of his mouth. Everything, it seemed, had come together – for her at least – within the last two or three days. She was now controlling her mental state as taught by her friends at the Buddhist monastery all those years ago, and she no longer had the distraction of wondering what Sandy was going to do.

'Sandy?' she asked.

'Yes, Charlie,' he replied without looking.

'I know you've asked me for my hand, but were you forced into it by the others?' she questioned, watching his every move and trying to read his body language.

'No, the only person bringing pressure upon me was myself; I should have mentioned it a long time ago. Meeting you was the greatest moment in my life, Charlie, and I mean that. If I had lost you, for whatever reason then I would only have myself to blame, no one else,' Sandy replied sincerely.

'Oh Sandy, do you really mean that?' Charlotte asked, a tear came to her eye.

'Of course, darling, you should know me by now – I do not say anything if I don't mean it,' he smiled at her.

'That is the nicest thing anybody has ever said to me, Sandy,' she remarked; her voice sounded full of emotion.

Sandy just glanced at her and smiled rather sheepishly. 'Charlie, I take it as a great honour that someone as sweet and as beautiful as you should even take the slightest interest in a great oaf like me.'

'You're no oaf! Sandy…?'

'Yes darling?' He looked a little concerned as her manner now became one of determination.

'I love you,' she said.

He smiled, a little embarrassed. 'I love you too, Charlie.'

He returned his attentions to the valley below.

She followed his line of sight down into the darkness below and smiled to herself as she remembered what Paddy had predicted over a year ago. Right as usual, she thought.

'Sandy?' she then again asked.

'Yes, sweet pea,' he replied again he did not look up.

'I was wondering, now that we're together – and you may, or may not, wish to spend some time together – what will you now have planned for when you go on leave?' Charlotte eventually asked.

'Oh, well – I think we may spend enough time together working, so I thought we would each have some time alone on leave,' he replied without hesitating; she did not notice his sideways glance and cheeky smile.

'Oh, yes, of course… so you intend to go home to Newcastle.' She tried to hide her disappointment.

'No, I thought Paris would be very nice at this time of year, or so I'm told,' he said.

'Oh yes, Paris… How I would love to see that city again, and just have a look around it this time,' she replied dreamily.

Sandy had now turned around and was smiling broadly at her. 'Your opinion of me must not be very high, Charlie,' he teased.

'What do you mean?' she challenged.

'Well, to think that I would forget what I said when I first heard you mention that you would at least like to see the city of Paris. I replied that it would be nice to return with your loved one, did I not?'

'Yes, you did,' remembered Charlotte. He had said that in the carriage as they were leaving Paris, over a year ago now.

'So I thought that is where I would take you this time – if, of course, you are agreeable to the idea,' Sandy explained.

'Of course, Sandy. Oh, how wonderful – oh, you are a treasure!' She hurried forward and embraced Sandy lovingly.

'Excuse me, but you are preventing me from executing my duties,' Sandy admonished playfully.

'I'm sorry, Sandy, but oh, Paris…' Charlotte was becoming excited.

'Don't apologise – I can easily get to like all these hugs,' laughed Sandy.

Barney sat above them still. I don't know who you are or what your business is but you do make a nice couple, he thought to himself.

He turned to look at Bob, who was fast asleep on the ground and snoring slightly, then looked around him in the darkness. The night reverberated to the various sounds of nature; nothing ever appeared to be close by, it always sounded some distance away. His eyes again fell upon Sandy and Charlotte. Ah wonder what it's like to have a woman in yer life, he thought. He began to think of the women he had known in his past. Could he have spent the rest of his life with any of them? Well, none had survived long in his life, so the answer must be no, he admitted to himself. He was soon to dismiss these kinds of thoughts anyway. He was here to do a job, not to reminisce. Who were these people? What were they doing in these parts? These were the thoughts that now began to slip into focus.

Charlotte had by now joined Sandy on the ground and together they observed the stars and listened to the sounds of the night. Not a million miles distant, Grey Wolf was looking at the same stars.

'It has been a good clear night; we have made good progress.' His spirits were high now that he felt safe. The same feeling had spread among his people and, because of this feel-good factor, they had made greater efforts to reach the crest of the valley. For the first time in many moons, his people were happy once again; sadness had given way to optimism.

'How are we doing?' he asked Black Eagle.

'As you say my chief, it has been a clear night; we are doing well. The next valley is called Pine River Valley; it is the one after that we seek.'

'Tell me – this Mad Dog, you did not tell me of which tribe he belongs,' stated Grey Wolf.

'As far as I know he belongs to the Scots tribe; they live far away across the great water. I do know, as I said earlier, that his chief is the Great White Squaw,' Black Eagle responded.

'Ah, so what is his purpose here in our lands?' asked the old chief.

'Many, many moons ago he was sent here by his chief to keep out the white man's war parties. He works with the redcoats.'

Grey Wolf nodded thoughtfully.

'I have heard that they are good and that they leave us alone to live in peace' he said.

'I have found them to be good people, my chief,' assured Black Eagle.

Grey Wolf smiled and patted Black Eagle across the back of his shoulder. 'Good, then let us move on – the quicker we are, the sooner we shall arrive. I look forward to meeting your leader Black Eagle; he appears to be a wise man.'

The Colonel was settling down by a campfire. He and his men had eaten and he stared into the crackling fire, watching the flames leap and dance.

'Vince,' he called at length.

'Yeah, Colonel,' a man opposite replied.

'Ah wants yer to ride point tomorrow,' the Colonel ordered as he chewed one nut at a time in his mouth.

'Yeah, sure Colonel,' Vince replied.

'Do yer think we'll catch these low-down, no-good sons o' bitches tomorrow, Colonel?' asked another man.

'The Colonel looked at him contemptuously, 'Do yer, Casey?' he asked.

Casey laughed nervously, and glanced about him to see if anyone could save his embarrassment. 'Well hell, Colonel, ah just don't knows.' He shrugged helplessly.

'Then why ask me? Ah ain't got a crystal ball, yer know,' the Colonel replied sarcastically.

'We should reach Fort Bastion tomorrow afternoon, sometime,' announced a third man.

The Colonel shot him a quick glance. 'Yip, ah guess yer about right there, Li'l Dave,' he replied. 'Remember, boys, ah wants these bounty hunters alive first. They have something that belongs to me and ah wants it back.'

The others just looked on; they knew when the Colonel fell into this mood he became a very dangerous man indeed.

A GATHERING STORM

Black Eagle and Grey Wolf were very happy with the exertions of
the tribe from the previous night. Not only had they managed to
ascend the crest out of Indian Creek but they had actually
descended into Pine Valley. However, as they reached the bottom
where the ground began to level out by the river, Grey Wolf
finally called a halt.

'My people have achieved much this night. It is the thought of
sanctuary and freedom that drives them on, but we must now
rest,' he said as he sat down. So did his followers and soon there
was a large camp set up in the open upon the valley floor. The air
became filled with woodsmoke and various aromas of cooking.
Some people sat by the fires, some were busy, and some sat with
their feet in the water. Black Eagle sat next to Grey Wolf; they
were both quietly, taking in the various scenes around them.

Then Grey Wolf stirred. 'I have been chief of my people now
for many, many moons. They have fought bravely when asked,
they have given comfort when required – I am proud to have led
them,' he declared admiringly. 'I have always sought the council
of the elders, so that I may represent the wishes of my people at
all times. I rode with Geronimo and fought alongside Sitting Bull.
Then, when my people could not fight any more, we sought
peace with the white man – only to be betrayed for the area we
were supposed to be given when making peace was taken from us,
and we were herded like cattle to another place, a place that even
the white man could not make use of. The tribe has lost many
brave warriors recently; we had to flee to survive.'

'Chief Grey Wolf,' Black Eagle began, 'Mad Dog is a wise
man; he will not turn you away to be ravaged by wolves. He will
give you shelter and food and will help your sick.'

The old chief now looked at Black Eagle. 'You say this with a clear heart, I can see that. But what makes this white man any different from the others?' he asked sadly.

Black Eagle glanced at his chief and smiled. 'Chief, with all respect, you should not judge him because he is white; he will not judge you because you are an Indian. I know he will do this, for he did it for me and Two Crows as well as Brown Buffalo and his wife Starlight. I know he will do it for you.'

'Brown Buffalo and Starlight are here, at Paradise?' asked a surprised Grey Wolf.

'Yes – do you know of them?' It was Black Eagle's turn to sound surprised.

'Starlight is my daughter; Brown Buffalo was one of my bravest warriors. I thought they had both died some moons ago,' replied Grey Wolf.

'Well, if we rest here today and make as much progress again tonight, then you shall see them once more tomorrow,' remarked Black Eagle.

'Yes, we shall rest now,' ordered Grey Wolf and with that the word was quickly passed around to make camp and to rest. Scouts were sent off just in case, but not as many as before.

Will and the team sat in their saddles as the sun rose above the nearest crest of hills to the east.

'Isn't that a wonderful sight!' exclaimed Charlotte.

'It certainly is – it means you're still alive,' agreed Paddy.

'And there was me just thinking it was a nightmare,' responded Sandy.

'Before we go, does anyone have the feeling they are being watched?' asked Charlotte.

'Why?' enquired Will.

'I've had that feeling all night,' she explained.

'So have I,' responded Paddy, 'and it is not nice.'

'Have either of you seen anything?' Will enquired further.

'No, it's just a feeling I've had,' Charlotte replied.

'I haven't seen anything either,' said Paddy, shaking his head.

'Right, then, the pair of you keep your eyes peeled. If it's this Colonel Cody fellow, then woe betide us,' warned Will.

'I'll watch our backs,' declared Sandy as they began to trot out of the camp area and descend the steep slope towards the valley below and Fort Bastion beyond.

They did not see Barney and Bob, who sat above them, watching.

'We'll give 'em half an hour, then we'll set off in pursuit,' announced Barney.

Bob nodded. 'So you think they may lead us to Ted and his gang?'

'Ah don't know. Ah don't know what their business here is, but ah aims to find out,' Barney declared determinedly.

They observed Will and the team leave camp and descend the pass on the west side. Barney began to toss small stones aimlessly to one side as he waited.

About this time, a US cavalry patrol was riding out of the local barracks just across the river from Harper's Crossing. It was being led by a keen and very observant young lieutenant by the name of David Benjamin Hudson, and it consisted of himself, a guidon bearer carrying the troop colours, a sergeant and half a troop of men – twenty-six in all. To help the young lieutenant, the sergeant was a tough, long-serving member known as Sam Rodgers; he had joined the army in 1878 and had just completed thirteen years of service. A rough, well-built man, who had the respect of the men, he had fought many battles against the Indian and, unlike his youthful officer, held them in great esteem. He always rode with an Indian scout known by the men as Tomahawk Jo; his native name was unpronounceable and, although he too had fought the Indian many times, he did not always approve of the methods used against his fellows. But unfortunately, if he was to say anything out loud then he would be sent back to his own reservation. Only his sergeant, Sam Rodgers, knew his true feelings – they had been through much together and had great respect for each other.

From the other side of town, Billy Joe sat upon a hill watching the bridge through a pair of field glasses when he noticed the army patrol crossing the river. He quickly counted the men, then prepared his horse, mounted up and rode off to find the Colonel. As they entered the town of Harper's Crossing, Sergeant Rodgers turned to his lieutenant.

'Would yer like to stop by the sheriff's office, see if there have been any sightings, sir?' asked Sergeant Rodgers.

'Sergeant, if there had been, don't you think it would have been passed on to us,' retorted the young officer arrogantly.

'Best be safe than sorry, sir,' replied the sergeant patiently.

'Sergeant, I know what I'm doing. Now ride on,' ordered the officer.

The cavalry column trotted through town and took the Richmond road north.

'Der yer know where yer goin', sir?' enquired Rodgers as the pace began to pick up once they had left town behind them.

'Yes, Sergeant, I most certainly do. Grey Wolf and his people have had a few days' head start on us. But I know they will have gone north; they'll be heading for Canada and I reckon they'll be found in the Richmond area.' He threw the sergeant a casual glance.

After a few more miles the young lieutenant halted the column. 'OK, Sergeant, I want you to throw out six scouts: two on either flank and two on the road. We'll be more cautious from here on in – I don't want any nasty surprises.'

'Aye aye, sir,' the sergeant replied, saluting. He then turned and calling over Tomahawk Jo, explained what was required. The sergeant always left it for Tomahawk Jo to pick his own assistants; once chosen, the Indian then put the men where he wanted.

'Sergeant,' the lieutenant called him over.

'Yep, sir?' Rodgers rode over to him.

'What are you doing?' the officer asked him abruptly.

'Sorry, sir?' The sergeant shook his head as if he hadn't quite heard correctly.

'You heard me, sergeant! Now tell me, what is this man doing?' He began to raise his voice and pointed towards the Indian scout.

'But Tomahawk Jo always picks his own men, sir,' protested the sergeant a bit puzzled. All the officers knew how he and Tomahawk Jo worked; they had never failed yet.

'These are not his men, Sergeant, they are *my* men,' shouted the young officer. 'I say who goes and who stays!' he raved.

'Yeah, sir,' the sergeant replied slowly. This was going to be a long patrol, he felt.

The officer now rode along the column. 'You, you, you and you.' He picked the men as he rode along the line of cavalrymen. 'Now then, Tomahawk Jo, you ride on the road where I can keep an eye on you, you two take the right point and you two the left. I want to know about anything that looks untoward.' He then rode back to the front of the column.

Those chosen as scouts rode past and took up their positions, Lieutenant Hudson gave his sergeant a sneering look as he ordered the column forward once more.

Billy Joe had seen enough and was riding north to find the Colonel when he rode into Hank and the Richmond posse heading south.

'Well, howdy, Billy Joe! Who yez runnin' from to be ridin' so hard?' mocked Hank.

'Ah'm looking for the Colonel, Sheriff. Der yer know where he's heading?' asked Billy Joe, ignoring Hank's sarcasm.

'He's headed west, rode out yesterday for Fort Bastion. Why, have yer found those bounty hunters?' Hank questioned.

'Hell no,' laughed Billy Joe, 'But ah got to report an army column coming up the road behind us.' He thrust his thumb over his shoulder where he had just come from.

'Really?' mused Hank.

'Yer still goin' to ride south, Hank?' asked Billy Joe.

'Yeah, it would look suspicious if we were to turn around now. Ah shall carry on to Harper's Crossing then turn west, mesel',' Hank explained.

'I'll see yer later then,' stated Billy Joe as he spurred his horse onwards in search of the Colonel.

Hank and his men watched him disappear from sight, then turned their own horses south. 'Come on, boys, we'll head towards Harper's Crossing first before doubling back towards Jefferson's Ranch,' he said.

They had not gone far when they met firstly the army scouts then the young lieutenant and his men coming the opposite way.

'Howdy, Lieutenant, now what brings yer into Greendale County?' greeted Hank.

'Good morning, Sheriff. We're on the lookout for some

Indians that escaped from their reservation a few days ago. Have you heard of anything?' he asked.

'Yeah, there appears to have been a bit of a shoot-out over at Beaver Creek, day afore yesterday. But ah reckons the Indians have gone north now,' Hank replied.

'Oh? So why are you and your men riding south?' asked the lieutenant.

'Well, we're huntin' some murderers who shot up the Jefferson ranch. We wants to take 'em in for a trial,' smiled Hank.

'Oh, those men that shot up the ranch – could they have been responsible for the incident with the Indians, do you think, Sheriff?' asked the young lieutenant.

'Couldn't rightly say, but whens we catch 'em we'll ask them fer yer,' laughed the sheriff.

'Sadly, we have not met anybody upon the road this morning, Sheriff, so I suggest you look elsewhere,' said the officer.

'They may have left the road. We'll carry on towards Harper's Crossing and search the riverbank all the same, Lieutenant.' And with that Hank spurred his horse on and past the soldiers.

The young officer watched them disappear with contempt. 'We shall carry on towards Richmond, there we shall camp for tonight,' he ordered his sergeant.

Ted and his boys had now arrived at the old prospectors' mine. Not only was the old tunnel opening still there but an old shack stood nearby.

'OK, boys, we'll make camp here,' ordered Ted.

'Joshua, go get some brushwood, will yer?' Abe asked his brother.

'Why, Abe?' Joshua queried looking perplexed.

'So as we can make a fire, goddamn it,' Abe replied sharply.

'Now boys, yer getting' tetchy,' mocked the Kid.

Abe threw him a sneering glance, as he and his brother began to get the fire going. They were soon joined by Ted, who sat down next to them.

'Well, ah reckon we should go back to Pinewood an' get our stone,' suggested the Kid for the umpteenth time.

'All right, then, big boy – what happens if we run into the Colonel? What are yer goin' to do then?' asked Ted.

The Kid looked at Ted, surprised, silent for a moment. 'Well, this is not the same Ted Skerrat that killed seven men at Red Bridge, or fought that shoot-out with the sheriff and posse from Daisy Hill, is it? Who is now a little worried about some old clapped-out Johnny Reb, surviving on reputation alone,' he added sarcastically.

Ted stood up slowly so that he looked the Kid in the eyes; he half turned away, then quickly swung back, hitting the Kid clean upon his chin. This knocked the Kid backwards off his feet, and when he'd realised where he was, Ted was already stood over him with his gun in his hand.

'Go on, Kid, pull yer gun. Ah'll drill a neat hole right through yer guts,' Ted snarled.

'Now come on, Ted,' said Abe as he stood up. 'Yer know the Kid, he speaks afore he thinks, there's ain't no need for this.'

'Ah reckons he needs a lesson taught,' laughed Joe, who always enjoyed watching the Kid get brought down to earth.

Ted kept his eyes on the Kid. Neither moved, then slowly Ted re-holstered his gun and stepped away from the younger prostrate man. 'Just once more – just once – an' ah'll drill yer full o' lead,' he growled.

Ted walked over to the edge of the camp that they had set up. He looked about him. 'Who's lookout?' he asked as he noticed a large rocky overhang.

Each member looked at each other, shaking his head.

'No one is, ah guess, Ted,' replied Joe.

'Danny, can yer keep lookout for me? Ah know ah can trust yer,' Ted asked.

'Yeah, sure thing, Ted,' replied Danny, surprised at the compliment. He hurried away after lighting a cigar.

Ted walked back to the fire and poured himself a mug of coffee; he looked neither left nor right and said nothing. In fact no one said anything; they were all waiting with bated breath to see how Ted was going to react.

He walked across to the far edge of the clearing, and sipped his coffee in silence. He remained standing, staring along the old road which led away from the mine eastwards. Abe walked over to his side.

'It'll soon be over, Ted, yer'll see,' he tried to reassure his old friend.

Ted turned to him. 'Of that ah'm sure, Abe,' he replied. 'But ah'm sick an' tired o' runnin', ain't yer?'

'Ah guess ah am, Ted – well hell, we all are,' Abe replied.

'Naw… ah'm thinkin' o' makin' a stand, Abe,' Ted revealed.

'Well, Ted, most of us would stand with yer,' responded his friend.

'Naw, this is sumthin' ah've got to do myself,' Ted sighed.

Joshua now approached them with two plates of beans. 'Here's yer breakfast, Ted, Abe,' he said hesitantly.

'Thanks, Josh,' replied Abe. Ted just took the plate and nodded.

Joshua then returned to the campfire. Ted watched him walk away, deep in thought. 'See, Abe, yer first responsibility is to yer brother. Take him west to San Francisco; ah've heard it's a great place to go. The Kid's right; we should ride back to Pinewood Falls an' split the haul that we've collected an' go our own ways. We've been together too long now.' With that Ted drank a mouthful of coffee and threw the dregs upon the ground. He turned and marched back to the camp. 'Right, fellas, we'll rest up here a while then ride east.' He looked at the Kid. 'Yer right, Kid, it's time to go our separate ways. Yer'll get what's comin' to yer when we get back to Pinewood Falls,' he explained.

'All right!' exclaimed the Kid in his excitement.

Abe sat forward and slapped the Kid across the arm with a cloth. 'Hey, Kid show some respect,' he warned.

'Ah'm not being, disrespectful. But ah do think it's time to split,' the Kid argued.

'So where yer headin' Kid?' asked Joe.

'As far away from you as possible,' the Kid answered sharply.

'Why, you—!' Joe reached for his gun at the same time as the Kid.

Frenchy stepped between them. '*Non*, not this way. We should part as friends.'

'Well, Josh an' me, we're off to San Francisco,' announced Abe. 'What about yer, Danny?' he then asked.

'I dunno, I may stay at Pinewood Falls for a time,' he replied, rubbing his chin.

'Ah'm goin' west, for as far as ah can,' announced the Kid.

'Good, 'cause ah'm a-headin' south, to Texas,' declared Joe, with a sneer.

'Oh, an' what about Alice?' asked the Kid.

'She can come if she wants to,' Joe replied indifferently.

'I shall go north once more, and I shall take Sally with me back to Quebec,' stated Frenchy dreamily.

They all now sat silently as they turned to watch Ted. He had walked off a little distance from the group and remained with his back to them. He did not say a word, but merely stood staring east once more.

'Well, come on then,' he said at last. 'The sooner we rest the sooner we get started.' He walked over to his horse, brought back his blanket and laid it down to sleep on.

Two Crows halted; ahead of him stood a large rocky edifice which was split by a very narrow gorge. He turned to Will. 'Wolf Pass,' he announced, pointing. 'Beyond that lies Fort Bastion.'

'All right, Paddy. Ride up to that point there and make sure the pass is clear. If you suspect anything, fire off that bloody cannon of yours,' ordered Will.

'Certainly, Will,' Paddy replied and rode on towards the craggy outcrop.

The others sat motionless in their saddles.

'If Paddy gives us the all-clear, we shall ride through in single file. Charlotte, you take point – any shooting, just ride as fast as you can out the other side. Sandy, watch our rear; make sure no one is coming up behind us,' Will instructed.

Sandy nodded and turned his horse to be more comfortable watching the road they had just rode along.

Paddy had now reached the point where he could check the pass and the surrounding area. Everything appeared peaceful, so enough he turned back to Will and held up his shotgun. This was the all-clear signal. Charlotte set off first; she was just entering the pass when Two Crows set off, then Will, Paddy and finally Sandy. Once on the other side, they found an old riverbed, which was lined with small trees and shrubs. Beyond that the area flattened out rather like a small plain, then they came to the outskirts of the town. A small trestle bridge carried the road across the dry riverbed.

'We shall follow this riverbed around to the back of the town,' announced Will as he led them down into the ditch.

This they followed carefully, for fear of being seen, until they arrived behind the town itself.

'So, Will, what now?' asked Charlotte.

'Paddy and I shall ride into town and simply ask for the whereabouts of Ted and his gang,' Will responded.

'Just like that,' Charlotte replied, amazed.

'Why not? It worked last time, didn't it?' Will argued. 'Anyway, you, Sandy and Two Crows wait here for half an hour. Make sure no one is following us. Then, keeping to this riverbed, ride around the town and we'll meet you on the other side.'

'All right, Will,' answered Sandy.

Will walked his horse to Sandy's side. 'Here, I want you to hold these for me.' He handed the diamond over to Sandy.

Sandy took it and then glanced back at Will. 'Are you expecting trouble, Will?' he asked a little surprised.

'Out here, I always expect trouble,' he replied as he looked about him. As Sandy placed the precious stone into his saddlebag, Will then handed him the bag full of money. 'Here, take this as well... Now, I don't want you running off with Charlotte and spending it all.' He smiled as he wagged a finger at the pair of them.

They both smiled in return and glanced at one another. Sandy dismounted and, climbing the near bank, lay upon the ground, placing his rifle in front of him. Charlotte lay down next to him, while Two Crows held the horses and watched the line of the river. Will and Paddy rode back to the bridge where they then rejoined the road. They did this so as not to give away their friends' position and also not to attract any attention to themselves by entering the town from an unusual direction.

'Here they come,' announced Charlotte, as she and Sandy watched Will and Paddy ride past them and into Fort Bastion. They trotted into town rather than galloping.

'Are you still wearing your wrist gun?' Will asked Paddy.

'Certainly, a young up-and-coming gent like myself should not be seen without his new-fangled gadgets,' Paddy replied sarcastically.

'Good, make sure it's cocked,' warned Will, ignoring the sarcasm.

'Do you think Ted and his gang are still in town?' Paddy asked.

'No, I don't. I'm half expecting them to have doubled back on themselves and to be halfway to Pinewood Falls by now,' replied Will.

They rode as far as the saloon and stopped. There they dismounted from their horses; they were aware of one or two people turning to look.

'I'll do the talking, Paddy, you watch our backs,' Will warned as he stepped into the saloon; Paddy followed.

The bar itself was not too busy. The bartender was stood behind the bar wiping out some glasses, while two men sat in one corner, hunched over a table talking quietly. Sat at a another table and in the far corner were three gentlemen playing cards; next to one of them stood a lady dressed in bright pink, with what looked like black ostrich feathers in her hair, with her arm around his neck. Neither group paid the strangers much notice. In the shade of the corner behind the door stood another gentleman, quietly taking the scene in around him.

'Well, howdy fellas! What can ah get yez,' greeted the bartender.

Will glanced at Paddy.

'Milk, please?' Paddy asked quickly and quietly.

Will sighed. 'I might have known you would get in quick,' he replied. Then, looking at the bartender. 'Nothing for me, but my friend here would like a glass of milk, please,' he ordered.

'Sure thing, comin' up,' remarked the bartender in a cheery fashion. He poured out the drink and placed the glass in front of Paddy.

'Thank you kindly, sir,' responded Paddy as he touched his brow with an index finger.

'Where are yez from boys? Yer certainly not locals,' said the bartender, more out of desire for conversation than malice.

'You would not believe us, sir. But can you tell me where we may find a Ted Skerrat?' asked Will quietly as he leaned across the bar.

The man in the corner slowly placed his glass down upon the bar and walked out of the saloon. Paddy stood and watched him leave; their eyes never left each other until the man finally had to turn.

'Must be me cologne,' muttered Paddy as his attention returned to his drink.

The bartender stood in deep thought rubbing his chin, then raised a finger. 'Now, there was a man by the name of Ted in last night, travelling with two other fellas, one of whom was called…' he paused as he thought a bit more… 'Kid, that was it. Kid, he called him.' He stood proudly, as if having achieved great things with that statement, with a broad smile and a nod.

'That's our man,' whispered Paddy.

'You don't happen to know where he is now, do you?' asked Will hopefully.

'Oh yessiree, ah sure do. The bartender kept that silly grin across his face and winked. 'They're heading for the old prospectors' mine just to the north-west of here,' he whispered as he too leant across the bar.

'That's enough, Curly,' warned a man's voice from behind Will and Paddy.

Both spun round to find the town's sheriff, the man from the corner and the sheriff's deputy standing in the doorway.

'Now boys,' began the sheriff as he walked into the bar, 'this here is a peaceful town, like, so why the interest in Ted Skerrat?' he asked. As he reached the bar he leaned against it, placing his foot upon the bar rail.

'Hello, Sheriff. We would like to question him, regarding a robbery and a murder,' replied Will politely.

The sheriff laughed, on hearing this, so did the other two men.

'Where's your cannon?' Will whispered to Paddy.

'It's still attached to my horse,' Paddy shrugged in response.

'Ah'm sorry, mister, but that's a mighty fine voice yer have there. What part of America do yer come from anyhow?' the sheriff asked mockingly.

Will and Paddy glanced at each other. They both edged away from the bar and Paddy turned to face the two men at the door.

'OK, boys,' the sheriff said cautiously. He too stepped clear of the bar and withdrew his gun from its holster. 'Now just place yer guns on the bar, boys, and put yer hands in the air,' he ordered, as he pointed his gun at Will.

Again Will and Paddy glanced at each other. Will sighed.

'Hang on a minute, Sheriff,' he tried to explain.

The sheriff stepped back, 'Just do as a say, no funny business. Ah have a very itchy finger here,' he warned.

'Well, I did try to warn you,' replied Will, he glanced at Paddy and nodded slightly.

Both raised their hands; two shots rang out, almost simultaneously. Will shot the sheriff through his shoulder, while Paddy shot the deputy through the head, who fell back through the door, dead. All those in the room dived behind tables and chairs for cover. The man who had stood in the corner now looked on totally aghast; his jaw dropped as he glanced at Will then at Paddy. He held his rifle in his hands but did not move.

Will glanced briefly at Paddy. 'What have you done now!' he exclaimed agitated.

Paddy shrugged. 'Sorry,' he apologised. 'I didn't intend to kill him.'

The man in the corner still nervously glanced at Paddy, who smiled sheepishly in return. Then, without warning, Paddy threw a right hook which caught the man under the chin, throwing him bodily across the room and over two tables; he landed on the floor on his back, out cold.

Will looked back at the sheriff. 'I do apologise, Sheriff, but I did warn you.' He shrugged as he reached down to the ground and picked up the sheriff's gun; he looked it over then placed it back upon the bar, out of the sheriff's reach. As he did so the sheriff flinched instinctively. Will glanced at him again; he lay upon the ground clutching his shattered left shoulder and grimacing in pain.

'You really ought to have that seen to, Sheriff,' Will said. He then turned his attention back to the barman, who in turn took a step or two back.

'Thank you ever so much; would you like a drink?' asked Will.

The bartender almost jumped out of fright. 'Well, thank yer

kindly sir, ah don't mind if ah do – ah'll have a whiskey. If that's all right?' he managed to answer. Paddy finished his drink off and placed the glass back upon the bar.

Will paid for the drinks; then, wishing the bartender and sheriff good day, they both left, stepping over the dead body of the deputy which was lying in the doorway.

Sandy and Charlotte were just getting ready to creep back to their horses when two riders came into view. They were not riding hard, just trotting along.

Sandy grabbed Charlotte's arm to gain her attention, and she turned to see what he was looking at.

'What do you reckon, Sandy?' she asked.

'Do you still have that feeling of being watched?' He half turned to look at her.

She glanced again at the two riders. 'Do you think they are following us?'

'Could be – who's to say the Colonel has not split his men up to find us?' warned Sandy.

The realisation now began to sink into Charlotte's face. 'Oh dear, we must inform Will and Paddy,' she blurted.

'Yes, we must. Come on, sweet pea, we'll meet them on the road as planned,' Sandy said.

They crept back to where Two Crows was holding the horses; they mounted up and together all three rode along the riverbank in the opposite direction to the way Will and Paddy had gone earlier.

Will and Paddy rode out of town casually. Although they could see that no one was paying them much attention, most people were now hurrying to the saloon as news spread of the shooting. Within minutes, though, their places outside the saloon were taken by two further strangers. Barney dismounted and glanced about him while he adjusted his saddlebags.

'Are yer comin' in, Bob?' he asked.

'Yeah, ah could do with a drink. Ma throat's feelin' like a donkey's armpit,' groaned his companion.

Barney smiled to himself; his friend was not usually one for words, but sometimes when he did speak he came out with some one-liners.

They pushed their way through the crowd and into the saloon.

Sandy, Charlotte and Two Crows were waiting upon the road for Will and Paddy.

'Any luck, Will?' asked Sandy.

'Yes, we must ride for the old prospectors' mine which is situated to the north-west of here,' Will pointed.

'Right, because two riders have just rode into town,' replied Sandy and, as if to emphasise the point, he flicked his head towards the town.

Both Will and Paddy turned their heads over their shoulders instinctively.

'Were they Dixie riders?' asked Paddy.

'Hard to say, but they were well armed and they were not dressed in grey,' answered Sandy.

'Well, we must assume the worst; let's ride for that mine,' prompted Will. 'Sandy, watch our backs,' he ordered as he rode past him.

Two Crows as always took the point, closely followed by Paddy.

Barney and Bob approached the bar; they walked slowly and purposefully. All eyes were upon them, but no one said a word.

'Bartender,' called Barney, 'two whiskeys, please.' He glanced about him, and noticed the sheriff receiving some sort of aid and the other man nursing a bloodied nose.

'Certainly, stranger,' replied the bartender as he poured out two drinks in whiskey glasses.

'Tell me,' Barney went on, 'has anybody been askin' about the whereabouts of a man called Ted Skerrat?' he asked the barman.

The bartender stopped what he was doing and just looked open-mouthed.

'What's the problem?' asked a puzzled Barney.

Just then a doctor arrived and began to deal with the sheriff.

'Well, ain't that something! Just five minutes ago, two men not unlike yourselves were askin' the whereabouts of this Ted Skerrat,' responded the bartender.

'Oh? An' what did yer tell them?' Barney queried.

'That just prior to them comin' in, there was a group of men in here, an' one was called Ted,' replied the barman.

'What did this Ted look like?' asked Bob, as he gulped down his whiskey and replaced his glass for another.

'Well, sir, ah couldn't rightly say… ah didn't really pay much attention to him, but he was ridin' with a man called the Kid,' the barman explained.

Barney and Bob looked at each other.

'Where were they headin', did they say?' asked Barney.

The barman swallowed and threw a fleeting glance at the sheriff.

'Sure did,' moaned the sheriff as he grimaced with pain. 'The old prospectors' mine, just to the north-west of here – but ah'd be quick, fer the pair that were in here a minute ago are also after them,' he warned.

'Thank yer kindly, Sheriff, ah'm much obliged,' responded Barney, as he produced a coin from his waistcoat pocket and flicked it at the man behind the bar. He then turned, and as Bob gulped yet another drink down, Barney slapped him across the shoulder and began to walk back out of the door. Having put the glass down, Bob followed him.

'There's a-goin' to be an awful lotta shootin' goin' on when they all meet up,' said the barman shaking his head.

When Barney reached his horse he paused thoughtfully, then slowly turned to Bob.

'Bob, if yer were in Ted's boots, what would yer do?' Barney asked.

Bob slowly untied his horse. 'What d'yer mean, Barney?' he asked, puzzled.

'Well, think of it this way: Ted is a very proud, dangerous character, he will not be enjoying this runnin' about. He tends to draw his hunters on to himself, don't he?' suggested Barney with a wry smile.

'So yer think he'll try to double back an' give them the slip?' replied Bob.

'Hmm, that's what ah was thinkin',' Barney mused.

'But where d'yer think they'll run to?'

'Where they feel no one will think of,' Barney responded. 'Pinewood Falls.'

'An' what if these other guys capture them afore us, Barney?' asked a concerned Bob.

'Then good luck to 'em, but somehow ah don't think they will,' he responded. He then began to ride back out of town the way they had entered.

Bob shook his head slowly. 'Ah don't know where yer get these thoughts from, Barney, ah just hope yer right,' he muttered to himself as he followed his companion.

As they rode out of town Barney decided to follow the route they had taken on arrival into town. This would take them towards Jefferson's Ranch, first then north to Richmond. Barney decided on this way, sure that Ted would return along the northerly route and would most likely travel faster than Bob and himself. At the moment he and Bob wished to remain anonymous – the less Ted knew the better.

Abe began to stir upon the ground; he turned upon his side and opened his eyes, to be confronted with the sight of Ted by the campfire. His jacket collar had been turned up and he sat with his face turned down so that it was hidden by his hat. To most people it would appear that Ted was sleeping, but Abe knew Ted was thinking deeply. He kicked off his blanket and sat up.

'Howdy, Ted,' Abe called as he stretched out his arms and yawned.

Ted did not reply but merely glanced at him sideways.

'What time is it?' Abe asked.

Again Ted sat motionless. Abe began to look around him. Some of the gang members were still dozing, while others were up and about. Suddenly, Ted stirred himself and stood up.

'OK, everyone up – it's time to get movin'.' He walked about kicking firmly with his foot those that still lay upon the ground.

It had the desired effect, as the camp now stirred as one and became a hive of activity. The fire was dowsed quickly, the horses were prepared, and every member wrapped up and tied his own blanket roll.

'We will not follow any road, just in case we happen to meet the Colonel or any chancin' bounty hunters,' warned Ted. 'Ah'm simply not in the mood to go about justifyin' myself at present.'

'What are we to do if someone *does* try to stop us, Ted?' asked the Kid, his hand resting upon the handle of his gun.

Ted looked at him. 'Yer obviously know what to do,' he replied, flicking his head towards the Kid.

They then all mounted up and rode out.

'Surely, yer don't intend to shoot yer way back across the county, Ted?' asked a concerned Abe.

'Not if they leave us alone, ah don't. Look, Abe, ah'm sick and tired of all this runnin' about. If they want me, they know where to find me. Ah'll make a stand at Pinewood Falls, ah ain't runnin' no more!' growled Ted.

Grey Wolf approached Black Eagle. 'You say that today we shall meet with the white squaw, White Feather, and the great white warrior, Mad Dog, and that both are free from the double tongue.' He placed his withered hand upon Black Eagle's shoulder.

'Yes, Chief, you shall meet both; today you will sit at the white man's table and your people shall be free and safe,' replied Black Eagle.

Grey Wolf glanced about him. People were already up and moving, instinctively climbing towards the next crest. He turned back towards Black Eagle. 'In years to come, when our children's children are sat by the campfires, they will tell of this journey and that when the tribe was in its moment of despair it fell to the young warrior, Black Eagle, who returned from Paradise to lead their ancestors to safety,' declared the aging chief.

Black Eagle paused, his face flushed with pride. 'If that is indeed the case then I shall be honoured – yet, let us not forget of the great warrior chief himself, who, having ridden with the likes of Geronimo and Sitting Bull, also led his people to safety.'

He turned and, picking up his rifle, he marched off to lead the front people towards the crest along the safest track. Grey Wolf stood and watched him go; a feeling of personal joy overcame him as he thought of meeting his daughter Starlight and his old friend Brown Buffalo once more. He then shook his head slowly and smiled as he followed the youthful Black Eagle up the track.

Murdoch sat back in his rocking chair upon the porch of the house; he slowly rocked back and forth, deep in thought. It was not particularly cold, but it was a clear evening and the first stars were beginning to shine. Storm Force were now late and although he was not yet too concerned, there had been no word, no news at all. If I hear nothing tomorrow, I shall drive into town. We need some supplies anyway, he thought.

The branding of the cattle was now complete and his mind turned towards the ranch and the events that had taken place over the last week or so. The place had rocked to the sound of laughter – a woman's laughter at that, as he thought of Charlotte, then of Lucy. It was nice to have a woman about the house – oh, there was nothing wrong with Starlight, but native women were so quiet, not like European women, who would sing and hum. Plus it had only been through Charlotte's insistence that the place had actually been cleaned. Murdoch had forgotten about the sweet smell of polish, or even flowers. He smiled to himself. The place doesn't know what has happened to it, what with polished floors, clean rugs and even washed curtains... He shuddered at the thought of what had become of himself since he had moved out here. He had not realised – no wonder they called him Mad Dog. The closing of the door brought him back to the present; he turned to see Lucy.

'Good evening, wee lass, please mek yersel' at home. Come sit here,' he gestured to her. 'Ah wish to have a wee word with yer,' he said as she sat down.

'Murdoch,' she interrupted; she was nervously rubbing her hands and she kept her eyes firmly fixed upon her feet. 'There is something that I need to say,' she blurted out.

'Oh, what's troublin' yer, lassie? Don't be nervous now, just tell me if it's something' ah said, then ah can apologise,' replied Murdoch cautiously.

'No it's nothing like that. I wish to thank yer for yer kindness in puttin' me up, an yer friends for being so helpful.' She glanced at him and smiled nervously.

'Ah now, ah wish to talk to yer about that,' began Murdoch as he sat forward.

'It's all right, I shall be out o' yer hair within the next couple o' days,' she said quickly. 'All ah ask is a bit o' time to get myself sorted.' She paused and sniffed slightly. 'I lost everything in that fire; all I possess at the moment is what ah'm wearing and two silver picture frames.' She looked forlorn.

Murdoch swallowed. He was not usually a man of soft emotion, yet the plight of this poor young woman brought a lump to his throat; he cleared it quickly. 'Och, ah was about to ask ye what yer plans were, lassie. Yer welcome to stay fer as long as ye like. It has been a pleasure havin' a woman about the house fer a change.'

Lucy stared at the big Scotsman. 'Do yer really mean that?' she whispered with an embarrassed smile.

Murdoch smiled in return. 'Please allow me to be so bold as to state that if ye wish, ye can even live here with me,' he remarked softly. 'Now, ah don't mean anything by that, ah'm not implying anything...' His tone changed and he held up his hands.

Lucy began to weep, so Murdoch quickly pulled out a handkerchief. 'Here lassie, use this, it's clean. Ah'm sorry, ah dinna mean to upset yer,' he apologised.

'I'm sorry, Murdoch.' She laughed a little, between sobs. 'No one has ever been so kind to me. I have no money to pay yer.' She paused. 'Ah could work fer yer though,' she added hopefully.

'Ye'll do no such thing, lassie!' barked Murdoch. 'When yer here, yer ma guest; besides, ye've done enough about the house already,' he added soothingly. 'As for personal necessaries, write down a list, an' seal it if yer wish. Ah'll take it into town the day after tomorrow an' get yer wants an' needs. Ah'll not read it, ah'll give it to Mrs Perkins – yer know – Ernie's wife, at the hardware store,' he explained.

Lucy nodded meekly. 'Thank yer, thank yer kindly,' she whispered, then quickly stood up and hurried back indoors.

Murdoch was left scratching his head. 'Och, yer great oaf, look what yer've done now,' he cursed to himself.

He continued to sit on his chair, yet he was not destined to get much peace that night. For shortly after, Black Eagle walked into the ranch compound.

Murdoch leaped to his feet. 'Black Eagle, what news?' he asked. Then he noticed the others. Most had stopped by the gate, but five elderly Indian men followed Black Eagle up to the house.

Murdoch stood silent and watched waiting for an explanation from his trusted Indian scout.

'Mr McLeod, this is Chief Grey Wolf.' Black Eagle swung his arm towards the first elderly looking Indian. 'Grey Wolf, meet my leader, Mad Dog.'

Murdoch nodded but remained silent, as he tried to take in the enormity of what stood before him. He had aided Indian refugees before, but this looked like a whole tribe.

The old man stepped forward. 'Black Eagle speaks highly of you. He say you are wise man and that you do not speak with double tongue. I am Grey Wolf, chief of my people.' He swung his arm in a wide gesture. 'To survive we had to leave our reservation. I was not going to leave anybody behind to suffer the consequences of our escape, so we brought everybody, even the weak and sick. I seek White Feather, but my people are tired and hungry. Black Eagle, he say that you will feed my people and allow them to rest here,' Grey Wolf announced.

'Did he, by heavens?' Murdoch replied, shaking his head in disbelief. 'Well, ah suppose we will ha' to feed 'em; they can rest where they are for noo.' Murdoch's eyes were fixed upon the gathering throng at the gate as he spoke. Now he turned his attention to the chief. 'As for you, Chief, White Feather is inside the house, so if yer care to step this way...' He led him towards the door. Then realising that the elders were still patiently waiting, he turned back to face them. 'Ah suppose you had best come, too,' he said, gesturing for them to follow.

They all entered the house, 'Buff? *Buff*!' shouted Murdoch. 'Can yer show these, er, guests to the lounge, please?' As Buff stepped forward, Murdoch introduce him to the chief.

The chief gave a wry smile, then, holding up his hand. 'We know each other, white man; Brown Buffalo is married to my daughter.' He placed his hand upon the now kneeling Buff's head.

'Well, ah suppose ah better get Starlight as well, then,' shrugged Murdoch as he left the Indians in the lounge. He found

Lucy in the kitchen as usual, then found Starlight, whom he led back to the room. He decided not to enter the room straightaway but to wait until called. So, feeling a little lost, he waited out on the porch once more.

He sat there for some time; it felt longer than it actually was. Eventually Lucy came hurrying out of the house. She quickly glanced about her and when she saw Murdoch sitting in the chair, she hurried over to him.

'Murdoch, Grey Wolf wishes to speak with yer. But first I have something to ask…' Her expression became a little shy.

'Well, what is it, lassie? Ah cannae fix what ah don't know is broken,' replied Murdoch.

Lucy swallowed hard. 'Murdoch, yer now know that it was me that was sendin' these Indians over to yer. At first it was in the hope that yer would help. Later ah knew yer wouldn't turn them away, an' yer never did. But now ah must ask one last favour: can yer find somewhere for the whole of Grey Wolf's tribe?' She paused, then threw herself at his feet. 'It'll be the last thing ah ask of yer; it's just they are desperate, an' ah was their last hope,' she pleaded.

Murdoch sat forward and with his great hands he picked Lucy up from the ground. 'Lucy, yer puttin' me an' ma organisation in a compromised position. Ma government has agreed now to send any Indians that are captured north of the border back for repatriation. Ah must seek advice from Sergeant Hackett.' He paused. 'Still, firstly tell me, how on earth did yer become involved in all this?'

Lucy sat down next to him upon the chair. 'Ah could associate with them; since ma folks passed away, ah have become the butt of all jokes and scapegoat for everythin' that has gone wrong in Pinewood Falls, an' ah could see the same thing happenin' to these folks here. So ah tried to help.' She shrugged her shoulders.

Murdoch smiled. 'Lucy, has anybody ever said what an amazing person yer are?'

Lucy smiled shyly again and lowered her face.

'Now, inform Grey Wolf ah'll be in shortly; ah'm just goin' to speak with Sergeant Hackett,' he explained as he stood up and helped Lucy to her feet.

He walked across the compound and found the Mountie Sergeant, stood upon the porch which led to the cow hands' dormitory. He was watching the Indian campfires burning in the growing gloom.

'Evenin', Hackett,' Murdoch greeted him.

'Hello, Mad Dog. Any news?' he asked his host.

'No – no' about our friends, anyway. Though ah wish to talk to yer about all these Indians.' Murdoch waved his arm in their direction. 'Now, ah know the official line, and there ain't goin' to be any more Indians after this,' he began.

'As you have just said, Murdoch, you know the official line, so you will know my answer. On the other hand, if I walk inside here, I won't see any Indians, and if they have moved by tomorrow lunchtime when I come out again, I won't know they were even here, will I? After all, you own a great deal of land and you simply cannot be everywhere at once... can you?' Hackett replied, then stepped away from Murdoch and disappeared indoors for the evening. He gave Murdoch a wry wink as he disappeared. Murdoch smiled to himself. He had known Hackett for a long time now, and he was a good man at heart. A loyal Mountie first and foremost, he was not afraid to use common sense.

Murdoch returned to his house; as he entered, he found the Indians all sat either upon the sofa or in his large comfortable chair. He shook his head mockingly. 'Ah don't know what the world's comin' to when a man cannae find a seat in his own house!' he smiled.

Grey Wolf stood tall on McLeod's entry to the room and Lucy looked on, concerned. Murdoch smiled broadly at her. 'It's all right, we can sort somethin' out.'

'Oh Murdoch!' Lucy rushed forward and instinctively threw her arms around the big Scotsman; then, quickly realising what she had done, she stepped away and put her arms behind her back. 'Sorry – ah'm so sorry,' she apologised.

Murdoch cleared his throat and his index finger struggled with his collar. 'Grey Wolf, you and your people can settle to the north of here. It is ma land, and I shall put yer near the fish burn – Black Eagle here knows of it. It has green meadows, running water full of fish, trees and, if yer require, yer can help yersel' to ma cattle. Take only what yer need. Sergeant Hackett has said he will turn a blind eye, so long as yer live peacefully, and leave tomorrow morning at first light. But,' Murdoch turned to Lucy, 'this must be the last – White Feather must pass on into mythology,' he warned.

Grey Wolf stepped forward. 'Black Eagle was right, you are a great warrior – your words and actions are great for all to see and hear. My people and I shall for ever be in your debt; for as long as my people survive they will for ever tell of the great white warrior.' He bowed in front of Murdoch. Then, straightening up, he raised his right hand. 'First though, I have some news which may be of interest to you. Black Eagle told me that your friends are riding abroad against the grey riders. I saw them two days ago; they helped us against the grey riders and left us food,' he explained.

'Chief, what do yer mean, helped yer?' asked Murdoch, becoming concerned.

'The grey riders tried to ambush us at a place called Beaver Creek, but your friends swept down upon them and defeated them, scattering them to the winds and killing some,' Grey Wolf elaborated.

'So, the Colonel will know about 'em, then,' Murdoch muttered to himself. 'Thank yer,' he said, his mind racing.

'They will be all right, our great warrior ancestors will protect them,' announced the Chief. Then he stepped out of the room majestically, followed by the others. Murdoch followed them to the door; watching them walk back to their people, he closed the door and turned to come face to face with Brown Buffalo and Starlight. They too bowed quietly and solemnly.

'My wife, Starlight, wishes to thank you and says she will always pray for you to our great ancestors,' announced Brown Buffalo.

'Now, now, yer two should know me well enough by now. Ah'm not into this prayin' lark, but so long as ah can help somebody...' Murdoch replied and rather timidly slipped back into the lounge. Ah think tonight, this may just call fer a wee dram, he thought to himself. Just then, Lucy reappeared.

'Murdoch?' she asked.

'Yes, lassie,' he replied pouring himself out a drink.

'Ah would just like to thank yer once more,' she responded as she sat down and watched him almost dreamily.

He half turned and held up the bottle. 'Care for a wee dram, lassie?' he asked.

'Ah don't mind if ah do,' she smiled.

'Good – an' we'll have a good blether, get to know each other better.' He smiled back as he waved his arm back and forth quickly.

'Yer worried about yer friends, aren't yer?' remarked Lucy as she took the glass Murdoch offered her.

'Yes, ah am. The Colonel knowin' about them does not bode well. If ah haven't heard anything tomorrow, ah shall go into town and get some supplies,' he stated as he drank his whiskey.

'Yep... here's to yer friends. Let's hope they are all right; I would hate to see any harm come to them.' Lucy held up her glass, then swallowed her drink almost in one.

Murdoch smiled, 'Aye, lassie, a woman almost after ma own heart,' he declared, and he reached for the bottle once more.

NEVER SAY DIE

The next morning, Brown Buffalo entered the lounge to tidy up after the previous evening. He noticed the empty bottle of whiskey and two glasses still upon the table. He shook his head slowly. Boss should leave well alone, boss should not drink firewater, he thought.

Murdoch was about to enter the room when he noticed Buff picking up the bottle and glasses. He smiled to himself. Probably thinks I'm steamin' drunk again, Murdoch thought. 'It's all right Buff, ah know what ah'm doin',' he assured the Indian as he walked in.

'You should give up firewater, it make you loopy,' argued Buff.

Murdoch smiled. 'Ah'll never give it up, it's in me blood, man – but ah'll no' drink as much as ah did,' he said as he strolled over to a small box room, where he soon sent another telegram off to Lord Porter.

As Britain was some six hours ahead, it was lunchtime when Hannah received the message. She quickly read it, then hurried off to Lord Porter's office. She knocked upon his office door and waited.

'Come in!' came his usual husky voice.

'A telegram from the intelligence agent in Canada, my lord,' stated Hannah as she held up the slip of paper. She hurried across the room and handed it to him.

'Thank you, Hannah,' he replied, and settled back within the chair to read it. 'McLeod is rather concerned about Storm Force, as they're a little late. I know this man very well; it must be something for him to become concerned.' Lord Porter placed the sheet of paper down on the desk, then stood up and limped with the aid of his stick towards the window. There he stood for a short time just looking out across the loch. Turning to face Hannah once more, he asked, 'When do you plan to visit Madeleine again?'

'I plan to pay her a visit tonight, my lord,' responded Hannah, a little puzzled.

'Hmmm, let's hope they turn up shortly. I certainly would not wish to tell her bad news so close to her wedding.' He limped back to his desk.

'No, my lord, they will turn up, you'll see,' Hannah tried to assure him.

At that very moment, Will and his team were just arriving at the old prospectors' mine. They had ridden all night in the twin hopes of putting a bit of space between themselves and their alleged pursuers, and finally catching Ted and his gang resting; but regrettably the latter had already gone on. Paddy and Two Crows rode cautiously into the miners' camp; it looked every bit as deserted as it actually was. When he reached the black circle of scorched earth that represented where the campfire had been, Paddy dismounted and, kneeling, gently placed the back of his hand against the cinders. As Will approached, Paddy then stood up.

'It is quite cold – they've been gone for some time, I'm afraid,' he declared to Will.

'Damn!' cursed Will, and glanced about him. 'We can't keep riding around like this, we'll have to head back soon,' he announced.

Just then Two Crows who had rode on ahead to the end of the camp, came hurrying back.

'Mr Will, Mr Will!' he called excitedly. 'Seven riders, head east.' He pointed to where he had just come back from.

Will and Paddy glanced at each other. 'That'll be them,' commented Paddy.

'So, at last they've decided to double back.' Will leant forward in his saddle and pushed his hat back upon his head.

'Well, before we go chasing them further, I suggest we have a rest,' announced Charlotte as she dismounted.

'I'm all for that,' declared Sandy, as he too dismounted.

'All right, but we must not be long here,' warned Will.

'I'll go and make sure we've not been followed,' stated Paddy. He withdrew his shotgun from its holster and ran back towards some rocks which overlooked the prospectors' mine.

'Two Crows, how long since these riders rode out of here?' asked Will.

'Eight, maybe ten hours,' replied the Indian without hesitation.

'All right, thank you,' replied Will, as he pursed his lips and patted Two Crows's shoulder. He sighed heavily as he sat down by the campfire that Sandy had lit.

'So what now, Will?' Sandy asked him.

Will glanced at him, then rubbed his chin. 'They go back, so must we,' he decided, shrugging his shoulders and raising his hands.

'That's fair enough, but what about the Colonel and his merry men?' quizzed Sandy.

'I know. I think it will be best to split into pairs. Paddy and I will go on a southerly route, while you, Charlotte and Two Crows follow the actual tracks. We shall rendezvous just before Richmond. Hopefully we will miss the Colonel or slip through his net,' said Will, as he scratched his head.

Sandy leant to one side so that only Will could hear him. 'Now Will, you know as well as I do, if the Colonel is on our tracks – which he most probably – there will be little chance of "slipping through his net",' he said quietly.

'I know. That's why I would send you and Charlotte together,' Will replied with a wry smile.

Charlotte now joined them. 'You two are looking serious,' she noted.

'We've good reason to be,' remarked Sandy.

'Do you think this could be a trap?' she asked looking very concerned.

'No, I don't think so. Not intentionally, anyway, but we will have to be quick and wily to get back to Richmond unseen,' responded Sandy.

'What, trust in God and chance to luck?' remarked Will.

'Ha, no, more like trust in luck and chance to God,' smiled Sandy.

Paddy returned and sat down by the fire. Charlotte handed him a cup of coffee.

'Ahh, thanks. That is mighty fine,' he said as he savoured the drink.

'When you're refreshed, Paddy, you and I will ride in one direction, while Charlotte, Sandy and Two Crows follow Ted's tracks,' explained Will.

'Are we not going to rest, Will?' asked Paddy, his eyes narrowed as he suspected there was a little more to it than what Will was telling him.

'No – not yet, anyway. I would prefer to be on the other side of the Colonel and his men when we do, though,' replied Will.

Paddy nodded slowly as the seriousness of their situation dawned upon him. 'Well, the sooner we get going the better, then,' he said at length.

They checked their weapons and their horses; luckily they had not ridden hard, so the horses were still in fine shape. Finally Will approached Sandy.

'Sandy, you keep the diamond, and I will take the cash with me.' He took the bag from Sandy's saddle and hooked it upon his own. 'This way, if either are caught then the Colonel only has half of the ill-gotten gains.'

Sandy smiled. 'Don't you spend any of that in Richmond, mind,' he joked.

Will smiled as he mounted his horse. Sandy followed; the others were already mounted. Together they rode as far as the end of the mining compound.

'Good luck, the three of you. We'll meet just before Richmond in two nights' time.' With that, Will and Paddy rode off together, leaving Charlotte, Sandy and Two Crows watching them disappear.

'Do you still have that feeling of being watched, Charlotte?' asked Sandy.

Charlotte glanced at him and paused for a moment. 'No – not at present, anyway,' she replied.

'Well, that's something,' mumbled Sandy as they rode on.

The Colonel led his Dixie riders into Fort Bastion. As it was still early morning, there was not much activity going on; the little town was peaceful and the air still. He rode up to the sheriff's office and halted; his men stopped behind him.

'Wait here.' He dismounted and removed his gauntlets. 'Josey, Li'l Dave and Vince, follow me,' he ordered as he stepped into the jailhouse.

The three men dismounted and followed. The Colonel, though, stopped abruptly in his tracks when he entered the jailhouse, for behind the desk, slumped asleep, sat an unfamiliar figure.

'Who the hell are yer?' demanded the Colonel as he slapped the sleeping man across the side of the head with his gauntlets.

The man sat up bolt upright with a start, coughing and grunting. 'W-well, howdy, Colonel! What can I do fer yer?' the man spluttered.

'Ah asked who the hell yer are,' demanded the Colonel a second time with a sneer.

The man jumped up, then fell backwards over the chair as he lost his balance.

'They calls me, Morgan, Colonel – Luke Morgan,' he said as he lay on the floor.

The Colonel rolled his eyes. 'OK, Luke, where is the sheriff?'

'Ah'm here, Colonel,' groaned the sheriff; he leaned against the open door of a cell holding his left arm, which was bandaged up in a sling.

The Colonel turned to face him and placed both hands upon his hips. 'Sheriff, tell me what happened here?'

'Luke here came for me last night, to say that there was two fellas in the saloon askin' about Ted Skerrat and the boys,' he began. 'So, following yer instructions ah ran across sharpish, and as ah tried to apprehend these men, one shot me in the shoulder and the other shot Brewster dead.'

'So they escaped?' clarified the Colonel.

'Yeah, but that's not all. Shortly after they left, two other strangers rode into town and asked the same question.'

'Really? D'yer think they were together or separate?' asked the Colonel.

'To be honest, Colonel, ah think they're ridin' together, but they want us to think they're ridin' separately,' replied the sheriff.

'Oh? What makes yer think that?'

'They was too close together; it was too coincidental. And the second pair, although they knew that Ted had gone to the old prospectors' mine, they rode out o' town in the completely opposite direction,' the sheriff responded.

The Colonel nodded thoughtfully. 'Yep, makes sense,' he muttered.

'Der yer think they're tryin' to herd Ted and the boys into a trap, Colonel?' asked Vince.

'It certainly looks that way. Very intelligent plan,' he said almost to himself, as he sat down opposite Luke, who was now standing. 'But if Ted and the boys have turned back – which it looks likely that they have – ah'll have their guts for garters,' he threatened. He fell into a thoughtful silence.

'All right boys, here is what we'll do. Vince take four men and ride to the old prospectors' mine. Be careful if the two bounty hunters are still there – ah want yer to ambush them, not the other way around. They're leavin' far too many dead men about fer my likin'. The rest can come with me, north,' he ordered as he slapped the desk hard with his hand and stood up.

'North, Colonel?' questioned Li'l Dave.

'Yep, if Ted and his boys are ridin' back, that's the route they'll take, and our quarry will not be far behind.

'Just one thing, Colonel,' called the sheriff as the Colonel was about to walk out of the jailhouse.

The Colonel stopped and turned. 'Yeah?'

'Be careful when yer ask them to raise their hands – they have some kind o' gun under their sleeves or something which they shoot at yer,' the sheriff warned.

The Colonel thought a moment then nodded as he stepped back outside and mounted up. 'Remember, Vince, no slip-ups, or yer'll pay!' he warned.

Vince turned his horse and nodded. Then, together with four men, he rode out of town along the same road as Will and Paddy had rode earlier. The Colonel watched them disappear, then turned back the way they had entered the town and rode out retracing their steps before turning north once through the pass.

Sandy and Charlotte rode side by side; they were walking their horses rather than trotting them, for fear of tiring them out. Two Crows rode slightly ahead acting as scout.

'Isn't this country lovely?' declared Charlotte as she glanced about her.

'Oh yes, and rather deadly too,' warned Sandy.

'How – in what way?' she asked.

'Well, there are any number of places around here where a good shot could take either one of us out without us even having a chance to reply. Likewise, with all these rocks and outcrops we could easily be surrounded and not even know it,' he explained.

Charlotte smiled. 'Dear Sandy, ever the optimist.'

'I like to think I'm careful, that's all.'

'Do you think we'll sneak past the Colonel's screen?' she asked.

'If he has one, I'll be able to answer that tonight, Charlie,' Sandy replied with a smile.

'When we make camp, right?'

'Right.'

'I wonder how Will and Paddy are getting along,' she wondered aloud.

'Oh, they'll be just fine, they're big lads and can take care of themselves,' laughed Sandy.

Alas, Will and Paddy were still riding in a south-westerly direction. They were riding alongside each other, chatting, when a shot winged past them and ricocheted off a nearby rock.

'What the hell!' cursed Will, as his horse instinctively reared, throwing him upon the ground. Paddy immediately made for the nearest rocks to give himself some cover, while Will now rolled over to hide behind a rock. He now became the focus of several shots which rained down upon the rock in front of him.

Paddy had got behind the rocks where he jumped out of the saddle, taking Macootcha with him, and began to climb the rocks for a better view. Will at present was still pinned down behind the rock, trying to fire back, but his revolver was no match for the rifle fire coming in on him and it did not have the required range.

He tried to crawl across the grass towards the rocks where Paddy was, but the fire was becoming so intense he did not get far and had to return to the rock.

'Will, Will! Are yer all right there, lad?' called a concerned Paddy.

'Yes, I'm fine – how many are there, do you reckon?' Will shouted in return.

'Quite a lot,' Paddy replied – he had actually counted about thirty, but did not wish to concern Will too much.

'How many?' Will insisted.

'I know there is more than one,' Paddy responded as he fired one shot from his shotgun. He knew that it too did not have the range, but it might keep a few of their heads down, he reasoned.

He then checked his belt – he still had one hand bomb left. This he raised in his hand; removing the pin with his teeth, he threw it towards where the shots appeared to be coming from, in the hope of giving Will a break. It appeared to have the desired effect, as there was a short pause in the firing. Will once more saw a possible chance of dashing towards Paddy's position, but the firing immediately started up again, which again forced Will back to the rock; Paddy firing a second shot off did not work this time.

'It's pointless yer carrying on, we will be able to pick yer off one by one. Just give yerselves up,' a voice shouted.

Will fired off four quick shots in return, which brought a rain of fire down upon him – it felt as if there was a gun behind every rock and tree.

'What do you think, Will?' called Paddy, feeling helpless behind his rock.

'I think the man could be right,' Will called back dejectedly. A few more shots were fired. 'All right, all right, we're coming out,' shouted Will, as he put the hand holding his revolver in the air.

'An' yer friend?' came another sinister voice – the Colonel.

Will stood up in the open and glanced where Paddy had been. 'Yeah, me too,' came his voice as he stepped into the open, holding his shotgun in front of him.

'OK, boys, place the guns an' any other weapons on the ground in front of yer,' demanded the voice. 'An' don't forget yer wrist toys,' it warned.

Will and Paddy glanced at each other as they placed their weapons upon the ground. Finally, Will dug out his throwing knife.

'That's an impressive arsenal yer have there,' the voice mocked. Then an elderly man stepped into the open, wearing a grey military uniform and holding a revolver. This had been the Colonel's official Confederate uniform. 'OK, boys,' he called and smiled pleasantly at Will and Paddy, who had by now placed their hands in the air. Within an instant bodies were coming out of the trees and from behind rocks. Will sighed as he realised it would have been pointless to fight on. In the end, Paddy counted fifty men.

The elderly man walked up to Will and Paddy and glanced at both. 'We now have the small matter of a trial and getting justice for our boys at the ranch,' he said calmly. 'Now, where's ma money?' His tone was now threatening.

'What money?' asked Paddy.

'It's here, Colonel, ah've got it here,' called a man who had collected Will's horse; he held the bag up triumphantly.

'So what's that, moon dust?' he jeered Paddy then pistol-whipped him across the face. 'Don't ever try to make a fool of me, boy. Yer'll not live to see the outcome,' the Colonel snarled into Paddy's face. 'Tie them up, boys, good an' proper.'

Several men jumped forward and, in the ensuing melee, they quickly tied both Paddy and Will's hands behind their backs. More menacingly, someone had thrown a noose around Paddy's neck.

'Now then,' began the Colonel, 'afore we hand yer over to my authorities –' he laughed – 'ah wants some answers. Now ah'll bring this big fella down to size first. String him,' he ordered.

Paddy was pushed back onto his horse, then led to below a branch obviously wide and strong enough to take a man's weight. Paddy did not flinch, nor did he remove his eyes from the Colonel – an act of defiance. Several hands then seized Will and pushed him so that he now stood facing the scene of a rider sat next to Paddy – both mounted. Paddy had his hands tied behind him and a noose around his neck. The other man held this in his hands.

The Colonel stepped forward and turned to Will. 'We will now play a game of blind man's bluff. Yer friend's life is now in yer hands, boy. Answer any question wrong and he will die, bit by bit,' the Colonel chortled.

Will stood defiantly looking on; he quickly glanced at Paddy, who was watching him just as determinedly.

'Where's the other two riders?' asked the Colonel.

'What other two?' Will replied, puzzled.

The Colonel calmly turned to look at the mounted man next to Paddy, he nodded once and the man threw the rope over the branch. The Colonel turned back to Will. 'Now, ah shall ask just once more. Where are these two other riders?'

Will quickly glanced at Paddy, who was watching him intently; he shook his head surreptitiously, as if to say 'don't tell them'.

'I don't know what you're talking about,' replied a defiant Will.

Again the Colonel casually glanced across at those surrounding Paddy; again he nodded. This time they took the rope and tied it against a stub upon another tree trunk. This had the effect of pulling Paddy back a little as he sat on the horse.

'D'yer still want to play?' the Colonel asked, as he punched Will in the abdomen, hard. This forced Will to his knees, from where he was physically hauled back to his feet.

'One last time... *where are the other two riders?*' The Colonel again smiled, but this time callously.

Will looked at his feet. 'All right... They've gone south; we knew you were on to us, so we split up,' declared Will.

The Colonel looked about his men triumphantly. 'Good,' he stated. 'Now, I will show yer just how serious we are about dealin' with bounty hunters in these parts,' he said calmly.

The Colonel turned and nodded at the man sat upon the horse next to Paddy; he dropped his arm as a signal. The man then whacked the horse across its flanks so that it bolted forward. This left Paddy dangling in mid-air, hanging and fighting for his life as his body now swung to and fro. Will hung his head in despair, unable to do anything, his mind frantically racing to find an escape. Paddy in the meantime gasped and struggled, trying vainly to force air into his lungs somehow, but he began to choke and a red mist began to swell up behind his eyes as he slowly lost consciousness. He also became aware of a bright white light as he kept his eyes tightly closed, not wanting them to bulge, and appearing more and more clearly in this light was Erin. She was smiling and waving at him. She was just as he remembered her, beautiful, innocent and as peaceful as she had lain in her coffin... Something in spite of this made him jolt back to reality and he realised just how painful his throat was becoming as the noose tightened.

'We're not bounty hunters!' cried Will indignantly.

The Colonel quickly glanced at him, the cruel smirk temporarily wiped from his face. He then quickly looked at his man still mounted and nodded. The man urged his horse forward and, withdrawing a knife, he cut the still struggling Paddy down. The Irishman fell to the ground into a crumpled heap, coughing and choking.

The Colonel again punched Will in the abdomen, with the same effect as before. 'If yer not bounty hunters, then who are yer?' he demanded. Then, as he thought about it, he broke into a large smile, 'Mounties, yer must be Mounties,' he said, answering his own question. 'Well, we have not finished playin' with yer yet, but we must move on. We will tie these two up on horses and take them back to Richmond. Then we will scour the border regions to the north.' He paused and smiled once more at Will. 'We'll find the other two afore they reach Canada.' He turned and walked off to his own horse. Will and Paddy were dragged and pushed up on to two horses; Paddy was still coughing and trying desperately to clear his throat.

'Are you all right?' Will whispered hoarsely.

Paddy could only nod in response. They then all rode off behind the Colonel.

Will leant across as best he could to Paddy's side. '*Nil desperandum*, Paddy,' he hissed. Paddy looked at him, puzzled. 'Never say die,' Will explained as he broke into a smile. Paddy smiled back and winked quickly in return.

They had not gone far before they were caught up by Vince.

'Howdy, Colonel,' he said in greeting.

'Well howdy, Vince. What did yer find out, then?' asked the Colonel.

'Yer were right about Ted and the boys; they've all rode east back towards Richmond, followed by these bounty hunters.' Vince flicked his head towards Will and Paddy.

'Did yer see any tracks?' asked the Colonel.

'What, theirs?' he replied.

The Colonel glanced over his shoulder. 'Of course.'

'Yeah, there was four of them at the mine, but they split shortly afterwards – these two, and two that rode north,' he replied.

'Are yer sure?' asked the Colonel.

'Oh yeah,' Vince smiled.

The Colonel turned to Will. 'Regrettably, yer elaborate plan to throw us off yer trail at Fort Bastion wasn't too clever after all,' he laughed.

Will and Paddy glanced at each other, puzzled. The Colonel quickly explained his plans to Vince, and soon they were all riding east once more.

Ted peered over the rocks in front of him and looked down upon the small town of Richmond. He rubbed his chin as he took in the view, for next to the town was an army camp complete with tents.

'What'll we do now Ted?' asked Abe, who knelt beside him.

Ted looked at him slowly. 'What d'yer suggest?' he questioned back.

'There's nothing for it, we'll have to ride round town,' interjected Danny.

Ted glanced at him. 'Ah guess so,' he replied, 'but we'll walk rather than run, saves creatin' dust clouds.'

They crept back to their horses where the others were waiting for them.

'What's the problem?' asked the Kid.

'Oh, there's just an army patrol between us and town, that's all,' replied Ted a little sarcastically.

'So what are we goin' to do, Ted?' asked Joe.

'We'll walk our horses around town, so as not to kick up any dust an' bring an army patrol down on us.'

'Was there many?' asked Joshua.

'Why, d'yer fancy shootin' 'em all up?' laughed Ted.

'Nope, just wondered,' he replied quietly.

'There was about thirty of 'em, Josh,' answered his brother.

'Yeah, ah'd say a half troop of 'em,' affirmed Ted.

He led them slowly around town; he was careful to keep rocky outcrops and trees between themselves and the army patrol.

'Hey, Ted, whut's goin' to happen when the Colonel finds us gone?' asked Joe.

'Gone? Gone from where?' asked a puzzled Ted.

'From the old prospectors' mine.'

'Oh well, what d'yer think?' questioned Ted.

'He'll not be over-pleased,' commented Danny.

'He can go to hell,' remarked the Kid.

'Well, he may just want to visit us in Pinewood Falls first, boys,' Ted reminded them.

'What d'yer think he'll do?' asked Abe.

'Oh, he'll rant an' rave a little. Then when he calms down he'll want us fer another job, ah suppose,' replied Ted.

'Have yer not told him that we're breaking up?' asked a surprised Kid.

'Nope, never – saw no reason,' Ted replied casually.

'So d'yer intend to tell him, Ted?' questioned Abe a little concerned.

'Nope, ah thought, if we do whatever he asks and cash in the stone, Joe, Frenchy, Danny and myself could ride back. The rest of yez could go wherever yer please. The Colonel would be none the wiser. He'll get what he wants, an' we'll get what we want.'

'Hey, that's actually a good plan, that,' exclaimed the Kid.

Ted just looked at him and smiled.

Eventually they had regained the road on the eastern side of town. There they all stopped and glanced over their shoulders.

'What are yer thinkin', Ted?' asked Abe.

'Well, boys, no matter what happens now, there is no turnin' back,' he replied.

'What d'yer mean, Ted?' asked Joshua.

'He means that if yer get cold feet, not only d'yer have to sneak past an army patrol – with us wanted men an' all – but yer'll also have to convince the Colonel no doubt that he may be goin' blind,' the Kid translated.

'Why, blind?' Joshua asked again.

' 'Cause when he searches the old mine, where are yer? Or us, fer that matter,' explained Joe.

Joshua looked at his brother for some support. 'What'll *we* do, Abe?' he asked nervously.

'Shut up, Josh,' Abe replied sharply.

'But they're sayin' that the Colonel will come lookin' fer us,' he pleaded.

'Ah'll bloody hand yer over myself if yer don't shut up,' scolded his brother, annoyed.

'When d'yer want to make camp, Ted?' asked Joe, as they began to trot along the road.

Ted looked up at the sky and sniffed, 'Probably nightfall, Joe. Ah wants to put as much distance between us and Richmond as possible,'

'Yer wished to see me sir?' asked Sergeant Rodgers, as he bent down to step into the lieutenant's tent.

'Yes, Sergeant. I wish you to take a detachment north tomorrow, as far as the border, and scour that countryside. Do not leave a stone unturned,' he warned. 'I myself will take the rest and ride to the north-west around here.' He circled a large area on the map. 'I wish to return by nightfall, you do the same and we shall compare notes – any questions?'

'Yeah... What happens if they went off to the north-east area? There's a pass over here which is quite accessible, and if, the reports about a skirmish at Beaver Creek are anything to go by, then—' the sergeant stated.

'Yes, Sergeant, I'm well aware of the skirmish at Beaver Creek. I'm of the opinion that it was a ruse and Grey Wolf is somewhere in this region here. He wishes to rest up then begin a guerrilla war, I'm certain,' the lieutenant proudly declared.

'What, sir? With women an' children? I think Grey Wolf would—' Again the sergeant was cut short.

'Would what, Sergeant? This man – this Grey Wolf – has done this before; he is nothing but a savage.' The young officer raised his voice so as to get his point across.

'Sir.' Sergeant Rodgers saluted his superior, turned and left the tent. Grey Wolf may be a lot of things but savage, naw! he thought. More importantly, he realised that he would most certainly reach Canada, if he had not already.

He began to organise the men for the next morning; as always, Tomahawk Joe was to travel with him.

The young lieutenant remained in his tent staring at the map on his desk in front of him. 'Where are you, Grey Wolf? Show yourself just for one day – five minutes, even – and I'll have you. Then I shall be certain of promotion. I'll become the youngest ever colonel yet; you never know, I could even run for the White House. Yes, politics, that's where I'm heading, and anyone who stands in my way shall be crushed. I shall have to keep an eye on that Indian-loving sergeant of mine, though – I can't afford any marks upon my record. He thinks he knows it all, but he does not, really; yes, I must keep an eye on him.' So he chatted away to himself.

Barney and Bob continued to ride towards Jefferson's Ranch; they rode confident in the knowledge that there was no rush, for they knew that Ted and his gang would hurry back towards Pinewood Falls or Richmond and wait for people to come to them.

'Remember, Bob,' remarked Barney, 'we need Ted alive in order to collect all of our bounty. Ah'm not so worried about the rest, but do we need Ted.'

'Yeah. Ah must admit though, ah was surprised that they are not so fussed about the Kid,' replied Bob.

'How d'yer mean?'

'Well, they want Ted "alive", but the rest "dead or alive", and there is more bounty money on Ted's head than that deranged killer's,' Bob explained.

Barney chuckled almost to himself. 'They are not so fussed about him, because it is Ted they want to make an example of. The days of the gun-totin', train-robbin' outlaws are over, Bob; they'll be almost the last. An' besides, the price on each member reflects the risk factor involved. The authorities know that if yer have an ounce of sense yer not even goin' to bother trying to take the Kid in alive; yer'd just shoot him dead – less hassle.'

'Yeah, but three and a half thousand dollars – ah mean, that's a lot o' dough, Barney,' argued Bob.

'Ah guess so, but that's the risk factor. If Ted ain't alive then the price drops, don't it?'

'Fair enough... so ah can shoot everybody else but Ted,' laughed Bob.

Barney was about to reply when a shot rang out and winged away harmlessly from a nearby rock, startling their horses.

'What the hell?' declared Bob, as he slid off his horse and drew his gun simultaneously.

He was closely followed by Barney. 'Did yer see where that came from?' he asked, as he quickly glanced around. Bob was already quickly scrambling up a rock to gain some height and hopefully a better view.

'Can yer see anything, Bob?' called Barney after a short pause, another shot winged its way past them.

'Nope, not a darn thing,' Bob hissed.

They both looked about earnestly. 'Ah guess there's only one, yer know?' mused Barney.

'If there is ah'll kick his backside so hard…' threatened Bob, as a third shot pinged off the rock not far from him. Barney peered around the rock to where the shots were originating from, and thought a moment. 'Hang on a minute, what if—?' He did not say another word as he was interrupted by a dozen or so clicks of various guns being cocked. He had spun around and came face to face with Hank and Billy Joe.

'Carry on – "what if"…?' smiled Hank.

Uncertain as to how to react, both Barney and Bob stood with their hands in the air.

'Ah'd put the guns down, boys,' Hank said to them. 'Are these the two yer saw this morning, Billy Joe?' he asked.

'Yep, they'd be the ones,' he replied.

'Whoa there, Sheriff,' cried Barney as he stepped forward, only to be pistol-whipped by Hank and pushed back against the rock. This prompted Bob to clamber down from the top of the rock.

'Yer were at Jefferson's Ranch, the pair of yez, the other night, weren't yer?' demanded Hank.

Barney and Bob glanced at each other dejectedly. 'Yeah,' replied Barney solemnly.

'Good, we're takin' yer into Richmond – to be tried,' remarked the sheriff triumphantly. 'We'll catch the other two, in time,' he added.

'What – what other two, an' tried for what?' demanded Barney.

Hank stopped and looked at him. 'The cold-blooded murder of them there cow hands,' he sneered.

'But, hang on a minute, Sheriff, that was not us!' argued Barney. 'The place was fine when we left.'

'Save yer cryin' for the jury,' sneered Billy Joe. 'If it were up to me ah'd hang yer now.' He glared at Barney then spat at his feet.

Then several willing pairs of hands pulled both Barney and Bob's hands behind their backs and tied them up, before pushing them off towards their horses. There they were bodily thrown on to their mounts before being led away.

'Go tell the Colonel we've got two of them there bounty hunters and we're takin' them into Richmond,' Hank ordered Billy Joe.

'Sure thing, Sheriff,' he replied and with a sneering grin he turned his horse and galloped off towards the north-west.

'Yer makin' a big mistake here, Sheriff,' warned Barney.

Hank paused and waited until Barney's horse had come alongside his own. 'Yeah and how's that?' he scowled.

'We're not murderers, we're bounty hunters,' Barney announced. 'And what's more we were hired by the Dakota Territory officials, as well as those from the State of Missouri, to apprehend Ted Skerrat and his gang.'

'Prove it,' replied Hank.

'Ah would if yer'd let me.'

'How?'

'I have a piece of paper in ma inside jacket pocket proving what ah say is true,' explained Barney.

Hank glanced at him, then slowly reached over to the inside pocket of Barney's jacket. Retrieving the piece of paper Barney was talking about, he opened it and read it, then glanced back at Barney. 'That's as maybe, but it ain't nothing an' it don't prove a thing, mister,' he snarled. He shoved the piece of paper into his top pocket and spurred his horse on.

Barney watched him ride ahead; his head fell slightly.

'Now then, *he* don't need to be taken alive or dead,' Bob hissed from the other side.

THE RETURN

Although they had travelled in a leisurely fashion, Two Crows felt that he, Charlotte and Sandy had made quite good progress that day – good enough to halt for camp early evening. They quickly found shelter behind some rocks and, while Sandy began the fire, Two Crows led the horses away to tie them up and hide them from view; Charlotte kept watch from the rocks, just in case they had been followed.

'Do you still have that feeling of being watched?' asked a smiling Sandy, after they had dismounted.

'No, funnily enough, I don't now,' she had replied thoughtfully.

'Well, just in case you're wrong, nip up there and keep an eye out,' Sandy had pointed to the top of the rocks with a smile.

Coffee and a bean stew were quickly cooked and served, then all three settled down. Sandy and Charlotte lay down either side of the fire, while Two Crows went off to lie with the horses – this was a custom he performed every night. At first Will and the group had felt it a little odd, but once they realised it was to keep an eye on the horses' welfare and to prevent predators from getting close, they readily accepted it.

Sandy lay watching the flames dance in the fire.

'Sandy?' asked Charlotte.

'Yes, Charlie,' he replied distantly.

'Do you think we're becoming as hard and as cruel as those we hunt down?' she asked.

'I don't know about being as hard or as cruel, but we have to remain tougher than them,' Sandy responded.

'Oh? In what way?'

'All ways – tougher to remain one step ahead and tougher to make them think twice about fighting back once we've nailed them,' Sandy explained.

'Do you think we are one step ahead of Ted Skerrat?'

Sandy glanced at her thoughtfully. 'I don't know about being one step ahead at present, but I'd say we are definitely tougher,' he replied.

'What makes you so sure?' she questioned.

'They are simply bullies, and bullies are by nature cowards. I'm looking forward to catching up with them, actually,' Sandy went on. His attention was now drawn back to the fire and he only glanced at Charlotte to observe her reaction.

She pulled herself up on to one elbow and looked back at him. 'You really have become involved in this case, haven't you?'

'Yes, I guess I have,' he admitted quietly.

'But why? Was it because of Lucy?' she asked softly.

'No, not just that. These are cold, calculating, callous killers, Charlie. They are cowards too, which has been proven, as they will shoot and kill poor defenceless people trying to do their job but will run at the first sniff of any gang looking for them,' he said disdainfully.

'Do you think they know we're on to them?' she enquired surprised.

'Most definitely, that's why they have turned back upon their trail. They are trying to lose us,' Sandy explained.

'Should we not be careful in case they try to ambush us, then?'

Sandy smiled. 'They will probably be in Pinewood Falls by now, tucked up in bed.'

'You don't hold them in very high regard, do you?' she said.

'Not really, but still I'll be happy when we are all together again,' he replied as he settled down.

She lay watching him, his features lit by the dancing embers of the fire. She began to wonder what the future would hold for the two of them. Would they be doing this type of work for long? What would they do when they have finished it? Would Sandy still love her? If so, who would be her bridesmaid – Hannah? Madeleine? Or even Elizabeth? She sighed heavily as she too then began to settle, forcing those thoughts from her mind. Remember, Charlie, you have this job to finish first. Concentrate on one thing at a time, take Paddy's advice, she told herself sternly.

Not so many miles away to the south, the Colonel drew his men to a halt.

'OK boys, we'll make camp here for the night. Take our

guests over there and tie them to that tree, back to back,' he ordered.

Will and Paddy were dragged from their horses to the tree, there they were forced to the ground and made to sit with their backs to its trunk. To this they were soon forcibly tied and beaten. Finally, for good measure, a rope noose was placed around both their necks, tied so that if one bent his head forward it would choke his companion. There, they were left for the time being while the Colonel's men went off to deal with their horses and sat around the campfires to eat and drink.

'How is your neck, Paddy?' asked Will quietly.

'Not so sore now,' replied the tough Irishman.

'You're lucky it was not broken.'

'Yeah, thanks for that,' retorted Paddy.

'Still, it proves one thing...' began Will.

'Oh, and how is that?' asked Paddy.

'That rope had to have been tough and solid to hold something as thick as that skull of yours up all of the time,' Will teased.

'When we are untied from here, remind me of that, will you please?' Paddy asked politely.

'Certainly, but why?' puzzled Will.

'So I can punch yer head in,' growled Paddy threateningly.

Having eaten and wound down from the day's riding, the Colonel stood up and walked over to some rocks at the edge of the glow of the fire, carrying the carpet bag with the money from the train robbery. He sat down alone upon a flat rock and opened the bag; he turned it upside down so that its contents fell out. Then he placed the bag upon the rock in front of him and picking up the money, he counted it then placed it back into the bag. Finally satisfied, he closed the bag and passed it on to Vince, who was close by.

'Here, Vince, guard this with your life.' He threw the bag at him.

Vince caught it and, looking worried and harassed, he placed it on the ground next to where he was sleeping.

'Yer life may depend upon it,' the Colonel warned him, as he returned to the edge of the fire.

Just then a warning shout was heard and everybody leapt to

their feet. Some ran to where the shout came from while others ran for cover, but all made ready with their guns.

'Who is it?' cursed the Colonel to his sentries.

'It's Billy Joe, Colonel,' came a reply after a few minutes.

'Oh good – and what has he to say fer himself?' wondered the Colonel aloud.

'Colonel, Colonel,' Billy Joe called excitedly.

He rode into the camp and stopped abruptly in front of his superior.

'Yeah, what is it?' retorted the Colonel.

'The posse, the posse – they've caught two of them there bounty hunters,' he declared, leaping to the ground from his horse.

'Well, ah declare! That calls fer a celebration, an' no mistake, fer we have the other two.' The Colonel smiled broadly at the messenger and, slapping him on the back, he led him back to the fireside.

Sitting down, Billy Joe told the Colonel of the army patrol and Hank's success capturing Barney and Bob. The Colonel sat, listening impassively; he generally gave an air of satisfaction. Nonetheless, when Billy Joe mentioned the arrival of the army, his expression darkened and he began to rub his chin with his hand, giving Billy Joe's account some thought.

'Right boys, tomorrow we shall have to be more careful. Ah shall post a screen of scouts ahead of us, as ah want to know where the army are camped. We must not ride through their camp; ah don't want them to know that ah'll be in town too,' he warned.

His men listened to his instructions then settled down for the night; sentries were posted and watch bill was drawn up.

As the camp quietened down and the glow of the fire began to fade, Paddy tried to get Will's attention by nodding his head forward. This, of course, had the effect of choking Will.

'What is it, you daft sod?' hissed Will as he tried to twist his throat and neck.

'Did yer hear that?' asked Paddy. 'Who are "the other two"?' he quizzed.

'I don't know; I'm hoping it was significant they only mentioned two and not three,' replied Will, as he became a little concerned.

'Aye, that's true enough,' replied Paddy contemplatively, 'but what about the army being involved?'

'Yes, we knew time was not on our side. We must hope for a chance to make a break in Richmond,' Will explained.

'Aye, an' maybe have some sort of fun between the Colonel here and the army,' mused Paddy in return.

The posse from Richmond decided not to rest up that night; they were not too far from town, so they chose to ride back. Hank of course led the way. He felt good – the townsfolk had proven that they did not require assistance from the Colonel or his troublesome Dixie riders to achieve something; they had two of the four bounty hunters responsible for the Jefferson Ranch shoot-out. Tonight they would spend their first night in jail and tomorrow morning he, as sheriff, would organise a jury to try the strangers.

It was dark and well past midnight when they finally arrived outside the jailhouse in Richmond. Hank jumped down from his horse.

'OK boys, bring in them two prisoners,' he ordered as he entered the jailhouse. He marched over to his desk and pulled out an old red-bound book, then placed it upon his desk.

'What yer doin', Sheriff?' asked his deputy, Mo.

'Ah'm goin' to swear in a couple o' spare hands, Mo. What does it look like?' Hank barked back. Then, looking up from his desk, 'Who wants to be sworn in as deputies for the trial?' he called.

Several men stepped forward and soon Hank had six new willing volunteers.

'Good. Now then, boys,' he addressed them, 'we need to set up a watch system on these two here gunmen.'

Barney and Bob watched silently as Hank organised the watches for their guardians.

'What d'yer reckon, Barney?' asked Bob solemnly, as he sat upon one of the bunks which lined one of the walls.

'We have to get out o' here, that's fer sure,' replied a pensive

Barney, as he watched the throng around the sheriff's desk.

'Now the rest o' yez can go back to yer beds tonight, boys; well done. The Colonel will be pleased. Tomorrow ah shall have a jury organised, an' when the Colonel returns we will start the trial,' Hank announced proudly from behind his desk.

Some of the men began to leave the jailhouse while those who had just been sworn in remained. Barney turned and glanced at his old friend lying upon the wooden bunk. They had been in some scrapes before, but Barney was struggling to think of a way out of this one. He was eventually brought back to reality by Bob.

'Stop yer worryin', Barney,' he announced.

'Ah thought yer were asleep, Bob,' replied a surprised Barney.

'It's not worth getting' yersel' worked up about, friend,' Bob then explained.

'Yer not under the fool impression that we may get a fair hearin' here, are yer?' argued Barney, he pointed towards the sheriff's desk as he spoke.

'Nope, but ah'm blowed if ah'm goin' to give mesel' a coronary over it,' retorted Bob. He still lay on his back with his arms folded and his eyes shut.

Barney was about to reply when he became aware of another man standing at the cell bars. He spun round to find the sheriff and one of the new deputies looking in at them.

'Now then, boys,' began Hank, off-hand, 'ah'd appreciate it if yer remain quiet tonight an' don't cause any disturbances. Ah'll organise a jury tomorrow so that we can proceed with the trial quickly, like. If in the meantime yer have any queries just ask one o' ma deputies here.'

'Oh, an' are yer goin' to signal through to the Dakota Territory to verify ma papers?' snarled Barney in return.

It appeared to have no effect upon the sheriff whatsoever; he simply carried on looking into the cell. 'There's no need to; it does not give yer an alibi,' he replied. Hank turned to walk away, then paused and glanced back. 'Oh, by the way... Ah'll have the undertaker in tomorrow, boys, just to measure yer up.' He smiled cruelly as he nodded then walked off, with the deputy.

As he left the office he turned to the two deputies sat there.

'Now remember, any hassle, just shoot 'em. Ah'll put it down as self-defence.' He then left the office.

A beautiful sunrise was breaking over Paradise Ranch as Murdoch prepared the wagon for the trip into Pinewood Falls. Liam, who had only returned to the ranch the previous afternoon, had volunteered to ride shotgun with him.

'Murdoch, Murdoch!' Lucy called as she hurried from the house.

'Yeah, what is it, princess?' replied Murdoch.

'Here, ah've wrapped up some home cookin' fer yez to eat on the way.' She offered a bundle wrapped in cloth.

'Well, thanks, Lucy, that's much appreciated,' responded a very happy Liam. Usually they had to make do with chewing tobacco and beef jerky on these trips.

Lucy stepped over to Murdoch. 'An' here, Murdoch – ah'd greatly appreciate it if yer could find the time to purchase these fer me?' She held up a small sealed envelope to Murdoch.

'Ah'd be glad ter, miss. But there ain't much there, mind,' he replied, looking at the small envelope.

Lucy blushed, embarrassed. 'Well, as ah ain't got no money ah kept the list to a minimum,' she replied shyly.

'Right, ah'll do as agreed an' give it to Mrs Perkins, but ah'll mek sure she adds bits an' pieces as she thinks fit,' he warned kindly as he placed the envelope into his top left breast pocket.

Lucy looked embarrassed as she stepped back; her eyes dropped to her feet. Murdoch and Liam then clambered aboard the wagon and set off. Lucy stepped upon the porch and watched, waving until the wagon had disappeared out of sight among the trees.

Sergeant Rodgers and Tomahawk Joe were casually strolling back to their tents when the young bugler began to play reveille.

'Well, that's it, ma friend,' announced the sergeant. 'Today's the day when young Lieutenant Hudson comes unstuck and Grey Wolf escapes,' he went on sarcastically.

Tomahawk Joe smiled. 'Good. Enough bloodshed has been spilled over this land,' he replied determinedly.

They then walked over towards the lieutenant's tent, where they found him fastening up his gun belt.

'Good morning… and are we ready for a successful day?' he greeted them jovially.

The sergeant looked at his scout and rolled his eyes surreptitiously, then saluted and stiffened to attention as he answered his superior. 'Yes sir, the men are now preparing their mounts,' he announced.

'Good. Sergeant, I feel today we'll finally catch up with this murderin' butcher.' The young lieutenant sniffed the air as he stepped out of his tent.

'As ah'm to lead one half of the men, sir, ah thought it best if Corporal Kennedy go with yer and Tomahawk Joe ride with me, sir,' suggested the sergeant.

The young officer paused and glanced at him. 'Sergeant, in future I would strongly suggest you leave the organising of the men to me,' he reprimanded his sergeant. 'On the other hand, that's probably what I would have done anyway,' he conceded, casting a cursory glance at the Indian scout before turning and walking away.

As planned the previous evening, they were to ride as one group as far as the border then split into two. The sergeant was to ride west before turning south while the lieutenant was to ride east as far as Beaver Creek. He felt that Grey Wolf and his tribesmen would be in this area somewhere, planning some sort of guerrilla war. By nightfall both detachments would be back safely in Richmond.

As they drove along the road towards Pinewood Falls, Liam turned towards his boss. 'Mad Dog?' he asked.

'Yeah,' replied Murdoch.

'The men back at the ranch have asked me to find out if all is well with yer…' Liam went on carefully.

'What d'yer mean, am ah all right? Of course ah'm all right!' cried Murdoch indignant.

'Well, it's just they're a little concerned – this is not the Mad Dog we're used to.' Liam struggled to explain.

'What are yer sayin', man? Just come out and explain yersel'!' demanded Murdoch.

'Well, the combed and trimmed hair, the smart clean clothes, the fresh-smelling aroma about the house... yer've even begun to talk to us.' Liam went on.

Murdoch laughed at his friend's awkwardness. 'So, because ah've begun to take an interest in mesel' an' ma men, ah've gone soft. Is that what yer sayin', laddie?' he turned to scowl at his companion.

'No, no – we were just concerned that something was wrong,' Liam tried to explain. 'We're used to a different you.'

'Och, yer should have seen me in ma army days! Oh, ah was hard – the best boxer in the Sudan – an' ma men were the smartest in the regiment. For a time ah may have forgot about those days. Maybe ah chose to forget, but not now.' He smiled at his friend and winked. 'Yer don't have to be hard to lead men, yer need to work with them, gain their respect,' he went on. 'Yer can't gain respect dressed as some vagabond, yer have to earn it.'

Liam nodded in understanding.

'So then,' Murdoch began, clearing his throat, 'what dress size d'yer think Lucy is?'

'Sorry – *what?*' asked a surprised Liam as he nearly fell off the wagon.

'What dress size d'yer think Lucy is?' Murdoch repeated.

Liam scratched the side of his head and looked back at his boss. 'Ah don't know,' he admitted.

Murdoch flicked his head in disappointment; they carried on in total silence, but Liam kept glancing sideways at his boss.

Eventually they arrived at Pinewood Falls. Murdoch drove the wagon up to the hardware store and stopped.

'Der yer have anything to do in town, Liam, while we're here?' Murdoch asked his companion.

Liam sat quietly, still struggling to take this new Murdoch in. He could only shake his head as a response.

Murdoch smiled and clambered down, 'Well, then, yer can look after the wagon while ah'm in here,' he declared.

Murdoch stepped into the hardware store; he looked about him as everyone inside stopped and stared at the new stranger. Murdoch paused and looked behind him. 'Sorry, ah ha' left the door open,' he apologised.

'Mad Dog?' asked a small, balding, dark-haired man from behind a counter.

Murdoch spun round. He walked over to the counter.

The small man, who was dressed in a beige apron, whistled. 'Well, well, well... an' just whose weddin' are yer goin' to?' he asked.

Murdoch stopped and glanced down at himself; he was wearing his old army jerkin and trews. These were in the government tartan, a distinction of the 42nd Regiment. 'Ah yes,' he laughed, embarrassed. 'Ah took to wearin' these again, to get out o' ma old clothes, yer know what ah mean,' he tried to explain.

The small man smiled approvingly at the sight before him. 'So then, how can ah help?' he asked with a smug smile.

Murdoch stepped up to the counter and leaned across it. 'Ah want yer wife,' he whispered seriously.

'Ah beg yer pardon?' replied a shocked Mr Perkins.

'Ah want yer wife, Ethel,' Murdoch repeated. He stood up to his full height and he nodded, smiling.

Mr Perkins stood dumbfounded; then, shaking his head, he looked Murdoch in the eyes. 'What fer, may I ask?' he asked nervously.

'Oh, ah need a hand wi' ma list,' announced Murdoch as he pulled Lucy's envelope from his top pocket.

'Oh, thank the Lord fer that,' smiled Mr Perkins. 'Jist wait a moment, ah'll go get her.' He hurried off.

As Ernie brought his wife into the store, the other customers had stopped and had begun to watch amazed; most were open-mouthed.

Murdoch glanced about nervously – he hated being the centre of attention. 'It can get draughty in here at times,' he said to the gathering crowd.

Some took the hint and began to go about their business once more, while others remained at the counter, soon to be joined by Ethel.

'Yer see, ah told yer Ethel, Mad Dog wants to see yer,' explained Ernie.

'Ah, thank yer, man. Now then, Ethel...' began Murdoch. He led Ethel away from the crowd towards the end of the counter. 'Ah would like a hand wi' ma list.' He produced Lucy's envelope once more, which Ethel took and opened. She glanced at it, then, shocked, looked back at Murdoch.

'This is yer list?' she asked suspiciously.

'Aye, but no…' replied Murdoch.

'What?' puzzled Ethel.

'It's fer a woman, a very special woman,' Murdoch tried to make clear.

'Oh…' replied Ethel, nodding in agreement.

'Now, if there is anything not on the list that should be fer a woman – yer know, smellies an' the like, please feel free to add them,' Murdoch went on.

'Certainly, but like what?' Ethel quizzed.

'Womanly things… ribbons, smellies, hankies, yer know,' Murdoch was waving his arms about as he struggled to explain himself; the big silly grin that he still wore only added to the surreal situation.

Ethel ran about, gathering bits and pieces, helped occasionally by Murdoch's own observations as he too added certain items.

'An' when yer finished, can yer wrap 'em up in two boxes in ribbons,' Murdoch asked.

Ethel could only nod her head in response; she was too taken aback to say anything. She followed Murdoch about the store as he glanced at each and every item in turn. He suddenly paused, stopping dead in his tracks.

'Whut's the problem?' asked a nervous Ernie.

'Them dresses, would they fit a woman this size?' asked Murdoch; he held his hands out in front of him as he tried to give an accurate account of Lucy's size.

Ethel and Ernie could only look at each other. Ernie scratched his head in frustration. 'Yer see, Mad Dog, yer cannot really go by that for a decent size,' he tried to explain.

'Well, it'll be for a young lady a little bit smaller than yer, Mrs Perkins,' smiled Murdoch.

'Ah beg yer pardon!' cried Ethel, offended.

'What? Naw – ah didn't mean to upset yer!' cried Murdoch in defence. 'Anyway, while yer wife an' I are getting these womanly things together, yer can be busying yersel' by getting ma provisions together,' he ordered as he handed Ernie a separate list.

'But Mr Mad Dog,' Ethel protested as Murdoch climbed into the shop window and admire the many fancy women's dresses there on the mannequins.

'Just call me Murdoch,' he smiled.

'But yer can't jist go wanderin' around our displays like that. What'll the townsfolk think?' argued Ethel.

Suddenly Murdoch realised what he been doing and where. He cleared his throat and quietly, rather embarrassed, he clambered back out of the window. He then noticed a woman looking in at him from the street.

'There – there, Mrs Perkins! What dress size is that woman?' Murdoch pointed excitedly.

'Oh, that's Nancy. I know her size,' announced Ethel triumphantly.

'Good, then we're in business.' Murdoch led her about the store once more. He purchased three dresses for Lucy; the first a claret dress, with white lace trim and V-neck inlay, the second was emerald green and the third – which Murdoch picked himself – was pure white with lace collar and cuffs, matching gloves, bonnet, purse and parasol. These he carried out to the wagon where Liam sat patiently waiting.

'What on earth kept yer?' he asked as Murdoch appeared under a bundle of clothing.

Murdoch handed all his goods over to Liam. 'Here, put these in the wagon fer me, will yer?' he asked.

'Yeah, sure,' replied Liam. As he placed them down carefully he noticed dresses and other female items. 'What the hell?' He could not contain his astonishment.

'Don't worry, they're not fer me,' assured Murdoch when he saw Liam's astonishment.

'Well, thank the Lord fer small mercies,' replied Liam, raising one eyebrow in return.

Murdoch turned to thank the Perkins for their assistance, then clambered aboard the wagon. Liam was watching him with interest, a wry smile fell across his face.

Murdoch glanced at him as he sat down, 'An' just who are yer lookin' at?' he demanded.

Liam shook his head and began to laugh. Murdoch was about to speak again when his attention was drawn to the street as passers-by began to chatter and become excited. Ted Skerrat and his men had arrived. They rode slowly and arrogantly past the wagon, and Ted gave Murdoch and the wagon only a cursory glance as he led his men towards the saloon. There they dismounted.

'Ted, Ted!' called Rosie as she came rushing out of the saloon, arms outstretched to greet him.

'Well, honey, that's some greetin',' smiled Ted as they met. He handed Abe his reins and began to lead Rosie back into the bar. 'Take care o' ma horse, will yer?' he ordered Abe as he disappeared inside.

Calvin too had noticed the arrival of Ted and his men; he stood observing them through his window. 'Ned, go see if yer can find Blue. If he don't already know it, tell him. Ted has just got back,' he told his deputy.

'Sure, Calvin.' Ned jumped out of his seat and made for the door.

'An' be sure to go the back way,' barked Calvin.

Ned did a complete U-turn and left the jailhouse by the back door. Calvin watched him leave and rolled his eyes.

By now Murdoch had turned the wagon and was making his way slowly out of town. As they crossed the ford he turned to Liam. 'Ah'm goin' to drive around Buffalo Mount there an' drop yer off, Liam. Pop up to the veranda an' keep an eye on events for me. Ah'll send a relief when ah get back to Paradise.'

'All right, Murdoch, but what's the concern?' asked his puzzled companion.

'Ah'm concerned that Ted an' his boys have just shown up back in town, but our friends from home are still missin',' he replied, perturbed.

As he drove away leaving Liam behind, he was deep in troubled thought. Where were Will and his team? They were definitely overdue on a mission that they expected to take only four days. Where was the stone? Did Will hold it? Or did Ted still hold it? Or even had the Colonel now got it? Had Will reached the Colonel? Had they managed to deal with him? It appeared more unlikely the longer they became overdue. Were they still alive? All these thoughts were now spinning through Murdoch's mind.

At about that time, Sandy and Charlotte had arrived at the agreed rendezvous point. Two Crows as usual led the horses out of sight.

As Sandy now crept towards a grass verge below a bush, he had a clear view of the approaching road without making himself obvious. As a precaution he now made his rifle ready. Charlotte now lay by his side, observing him carefully. 'Are you suspecting trouble?' she asked.

'No, just a precaution,' he smiled back.

Yet as time passed he became visibly more and more concerned.

'What do you think is keeping them?' asked Charlotte eventually anxious.

'I don't know – let's hope it isn't too serious,' replied Sandy; he did not remove his eyes from the road.

Eventually two riders appeared.

'Scouts,' whispered Two Crows; he too had now joined Sandy and Charlotte by the verge as they waited.

'Dixie riders?' asked Sandy, he shouldered his rifle, in case they spotted them.

'Yeah,' nodded Two Crows, 'The main body will soon follow,' he then added.

Sure enough, the main body of Dixie riders appeared, led by a jolly-looking gentleman dressed in a very smart Confederate officer's uniform. But it was the following sight that worried the hidden agents, for, being pulled along by ropes tied to two riders' saddles, there were both Will and Paddy. They were on their own feet and tied by the hands. Sandy instinctively raised the rifle to the firing position.

'Oh dear, are they all right?' asked Charlotte as she raised her hand to her mouth.

'They are at least on their own feet,' hissed Sandy; he visibly tensed.

They lay and observed the column pass along the road; thankfully it moved along at walking pace.

'How long do you think it will take to reach Richmond at that pace, Two Crows?' asked Sandy.

The Indian looked up at the sky. 'About two hours, maybe three,' he replied thoughtfully.

'Fine, we shall follow them to town,' he announced.

'Then what?' questioned Charlotte.

'Hopefully we can free them before they reach town. If not, then we shall have to hope we can do it there,' said Sandy.

'But what if the opportunity does not arise?'

'We will have to hope it does,' replied Sandy as he mounted his horse.

Two Crows and Charlotte followed; they all rode out after the column. Sandy remained pensive and tense as he rode along. They did not follow the Dixie riders directly but followed behind and to the left, staying deliberately off the road and sticking to the bushes.

'Well, we've passed the rendezvous,' hissed Paddy as they walked along. The heat was beginning to increase and along with the dust made for an uncomfortable time.

'Do you think they were there?' questioned Will quietly.

'Let's hope... but I am concerned about that message last night,' replied Paddy.

Although they were being hauled along at an even pace, they did not dare fall or trip, for the riders would not stop and they would have difficulty getting back on to their feet – as Will found to his discomfort at one stage.

'Could we not take out those two scouts and get close that way?' suggested Charlotte as they rode along.

'I don't think we would have time; they are not that far ahead of the main body,' replied Sandy.

Unbeknownst to Sandy and Charlotte, the lead scouts had now discovered the army camp and were informing the Colonel of its position. The Colonel in turn, realising that the day was drawing on, took the news as he walked his horse along rather than stop.

'OK boys, we shall turn south at this point.' The Colonel indicated with his arm and the whole column turned and followed him.

Unluckily, because of the positioning that Two Crows, Sandy and Charlotte had taken, they actually missed this and arrived at a crest of a ridge which overlooked the army camp set out in front of them before the town.

'Oops,' remarked Sandy.

'What do you mean, oops?' questioned Charlotte.

'Well, you have minor oops and major oops', remarked Sandy. 'This is a major oops.'

'So where on earth is the Colonel?' asked Charlotte as she scoured the valley in front of them.

'He is certainly not down there,' stated Sandy.

'Dixie riders,' announced Two Crows, pointing to the south.

Sandy and Charlotte looked in the direction to which he was pointing. From their elevated position they could just make out a line of riders, slowly working their way round to the south of the town.

'Are they heading for the Jefferson's Ranch road?' asked Sandy.

'Yes,' replied their scout now sounding anxious himself.

'All right, come on – let's follow,' announced Sandy; a little urgency had now entered his voice.

That afternoon, Hank had busied himself organising a jury for the coming trial. It was quickly becoming an eagerly awaited event and it was soon deemed that the town hall was to be too small. So they decided to stage it within the church hall, to this end Hank began to organise the setting up of seats, the judge's position, the jury's benches, the dock and the witness stand. He even began to build some gallows upon slightly raised ground next to the cemetery which lay upon the Beaver Creek road. Barney and Bob could watch the erecting of the gallows from their barred cell. Bob gave a deep sigh of dejection as he watched.

'Well, Bob, have yer come up with any ideas on how to get out o' here?' asked Barney as he sat down.

'Nope, have yer?' Bob replied over his shoulder.

Barney only shook his head in response.

The Dixie riders now reached the Jefferson's Ranch road; here the scouts paused and waited for the Colonel to catch up.

'What's the problem, boys?' he asked as he arrived on the road.

'We were unsure as to which way yer would want to turn, Colonel,' announced one of the men.

'What d'yer mean?' questioned an annoyed Colonel.

'Well, ah jist thought yer might wish to ride fer Jefferson, Colonel,' the rider argued his defence.

'With these two, low-down yella-bellied rattlesnakes?' the Colonel declared as he pointed towards Will and Paddy.

'Sorry, Colonel,' the man apologised and immediately set off to the north. It was not long before they entered town. The Colonel led them up to the jailhouse door. Hank had seen them arriving and crossed the street to meet the Colonel on the porch.

'Howdy, Colonel,' he greeted the elder man.

'Howdy, Sheriff. Ah believe yer have been busy an' caught the other two bounty hunters,' the Colonel remarked.

Hank looked proudly around the gathering crowd. 'Yep, we sure as hell did,' he boasted.

'Good, then we can add these two to yer collection,' the Colonel then announced as he stepped into the sheriff's office, removing his gauntlets as he did so.

Will and Paddy were forcibly pushed into a cell next to Barney and Bob. Their weapons were deposited at the desk; one of the deputies then unlocked a cabinet and placed the weapons inside.

Will and Paddy glanced at each other as both made a note of the other two prisoners. Will caught Paddy's eye and nodded surreptitiously, to which Paddy shrugged his shoulders slightly.

'Hell, Colonel, that was some arsenal, that,' announced a duly impressed Hank.

'It certainly is. Now, before we hang these, ah wants some answers as to where they're from and who sent them,' the Colonel declared.

'OK, Colonel. Ah've organised a jury, moved the courthouse over to the church hall an' had the gallows built,' Hank announced proudly.

'Church hall?' asked the Colonel.

'Yep, because of the popularity; there's a lot o' folks in town wantin' to see 'em hang,' Hank affirmed.

'Hmmm, OK... We'll gave them their hangin', but first ah want some answers,' the Colonel replied.

'Sure, Colonel, but ah would suggest we have the trial first,' said Hank.

The Colonel turned on him immediately. 'Of course – d'yer take me fer an idiot?' he barked, then stormed out of the jailhouse.

Two Crows, Sandy and Charlotte had now reached the road. Two Crows dismounted and checked the tracks.

'They go this way.' He stood up and pointed back towards town.

'All right, Two Crows, we'll ride north, but we'd best stay off the road,' warned Sandy.

'I hope no harm has come to them,' expressed Charlotte.

'We shall try to spring them out of jail tonight,' suggested Sandy.

'Do you feel that's where they'll be?' she asked.

'The Colonel will want to keep them under lock and key. We cannot afford to announce our presence, so it will be down to you and your fancy footwork, Charlotte,' stated Sandy as they rode along at a quickening pace.

The Colonel took the carpet bag from Vince's saddle and carried it over towards the bank. He marched into the building straight past the counter and into the manager's office. A well-dressed man of nervous disposition jumped up from behind his desk.

'Colonel, Colonel!' he cried. 'What can we do fer you today?' he asked nervously.

'Ah wish to deposit this money here in yer bank,' the Colonel announced sitting down at the manager's desk.

'Oh, Lord – good, I mean. May I ask how – how much there is in the bag?' he stammered as he now wiped his brow with a handkerchief.

'Yer may – three thousand pounds,' declared the Colonel; he turned in his seat to face the nervous manager.

The man swallowed hard. 'Thr-three tho-thousand pounds, Colonel?' he stammered, wiping his brow all the more.

'Yep, that's right,' the Colonel replied confidently. 'Sterlin',' he added after a short pause.

'Ohh,' remarked the manager, sitting down, still dabbing his brow frequently.

'An' ah don't want it removed from the bag,' the Colonel declared, standing up so that he now loomed over the anxious man.

'Ye-yes, Colonel. As you wish.' The man leant forward and held the bag with one hand while he quickly rang a bell with the other.

A young clerk immediately appeared in the doorway. 'Yes, sir?'

'Harding, take this bag to the small safe and deposit it there, please,' the manager ordered, handing over the bag. The clerk took it and hurried off.

'An' remember, Watts: this is now yer responsibility.' The Colonel pointed at the manager sitting terrified in his seat.

'Ohh,' was his only response, as the Colonel, now satisfied, stormed back out of the bank.

'Come on, boys, we'll ride back to the ranch an' prepare ourselves fer tomorrow,' he ordered as he clambered back upon his horse. Then, turning he led his men out of town.

Sandy and Charlotte watched them ride past from behind the cover of rocks and bushes.

'Good – at least they've left Will and Paddy behind,' announced Charlotte.

'Yes, I didn't see that carpet bag either,' mused Sandy.

'No… Do you think he may have left that behind, too?' Charlotte asked hopefully.

'Let's hope; Richmond does have a bank, after all,' smiled Sandy.

'Let's get… Will and Paddy out of jail first,' she warned.

'Of course, you're quite right, come on,' urged Sandy.

'It's lovely to have yer back, Ted,' said Rosie softly as she lay back on her bed.

'Yeah, me too, honey,' replied Ted absently. He then opened her wardrobe and began to feel around inside among her dresses.

'What the hell? That's ma wardrobe!' declared a flabbergasted Rosie.

'Yeah, so where is it?' demanded a now concerned Ted, turning to face her.

'Where's what, Ted?' she asked, almost crying in fear; she knew that look he now threw her.

'*Where's the stone?*' he snarled; he walked over to her side slowly.

'What stone? Ted, ah don't know what yer talkin' about?' she pleaded.

He grabbed her arms and twisted her round so that she lay face down, her face almost buried in her own pillow.

'If yer don't know what ah'm talkin' about, then where's the velvet pouch containin' the stone?' he demanded.

'Ah don't know, ah don't know what yer talkin' about,' she again pleaded, crying.

Abe had just poured himself a drink when those in the bar heard the crashing of furniture and the shrieks of Rosie as she vainly called for help. Kate, who had sat next to the Kid, stepped forward as if to ascend the stairs to go to the aid of her friend, but the Kid held her back by the arm.

'Ah wouldn't, if ah were yer,' he warned.

'But Rosie – she's callin' fer help,' Kate said, frightened.

'An' so will yer if yer get involved with Ted when he's in this mood,' warned Abe.

Kate sat down again, reluctant and fearful.

The cries became more desperate and Ted's voice more threatening, until both stopped suddenly. Abe, who had poured himself another drink, glanced up the stairs as Ted came out of the room. His shirt was covered in blood down his chest; he breathed deeply as if out of breath and he looked wild-eyed about the saloon.

'*You,*' he snarled, as he pointed at Kate.

She shied backwards. 'Who, me?' she eventually answered. Kate hardly recognised her own voice, she was so frightened.

'Where is it?' Ted began to descend the stairs.

'Wh-hat?' Kate stammered. She realised that her only chance was to run, run out of the bar as fast as she could to safety, but she could not move; she could only cower deeper into her chair.

Ted stepped closer; his eyes never left hers, he now drew his gun. 'Where is it?' he snarled menacingly.

'A-ah don't know what yer on about.' She began to weep as she shook her head in denial, as if trying to shake the threatening scene from her mind.

Ted cocked his gun. 'Where is it?' he finally snarled.

Kate could no longer answer; she simply shook her head. Then the silence was broken by a loud bang, and Kate's body was hurled backwards across the bar. Ted's six companions and the other girls in the bar all stood rigid, silent and open-mouthed as Kate's dead body lay upon the floor. The bullet had entered Kate just below the neck. A neat hole indicated its entry point, likewise a large gaping hole indicated its exit point in her back.

The saloon bar was eerily quiet for a few moments, until Ted regathered his thoughts.

'Right, boys, line the girls up against the bar!' he shouted.

'Why, Ted?' queried Joe, who sat next to Alice.

'Shut up, an' just do it.' Ted turned to him, and drove his face threateningly into Joe's.

'Hey, Ted, what's Alice done?' pleaded Joe.

'Jist line them up, or ah'll drill a hole through yer!' He raised his gun and pushed it into Joe's throat. 'An' get that bartender in here too,' he snarled as he turned to Abe.

Abe jumped into action; it was a long, long time since he had seen Ted this annoyed, but he knew not to argue. The Kid stepped forward.

'Come on, Ted; enough is enough,' he declared as he tried to calm Ted down.

Ted turned sharply and pointed his gun at the Kid. 'Now ah've warned yer afore, Kid; one word out o' yer an' ah'll blow yer away.'

'But whut's wrong, Ted?' asked a surprisingly calm Danny.

Ted stopped and glanced about him; he began to waver slightly and he sat down, confused. 'They've taken the stone, boys,' he said quietly.

They all stopped and looked at the terrified girls stood along the bar, soon joined by Bert the bartender.

'So yer think they took it then?' asked Joe, almost in disbelief.

'Who else could 'ave taken it? Ah hid it in Rosie's wardrobe,' explained Ted, 'So it's got to be one of these here.' He waved his gun at them.

'Could it not have been one of Rosie's clients?' quizzed Abe.

Ted stopped, the thought finally dawning on him. 'All right...'

He reached out, grabbed one of the girls by the scruff of the neck and pulled her down towards him. 'Who visited Rosie while we were gone?' he growled.

The girl cried out in pain. 'She had several callers—'

'Like who? Names – ah wants names, goddamn it!' He cocked his gun and held it to the side of her head.

'Ah'll give yer a list, Ted, but ah need time to think,' offered the bartender.

Ted's attention was now drawn; he threw the helpless girl to one side and stepped over to the cowering bartender.

'Give him a piece o' paper and a pen, Abe,' he ordered his friend. Then turning to Bert, he hissed, 'Ah'll give yer time to write down their names, then tomorrow ah'm goin' to hunt each an' everyone o' them down till ah find the stone,' he threatened.

He glanced up and down the bar. 'No one is to leave the saloon tonight, no one is to get a warnin'. This town has not seen Ted lose his temper yet – tomorrow it will.'

Murdoch had now arrived back at Paradise; he drew the wagon to a halt outside the house and hurried over to the cow hands' dormitory. There he quickly organised a rider to return to Buffalo Mount with a spare horse for Liam. Then he quickly returned to the house, where Lucy was now standing.

'Is everythin' all right, Murdoch?' she asked alarmed.

'Ah don't know. It doesn't look it, ah'm afraid,' he replied solemnly.

She gave him a look of concern.

'Anyhow, there's me forgetting ma manners.' He paused and his face broke into a large smile as he faced Lucy.

She looked up at him like a little girl lost, as he clambered back on to the wagon.

'Here.' He held out a medium-sized box, no bigger than a shoebox; it was tied by a broad pink and white ribbon. 'These are yer things.'

'Murdoch!' she exclaimed. 'Fer me?'

Murdoch smiled and nodded his head. 'Also, ah took the liberty, Miss Wightman, to get yer these.' He had now stepped on to the back of the wagon, and there he held up the crimson dress.

Starlight gasped as Lucy just looked on; tears fell down her face as it broke into a beautiful grin.

'Ah hope yer don't mind, miss,' Murdoch said quietly.

'Mind? Mind? Oh Murdoch, yer've made a simple country girl very, very happy,' Lucy replied as she wiped away the tears.

'Good, so yer'll not mind these, then.' He now handed down the other two dresses.

'Oh my, oh goodness!' Lucy gasped as she smoothed her hand over the fabric. 'But why?' she asked Murdoch incredulously.

'For services rendered, Miss Wightman,' he replied softly. Then, turning his attention to his cow hands, he gestured them to the wagon and began to hand out the supplies, which they carried into the house.

He jumped down from the wagon and began to walk towards the house. Lucy was still stood on the porch by the door. She was smiling as tears still fell down her cheeks.

'Thank yer, Murdoch, thank yer, but how will ah ever pay yer back?' she asked.

'Yer already have,' he smiled as he led her indoors. 'Now come on, try them on for size.'

BID FOR FREEDOM

The townsfolk of Pinewood Falls had almost all been awakened by the shot that was fired in the saloon. Calvin and Ned hurried over to the bar.

'Wait here, Ned. Cover me if yer have to,' warned Calvin as he paused upon the porch outside the saloon.

'Should ah go round the back, Sheriff?' asked a very nervous Ned.

Calvin glanced at him and smiled. 'Yep, go round the back, Ned, but don't do nothing rash.'

He watched Ned hurry off; as he disappeared Calvin took a deep breath.

'What the hell's goin' on, Sheriff?' interrupted Blue.

Calvin turned to see Blue and two Dixie riders run up towards him. He was not a Dixie rider fan, but he was pleased to see them now.

'Ah don't know – ah'm about to find out, though,' he hissed as he straightened up once more.

'Well, Sheriff, we're right behind yer,' offered Blue.

Calvin nodded, then stepped through the saloon doors. There he found a line of girls stood along the bar. At the far end stood the bartender Bert, busy scribbling something on a piece of paper. To Calvin's right lay the prostrate body of Kate. 'What the hell's been goin' on here?' he demanded.

'What's it to yer, Sheriff?' snarled Ted, stepping clear of the people at the far end of the bar.

'Are yer responsible fer this, Ted?'

'An' what if ah am, what are yer goin' to do about it?' demanded Ted.

The three Dixie riders stepped to one side of Calvin so that each could get a clear shot. The saloon fell silent as Ted's gang members also began to spread out.

'Ah've warned yer about this afore, Ted. Yer can come quietly, or yer can come screamin'. Either way ah'm takin' yer in,' warned Calvin. In the uneasy stand-off he appeared to be the calmest man in the bar – apart from Ted himself.

'Yer fancy yer chances, d'yer, Sheriff?' Ted smiled wryly, resting his hands upon his gun belt buckle.

Just then the back door crashed open and in fell Ned, although he managed to keep his feet and his rifle pointing at Ted.

Ted turned to face this new threat, then sighed. He retained the wry smile. 'Well, Sheriff, it appears first battle to yer. But ah'm warnin' yer now yer've started yer'd best finish it,' he snarled as he turned back to Calvin, as he did so he raised his hands.

'OK, boys, take his guns.' Calvin now drew his gun out and directed the Dixie riders to take position of Ted's guns. 'You boys...' Calvin now addressed the other gang members. 'Yer are all to stay within the confines of the saloon. Any one of yer found leavin' and ah'll arrest yer too,' he warned as he glanced about them slowly. 'Take their guns, Ned,' he ordered his deputy. Finally he glanced at Bert the bartender. 'Now then, what's that yer writin' down?' he demanded.

'A list of Rosie's clients from while Ted were away, Sheriff,' the bartender replied anxiously.

Calvin stepped up to the bar and took hold of the sheet of paper; he glanced at it. On it was indeed a list of names. 'Uh-oh.' He glanced at Ted. 'An' what's this fer?'

'They have something belongin' me, Sheriff,' replied Ted calmly. 'An' ah intend to get it back,' he added threateningly.

'Not from where ah'm sticking yer,' smiled Calvin, as he gestured Ted towards the door and out into the street.

Once he had locked Ted up, he sent Blue off to ready a rider to inform the Colonel of the events at Pinewood Falls, while he and Ned planned to take turns watching their new prisoner.

'Ah'm not goin' to let that jumped-up fat sheriff get away with this,' declared the Kid as he stood at the saloon window and watched them march Ted away.

'Neither am ah,' added a disgruntled Joe.

'So then, boys, what d'yer suggest?' asked Abe.

'Ah'm fer gettin' ma gun back,' snarled the Kid.

'Ah agree,' declared Abe.

They stood around the window and observed the sheriff's office across the street.

Now that it had become a little quieter around the jailhouse in Richmond, Will sidled over to Barney and Bob's cell. Bob looked as if he was asleep but Barney sat forlornly upon his bunk. He was looking at his hands but his mind was obviously elsewhere.

Will hissed across at him, which immediately caught his attention.

'Good evening, I'm Will and this is my colleague Paddy. Who, may I ask, are you?' he whispered hoarsely.

Barney smiled; he stood up casually and strolled over to the separating bars. 'Howdy, ah'm Barney. This here is ma partner Bob.'

'Oh, and what are you in for?' asked Will.

'Why, what concern is that fer yer?' Barney replied, becoming suspicious.

'Oh, I just wondered. We're in for murder,' Will shrugged nonchalantly.

Barney looked at him his eyes narrowing. 'Yer not responsible fer the Jefferson Ranch shoot-out, are yer?' he quizzed.

'I'm afraid so,' replied Will.

Paddy now joined them at the bars.

'So where is yer two partners – the woman?' asked Barney, his tone now changing to one of annoyance.

Will glanced at him suspiciously.

'How do yer know of her?' asked Paddy.

' 'Cause we followed yer as far as Fort Bastion, that's how.'

'Why?' It was now Paddy's turn to become suspicious.

'It appears that we are after the same gang, boys,' smiled Barney.

'Are yer bounty hunters?' asked Paddy.

'Yep, we work fer the Silver Star Agency, an' were hired by the Dakota Territory an' the State of Missouri to hunt an' bring in Ted Skerrat and his gang – dead or alive,' Barney explained.

'Better alive, I take it,' remarked Paddy.

'Of course, although they were only interested in Ted being alive... the others we can shoot.'

'I see. So where were you picked up?' asked Will.

'South of here; we were trying to avoid the town but ran into an organised posse out looking fer yer,' Barney explained quietly.

'When?' questioned Paddy.

Barney smiled. 'We turned back from Fort Bastion. I had anticipated that Ted would run fer Pinewood Falls. We wanted to get there afore yer boys.'

Paddy and Will glanced at each other; Paddy raised his eyebrows and cleared his throat. 'So what would yer do if we got out first then?' he queried.

'Yer wouldn't leave us in here to face the Colonel's wrath alone, would yer?' asked a now very suspicious Barney.

'Well, surely you now realise that if we are after the same gang we would benefit by leaving you here, wouldn't we?' Will smiled cruelly.

'OK, an' jist how d'yer think yer goin' to get out?' Barney challenged.

'You appear to forget, my friend, that we still have two colleagues on the outside,' smiled Paddy.

'And as far as we are concerned, they are trying to get us out of here,' added Will. He turned around so that he sat with his back against the bars and crossed his arms.

Barney smiled wryly. 'Now then, yer boys don't sound as if yer from round these parts?' he questioned.

'So?' queried Will.

'Well, ah guess yer from Canada.' Barney stood up and stepped closer to the bars; he rested each hand upon a bar as he looked at Will closely. 'Ah reckon that if yer are, then yer government will want to avoid any embarrassing incident, won't it?' He smiled mischievously.

Charlotte stepped along the boardwalk, moving silently and swiftly among the shadows as she carefully approached the jailhouse. She had changed into the all-black combat suit that they each carried with them wrapped neatly in the blanket roll upon their horses. As she approached the door she paused and glanced about her. The street was deserted and, apart from the sounds of a piano and people laughing and chatting emanating from the saloon, the place was quiet. She took a deep breath, calming herself before she pushed the door open and stepped inside.

'Good evening, gentlemen,' she smiled.

There were two men inside: the first was sat behind the desk while his buddy sat to one side by the back door. The first man leapt up out of fright.

'Well howdy, missy,' he smiled; in return, he began to look Charlotte up and down as he rubbed his hand down his shirt. 'How can ah help?' he offered.

'Oh good, you've kindly stood up for me,' remarked Charlotte quietly.

'S-sorry?' exclaimed the man surprised.

'So I can knock you down again,' she smiled casually, before punching him in the diaphragm, which had the effect of literally knocking the wind out of him and forcing him back a step. Charlotte followed this up by stepping forward and bringing her arm up in a punching motion so that her elbow connected with the unfortunate man's chin, knocking him clean over the desk.

Bob stood up quickly in his cell. 'Who the h—'

'Just smile, Bob, just keep smilin',' interrupted Barney as he too looked on stunned.

Will and Paddy remained seated, calmly waiting for Charlotte to finish. The second man now leaped up and reached for his gun.

'What the hell!' he shouted, surprised.

Charlotte spun round and calmly ordered. 'Pick a cell.'

This forced the man to stop. He looked on, incredulous, 'Sorry?'

'Deaf as well as daft! Now pick a cell,' she repeated.

'Why?' he replied puzzled.

'Because you're going in it,' she replied. She then immediately side-kicked him in the chest, which forced him to bend over winded; then she launched herself into a roundhouse kick to his head, which sent him sprawling along the passageway and left him prostrate upon the floor outside the open door of the empty cell. All this took only a few seconds; she then took a deep breath and steadily opened the back door. There stood Sandy; he too had changed into black combat gear so as not to be seen among the shadows. He stepped inside. 'Aha, I see I've missed the party,' he said casually.

Charlotte walked over to the desk where she picked up some keys and hurried towards the cell where Will and Paddy were sat waiting. Sandy followed and began to tie the prostrate man up, dragging him into the empty cell; there he was gagged with his own neckerchief.

'What kept yer?' asked Paddy coolly.

Sandy had by now hurried to collect the first man, who was still flat out upon the floor behind the desk. He gave him the same treatment as the first.

'Hello, Charlotte – this here was your awkward feeling.' Will introduced Barney and Bob, who were still stood by the bars, each bearing a silly grin upon his face.

'Hello,' she said serenely.

Paddy rushed up the passageway and unlocked the cupboard that held their guns.

'What now, Will?' asked Sandy.

'What about these two?' asked Charlotte.

Will turned and glanced at Barney. 'Leave them here; we need as much time as possible – they can be our decoy,' he announced as he received his guns from Paddy and they all hurried out of the back door.

Will led them around to the side of the jailhouse. 'We need to rob a bank,' he declared. 'That bank,' he said pointing to a large building across the street.

'Where are the horses?' asked Paddy.

'Two Crows has them at the end of the street, just down there,' directed Sandy.

'All right, let's get on with this. Sandy, do you have any bombs left?' asked Will.

'Of course,' replied Sandy.

Will quickly glanced about him and around the street. 'Can you cause a diversion with that shop there, the one almost opposite the saloon?' He pointed up the street.

'No problem,' hissed Sandy with a smile.

'Good, the rest of us will cross the street and get into that bank – come on!' urged Will. He led both Paddy and Charlotte across the street and down the side of the bank. As they crept around the bank, Paddy tried the back door.

'Locked,' he hissed.

'Then kick it in,' ordered Will.

'Hang on a minute,' hissed Charlotte as she glanced about. Not far from the back door there was a small sash window.

'Ah'll deal with that,' declared Paddy, stepping up to the window. As he had done in Pinewood Falls, he twisted and pulled at the lower frame; as it was just about to drop he caught hold of the top sash frame.

'There you go,' he smiled.

Charlotte and Will glanced at him suspiciously.

'I'd like to know who taught yer that one,' said Will with a wry smile.

'Just shut up and climb in,' urged Paddy as he lifted both window frames up.

'Charlotte, creep around the side and watch the street,' ordered Will as he clambered inside, followed by Paddy.

Sandy had crept back along the rear of the street opposite the bank and saloon. There he stopped and glanced about him. It was very dark; little light found its way around this side of the buildings. He removed his handkerchief from his pocket, and wrapped it around a medium-sized stone; this he did to dull the noise of breaking a window as he smashed through the rear door. Again he checked about him, just to make sure he had not been heard... he had not. Next he removed two bombs from his belt; he pulled each pin out with his teeth, spitting them on to the ground in turn.

'Here goes,' he said to himself as he dropped both through the door and hurried back down through the shadows.

He made the jailhouse once more, which he sheltered behind when the bombs exploded. Unluckily – and unbeknownst to Sandy – one had rolled below a paraffin lamp when it exploded. This turned into a large fireball and immediately began to burn not only the shop he had chosen but the one next door too.

Oh, bloody hell! he thought as he turned and hurried off towards where Two Crows was waiting.

Charlotte nodded and quickly hurried towards the front of the bank where she could observe the street and saloon; there she knelt within a shadow at the corner of the building and the street, while Will and Paddy crept around inside.

'What are you looking for?' asked Will.

Paddy stopped and looked at him. 'Are you for real?' he asked astonished.

'Well, I know it is a safe we are looking for, but why have we walked past that one?' He thrust a thumb back over his shoulder towards a small safe behind the counter.

' 'Cause ah didn't see it, that's why,' explained Paddy; he walked over to the safe and, kneeling down next to it, he began to flex his fingers.

Will knelt down next to him watching intently.

Paddy gave him a cursory glance as he removed his pocket watch from his waistcoat. This he then wound to set the alarm and, placing it upon the safe door, they both hurried out of the room into the passageway. They did not have long to wait before there came the crumpled thump of the watch exploding. Both glanced around the corner at the safe.

'Bingo,' Paddy said triumphantly as he hurried over to the safe.

It swung open to reveal the carpet bag that the Colonel had recently relieved Will of. Will reached in and picked it up; he opened it and almost hesitantly looked in.

'Well?' Paddy asked, finding the suspense almost unbearable.

Will's face broke into a broad smile. 'Come on, let's go while the going's good,' he said, and with that he sprang to his feet.

Just then the whole room was lit up as Sandy's two bombs exploded and shook the whole street.

'Come on, we have not got long,' urged Will as they hurried out the way they had come in.

They met Charlotte at the window, as she had hurried back up the alleyway. Together they hurried off down the rear of that side of the street, which was now beginning to fill with shouting, chattering people.

'Where did these two horses come from?' asked a curious Paddy as they arrived at the point where Two Crows and Sandy were waiting.

'What on earth do you think I was doing at the back of the jailhouse?' questioned Sandy.

'We borrowed these off the two men in the sheriff's office,' replied Charlotte.

'You!' exclaimed Will to Sandy.

'But of course – I'm not just a pretty face, you know,' Sandy retorted.

'Who's been telling yer lies?' interjected Paddy with a wry smile.

The townsfolk were now hurrying to and fro as they fought desperately to try to extinguish the flames. The first shop was now just a burning mass, but the second was brought under control. Hank was organising the fire control and the townsfolk when he realised that neither of his two guards had approached him from the jailhouse.

Strange, he thought, as he hurried over to the jail. He stopped when he found the door ajar and slowly stepped inside. He sighed dejectedly when he found the two guards tied up in the spare cell and Will and Paddy gone. He looked at Barney and Bob menacingly. 'Where the hell have they got to?' he challenged.

Barney shrugged. 'Dunno, Sheriff. As ah said earlier, ah'm not with them there boys.'

'We'll see about that,' Hank replied, then looking over his shoulder. 'Buck!' he shouted.

'Yeah, Sheriff,' replied a man from the doorway.

'Go ride over to Jefferson's Ranch – tell the Colonel what has happened, d'yer hear?' ordered Hank.

'Yep, sure will, Sheriff.' The man turned and walked out of the jailhouse.

'An' hurry!' Hank urged after him, as he followed him through the door.

The Kid, Abe and Danny sat around the table in the bar; there they planned their freeing of their leader, Ted.

'Remember, it has got to be quick and silent, and we must not forget our weapons,' warned the Kid.

'Yeah, so what d'yer suggest, then?' remarked Abe.

The Kid sat silent as he mulled the idea over in his head.

'Ah suggest we wait until the sheriff is out o' the way – that would leave Ned in there on his own,' offered Danny.

Just then Joe came hurrying over from the door. 'Ah think that's the rider been sent to inform the Colonel,' he said as he sat down.

'That wouldn't surprise me; Calvin would be desperate to squeal an' get some credit,' snapped the Kid.

'Well, whatever we come up with it will have to be afore daybreak,' suggested Abe.

The Kid nodded in response.

'So are we goin' to tie up the girls then?' asked Frenchy.

The others looked at him puzzled.

'Why?' asked Abe.

'Well, if we're planning to spring Ted, they can easily slip away and inform Calvin of our plan. After all, ah don't expect much loyalty from them now,' Frenchy explained.

The girls had up to that point been locked in a room upstairs, but nobody had thought of tying them up, conveniently forgetting about the incident in the bar earlier.

'Yer right, Frenchy,' admitted Danny; he then stood up.

'An' where are yer goin'?' asked The Kid.

'To find some rope,' replied the Irishman. 'Frenchy, come with me,' he ordered and the two of them soon disappeared.

The Kid, Abe and Joe settled around the table once more. Joshua sat by the window watching the street for any further developments.

'So then, Danny goes across to the jailhouse, on the pretext of seeing if Ted requires anything. Then we follow; Abe, yer an' yer brother go collect the horses. Ah'll get the guns, then we'll make a run fer it towards that abandoned settlement up Pine River Creek,' explained the Kid.

'Why Danny?' asked Abe.

' 'Cause no one suspects him o' anything, with him bein' quiet an' all,' explained the Kid.

'Why, he could knock poor Ned into the middle o' next week with his li'l finger,' sniggered Joe.

The Kid smiled as he sat back in his chair nonchalantly.

'So when do we put this plan into action?' hissed Abe.

'Ain't yer been listening?' retorted the Kid. 'When Calvin leaves the office.'

They all sat back, then Abe produced a deck of cards. 'Anyone fer a hand or two?' he asked hopefully.

Both Joe and the Kid agreed; Abe began to deal the cards about the table.

It was still very early when Liam arrived at Paradise Ranch. Daylight was still some hours away, but Murdoch had stayed up. He sat in his chair upon the porch at the front of the house. He stood up when he saw Liam arriving.

'Well?' he demanded as Liam dismounted in front of him.

'There appears to have been some sort of bother at the saloon,' began Liam.

'Oh? Go on,' Murdoch urged.

'Well, after Ted and his gang arrived, not much happened at first, then later ah thought ah heard a gunshot. Ah wasn't sure exactly where it came from, or who it involved, but soon after that ah saw figures milling around in the street outside the saloon. Ah believe one was the sheriff,' Liam explained.

'Go on,' repeated Murdoch pensively. He had sat back down and rocked in his chair as he clasped both his hands in front of his face thoughtfully.

'Soon after that, ah noticed one man entering the saloon through the back door. After a short pause one was led out of the front by a group of men and frogmarched across to the jailhouse,' Liam went on.

Murdoch glanced up when Liam had finished. 'Is there anything else?' he asked urgently.

'Nar, that's all ah saw.'

'Good. Well, thank yer, Liam. Now go an get yersel' something to eat an' some rest,' gestured Murdoch. He sat deep in thought. Who fired the shot? The omens actually looked good. Obviously the stone had gone and Ted had not retrieved it. Which in turn meant that his path had not yet crossed that of his friends. But where were they? He would have to report to this to Drumloch Castle, but what would he say? He scratched his head.

Then, to his surprise, Lucy stepped out into the early morning air.

She looked beautiful in her new crimson dress; she had also put her hair up and had put on some ladies' cologne. Murdoch's jaw dropped when he saw her; then, as if prompted from a trance, he stood up.

'My, but yer do look a pretty picture!' was all he could say.

She smiled. 'Thank yer, Murdoch, ah thought ah'd put it on fer yer. Yer so kind, but yer never came in, so ah thought ah'd come to yer.' She gave a twirl in front of him then sat down next to him upon the chair.

Soon, Murdoch's mind was evidently elsewhere; his eyes remained fixed upon some distant object in the darkness.

'What troubles yer?' Lucy eventually asked out of concern.

'Oh, it's nothing for yer pretty little head to worry about,' Murdoch smiled sadly.

'Yer've been so kind, not jist to me but to others. Yer not only try to help but yer listen – that's a skill not many people have. But yer've got to remember that yer like a well. Yer've got to replace some of that water comin' out, and yer don't appear to have someone that yer can turn to.' Lucy said.

'Ah well,' Murdoch sighed. 'Ah've been called many things, but a well, never.' He laughed.

'Yer can talk to me if yer like,' she offered.

Murdoch turned to her and smiled gently; she slipped her hand into his. 'Och, Miss Lucy, that is very good of yer, but this is business and the less yer know the less chance yer have of being hurt. But thanks all the same.' He patted her hand gently and replaced it back upon the seat. He then stood up as if to walk back into the house.

'Where are yer goin', Murdoch?' she asked quietly.

'Ah need to send off a very important message,' he replied. He held out his hand to aid her to stand up, and together they returned to the house.

Hannah was chatting to the Storm Force Delta leader, John Proctor-Williams, when the telegram arrived. John's team was in charge of security that month, while Charlie's team, Storm Force Charlie, was training. The rota system that Lord Porter had worked out usually placed two of the teams on operations, while the third trained in new techniques and kept fit. The fourth team maintained security around the castle itself. It was a method that had worked well for the first twelve months of the organisation's existence.

Hannah returned to the telegraphy office, where she picked up the message from Murdoch. She sighed heavily when she read it, then hurried out of the room and went straight to Lord Porter's office. She knocked on the door.

'Come in,' came Lord Porter's distinctive husky voice. He stood by the large window looking out over the loch. The morning was beautiful and the sunshine was illuminating the west side of the loch in several shades of the most exquisite shades of green and purple hues.

'Och, it's beautiful is it no',' he said to his lovely assistant as she entered the room.

'It is, my lord, but I feel you should read this,' urged Hannah, paying little attention to the actual view. She handed him the slip of paper.

Lord Porter took the slip of paper. 'Hmmm,' he sighed as he read the message. 'When did this arrive?'

'Just a moment ago, my lord,' replied Hannah.

'Which team is on training schedule this month?' he enquired as he limped back to his desk.

'Storm Force Charlie, my lord,' she informed him.

Lord Porter glanced up at her. 'Regrettably we must prepare Charles's team. We must, I'm afraid, prepare for the worst my dear,' he said softly. 'But do not say a word of this to Madeleine as yet,' he warned as an afterthought.

'No, my lord, I shall not. But she must be told that something is amiss soon. It is, after all, only fair,' she argued.

Lord Porter nodded; he was deeply troubled. Teams had been a little late before, but he had know Murdoch for a long time; he was a good asset to have. Lord Porter had even wanted him in on his bureau, only the agency McLeod was employed with refused to allow him to leave, as he was still operational. If Murdoch was worried about the delay then something was amiss.

Of course the Bureau was prepared to take losses – the nature of the work dictated such – but fortunately so far no one had died on operational work. Yes, one or two injuries had occurred, but so far no deaths. It would be ironic and a terrible shame if Storm Force Alpha were the first; for not only had they proven the best team the organisation had produced but they were probably the best liked among the organisation and would be deeply missed. Lord Porter leant upon his right elbow. During his military career he had had to deal with many losses of many good men, but he felt a different sense of loss this time – as if it were a member of the family he was at risk of losing. Lord Porter felt the same about everyone within his organisation no matter who they were; they were all his family – the only one he ever had.

Elizabeth had just pulled Charlie out through the half-filled tunnel when they turned they ran straight into Archie.

'Oomph, sorry, Sergeant,' apologised Charles as he picked himself up from the ground, he was brushing the dirt and dust from his trousers. 'Oh, excuse me.' He quickly turned around and pulled Elizabeth up to her feet. Spud and Hector, the other two team members, now joined them.

'What is it, Sergeant?' asked Elizabeth.

'Yer've to get yerselves ready, miss. Yer security status has just been raised to standby,' warned Archie.

'Which team is it?' asked Charles. Other teams had been brought to this level of security before, but not them.

'Hannah will fill yer in on the details back at the castle,' replied Archie. He then turned and marched away, leaving the members of Storm Force Charlie looking at each other. They quickly gathered their thoughts and hurried back to the castle. After cleaning themselves up they hurried down to the conference room. There sat Hannah and Lord Porter, who looked solemn.

'Good morning, Hannah... my lord,' greeted Charles as they entered the room.

'Ah, thank you for being so prompt. Please take a seat,' gestured Lord Porter.

The four members of Storm Force Charlie all sat down.

'I shall be as brief as possible. I have raised your status to stand by, as Storm Force Alpha are now overdue,' began Lord Porter;

he was interrupted by Elizabeth as she gave a quick shriek. He glanced at her caringly and sadly. 'Yes, my dear, I am well aware that they are a very popular team. Nevertheless, the nature of our work dictates that we must prepare ourselves for the worst. If we have not heard anything within two days' time, then you yourselves will be sent off to Canada.'

'What is our task to be, my lord?' asked Charles.

Lord Porter took his time to answer. 'You are to catch a boat for Halifax, Nova Scotia from Liverpool. There you will catch a train which will eventually bring you into a small town called Jamestown, which sits in the north-western province of our dominion. There you will be met by the North-West Mounted Police and escorted to Paradise Ranch, where an agent shall meet you and give you up-to-date information. Hannah shall give you each an info pack with the background information you require.

'Forgive me, my lord, but has anyone informed Madeleine as to the present situation?' asked Elizabeth.

'Not yet, Elizabeth; we are waiting until it becomes absolutely necessary,' replied Hannah softly. 'We do not wish to cause any undue stress at this present time.'

'Yes, yes, of course,' answered Elizabeth quietly. 'I'm sorry, please forgive me.'

'Right, any more questions?' Lord Porter glanced about the small group. There were none; so, gathering up his papers, he shuffled them together and walked towards the door.

Daylight was not far off when Calvin finally left the jailhouse in Pinewood Falls.

'There he goes!' exclaimed Joshua from his vantage point in the saloon window.

'Good – at long last,' yawned the Kid.

'Gawd, ah thought he'd fallen asleep in there,' remarked Abe.

They gathered around the door, while Abe watched the street until Calvin disappeared from sight.

'OK boys, he's gone,' he declared.

'Right, everyone knows what they are about?' asked the Kid, before he allowed Danny out of the door.

They observed Danny as he crossed the street and knocked upon the sheriff's door.

'Yeah, who is it?' came a voice from within.

'It's me, Ned – ah wants a word with Ted, to see if he needs anything,' Danny shouted back through the door.

The door creaked open a little and Ned peeped out. 'Is it only yer, Danny?' he asked.

'Yep,' replied the Irishman.

Ned opened the door and allowed him inside. Once the door was shut behind him the others swiftly moved into action. Abe and Joshua hurried up the street to collect their horses, while the others hurried across the street and listened at the door.

They did not have to wait long, as Danny opened the door almost as they reached it.

'Come on, hurry up,' he said, urging them inside.

'Where's Ned?' asked the Kid quietly.

'Don't worry about him, he'll not be botherin' us again from where he is now,' replied Danny, he flicked his head to where the crumpled body of Ned lay against the wall. He had broken his neck – a quick silent death, and one that Ned would not have known anything about.

'Hurry up an' get me out o' here,' demanded Ted, clapping his hands in anticipation.

The Kid quickly dug out the keys for the cells then hurried along to his cell.

'Where's Abe and Joshua?' Ted asked suspiciously.

The Kid smiled cheekily. 'They've gone fer the horses,' he replied.

Just then Abe burst in through the back door, out of breath.

'Everyone OK?' he asked as he looked about.

'Have yer got the horses?' asked Joe.

'Yeah, they're outside with Joshua,' Abe replied.

'Good,' said Ted as he hurried past.

The Kid had now unlocked the cabinet that contained their guns and was passing them out among the group.

'OK, Ted, what now?' questioned Abe.

Ted glanced about the group. 'The best place at present, ah think, will be at that abandoned settlement up Pine River Creek,' he replied.

'Ah said the same exactly,' announced the Kid.

'So we are agreed, then,' Ted stated with a smile. 'Come on, ah'm not goin' far, ah've a few scores to settle yet. But we shall weather out the storm there fer now,' he declared.

The first cracks of dawn were just appearing over the eastern hills, when reveille was called within the army camp. Sergeant Rodgers was as usual already up and about as he performed his morning rounds of the outlying sentries. That night had been a hectic one, as they had assisted in putting out the fires. The cause of these had been blamed by the sheriff upon a paraffin stove being left alight, although having noticed one or two of the townsfolk and their shifty glances, neither the lieutenant nor Sergeant Rodgers were sold on that idea.

Once the rounds were completed, he returned to Lieutenant Hudson's tent. The young officer was not in the best frame of mind, especially as his hunch had proven to be completely wrong the day before and he was still weary. They had not so much as found an old cold campfire, let alone any Indians, a point which Sergeant Rodgers had mentioned earlier. So to gain some kind of credibility with the men once more – not that he had any in the first place, but he was not to know that – he informed Sergeant Rodgers of his plans for that day. The sergeant saluted, then went about his duties. His orders were to take half the troop out that morning and ride to Beaver Creek, find the Indians' campfire and try to find the tracks of Grey Wolf and his people. He was to track them as far as possible that day, then return to camp by nightfall and report.

The sergeant was to take Tomahawk Joe with him, while the young lieutenant would remain behind in camp. Of course, this was the very thing that the sergeant had argued for the day before – a point of irony not lost on the wizened old hand or his loyal scout. But the longer they remained at Richmond, the more questions required answering, and at present the young officer's mind and time was occupied with catching those Indians.

The Colonel too rode into Richmond that morning; he had dispensed with his Confederate uniform and wore civilian clothing. This he felt necessary especially with the army being camped at the edge of town and becoming more involved that previous night. Buck had passed on the sheriff's message, which made the Colonel furious. 'If ah need a job done, do ah always have to do it mesel'?' he shouted in temper. Now a little calmer, he led his men towards the jailhouse, although this morning Hank was not there to meet him as he usually did. Mystified, he clambered down from his horse.

'Here, Li'l Dave, hold these, will yer.' He gave his companion his reins.

Stepping up to the porch he opened the door and stepped inside the sheriff's office. There he found Hank sat behind his desk; facing him were two of his deputies.

'Howdy Hank, how are yer?' asked the Colonel with a broad smile.

Hank glanced up nervously. 'Colonel, did Buck find yer?' he asked hesitatingly.

The Colonel paused and looked at Hank hard. 'Yep, he did. Now tell me what happened.'

The sheriff explained what his deputies had told him; the Colonel looked on silently, then walked past, struggling to hold his temper. Barney was by the bars as the Colonel walked towards him while Bob lay on his back upon the bunk.

Hank followed the Colonel down the passage towards the cells.

'I see the two that yer brought in, Sheriff, are still here. Have yer interviewed them?' he asked; his eyes did not leave Barney's.

'Nope, ah've not got round to that. But it does appear that two others came in from outside and sprung their companions from Jail, leavin' these two to face yer wrath,' explained the sheriff.

The Colonel withdrew his gun and nodded slowly, still watching Barney; then he fired sideways into the sheriff, slamming his body against the passage wall. Hank's body slid to the ground, dead. The Colonel turned around to face the cowering deputies, recocking his gun. 'Now then, did either of yer stay awake long enough to find out where they are headed?' He pointed the gun at the first deputy, who cowered further back and closed his eyes in pure fear.

'N-no, Colonel,' replied the second deputy.

'But ah know, Colonel,' interrupted Barney as he smiled wryly.

The Colonel slowly turned around. 'Der yer now? An' where may that be?' he asked threateningly.

'If yer let us out o' here, Colonel, ah'll take yer to them,' offered Barney, raising his eyebrows.

The Colonel smiled. 'Der yer really think ah'm that stupid?' he mocked.

'Nope, ah don't think yer stupid at all, Colonel. But neither am ah, an' ah'm not willin' to stay here to face the wrath of these townsfolk,' replied Barney.

The Colonel re-holstered his gun and placed his hands on his hips. 'Go on,' he said after a short pause.

'Ah'd ask yer to take us with yer, not only so that ah could lead yer too 'em, but also to see ma day with 'em fer leavin' us in here to face yer wrath this mornin'.'

The Colonel smile. 'So ah take it yer had nothing to do with them bounty hunters then?'

'Nope, Colonel, we were jist travellin' through the county when they fell upon us,' explained an innocent Barney.

'Hmmm.' The Colonel sighed through his nose, then turning around 'OK, Clyde, let 'em out,' he ordered as he walked back to the door.

As he reached the street, his men were passed by Sergeant Rodgers and half of the army troop. The sergeant was well aware of these cow hands riding about of late in a large group; there had also been a posse looking for some outlaws on the loose. He wondered if they had found them yet. By the time he reached the end of the street his mind had returned to his own duty – to track down Grey Wolf and those Indians.

The Colonel watched the soldiers pass before crossing the street and walking into the bank; he was followed by Vince and Li'l Dave.

'Wait here, don't let anyone in or out,' he ordered Josey as he stood at the doorway.

The bank had fallen silent as he marched towards the manager's office. He stormed into the office. The manager, a man of nervous disposition, almost fell off his chair, then quickly ran round the side of his desk and threw himself upon the floor at the Colonel's feet.

'Please, please, it was not my fault! Think of my family – the children,' the poor man pleaded.

This only added to the Colonel's annoyance. 'Mr Watts!' he exclaimed.

The manager stopped pleading but remained face down upon the floor, sobbing like a baby. The Colonel rolled his eyes in pure disgust, and turned to Li'l Dave. 'Go find out if they took ma money, will yer,' he asked, although he was already expecting the answer.

Li'l Dave nodded and left the room. The Colonel turned back to the manager; he gestured to Vince to pick the prostrate man off the floor. The manager was now a shaking, sobbing wreck.

'Mr Watts, pull yersel' together, man! Yer a disgrace, a coward.' He thrust his face into the poor man's. 'Ah should pluck yer eyes out,' he threatened.

Just then Li'l Dave walked back into the room; the Colonel turned. 'Well?' he growled.

'They've taken the bag, Colonel,' Li'l Dave replied with a sigh.

The Colonel glanced back at the weeping, shaking man. 'Ah should blow yer away, Mr Watts, but yer know what? Ah wouldn't waste the bullet,' he snarled into the poor man's ear. He hit him across the face with his pistol then turned and stormed out.

As he reached his horse once more, he glanced about him. 'Where are those two prisoners?' he demanded.

Barney and Bob were pushed in front of the Colonel, who mounted his horse. 'Right, boys, yer shall have yer wish. Ah'll take yer with me an' yer will see yer day with these rogues. But any funny business an' ah'll blow yer to kingdom come. Do ah make mesel' clear?' he snarled.

'Yer sure do, Colonel,' smiled Barney, as his gun was thrust into his hands. Bob also received his gun; they then mounted their horses and followed the Colonel out of town. Once out of sight, the Colonel led the men slightly to the north of the road so as to avoid the army patrol that they were following. They had not ridden far when one of the Dixie riders from Pinewood Falls rode up to them.

'Colonel, Colonel! Ted Skerrat and his gang rode into Pinewood Falls and shot one of the saloon girls,' he announced.

'So what has Calvin done about it?' The Colonel demanded.

'He's locked Ted up and confiscated the others' guns,' he declared.

'Good, so *someone* can do the job ah've given them without me havin' to help them along.' The Colonel smiled sarcastically.

'So what d'yer want me to tell them, Colonel?' asked the rider.

'What d'yer mean, "me to tell 'em"? They've done their job, what do they want – a pat on the back?' the Colonel replied indignantly. 'Ride back to Pinewood, tell the sheriff to hold Ted until ah arrive. Ah've some important business to deal with first.'

Ahead of them, Will and the team rode on till nightfall. Then they set up camp; they had just arrived at the beginning of the Indian Creek.

'We should arrive back at Paradise tomorrow night,' announced Will as he lay down next to the fire.

'Do yer think they'll have missed us?' asked Paddy sarcastically.

'Ha, well, we are a little late,' remarked Sandy, shaking his head.

Charlotte sat up and looked at Paddy. 'What's that?' she asked.

Paddy sat up and glanced back. 'What?'

'That mark about your neck.'

'Oh, that's ma war wound,' he replied proudly.

'Are you all right. I hope it's not painful.' Charlotte crawled over to him and began to fuss over to him.

'Ah, yes, that's where he was hanging around,' smiled Will.

'Kept dangling, were you?' smiled Sandy.

'He was just swinging about!' laughed Will.

'All right, all right, I came close to breathing my last out there,' argued Paddy.

'Obviously a tight call,' sniggered Charlotte.

Paddy sat back and scowled at her. 'Charlotte, ah would have expected better from you.'

'Sorry,' she giggled again as the others laughed.

Charlotte bathed Paddy's neck all the same, then dressed it as best she could.

Sandy stood up. 'Well, it is my turn to keep watch,' he announced, and walked away.

BATTLE OF PARADISE

Ted Skerrat and his gang crossed the ford and turned north upon reaching the east bank of Pine River. Their intention was to ride as far as Valley, the old abandoned prospectors' settlement, and there to wait until things calmed down – possibly within a week or so. Ted then intended to return to deal with those who were holding their precious stone. Unbeknownst to them, as they turned north, another rider who had observed them from the top of Buffalo Mount set off in a north-easterly direction towards Paradise to inform Murdoch of the unfolding events. The first rays of dawn had still to show themselves, and not a million miles away Paddy was now shaking his comrades, as they wished to set off early.

'Is everything still quiet?' asked Will as he sat up and stretched.

'Yep, thankfully, but I won't be sorry to be rid of this country and back in Paradise, I can tell you,' admitted Paddy.

'Why, it's unlike you to be uneasy,' remarked Charlotte; she had already washed and was now just putting her jacket on.

'I just feel the need for urgency,' Paddy retorted.

This made Will pause and he glanced at his larger-than-life Irish friend. 'All right, we'll have a quick brew, then get on our way,' he ordered.

Sandy nodded in response; he had just got the fire going and had hung their pot over it to boil water.

Murdoch too was up early, and he was strolling about the corral area of his ranch when Sergeant Hackett approached him.

'Good morning, Mad Dog,' the sergeant greeted him.

'Mornin', Hackett,' Murdoch replied with a sigh.

'What's the matter? Something appears to be troubling you?' the sergeant remarked as he tried to put his old friend at ease.

'Ah'm concerned about our English friends – they are runnin' late. Ted Skerrat an' the gang have shown up at Pinewood but we've had no word of our allies. Ah'm debating either ridin' to Pinewood or Indian Creek an' have the area observed,' Murdoch explained as he stood by the fencing looking south.

'I wouldn't worry too much just yet; no news is good news, Mad Dog,' explained the Mountie Sergeant pleasantly. 'Besides, if you go to Indian Creek or wherever, you're then placing yourself in danger. These are professional people. They will show up yet; then we will know just how to respond,' he reasoned.

Murdoch half turned and smiled to his friend. 'Yeah, yer right – of course. Did yer two constables turn up?' Constables Courtney and Adams had been away on patrol and were due to return any day.

'Yes, they returned late last night. I've told them to rest today. If necessary we shall patrol down to the border tomorrow for you,' the sergeant offered.

'Aye, thanks, Hackett. Let's hope it'll not be required though,' answered Murdoch as he led his old friend back towards the house.

As they reached the porch the sergeant stopped. 'Forgive me old friend, I may be speaking out of turn when I say that the idea of having a woman about the house has become very agreeable to you.'

Murdoch hesitated then smiled. 'Yeah, the same thing had crossed ma mind, too.'

It was reveille once more at the army camp set up on the outskirts of the small town of Richmond. Sergeant Rodgers had just completed his morning rounds of the outlying sentries and was approaching Lieutenant Hudson's tent.

'Ah, Sergeant, today we shall follow up on your report of yesterday,' began the eager young officer. 'As usual, I shall take half the men along the old riverbed from Beaver Creek, towards this old prospectors' settlement here in Indian Creek near the border.' He pointed to an old settlement marked upon map which was laid out on his desk. 'You shall lead the other half along the road, towards Indian Creek – here, just above the town of

Pinewood Falls.' Again he pointed to a part of the map. 'Then you'll turn north and we shall meet at the settlement,' the officer finished.

'What happens if the Indians have already crossed the border sir?' asked the sergeant. 'Are we to follow?'

'No, Sergeant, we are not. I have strict orders not to cross into Canada.' The officer paused and took in a deep breath. 'Yet, I feel that these Indians are still this side of that border, and that we have not heard the last of them,' he said finally.

'Right, sir.' The sergeant saluted. His thoughts immediately turned to his Indian scout, Tomahawk Joe. He would be pleased to know that they were not going to pursue his brethren north into Canada.

'Now, Sergeant, get the men ready, and tell them that today we shall have to be on our guard, for we will finally ascertain the whereabouts of our quarry – it may become very perilous,' announced the young officer theatrically.

The sergeant looked on impassively. 'Aye aye, sir.' He saluted and left the tent.

Through the night, the Colonel had regained the Pinewood Falls road; he led his men all night in his quest to regain his money. Now, thanks to Barney, he knew exactly where Will and his colleagues were heading.

'They will head for the Canadian border here at Indian Creek, then they may turn north-east and head for Paradise Valley,' instructed Barney.

'OK, then we shall ride on through the night to try an' head 'em off at the border. But if we miss them there I shan't stop, for we shall follow them into Canada. What's good fer them is good enough fer us,' decided the Colonel determinedly.

No one had got the better of him in thirty years – he was not about to let people start now. These bounty hunters, opportunists, whatever they were, had managed to get the better of him thus far. He would now make an example of them so that in future people would think twice before messing with Colonel Cody. He was not that far behind Will and Storm Force Alpha, but because of the lay of the land they remained out of sight of each other.

By now Will and his colleagues had turned into Indian Creek and rode past Lucy's old cabin that marked the old settlement. They then turned east and began to climb towards the crest of the valley and safety. Their tracks were still visible when the Colonel arrived; some of his men were renowned hunters and trappers, and the lead horsemen leapt to the ground to check the tracks.

'Well?' asked the Colonel.

'It's them all right, Colonel. Five horsemen headin' off in that direction.' The man pointed east. 'Not more than two hours ago, ah'd say,' he added in a promising manner.

'Good, then come on. Let's track 'em down like the dogs they are,' the Colonel growled.

In the intervening time, Ted and his gang arrived at Valley. Ted looked about him. A line of old derelict cabins marked out the old road through the settlement as far as an old square or green had once been. Here the cabins were set back and ran in a semi-circular line around the area back to the old road, which then disappeared onwards up the creek. Each cabin's pitch was still marked out by old log fencing in various states of dilapidation. Ted led his men over to the middle of the green, where stood a large old oak tree, and again two areas marked out by an old fence.

'OK, boys, we shall camp here. Set the fire goin', Abe,' he ordered as he dismounted.

'Der yer not think it's a bit open here, Ted?' asked Joe.

Ted looked at him suspiciously. 'Looky here, if anyone is to approach, they are goin' to come up that road there. One of us can keep watch from the end of the street an' give enough warnin' to use these fences and old cabins fer cover,' he explained.

'But what if they come from the north?' asked Frenchy.

Ted, sighed through his nose, totally disgruntled. 'An' jist who the hell is goin' to come that way? Who the hell knows we're here?' he cried.

'Sorry, Ted,' apologised Frenchy, as he sat by the fire.

'Who is taken first watch?' asked Ted as he looked about.

The others glanced at each other.

'Ah'll do it,' said the Kid; he stood and walked down to the end of the street.

Ted was now becoming impatient with the group. It was high

time they split up and went their separate ways, he thought, before he finally lost his temper and lashed out.

The young army lieutenant led his men along the main street of Richmond. As he did so two things struck him. All those grey-clad riders that he'd noticed about town were now gone. In actual fact, so was the sheriff and his posse. The second thing was the erection of the gallows at the end of the street next to the cemetery. He was unaware of any outlaw being caught since his conversation with the sheriff; even during the fire nothing had been mentioned about removing prisoners. He made a mental note to have a word with the sheriff on his return.

'Sergeant?' he asked at length.

'Yes sir,' replied Rodgers.

'Did that posse catch the gunmen they were searching for?'

'Nope, can't say that they did, sir. But this here county is ruled by one o' those land barons. Ah've heard an he tends to keep the lid on any petty crime,' explained his sergeant, 'so ah was surprised to learn of the posse chasing anybody in these here parts in the first place.'

'Hmm... what's his name?' Lieutenant Hudson asked.

'Everyone knows him as the Colonel, sir,' the sergeant replied.

'Does he live in Richmond?'

'Jist outside, sir – ah believe at Jefferson's Ranch.'

'That was where the shoot-out was supposed to have taken place, wasn't it?' asked the officer.

'Yep, sure was,' smiled the sergeant.

'Hmmm. On our return we must pay this Colonel a visit,' the young officer announced.

'Certainly, sir, but may ah ask why?' puzzled Rodgers.

'Did you not notice the gallows, man!' exclaimed Hudson. 'And what about the other night? Even you weren't sold on what the sheriff had to say, now were you, Sergeant?'

'Aye, sir, that ah was not, sir,' replied his sergeant as they rode on together.

Murdoch's scout rode into the corral at breakneck speed, just as Murdoch stepped out of his house. He hurried over to his man as he dismounted from his horse.

'Well, what news, man?' asked Murdoch.

'Ted Skerrat and his men rode out of town this morning, heading north for the border,' declared the panting man.

'North!' exclaimed a surprised Murdoch.

'Yep, cool as yer like,' remarked the man.

'All right... get yersel' sorted an' see to yer horse,' replied Murdoch as he scratched his head in puzzlement. North, what on earth were they going that way for? he pondered. Then it suddenly dawned on him that was where the abandoned settlement was – Valley. Murdoch clicked his fingers as he realised that Ted and the gang were riding to Valley to hole up. 'We've got him!' he remarked aloud to no one in particular.

Sergeant Hackett joined him. 'What news, Mad Dog?' he asked.

'Ted and his boys have just ridden north to Valley to hole up,' Murdoch replied with a broad grin. 'We could easily apprehend him from there and bring him in, Hackett.'

'Just remember, it is a couple of miles south of the border; neither my men or I could actually *go* there,' remarked Hackett.

'Maybe so, but there's nothing stopping *me*.' Murdoch gave a cheeky smile.

'So what about the four agents?' asked Hackett.

'We can wait fer a day or two, there is nothin' pressin'; but we've got them.' Murdoch rubbed his hands with glee as he stepped back towards his house.

The US cavalry troop was soon approaching Beaver Creek. The young lieutenant halted the men.

'All right, men,' he announced. 'From now on, every one of you be on your guard. These Indians are a slippery breed. We know they've headed north from here, but I feel that they may actually have turned south at some stage. I believe we may find them at Indian Creek just north of a small town called Pinewood Falls. They will no doubt be desperate and will put up a bitter struggle, but we must take back as many as we can find.'

He then turned his horse round and, waving his men on, he led them across the creek. There the sergeant showed him the remains of the campfire and where the short skirmish had taken place. The lieutenant split the men; he took half with him up along the old riverbed – the actual route taken by Grey Wolf and his tribesmen – while Sergeant Rodgers took the others along the road, where with Tomahawk Joe's skill they eventually came across the Colonel's tracks.

'How many men?' asked Rodgers.

'Many, many riders,' Tomahawk Joe replied.

'Well, they certainly ain't Injun tracks,' replied Sergeant Rodgers; he pushed his hat forward as he scratched the back of his head. 'Ah wonder if it was that posse again.' He paused and glanced at his Indian scout. 'How long ago, Joe?' he asked.

'Not long – maybe three, four hours,' Tomahawk Joe replied.

'Well, we shall see where they were headed an' report it to the young lieutenant,' announced Rodgers as they rode on. They now rode at a steadier pace as they searched the road and its surrounding area for more clues. Eventually they came across the remains of the camp and the fire that Sandy had lit only that morning. Again Tomahawk Joe dismounted and scoured the area; he searched the strange-looking shelters for any signs. 'Five people,' he announced at length. 'At least one was Indian,' he added with interest.

'Really? How do yer know?' the sergeant asked.

'Look at footprints – one wear moccasins. Only Indians wear moccasins,' Joe announced.

'How long, Joe?' asked Rodgers.

'Last night,' he replied.

'Did the others stop?' the sergeant asked, as he glanced about the ground.

'No, it does not appear so,' replied the Indian as he too looked about the ground. 'They stayed upon the road.' He pointed.

'Ah wonder if they missed this camp then,' pondered Sergeant Rodgers. 'Well, these appear to be to headed the same way as us, so let's move on,' he announced, as Tomahawk Joe remounted his horse. Again they set off eastward towards Indian Creek.

Will looked down into the valley they had just scrambled out of. They had crossed the border and had been in Canada for the last two or three hours; ahead of them now lay the deep tree-lined valley of Paradise.

'Almost home,' he announced wearily.

'How long, do you think?' asked Paddy.

'Three hours,' Will shrugged.

'Do you still believe that the Colonel will be following?' asked Sandy, as he glanced behind him.

'Without a doubt,' smiled Will. 'He will be more determined than ever,' he added.

'Well, come on then, let's give him something to chase,' challenged Charlotte as she urged her horse forward.

They rode on; they were now going downhill which made for slower progress. Eventually the valley flattened out; at the bottom it was heavily shaded by spruce and Douglas firs, then the trees gave way to a wide grassy meadow. At the far end, it stopped abruptly at the base of a large rocky outcrop. They had now arrived at the Devil's Cut; the track carried on through a narrow defile with steep insurmountable sides. It ran like this through the rock for some twenty yards and was only wide enough for two riders at a time. Once they had ridden out of the pass they immediately came into trees once again. Will stopped and glanced back; the rock edifice was not as severe this side.

'Right,' he suddenly announced. 'Two Crows, ride on towards Paradise, and bring Murdoch and all available men. We shall hold the Colonel here for as long as possible.'

'But Mr Will, Mad Dog, he ask me to watch over you at all times,' the Indian scout protested.

'I'm sorry, Two Crows, but we cannot allow this rocky outcrop to fall into the Colonel's hands. He would only use it against us,' explained Will.

The Indian nodded in agreement. 'I shall not be long,' he said, and rode off at full speed. They watched him ride out of sight.

'Right, we have not long; the Colonel in my reckoning is only some two hours behind us. Sandy, if you and Charlotte take that side, Paddy and I will take this side. Together I believe we can hold this defile long enough for Murdoch to arrive and then we can capture our man,' Will proudly declared.

'All right – good luck everybody,' stated Charlotte as she hurriedly ascended the rock face.

She was quickly followed by Sandy, who settled down a little to her left behind and below a bush. He rapidly made his rifle ready, slipping a round into the breech and cocking his gun. Then he turned to Charlotte and smiled. Charlotte smiled back, then she glanced across at the opposite side of the gorge. There, Paddy and Will were making themselves ready. Paddy could be seen putting two cartridges into his shotgun, one to each barrel. Will caught Charlotte and Sandy's eye and waved across to let them know that all was well and they were prepared too. Then the four settled down to wait.

'Do you think we shall have long to wait?' asked Charlotte.

'About two or three hours, Charlie,' replied Sandy as he peered across the grassy meadow.

'Will we stop them here?' she continued.

'Will has picked a good spot. If we had passed this place by, the Colonel no doubt would have used it likewise; then we would have known about it,' Sandy commented.

Two Crows rode as fast as he could towards the ranch, only slowing when he entered the corral. There he quickly dismounted and ran up to the house. Murdoch had heard the approach of a galloping horse and had hurried to his door, along with Sergeant Hackett.

'Two Crows!' cried Murdoch when he realised his loyal scout had returned. He immediately glanced over the Indian's shoulder to see who else had returned, but his face quickly fell when he found that his scout was alone. 'Where are the others, my friend?' he asked quietly, placing his big paw of a hand upon the Indian's shoulder.

'They back down track – hold the Devil's Cut against Colonel,' panted Two Crows, pointing back down the track whence he had just come.

Murdoch tensed as his brain began to immediately calculate how best to react to this news. 'How long have we got?' he asked in his booming voice.

'One hour, maybe less,' Two Crows explained.

'OK, get yersel' a fresh horse, then take Black Eagle an' ride to Grey Wolf – tell him we may require help at Devil's Cut. Sergeant

Hackett, our moment has arrived; the lamb has brought the wolf to the door, an' now is the time to trap it! Get yer men ready an' inform Liam ah want to see him, please,' requested Murdoch; he turned to re-enter the house.

'Right, Mad Dog. But what of you?' asked Hackett. 'Where shall I send Liam?'

'Send him to the house. Ah'm goin' to get mesel' ready in ma best uniform, and ah have to send a message off to London immediately.' He hurried away.

Sergeant Hackett was left alone for a moment upon the porch, shaking his head. 'The man's really had his head turned... best uniform? What the hell is he talking about?' He too hurried away to get everyone ready.

Time was now of the essence, Murdoch quickly sent off a telegram to Hannah; it was short and sweet. It was all he had time for, and it read: 'Agents safe, am preparing to ensnare target. Further details to follow.'

Having sent that, he began to hurry about the house in various stages of undress as he quickly changed and struggled into his best uniform, which had not seen the light of day for many a long year.

'Lucy, Buff!' he shouted as he moved about and struggled with his jacket.

'Yes, boss,' replied Buff as he appeared and bowed several times.

Murdoch shook his head in frustration. 'Stop callin' me boss, it's Murdoch,' he said.

'Sorry, boss – Murdoch,' answered the Indian servant.

'Right, yer an' Miss Lucy...' Murdoch began.

Just then Lucy appeared in the room. Murdoch was still having trouble trying to fasten his collar button.

'What on earth are yer tryin' to do, Murdoch?' she exclaimed.

'Ah'm tryin' to get ready, that's what. But anyway,' Murdoch went on dismissively, 'ah wants yer both, to look after this house while ah'm gone. Yer will find guns and ammunition in ma locker in the study. If the Colonel does get here, do not try to surrender; he will have yer pretty guts fer garters, lassie, an' ah couldn't bear that.' Murdoch stepped over to Lucy and cupped her face in his big hands.

She touched his hand and rubbed her cheek in his palm. 'Please be careful, Murdoch. Ah don't have many friends left.' A tear formed in her eye.

Murdoch quickly cleared his throat. 'Aye, well, as ah said, try to get away rather than give yerselves up. Buff, yer in charge here,' he ordered. Just then Liam hurried in. He stopped short, open-mouthed when he saw Murdoch in his old infantry uniform.

'What's the matter with yer? Stop gawkin'! Have yer never seen a soldier before?' boomed Murdoch, fastening his regulation gun belt around his waist.

'Yeah, but ah mean... well...' struggled Liam.

'Look, ah ain't got time to explain. Get yersel' three men an' set up a barricade at the gate. Hold that till ah return; if ah don't, hold it for as long as possible so that Miss Lucy and Starlight can escape. Buff, ah know, will want to get to grips with the Colonel if it gets that bad,' Murdoch quickly ordered.

'Right.' Liam without thinking stood to attention; then, realising where he was, he turned and hurried out of the room.

'Aye, ah can still do it after all these years.' Murdoch winked after Liam as he left; then he too walked out of the room.

Lucy hurried as far as the lounge doorway; she could not drive herself to go any further, tears welled up in her eyes as she remembered her father – she was afraid of the same fate for this larger-than-life friend of hers. Murdoch stepped proudly upon the porch in his scarlet jacket with dark blue collar and cuffs, colours as deep now as they had been the day he was issued with it. The gold braid was still as bright as his buttons and his medals, which he now wore upon his left breast, pinned above his plaid, which was in the government tartan of dark green and dark blue. This was the tartan of the 42nd Royal Highland Regiment, which also made up his trews. His waist belt not only carried his revolver but also his skean-dhu, the traditional dagger worn by all Scotsmen in traditional dress. His boots were topped by a pair of brilliant white gaiters, that his trews were tucked into. Sergeant Hackett and his men sat upon their horses open-mouthed as they waited for him to lead them towards the Devil's Cut.

'Dear me, Mad Dog, we are not going on parade, are we?' questioned Hackett, sniggering at the sight that presented itself to him.

' "One cannot be too well dressed fer the enemy", as my old colonel used to declare,' Murdoch replied as he placed his white Wolseley helmet squarely upon his head. Then he too mounted up and led them out of the corral towards Devil's Cut. 'Come, we must hurry; our friends are trying to buy us time,' he said over his shoulder, as he quickly spurred his horse on to greater efforts.

Sandy and Charlotte sat upon the rock, chatting. Sandy held her hand gently as he kept her calm. Their conversation was not of anything important, he simply wanted to keep her mind occupied. Suddenly he noticed a slight movement across the meadow among the trees.

'Ah, here we go,' he announced as he let go of Charlotte's hand and picked up his rifle.

Charlotte followed his gaze. 'Thank you, Sandy, but I never get as nervous now as I used to.' She touched his arm. She quickly glanced across at Will and Paddy. They too were readying themselves, having also noticed the movement among the trees.

One rider then two appeared, soon they were all riding across the meadow. Halfway across, the Colonel called a halt, and from where they sat Sandy and Charlotte could see him issuing orders. He placed two or three riders ahead of himself in the line, then moved on.

Charlotte recognised the two riders immediately behind the Colonel as the two men from the jailhouse back at Richmond. Will had strictly forbidden any one to shoot them. 'They must be taken alive,' he had ordered.

'Aha – as expected, the big man wants someone else to take the first shot,' hissed Paddy, as he and Will also observed the Colonel ordering three riders ahead of himself.

'That's all right, Paddy. As you know, we shall not be shooting at the first three anyway,' smiled Will in response.

Sandy placed his two remaining bombs upon the rock in front of him. Will had done the same with his four.

As the riders drew ever closer, Sandy placed his hand upon Charlotte's shoulder. 'Keep your pretty head down, Charlie. Remember, set 'em alight,' he hissed.

Charlotte turned to glance at him; she placed her hand upon his and smiled, then nodded briefly in response.

Finally the first three riders rode past below where the four agents hid from view. Will crept to the edge and as Black Bob rode past him he fired the first shot into the man directly behind him. On that signal, Paddy, Charlotte and Sandy all opened fire; Sandy had turned his attention to the rear of the line, just to cause confusion.

Four riders fell dead immediately; some horses reared upon their hind legs, throwing men to the ground, while those who remained in their saddles turned and tried to ride through the milling throng behind them.

'Stand fast, stand fast!' shouted the Colonel as he and the first three riders dismounted and, hiding behind some rocks, began to fire back at the top of the rock.

His orders, though, went unheeded as his men panicked. Another round of shots rang out from the top of the rock above them and four more riders fell dead. Those in the gorge only had one thing on their minds at the present time, and that was to get out of the trap and attack on foot from the grassy meadow beyond. This is what most of them attempted to do now.

Charlotte fired into the milling throng below when she became aware of shots pinging away harmlessly around both her and Sandy. She quickly realised that these shots could only be coming from behind them, so she turned her attention towards the Colonel and the three riders with him.

Barney and Bob had ridden on a little way before they too dismounted and placed themselves behind some bushes for cover. From there they could quickly assess the situation and react as they saw fit.

Will had now tossed two bombs in among those trying to gain ground in front of them on foot.

Murdoch and those riding with him could now hear the shooting ahead of them. 'Der yer hear that, lads? Those are our friends. Come on!' he shouted. As they rounded a curve in the track they saw for themselves the defile ahead of them. It appeared that four of the men had got behind Will and his companions' position. These were the Colonel and the first three riders. Others were shooting from the grassy meadow beyond the defile.

'Come on, lads! Charge!' shouted Murdoch, and together as

one mass the seven men rode into the fray. The Colonel and one of the riders with him quickly hurried over to one side; each fired one shot at the oncoming riders as they did so. One shot whistled away harmlessly but the other passed through Murdoch's arm. He winced in pain as he quickly glanced at his arm, but as the bullet had just passed through flesh he carried on. The other two men belonging to the Colonel were not so quick and were gunned down where they stood.

'To hell with this!' cursed Bob, as he withdrew his gun and shot the man standing alongside the Colonel, while Barney quickly pulled his gun out and held it to the Colonel's head.

'Now then, Colonel, ah promised yer ah'd bring yer to the four bounty hunters. An' ah have, but ah think ah'd best take yer gun,' remarked Barney as he cocked his pistol in the Colonel's ear.

The Colonel turned to face him, hatred written all over his face. 'Why, yer yella-bellied snake! Don't ever turn yer back on me son, 'cause ah jist might shoot yer down like the dog that yer are,' he sneered as he handed over his pistol.

Murdoch and Sergeant Hackett had ridden on through the defile, followed by their men. Here, several dead riders lay around the ground while several others had taken cover and were returning fire at the rock face. Both Murdoch and the sergeant despatched two more riders, before those in the meadow realised and turned their guns on the newcomers. Within a very short space of time, Sergeant Hackett had been shot through the shoulder and Murdoch had had his horse shot from under him. Constable Courtney, who been directly behind them as they rode into the fray, now lay upon the ground next to Murdoch, dead, a single neat hole drilled through his forehead. As for the rest of Murdoch's men, they now quickly dismounted and began to use the cover of the rocks to force the riders back away from the defile.

Will, Paddy and Charlotte clambered down onto the ground, where they quickly joined Murdoch and Hackett.

Sandy remained upon the vantage point, picking off each of the riders in turn, as they struggled to deal with both his shots and those from behind rocks at them.

'Are you all right, Murdoch?' Charlotte asked as she began to administer first aid to his arm.

'Och, ah'm all right, missy, it's just a wee scratch,' Murdoch smiled back. 'But did yer see me charge in? Was ah no' a bonny fighter?' he boasted.

Sergeant Hackett was in a little more pain; the bullet had passed through his shoulder. Charlotte quickly bandaged it up in a sling for him after she had cleaned out his wound.

The shooting began to subside, as the remaining riders, having lost their mounts, surrendered. It was just as well that they did, for shortly after that Grey Wolf, Two Crows and Black Eagle appeared with several Indian warriors.

'Hello, Grey Wolf – ah'm afraid yer missed the party,' greeted Murdoch as he sat upon a rock, resting.

'I see the redcoats are still as brave and strong as our ancestors portrayed them many years ago,' Grey Wolf smiled as he took Murdoch's hand in friendship.

Their attention was now drawn by Will. 'Ah, here is our quarry,' he remarked, as he caught sight of Barney and Bob marching the Colonel towards them through the cutting.

'Ah thought yer might want this back,' suggested Barney jovially, as he pushed the Colonel forward.

'Thank yer, my friend, that's most kind of yer,' replied Paddy as he took control of the prisoner.

'Barney, Bob, meet Sergeant Hackett of the North-West Mounted Police and Murdoch McLeod, a landowner in this district,' Will introduced them.

'Howdy, that was some cavalry charge there yer performed, mister,' smiled Barney.

'Aye, ah was performing them properly when yer were still in yer nappies, laddie,' answered Murdoch.

They quickly assessed the situation. Both Hackett and Murdoch had but one man each with them, while there were still the Colonel and twenty riders to take into captivity.

'Ah wants to know on what grounds yer intend to hold me,' demanded the Colonel.

Murdoch and Will turned to face him. 'What did yer say?' growled Murdoch.

'What crime have ah committed here in yer territory?' the Colonel asked.

'Well, apart from taking arms against Her Majesty—' began Sergeant Hackett.

'Is that it? I should be out by the time I stand trial, then,' the Colonel went on arrogantly.

'Oh, an' what about murder?' questioned Murdoch.

'Murder? Ah've murdered no one,' stated the Colonel.

'Oh, but yer have – what about Mr Wightman?' asked Murdoch.

'Who?' snorted the Colonel. 'Ah don't know who yer goin' on about.'

'Yer'll hang fer that,' warned Murdoch with a smile.

'Prove it!' challenged the Colonel.

'That should be easy; we have a witness,' he retorted.

The Colonel sat down and glanced about him. Will had just placed the handcuffs that Sergeant Hackett had given him upon the Colonel's hands.

'Who is this witness?' he eventually asked.

'Yer'll see soon enough.' Murdoch stood up. 'So what now?' he asked Will.

Will looked about him, then sniffed the air. 'Back at Richmond, I made a deal with these two gentlemen: if they assisted us in bringing the Colonel into our net, then we would help them capture Ted and his gang,' he explained.

'Go on,' said Murdoch thoughtfully.

'Well, they led the Colonel to us, so we should now uphold our side of the bargain and ride for Pinewood Falls, where Ted is,' suggested Paddy.

'Yer can do, but ah'd hate to disappoint yer,' replied Murdoch.

'Oh – how?' asked Will.

'Ted is no longer at Pinewood Falls; he is more than likely at Valley,' Murdoch went on.

'Where?' asked Will.

'It's an old prospectors' settlement, just inside American territory. It's been abandoned for some years now; the settlers were driven out by yez truly here.' Murdoch jerked a thumb at the Colonel.

'Is it far?' asked Barney.

'Naw, ah'll take yer there myself,' offered Murdoch.

'But Murdoch, you've been hurt!' cried a concerned Charlotte.

'Ah, lassie, yer concern is most reassuring. But ah've had worse scratches fightin' the fuzzy-wuzzies,' he smiled.

'Who?' asked Charlotte.

'Don't ask,' retorted Sandy as he shook his head.

'More importantly, can you, Sergeant Hackett, take these prisoners back to Paradise?' asked Will.

'Certainly, with the help of our native friends here.' He gestured to Grey Wolf and Two Crows. 'That should be no problem.'

'Right, that means if you're willing to lead us to this abandoned settlement, Murdoch, it'll be seven of us against seven of them – even odds,' smiled Will.

'To be sure, to be sure,' smiled Paddy.

'Before you go, Sergeant, I have this bag for you,' stated Will as he walked over to his horse and removed the carpet bag. This he then placed upon Hackett's saddle.

'Now that's a fine sight,' smiled the sergeant as he patted the bag with his good hand.

They then began to collect their guns and horses, while Sergeant Hackett went about sorting out the collecting of the dead. He used Grey Wolf's men as well as Murdoch's. When all was ready the two groups left in opposite directions.

'Tell Lucy not to worry, ah shall be back by nightfall,' said Murdoch in parting to Sergeant Hackett, who nodded and waved in response.

'So we don't have far to go?' asked Will.

'Nope, just the next valley,' replied Murdoch.

'So they wouldn't have heard all the shooting going on here then,' guessed Charlotte.

'Nope, they won't even know we're coming,' smiled Murdoch.

Tomahawk Joe now scoured the grassy verge about the old settlement in Indian Creek. 'They go east.' He pointed towards the crest of the valley.

'Well, I'm afraid that's Canada, and I have strict instructions not to go anywhere near the place,' declared the young officer.

'It appears that Grey Wolf and his people may have gone that way too, sir,' admitted the wily Sergeant Rodgers.

'Unhappily that may be so, but orders are orders. I'm as disappointed as yourself, Sergeant. Are you sure these horse tracks are not Indian?' he questioned.

'No, they are not, sir,' answered the sergeant. 'These tracks show the horses had shoes; Injuns don't put shoes on their horses.'

'But one of those chased was an Indian, you say?' questioned the officer.

'That's correct, sir – at least one of those chased was, sir,' admitted the sergeant.

'Hmmm.' The officer rubbed his chin in thought. 'Most puzzling.'

'Well, sir, if it were that posse, they've chased them all the way into Canada,' observed the sergeant as he scratched his head.

'Quite,' replied the officer, as he looked up at the crest of the valley concerned. 'Sergeant, what is that town called down this valley?' he then asked, as if pulling himself back into reality.

'Pinewood Falls, sir,' replied Sergeant Rodgers.

'Then we shall ride down to there and rest a while, before returning to Richmond,' ordered the officer.

'Sir.' The sergeant saluted as he organised his men to set off once more.

'Missy, missy!' called Brown Buffalo, as he watched the procession enter the Paradise Ranch corral.

Lucy hurried to the door to see how Murdoch was, only to shriek in horror when she saw that he was not there.

'I'm sorry to have shocked you, Miss Lucy,' apologised Sergeant Hackett, as he observed her on the house porch.

'Murdoch, where is Murdoch?' she cried, fearing the worst.

'He's all right, ma'am; he has led our friends towards Valley. He asked me to assure you of his return this evening,' comforted Sergeant Hackett.

'Oh, thank heavens… when ah failed to see him, ah feared the worst, Sergeant. But come, yer wounded. Let me see to yer wounds.' She gestured towards the sergeant.

He quickly issued orders for the placement of the prisoners, which were quickly dealt with by Liam. Then, saying his farewells to Grey Wolf and his tribesmen, he followed Lucy into the house.

THE AVENGING ANGELS

Hannah and Elizabeth were strolling casually along the parapet of Drumloch Castle. The weather was warm and they chatted gaily about the lighter points of daily life.

'Ooh, excuse me, Elizabeth, I must check the telegraphy office before we return,' remembered Hannah.

Elizabeth squeezed Hannah's arm. 'Do you feel that Charlotte and her team will be all right?' she asked a little hesitantly.

Hannah placed a reassuring hand upon hers as they stepped into the corridor. 'I'm sure they will be fine, Elizabeth. Please wait here,' she said as they reached the office door.

Elizabeth stood, afraid to breathe, as she awaited Hannah, who had stepped into the office. She did not have long to wait, thankfully, as Hannah quickly reappeared. A broad radiant smile lit up her beautiful face.

'You see, I told you all would be well!' She waved a piece of paper in front of Elizabeth.

'Oh, Hannah, I'm so pleased,' replied Elizabeth as the pair clasped hands like two schoolgirls. Excited they both hurried towards Lord Porter's office, where Hannah took her leave and knocked upon the door. As Elizabeth hurried away to inform Charles, she heard Lord Porter beckon his assistant into the office in his usual husky tone.

The young lieutenant led his army half-troop of cavalry into Pinewood Falls; they rode slowly in pairs, so as to give the impression of an organised military bearing. The townsfolk lined the street to watch as they rode up to the sheriff's office. There Calvin stood awaiting them.

'Well howdy, Lieutenant,' he greeted the newcomer.

'Good afternoon, Sheriff,' replied the officer as he paused next to the jailhouse.

'It's mighty fine of yer to turn up so quickly; ah was fearin' the worst an' that Ted would get away,' Calvin commented.

The lieutenant looked at the sheriff sceptically. 'Oh, is there a problem, Sheriff?' he asked.

The sheriff paused. 'Why, ah'm sorry, Lieutenant, ah thought yer was here to help catch the Ted Skerrat Gang – after all what they did, an' all.'

The lieutenant dismounted, followed by his sergeant. 'I think, Sheriff, we should go inside and you may explain exactly what has gone on.' Then, turning to his sergeant, the officer said, 'Rodgers, come with me. Stand the men down, let them rest and they can cook their meals here,' he ordered.

The sergeant nodded and saluted, then relayed the orders. The cavalry rode towards the end of the street, where they set up camp and soon began to cook their meals.

The sergeant then hurried back to the sheriff's office, where he found the officer now sat behind the desk and Calvin opposite, pacing backwards and forwards.

'OK, Sheriff, tell me if you will what has happened here,' instructed the young officer.

'Well, it's like this, yer see,' began the sheriff, excitedly waving his hands about. 'Yesterday evening, Ted Skerrat an' his boys rode into town. They pulled up across the street at Texas Rose's. She was a close friend of his, yer see... Anyhow, this time he loses his temper with her an' kills her. He accused her o' stealin' something from her.'

'Do you know what it was that was stolen?' asked the officer, as he wrote down notes.

'Naw, nobody appears to know. Anyhow, after he kills her in his fit of temper he kills another girl, then threatens the rest of the staff,' the sheriff went on.

'And where were you, during all of this?'

'Well, that's when ah turned up, ah sent ma deputy round the back.'

'Oh, and where is he now?'

'They killed him later. But in the meantime, ah sent him rounds the back and entered the front with some support.' The sheriff paused.

'Go on, Sheriff,' urged the officer.

'Well, ah arrested Ted and disarmed the rest of his gang. Ah told them to stay in the saloon, but unhappily, through the night, they must have crept over here and broke poor Ned's neck.'

'Ned? Who was Ned?'

'He was ma deputy – didn't deserve to die,' the sheriff said quietly.

'All right, Sheriff, go on.'

'Well, they obviously sprung Ted and headed out of town.'

'Do you know in which direction they went?'

'Yep, they forded the river and headed north; they will be clear into Canada by now,' assured the sheriff.

The young lieutenant closed his notebook slowly. 'Regrettably, if they've gone to Canada there isn't much we can do about it,' he said forlornly.

'Well, they could be holed up at an old prospectors' settlement just this side of the border,' suggested the sheriff hopefully.

'Can you take us there?' asked the officer.

'Of course – would yer want me to gather in some of the boys?' offered the sheriff.

'How many are we chasing here?'

'Seven, including Ted.'

The officer smiled. 'No, I think thirty troopers should be sufficient,' he replied.

'Aye, that should do it all right,' nodded the sheriff thoughtfully.

'Good, we will ride in an hour, to give my men a chance to rest and check their mounts over,' the officer suggested; he stood and, followed by his sergeant, he left the jailhouse and walked towards the men's bivouacs.

'We may be able to salvage something out of this after all, Sergeant. I do not intend to go back totally empty-handed,' mused the officer to his companion.

'No, sir, but if the outlaws rode here into town last night, who was the other posse chasin' up Indian Creek?' asked a puzzled Sergeant Rodgers.

Murdoch led the little group down the small tree-covered track towards the back of the old settlement. He paused as he took stock of where everyone was. They could see Ted and some of his men sat by the fire; another two, one of whom was older, stood a little way down the street – this was Abe and Joshua. All of the horses were tied under the large tree in the centre of what had been the green at one time, not far from their fire.

'Ah suggest we leave our horses here, an' continue on foot,' whispered Murdoch.

They tied their horses up at that point and continued on foot in single file, taking their time to creep around to the base of the incline. This brought them out behind a deserted cabin, so that they were hidden from view where Joshua and Abe kept watch. Murdoch carefully peered around the corner towards the track that ran along the riverbank back towards Pinewood Falls.

'Now, ah reckon if two or three of us should creep along the back here…' he indicated with his hand which way to go, so there would be no misunderstanding… 'an' the rest of us go this way an' take out the two sentries in that cabin there.' He pointed at the next cabin along, where occasionally the shadow of Abe could be seen moving about.

'I'll go this way,' suggested Sandy, as he crept to the front.

'I'll come with you,' added Charlotte, with a gentle nod.

'And count me in,' added Will.

Murdoch glanced about him. 'Good, we shall give yer five minutes to get around the other side of the camp before we rush them here,' he suggested.

Will smiled. 'Thanks, good luck.' Then, following Sandy and Charlotte, he crept off along a broken-down log fence, then behind another building before reaching a ditch. Here Sandy and Charlotte waited for him before they continued, Sandy leading. They moved quickly and silently in short bursts from cover to cover. Not a word was said until they were level with the old village green. Sandy at this point left the ditch and crept up to the back of an old dilapidated shed. He carefully peered through a gap in the wall; then, turning back towards Will and Charlotte, he held up four fingers, indicating that four people stood or sat about the fire. There was one missing and he frantically searched around for him. At first he could not see anything, then he caught a glimpse of the missing person. It was the Kid, and he was searching through a cabin further to Sandy's right, looking for firewood. Sandy crept back to the ditch.

'Right, we're now opposite the fire. There are four men sat or stood by it, the fifth is over there.' He pointed with a jerk of his thumb to where the Kid was. 'I'll go and deal with him. You two stay here; when the balloon goes up, they will be stood right in front of you,' he smiled.

'All right, Sandy, but no heroics,' warned Will.

Sandy smiled. 'Just set 'em alight,' he said and hurried away.

Charlotte stopped him and touched his arm. 'Take care, Sandy,' she urged.

He glanced at her and smiled, kissing his fingers; he then placed them upon her lips. 'Don't fret, I'm allergic to pain,' and with that he hurried off.

He crept around the back of the cabins stealthily, trying to place where the Kid was. It was not really difficult, as the unsuspecting Kid was making enough noise to awake the dead. Sandy had now left the cover of the ditch behind him and had made the wooden fence which surrounded the cabin that the Kid was busy dismantling. Sandy carefully and silently climbed over the fence and edged slowly up behind the old water tub next to the door. Suddenly, shooting and shouting was heard from the other end of town – the five minutes that Murdoch had given them was up.

'Come on, lads, follow me,' urged Murdoch, but he was stalled by Paddy, who held his arm.

'Not this time, Murdoch. With Macootcha here ah'll blow anyone who tries to stop us away. Please follow me,' Paddy smiled and pushed past the big Scotsman.

'It's not worth dyin' fer,' Murdoch replied, slightly put out.

Paddy hurried around to the front of the cabin that Joshua and Abe stood in. Abe had caught a glimpse of Paddy hurrying past the window, but he moved too quickly for Abe to shoot at, so he then hurried out through the door, appearing right in front of Paddy. Both brought their guns up to shoot, but Paddy was by far the quicker with his shotgun. The blast caught Abe in the stomach and threw him backwards up the street. He lay upon his back, coughing and holding his wounds.

'Top o' the morning to yer,' greeted Paddy as he rushed past the prostrate body of Abe.

He was followed by Murdoch, who glanced down at the dying outlaw before hurrying on. Joshua hurried out of the house right in front of Barney, who clubbed him with the butt of his pistol as a matter of instinct and knocked him to the ground. Bob then stood over him and cuffed the younger McCabe brother where he lay, then dragged him over to where his brother lay dying.

Paddy's shot had the effect of making those by the fire leap up; they began to run in all directions, panic stricken. Will and Charlotte began to fire at the hurrying figures to add to the panic. Sandy had by now just settled behind the water tub when the Kid came bursting out of the cabin. Sandy hit him as hard as he could under the chin with the butt of his rifle, which sent the Kid flying back through the door. Sandy hurried into the cabin, but the Kid was not done yet. As he lay on his back upon the ground he kicked the door shut with all his might upon Sandy. This in turn knocked Sandy to one side and he dropped his rifle; both scrambled to their feet, and Sandy punched the Kid with the flat of his hand, bursting the Kid's nose, while the Kid in turn kicked Sandy hard in the groin, forcing him to his knees.

As Sandy doubled up in pain, the Kid punched him to the ground.

'Yer!' exclaimed the Kid when he recognised Sandy. 'Yer the hero with luscious Lucy. Well, ah said ah'd teach yer a lesson,' he sneered, and withdrew his hunting knife. The Kid lunged forward, as Sandy lay on his back upon the ground, dagger in hand, but again Sandy was ready. He quickly placed his foot upon the advancing Kid's stomach and threw him over his head into a pile of junk. As quick as he could, Sandy scrambled to his knees and pulled his bayonet from its sheath; by now the Kid was lunging at him once more. All Sandy had time for was to hold his arm out straight with his bayonet in hand. It all happened as quick as a flash as the Kid impaled himself upon the sword. He stopped abruptly and looked at Sandy, puzzled, trying to figure out where the pain was coming from and why he had stopped. He glanced down at his midriff; Sandy was still holding his sword bayonet at arm's length.

'Teach me a lesson, will you? Well, this one's from Lucy.' Sandy smiled callously into the dying Kid's face as he pushed him to the ground. There he placed his boot squarely upon the other man's chest and pulled his sword bayonet clear of the dead man.

'Far too good to waste on you,' Sandy added to the corpse. He then wiped his blade clean upon the man's coat-tails.

Charlotte had hurried around to the most northerly part of the village using the various cabins and buildings for cover so that she was now beyond Sandy's cabin. She had noticed Ted making for this cabin and could occasionally see him fire his pistol out of what used to be a window. She crept around the back of the building and peered carefully around the back door frame. Little did she realise, however, that she was being watched and tracked by Danny. He had also dived for cover in among these last two cabins, and as he looked about his new surroundings he had noticed Charlotte creeping ever closer to the cabin Ted was using next door. True to form, Danny fired off two shots towards the now oncoming figures of Paddy and Murdoch, before he began to creep carefully towards Charlotte.

Frenchy and Joe had panicked and run in the opposite direction to Ted and Danny, so that they actually ran towards Paddy and Murdoch. Random shots were now being fired all over the place at targets genuine and imagined. In between each shot the desperate voice of Joshua could be heard shouting.

'Ted, Ted, they've got Abe! He's a-dying, Ted!'

Murdoch had been running behind Paddy when two or three shots whizzed close by and Paddy threw himself into a cabin up ahead of them. Murdoch felt he could not make it and paused in his tracks; he threw himself behind a rickety old log fence, just as he was shot once more through his right arm. He glanced down and sighed disappointedly. 'Och, ma best clean uniform! Ah'm goin' to have more holes in me than one o' those tea strainers,' he cursed. He rolled on to his stomach and glanced through a gap under some logs. He noticed and heard running feet coming towards him, so he waited until they were almost upon him then leaped up, right in front of Frenchy, who stopped dead in his tracks.

'*Mon Dieu!*' he exclaimed in total surprise, dropping his gun. This had no effect on Murdoch, who quickly raised his revolver and fired one shot right through Frenchy's head, killing him instantly.

Murdoch paused as he recocked his gun. 'Ah can still knock 'em bandy,' he said, then instantly ducked behind a barrow as two more shots rained in from Joe.

Ted had noticed Paddy in the next cabin along from him and was now firing incessantly into the old building, which made Paddy duck down behind some cover. Charlotte saw her opportunity and quickly leaped into the cabin. Ted heard her and spun round, only for Charlotte to kick the gun from his hand.

'Well, well, looky here! Ah've got myself some blonde broad to keep me company,' he sneered contemptuously and pulled out his hunting knife.

Charlotte laughed. 'You'll need more than your toothpick to nail me.'

They stepped around the cabin, each trying to force the other into a sudden rash movement. Eventually Ted could wait no more and he lunged at Charlotte; this was what she had been waiting for and she stepped to one side as Ted's outstretched arm which held his knife shot past her. She then clasped it tightly by her side with her own arm, and swung her free arm, chopping his windpipe and knocking him to the floor. Quickly, and before he could react, she pressed her weight against his wrist, forcing him to drop his knife. This she kicked to one side, before he pushed her away.

Hoping that he'd knocked her off balance, he quickly rushed at her, but again she was able to grab his wrist as he rushed past her. This time she brought her elbow down hard against the back of his arm, breaking it instantly. He cried in pain as a loud sickening crack was heard, and slumped to the floor holding his now limp arm.

'Do you surrender?' she asked politely as she bent forward, holding out a hand with which to help Ted up.

As she did so, a shot whizzed past her shoulder and she quickly glanced around to see where it had gone. She was just in time to see Danny fall back out of the doorway. Charlotte turned to see who had fired the shot – there through the old window frame stood Will. He dramatically blew the smoke away from his gun.

'One should always check one's back,' he smiled.

'Who the hell are you?' groaned Ted as he scrambled to his knees and nursed his shattered arm.

'Think of us as the avenging angels,' smiled Charlotte.

Joe had been keeping both Paddy and Murdoch pinned against the cabin wall quite successfully. But Barney had crept up on him from behind, using the sound of the gunshots as a way of locating him. Joe was so engrossed with those ahead of him he neither heard nor saw Barney behind him until Barney cocked his gun in his ear.

'Howdy,' Barney said casually. 'Now, do yer wish to come peacefully, or do yer wish to join yer friends?'

Joe stopped and stood up slowly, raising both hands.

'Good lad,' announced Barney. 'Yer know it makes sense,' he added as he took Joe's gun.

The place fell silent except for Joshua, who still called for Ted. 'Ted, Abe's dyin', Ted!' was all he could shout.

Sandy strolled over to the old campfire, where he was joined by Charlotte. He smiled at her. 'Everything all right?' he asked.

'Yes, thank you,' she replied as she slipped her hand in his.

Will brought Ted over towards the fire; he had now handcuffed his hands to the front, owing to his arm being broken.

'Sit there and don't groan too loud,' he ordered.

'Would it make any difference?' moaned Ted through gritted teeth.

'No,' answered Will.

Paddy and Murdoch appeared, followed by Barney and Joe, who was also handcuffed but with his hands behind him. Then Bob appeared with a totally disconsolate Joshua, and almost threw him to the ground.

'Well, is that it?' demanded Bob, as he looked about the group.

'Yep, Abe's dead, that we know of.' Barney pointed back in the direction from which they had entered the village.

'The Kid is lying over there,' gestured Sandy.

'I nailed a Canadian or Frenchman,' announced Murdoch.

'That would be Frenchy,' corrected Barney.

'The seventh member I shot over there,' indicated Will.

'OK, we'll sort them all out an' have a brew,' declared Barney as he re-holstered his gun.

The dead were all quickly picked up and strapped across their horses; their guns were collected, while the prisoners were tied together below the old tree. Paddy and Charlotte had gone to collect their horses from the small track at the back of the settlement. They returned with them and tied them to the tree next to where Ted and his gang had previously tied theirs. Once they had cleaned everything up, the victors then sat around the fire.

'Well, I do declare that, that was a good day's work,' announced Will as he drank some coffee.

'Yip, certainly was – it was mighty fine of yer to help us get our man,' added Barney.

'Think nothing of it, old man. You assisted us in leading the Colonel into our trap,' smiled Will. At this Charlotte, Paddy and Sandy now sniggered.

'Yer caught the Colonel, too?' cried a startled Joe.

'Shut up, numbskull,' growled Ted.

'Ah wouldn't fret yersel', Ted. We know that yer were workin' fer the Colonel. That's why we went lookin' fer him,' informed Murdoch.

'Yer'll regret this – he'll get off an' set us free, too,' announced Ted defiantly.

His captors all laughed. 'Not this time, he won't,' predicted Charlotte happily.

'Nope, we've got him on a murder charge this time, among other things. He'll hang fer sure,' declared Murdoch.

'Ah don't think so; yer'll need witnesses,' snarled Ted.

'We have one – an eyewitness, no less,' smiled Murdoch.

It was at that point that Charlotte realised Murdoch had been shot through the arm a second time.

'Oh, Murdoch – you're hurt!' she announced as she hurried to his side, immediately investigating the hole in his sleeve.

'Och, lassie, as ah said earlier, it's nothing. A mere scratch, that's all,' he tried to assure her.

'I'll be the judge of that, thank you. Now come on, let me have a look at it.' She dismissed his argument and fumbled through her saddlebag for a bandage and some ointment. 'Now, Murdoch, please remove your jacket,' she ordered.

Murdoch began to moan and growl in protest.

'Ah wouldn't, if ah were you. She'll argue till the cows come home, and as always she will win,' warned Paddy.

'Och, woman,' moaned Murdoch as he removed his jacket.

Charlotte quickly began cleaning and dealing with the wound, placing a bit of lint upon the wound as she had done earlier, then she bandaged it up. 'You are prone to accidents, Murdoch, aren't you?' she smiled as she finished dealing with his arm and put everything back in her saddlebag.

'Och, well, thank yer anyway, lassie,' responded Murdoch awkwardly.

Once refreshed they prepared to leave the old settlement behind. Will shook Barney's hand.

'Thank you again for your assistance,' he said. Then, glancing at the train of horses all tied together. 'Will you manage these down to Pinewood Falls?' he asked.

'Yeah, sure; it's been a pleasure. It was worth the sight of him chargin' around in that red coat if nothing else,' replied Barney as he jerked a thumb at Murdoch.

'Hey – this is ma best uniform! Ah'd make soldiers of yer yet,' he declared defiantly.

The others laughed. 'Nar thanks, we have enough of our own,' remarked Bob as he sat in his saddle.

'It's a pity Marshall Roscoe and his deputy aren't here to witness this,' sighed a despondent Barney.

'Yer should ask yer friends here about the whereabouts of the marshal,' suggested Paddy.

'Oh? Why is that?' asked Barney.

'They shot them – didn't you?' challenged Charlotte.

Ted gave an arrogant snigger. 'It weren't jist us, yer'll need to see the sheriff, too.'

'What – the sheriff was in the Colonel's pay also?' questioned Barney.

'Everyone was,' answered Ted indignantly.

'Yer'll all pay fer that,' threatened a now annoyed Barney.

'Ah'll tell the authorities that we was set upon by the British. Yer won't get away with this, it'll cause a major incident,' snarled Ted.

'You will require proof,' remarked Paddy.

'What more proof do ah need?' he retorted as he held up his shackled hands.

'I'm sure Barney and Bob were able to set upon you as you all sat around the campfire,' mused Will.

'Yeah, an' what about ma broken arm?' questioned Ted.

'So the big Ted Skerrat is willing to admit he was beaten up and arrested by a beautiful lady?' mocked Sandy, he sniggered.

'Argh,' growled Ted in response.

'Don't worry, yer secret is safe with us,' assured Barney.

'Again, many thanks. At least we can say that we played our part in taming this wild border country,' smiled Will once more.

Finally they each wished the others farewell in turn, as the two groups parted. Barney, with Bob in the rear, led the prisoners south towards the town of Pinewood Falls, while Murdoch led the group back up the small track towards Paradise Ranch.

Back in town, the young lieutenant returned to the sheriff's office.

'Now then, Sheriff, if we manage to apprehend these gunmen, who were responsible for the saloon shooting, have you the men to keep watch over them satisfactorily while in the cell here? Or would you prefer us to escort them down to Harper's Crossing and try them there?' he asked Calvin.

'Actually, Lieutenant, that sounds like a mighty fine solution. Ah don't know if ah could find a replacement fer Ned in time,' responded the sheriff.

'Now then, did you take witness statements from all those present?' the young officer asked.

'Sure did,' replied Calvin, leaping to his feet; he hurried over to a cabinet and opened it.

Just then Sergeant Rodgers stepped into the office. 'Ah've gathered all of the witnesses together in the saloon, sir,' he stated to his officer.

Calvin glanced from one to the other. 'What's the matter? Don't yer trust me or something?' he asked suspiciously.

'It's not that, Sheriff, but as you're aware if I'm to go chasing after a bunch of no-good outlaws, I want to be aware of the full picture,' explained the officer, nonchalantly stepping out of the office.

He and his sergeant crossed the street. 'We need to keep an eye on our sheriff – there is something amiss here, but I do not know what it is,' the officer said as they entered the saloon.

Lieutenant Hudson then walked over to a table which was positioned so that as he took the various statements he could face the saloon door and see if anybody entered. His sergeant was to stand behind him and keep an eye on order. The first witness was brought forward and the lieutenant picked up his pen; it was one of the young girls.

'Now then, miss, I believe you were a witness to the shooting of the two girls in here last night,' he began.

The young girl nodded and began speaking; he wrote everything down. The sheriff was conspicuous in his absence. Finally, after all the girls were interviewed, it was the turn of Bert the bartender.

'You were the bartender, were you not?' asked Lieutenant Hudson.

'That ah was,' he replied.

'And you witnessed the shooting of the two girls?'

'No, 'cause Rosie was killed upstairs in her room, by Ted's own hands. Ah was only a witness to the shootin' of Kate.'

'Did yer hear Rosie getting killed?'

'Well, ah heard a lot of commotion, but we couldn't do anything as the rest of his men were down here in the saloon, as usual.'

The young officer paused and glanced at the man. 'What d'yer mean, "as usual"?' he asked deliberately.

The bartender swallowed hard, realising he had let slip a piece of information that he might suffer for. 'Well, whenever the gang was in town, they always stayed here… Ted and Rosie were quite close.'

Hudson now glanced at Rodgers. 'Was the sheriff aware of this arrangement?'

'Oh yeah – he was told by the Colonel to leave Ted an' his boys alone. If there was any bother, then he would deal with it personally.'

'So why was the Colonel not sought originally?'

'Oh he was, but he had other business to attend to – or so we was told.'

'By whom?'

'By one of his riders. The sheriff sent one of them riders off to fetch the Colonel, but he returned early this mornin' alone.'

'Who is in charge of the riders?' asked the officer.

'A man named Blue.'

'Where can I find this man, Blue?'

'He'll be over at the bank, ah guess,' the bartender replied thoughtfully.

Lieutenant Hudson stopped writing; he turned the sheet of paper around and offered the pen to the bartender. 'Sign here, please.' He pointed to a spot on the sheet at the bottom.

Bert took the pen and signed his name.

'I'm surprised the authorities have not investigated this before,' mused the young lieutenant.

'Well, Lieutenant, there was a US marshal and his deputy turned up, not so long ago,' the bartender replied.

'Really? And what happened?'

'Ted, declared that he was fed up o' runnin', so he shot him, as well as the deputy.'

'What did the sheriff do?' asked a surprised Lieutenant.

'Well, he warn't too pleased an' there was a lot o' arguin'. The Colonel called fer Ted to go to Jefferson's Ranch.' The bartender paused. 'That was the last we heard until Ted returned.' He shrugged.

'All right, Bert, thank you,' said Lieutenant Hudson, dismissing the bartender.

The two soldiers watched the bartender leave the saloon.

'Well, Sergeant, what do you make of all that?' Hudson asked at length.

'We've certainly opened a can o' worms, sir,' replied the sergeant.

'Who is our fastest horseman?' the lieutenant asked, as springing to his feet.

'That would be Tomahawk Joe, sir, the Injun scout.'

'Then send him to Harper's Crossing with a message,' the officer replied; he did not look at his sergeant but kept his eyes upon the sheriff's office. 'Require legal representation in the form of a US marshal and deputy as soon as possible. Have uncovered irregularities in performing of legal duties by local sheriff and dignitaries. Shall remain in Pinewood Falls to maintain law and order.'

The sergeant wrote the message down as quickly and as neatly as possible; when he had finished the lieutenant glanced at him.

'Come on, Sergeant, fetch me four men,' he ordered.

The sergeant stiffened to attention and hurried out of the saloon; he detailed four men off. They all stood to attention by their horses, waiting to ride out. Next Sergeant Rodgers gave his message to his Indian scout friend. 'Ride like the wind, and try to keep off the beaten track,' he warned.

Tomahawk Joe nodded in response and, mounting his horse quickly, he rode off at a fast pace. The sergeant returned to the saloon, where Lieutenant Hudson and his four men were waiting.

'That's taken care of, sir – what now?' asked the sergeant.

'We are to arrest this Blue fellow and these riders, whoever they may be,' Lieutenant Hudson responded.

It was late afternoon when Barney and Bob led their small party of captives into town. They rode across the ford and for the first time they were not challenged by a sentry. That's odd, thought Barney as he glanced about the main street. Apart from several rows of army tents being lined up, everything appeared quiet, too quiet... As they drew level with the sheriff's office, Sergeant Rodgers stepped out of the doorway.

'Howdy, folks, ah see yer've been busy.' The sergeant nodded his head at those sat behind Barney, all tied up.

'Yep, name's Barney Greenway an' this is ma partner, Bob. We've been on the trail of—' Barney jerked his thumb over his shoulder towards Ted and his men; the sergeant held up his hand.

'Yer'd best step inside, gentlemen, an' inform ma lieutenant – he may have one or two questions fer yer,' explained the sergeant as he held Barney's horse.

'What about these?' asked the bounty hunter, flicking his head towards his captives as he dismounted.

'Oh, don't worry about them. We'll hold them fer yer,' smiled the sergeant.

Barney stepped upon the porch; two soldiers now stood

sentry at the doorway. He pushed the door open carefully and stepped inside. There he found a young lieutenant sat behind Calvin's desk. The lieutenant glanced up. 'Afternoon,' he greeted Barney.

'Howdy, Lieutenant,' smiled Barney.

'I am Lieutenant Hudson of the US army; at present I am upholding the law in this town. How may I help?' he glanced up at Barney.

'Barney Greenway, Lieutenant, an' ah'm a bounty hunter. Ma pardner an' me were assigned to track and apprehend an outlaw by the name of Ted Skerrat,' began Barney.

'Ah, this Ted Skerrat – I would like to know just who on earth he thinks he is,' the young officer moaned.

'Well, yer can ask him if yer want, Lieutenant,' smiled Barney.

The lieutenant leaped to his feet. 'You've caught him? You've captured Ted Skerrat?' he cried excitedly.

'Yep, me an' ma pardner, Bob. As ah said, Lieutenant, we were given the task of apprehendin' him and his gang for trial by the Dakota Territory and the State of Missouri,' explained Barney.

'Well, done, man,' beamed the young lieutenant. 'How many have you managed to bring in?'

'Three alive, including Ted and four dead.'

'Would you require any help taking them into Dakota?' asked the lieutenant hopefully.

Barney smiled. 'Yip, that would be mighty helpful, Lieutenant. Could we hold them here until yer ready?'

'Of course; I believe we have a vacant cell. Slip them in next to the departing sheriff,' smiled the lieutenant.

Barney turned to leave, then paused; he glanced back at the officer and the pair smiled at each other.

Murdoch and Storm Force Alpha were now approaching Paradise Ranch. Word of their approach must have been passed back to the house, for Lucy and Sergeant Hackett stood by the gate to welcome them back. As they neared the gate Lucy hurried forward; she then held Murdoch's horse and led it into the corral.

'Der yer recognise this young lady, sailor boy?' Murdoch turned to Sandy and smiled.

Sandy scratched his head. 'Well, I'll be blowed… it's Lucy, is it not?' he asked, astonished.

'And very pretty, she looks too,' complimented Paddy with a smile.

They reached the house and dismounted. Lucy hurried round to Charlotte and they fell into a friendly embrace.

'It's so good to see yer again; we were beginnin' to worry about yez, especially Murdoch,' Lucy explained excitedly.

'Was he!' exclaimed Charlotte in mock surprise, as they all turned to Murdoch.

'Och well, ah dinna want to be responsible fer yer all bein' killed,' he replied deprecatingly and hurried into his house.

The others followed; Murdoch took Will straight to the telegraphy machine.

'Here, send yer report,' he said then turned and left Will alone.

Will stood for a short time, taking in the feeling of the task now being completed. Then, smiling to himself, he sent off his report.

After being refreshed and changed they all met in the dining room for something to eat.

'Ah, real food,' remarked Paddy, as he sniffed the aroma of cooking.

'Yep, an it'll be cooked by Lucy an' Starlight no less,' boasted Murdoch proudly. Turning to his Brown Buffalo, he asked, 'Buff, fetch the drinks, please.'

Buff bowed and did as he was asked; as Lucy joined them at the table, Murdoch lifted up a steaming silver pot. 'Coffee?' he asked.

'What is this, Murdoch?' questioned Charlotte; she narrowed her eyes in mock suspicion. The others sniggered.

Murdoch looked rather sheepish as he struggled with his jacket collar, 'Ahh, yes ah cannae get the hang o' that tea yet, lassie, so ah'll have coffee instead,' he replied bashfully.

His guests burst out laughing.

'I would never have believed it if someone had told me,' commented Sergeant Hackett incredulously.

The revelry went on long into the night, as the tension and stress of the past few days left them and they were able to let their hair down. Even Murdoch dispensed with the formality of coffee for the time being, turning to whiskey – 'For medicinal purposes, ye understand…'

Hannah hurried into Lord Porter's office.

'What is it, my dear?' asked a concerned Lord Porter as he glanced up from his desk.

'You will want to read this, my lord.' She proudly placed a telegram upon his desk.

He picked it up and read it:

STORM FORCE ALPHA RETURNED INTACT STOP SOUTHERN STAR AND MONEY RECOVERED STOP MASTERMIND BEHIND TRAIN ROBBERY COLONEL CODY STOP APPREHENDED AND IN THE SAFE HANDS OF THE NORTH-WEST MOUNTED POLICE STOP TED SKERRAT AND GANG ALSO APPREHENDED STOP FOR DIPLOMACY'S SAKE HANDED OVER TO US AUTHORITIES STOP PLEASE PREPARE TICKETS AND JOURNEY FOR RETURN STOP CAN TRAVEL AT EARLIEST MOMENT STOP WILLIAM PRICE

Lord Porter placed the slip of paper deliberately down upon his desk.

'Hmm, wants to return, eh?' He rubbed his chin. 'You know Hannah, I've been thinking, it has been rather quiet of late without them being here… I'm not altogether convinced that we should have them back,' he declared.

Hannah looked at him; she narrowed her eyes and a mischievous smile fell upon her lips as she detected his dry humour. 'My lord, unless you wish to feel the wrath of a lady upon you, I suggest we make arrangements for their return,' she warned.

Lord Porter smiled. 'Yes, you're right of course.' He sat back in his chair. 'Oh, and please inform Whitehall of our success,' he ordered as Hannah hurried out of the room.

On reaching the doorway, she paused and turned to face him. 'My lord, more importantly, we can now give Madeleine a date with which to set her appointment in church with her betrothed,' she smiled.

'Oh yes, of course... more distractions! How can we defend the realm with everyone enjoying themselves and all these distractions going on?' Lord Porter responded.

A NEW CHAPTER

Hannah worked feverishly to have all the travel arrangements in place for Storm Force Alpha's return. In the meantime, as they rested at Paradise, two more Mounties had turned up to assist both Sergeant Hackett and Constable Adams in the escorting of Colonel Cody back to Jamestown. Further, as soon as he had rested sufficiently, Sergeant Hackett had taken a written statement from Lucy as to the events leading to the murder of her father; the Colonel was to stand trial for that in Montreal.

'You will now see justice, my dear,' announced Hackett as he rolled the statement up and slipped it into his briefcase. Paddy, Sandy and Will had been busying themselves digging graves for those who sadly were not to return, including Constable Courtney, who had fallen at Devil's Cut. A special ceremony was held for him, and the agents paid extra tribute by providing the armed guard.

Soon it was time for Sergeant Hackett to return; all was in place as he stepped out of the house one bright glorious morning. He stopped and turned on the porch. 'Are you sure you do not wish to ride with us back as far as Jamestown, Will?' he asked, smiling.

'Alas, the telegram will arrive here with our travel details, Sergeant, so it would be wiser to wait here,' explained Will, as he placed his hand upon the sergeant's good shoulder.

'Aye, be off with yer, Hackett, an' stop tryin' to drag ma guests away!' Murdoch smiled as he followed his friends outside. 'Ah've organised four o' ma best riders to escort yer all into Jamestown; Liam is in charge. He's a good man, Hackett, so don't try an' poach him.'

'As you know, Murdoch, I'm always on the lookout for good men,' smiled the sergeant as he glanced at Liam then back at Will, to whom he gave a quick wink.

'Yes, and don't think of poaching him either, Sergeant,' warned Charlotte as she stepped forward and held Will's arm gently.

The sergeant smiled and, having shaken everyone's hand in turn, he mounted his horse. 'Well, farewell, my friend – until next time.' He offered Murdoch his hand again and shook it. 'And I hope to see you again, Miss Lucy,' he added as he sat up and turned his horse.

The money from the train robbery had now been transferred into saddlebags for ease of transportation; these were placed upon the Mounties' horses.

'Don't even consider the possibility of losing them,' warned Will as he patted the saddlebag over Hackett's horse.

The sergeant smiled at them, 'Why, you could get to like it here,' he commented as he looked about him.

'That's just it, I could, but I have a very important appointment to keep back home,' Will smiled in return.

'Now don't yer go telling yer friends in the department that ah'm getting soft, 'cause ah'm not!' shouted Murdoch after his friend as he began to ride out of the corral.

Hackett stopped at the gate and looked back. 'What, you, Murdoch? No one would believe me.' He smiled yet again and, turning his horse, he rode away with his captives and escort.

'Aye, it'll be a bit quieter now around here,' sighed Murdoch. Turning, he watched Lucy and Charlotte disappear in to the house. Paddy stood next to the big Scotsman. 'But at least the days will be a bit brighter from now on.' He smiled at Paddy, who slapped him upon his shoulder as they followed the ladies into the house.

Will had strolled over to where Sandy stood by the log fence; his hands were in his pockets as he looked aimlessly south.

'What's the matter, Sandy? There is no problem, is there?' he asked his friend.

Sandy spun round. 'No, good heavens. I was just thinking,' he replied softly.

'You're not getting cold feet, are you?' Will asked, concerned.

Sandy smiled. 'No, definitely not. I feel honoured that she has chosen me as her betrothed, Will, but I do not wish to put extra stress or strain either upon her or the team,' he began to explain.

'Then why not simply declare your love for her and get engaged for now? You don't have to marry until the time is right to retire from this role,' Will pointed out. 'And that is something the pair of you can talk about and agree,' he assured Sandy.

'But *you're* getting married on our return, Will, so why are you telling me to wait?' Sandy asked puzzled.

Will smiled and placed his hand upon Sandy's shoulder. 'With me, my friend, it is a little different. I have Rosie to consider. She and Madeleine are getting along fine, thank heavens, so she would make the ideal guardian for my daughter and give her the stability and security she has been lacking all her young years,' he explained; he too now looked aimlessly south.

'Yes, you're quite right, we must chat,' announced Sandy as he stood up, followed by Will. Together they entered the house.

It was only a day or two later when the long-awaited telegram arrived from Hannah. Murdoch had taken it to Will as he sat upon a pile of logs; a meeting was quickly called for, and the decision – if one was needed – was made to return the very next morning. Both Murdoch and Lucy, who had now formed a very special friendship with Charlotte, came out to wish them bon voyage. Will held the diamond in its velvet pouch within his saddlebag.

'It's a bit lighter in there now with all that money gone,' he declared as he removed the stone for one last look.

'Ooh, isn't it wonderful!' exclaimed Lucy; it was the first time she had set eyes upon it.

'Beauty is only in the eyes of the beholder, an' ah can see that there are several people here now who might disagree that it is the most beautiful sight in the world,' announced Paddy.

Will glanced at his Irish friend and smiled. 'As always, my friend, you are quite right.' He slipped the stone back into its pouch, which in turn he placed within the saddlebag.

Charlotte had led Lucy to one side. 'You take care, if you are ever lonely or you wish someone to talk to…' Charlotte began… 'then look to the North Star; I shall be watching it also.' She smiled as she pointed at the sky.

They fell into a loving embrace as if they were two sisters saying their farewells.

'Oh, Charlotte,' Lucy began; her eyes flicked to a point just above Charlotte's left shoulder. 'Yer've all been so kind to me, but ah shan't never forget the kindness of yer man.' She smiled, and in her eye a tear formed, which she quickly wiped away, with a sniff. 'He is a very special man indeed.' They embraced once more.

'Thank you, Lucy. Yes, he is,' Charlotte turned to look at her betrothed with pride.

'If ah ever wished fer a sister, she would have been jist like yer, Charlotte,' announced a very tearful Lucy; Charlotte rejoined her friends.

'Two Crows here has volunteered to escort yer all to Jamestown,' announced Murdoch. 'Old habits die hard, or so it appears,' he added softly, almost sadly. He then stepped over to Charlotte and, gently holding her hands, he raised them to his chest. He smiled as he looked her squarely in the eye, then gently kissed each hand in turn. 'Now, lassie, yer take care, an' if that sailor boy doesn't appreciate yer enough, send fer me – ah'll sort him out!' he warned as he quickly glanced at Sandy.

'I think I can sort him out myself, Murdoch. Though I do appreciate the offer,' smiled Charlotte.

As he helped her up into her saddle, he squeezed her hand to gain her attention. 'Thank yer, lassie, fer makin' a sore bear see the error of his ways afore it was too late.' He smiled and stepped back.

Charlotte smiled back.

They then turned their horses as one and rode out slowly. At long last they were riding home, thought Will. A smile played gently upon his lips as he thought fondly of Madeleine and Rosie. Murdoch and Lucy followed them down to the corral gate, waving at their departing guests as they walked.

'We'll have the house all to ourselves now, lassie,' mused Murdoch as they turned and strolled back to the house.

She gently squeezed his arm. 'An' yer don't mind ma being here?' she asked once more, just to put her own mind at rest.

He paused and looked down at her. 'Naw lassie – why would

ah mind that?' He smiled as he embraced her gently as a friend. 'Now, go an' put the kettle on, an' we'll have a coffee. Ah have to send off a telegram an' prepare a list fer town tomorrow,' he announced as he led her into the house.

She paused in the doorway. 'Pinewood Falls, tomorrow?' she asked.

'Aye lassie, we'll be needin' some provisions,' explained Murdoch.

'An' who'll keep yer company on the journey?' she then enquired.

'Och, ah'll take one o' the cow hands.' Murdoch glanced towards the dormitory and nodded his head.

'Yer'll do no such thing, Murdoch McLeod! Ah shall come with yer,' she announced with a broad smile.

'Aye, that'll be jist fine,' he replied, smiling in return.

Next morning Murdoch drew the buck wagon up to the house door. He jumped down to the ground and stepped on to the porch to call for Lucy. She anticipated his move, reaching the door before him. He stopped, stunned. His jaw dropped, for in front of him stood a vision he never thought possible.

Lucy was stood in her white frilly dress, the one that Murdoch had purchased from the hardware store for her. It fitted her like a glove. Upon her head she wore the matching white hat, which she had tied around her neck with pink ribbons. A similar pink sash was worn about her slender waist; in her right hand she held a white parasol, and in her left she carried her matching bag, slung about her wrist by a cord. The whole was set off by two perfectly white boots which were just visible below her dress. She looked at him and smiled, fluttering her eyelashes as she did so. Murdoch could not move; he swallowed hard but could not do or say anything.

'Are yer all right, Murdoch?' she asked concerned.

He nodded like a shocked schoolboy and closed his mouth. He then opened the door and stepped to one side as she strolled past him.

'Ah do hope ah'm not overdressed.' She glanced at him over her shoulder as he hurried forward to help her up on to the wagon. Still he could not say a word; he just shook his head, dumbfounded.

They set off, still in silence. As Murdoch had helped Lucy onto the wagon, Buff had placed a picnic basket upon the back. This had been prepared by Lucy the evening before, with the intention of taking their time and halting for a snack on the way. This they did, and it was only then that Murdoch finally found his tongue.

'Yer an' apparition, Lucy,' he remarked admiringly, as they now sat upon a blanket he had laid upon the ground.

'Why, thank yer, Murdoch,' she replied.

'Ah never thought the dress would suit yer so well,' he added.

'Charlotte showed me how to wear it – ah don't want to let yer down, Murdoch,' she declared determinedly.

'Yer would never let me down, lassie,' he stated defiantly.

They had lunch then carried on as before, only this time chatting and laughing together over the innocent things in life. This made the second half of the journey pass all the quicker, and it seemed that in next to no time they arrived at the ford by Pinewood Falls. Murdoch halted the wagon before entering the river.

'Here we are – it hasn't taken long, has it?

'Time flies, when yer enjoying yersel',' she observed, squeezing his arm tenderly.

'Der yer still wish to go through with this?' he asked.

'Yes. A nice man once reminded me that they are no better than ourselves,' she replied thoughtfully.

'Yer stand head and shoulders above that lot, Lucy,' Murdoch proudly announced, as he urged the wagon forward.

They drove slowly into town; people stopped to watch, and occasionally voices could be heard. 'Who is that with Mad Dog?' 'Who is the pretty lady?' There were more soldiers than Murdoch could remember, and no Dixie riders. Murdoch carried on; he visibly grew upon his seat as he drew ever closer to the hardware store. Eventually the wagon stopped children who had hurried after it now rushed about the wagon to meet the pretty stranger.

'Ooh, Mister, who is the pretty lady?' asked a small girl to Murdoch.

'Och, now, run along, lassie; yer should not ask a princess fer her name,' replied Murdoch with a wink and a smile. Then, to everyone's surprise – least of all the children – he tossed out a handful of coins upon the ground and walkway.

'She's the prettiest princess ah've ever seen,' declared the young girl, as Murdoch helped Lucy down.

Mr Perkins hurried out of the store to see what all the commotion was about and abruptly stopped when he came face to face with Lucy and Murdoch.

'Who is the pretty lady?' came a voice from the now intrigued crowd.

Lucy turned to face the townsfolk. 'My name is Lucy Wightman – and don't you ever forget that,' she announced defiantly.

'Another of Charlotte's ideas?' asked Murdoch.

She turned to face him and smiled. 'No, mine actually,' she replied as he led her into the hardware store.

Ethel too had hurried to the door to meet the newcomers; she chatted away excitedly to Lucy. At the same time Murdoch was gaining up-to-date knowledge from Mr Perkins, such as how two bounty hunters had caught and brought Ted Skerrat and his gang in, how the sheriff and the Dixie riders were implicated, and how Barney and Bob were given an army escort to the Dakota Territory with their prisoners, both dead and alive.

On their return, Storm Force Alpha gave Jamestown but a fleeting visit; they were soon winding their way eastwards towards the Atlantic seaboard. Their journey was to take them firstly to Montreal, then onwards to Halifax in Nova Scotia. There they would meet their ship that would carry them towards Liverpool and home. The Atlantic crossing was calm and mild, and it was while they were aboard the steamship *Mercian Queen* that Charlotte and Paddy found themselves strolling about the promenade deck one evening.

'You were right, Paddy,' remarked Charlotte casually as she held his arm and glanced out at the dark horizon.

'Oh? Right about what?' he asked.

'About me finding Mr Right.' She glanced at him and smiled.

'Of course I was. I keep telling you I have a nose for these things.' He smiled in return.

'You knew it was Sandy, didn't you?' She then squeezed his arm.

'Well, my dear, it was certainly not going to take a mathematician to work that one out.' He glanced down at her and gave a mischievous smile. 'Anyway, what plans have you now for your leave?' he asked.

'Oh, Sandy has promised to take me to Paris,' she explained excitedly, then realised what she had said. 'Oh, but Paddy... what of *your* plans? I hope it will not spoil them,' she said apologetically.

He laughed slightly. 'My dearest Charlotte, I have but a small confession to make.' He cleared his throat, as she now searched his face for clues. 'I never did actually make arrangements for yourself to travel this time to Ireland.' He paused.

'Sean O'Brien, you *knew*, didn't you?' she teased him, squeezing his arm again.

He smiled in return. 'Talking of which, where is our lucky fellow?' he asked, trying to change the subject.

'Probably up here somewhere sat watching the stars as usual,' she replied jovially.

Just then Sandy approached them from the opposite direction. 'May I cut in?' he asked Paddy, taking Charlotte's hand.

'Yer may – no doubt yer have a few things to discuss.' He released over Charlotte's hand and winked at Sandy as he strolled off on his merry way.

Sandy led Charlotte back the way she had come.

'What did he mean, "things to discuss"?' she asked searchingly.

Sandy stopped and smiled; he clasped her hand in both of his. 'My dearest Charlie, as we sat below the stars in Montana, I meant every word of what I said to you. I am more than honoured for you to declare me as your betrothed. However, because of the nature of our work and the fact that I do not wish to place any undue stress or threat upon your person, I feel that we should not get married until we retire from our posts...' he explained.

She walked along with Sandy step for step, listening to him intently as he spoke to her. Before they knew where they were they stood next to a seat, which they took advantage of and sat down together, their hands still clasped. She smiled at him once he had finished.

'Sandy, I have told you before that I never thought that I could find love within my heart for any man, let alone a sailor. Now that I have found you, I do not wish to let you go lightly.' She placed her free hand upon his.

He glanced down at their hands then quickly back into her eyes. 'Then we must make an appointment upon our return to England, my dearest,' began Sandy.

'Oh? With whom?' she asked, concerned.

'Before we hand that stone over to Her Majesty, my own princess shall have one for her own hand,' Sandy declared as he kissed her hand gently.

'Oh, Sandy!' she cried and they fell into a loving embrace.

The journey from Nova Scotia back to Liverpool took seven days. For Charlotte and Sandy it did not feel like five minutes; for Will on the other hand, it felt like four weeks. Each morning he would be found upon the boat deck looking eastward, as if urging the ship onwards at greater speed. He could not wait to be by Madeleine's side and to play with his Rosie once again. Since they had met just over a year ago now, Lord Porter had quite happily agreed to allow them to live together in one of his cottages on his land at Drumloch. They had become so, so happy and he could not wait for the sight of Liverpool. Eventually, the morning arrived when the vessel docked in Liverpool. Will and the others met in his cabin to await customs clearance; he held his rail tickets for Glasgow in his hands as a child would hold a bar of chocolate, when a knock came upon the door.

Will glanced about the group, surprised. They in turn looked at him, just as puzzled.

'Well, aren't yer going to answer it?' questioned Paddy at length.

The knock came again, and Will now opened the door to find a bellboy stood there. 'Sorry to trouble you, sir; there is a gentleman at the purser's desk who wishes to speak to you.' The boy hesitated. 'All of you,' he added, then turned and hurried off.

Will turned to the others; they all glanced at each other, surprised and not a little suspicious.

'Who on earth could it be?' Will asked, puzzled.

'Don't know, but let's not take any risks,' replied Sandy as he now placed his wrist gun on, then cocked it.

Paddy and Charlotte followed suit.

'As requested, I shall approach the purser's desk; you lot keep me covered. Any funny business, then let them have it – but don't let them see you,' ordered Will. He picked up his bag and, turning, left his cabin, followed by his friends.

They hurried down to the area in front of the ship's desk. Will glanced over his shoulder at his friends before turning the corridor corner. Then, with a deep breath he stepped around the corner to face Lord Porter.

'Ah, there you are, my man; good show, what,' Lord Porter declared as he caught sight of Will.

'My lord, what brings you here?' questioned Will suspiciously.

Lord Porter at first ignored him and glanced over Will's shoulder. 'Ah, there's your team. Come here.' He gestured them forward.

They moved forward quickly and he led them into the ship's office, where Hannah stood quite alone.

'Hannah!' cried Charlotte; the two ladies met and embraced one another like two long lost friends.

Lord Porter stood apart, looking Will up and down. 'I informed Whitehall of your success, and they quickly passed the message on to Her Majesty. She was so grateful for what you had done that she wishes to thank you personally at Buckingham Palace.' He patted Will upon the arm and looked him in the eye proudly.

'Oh, I shall need to purchase a new dress,' announced Charlotte excitedly.

'Well, I, er… That's wonderful, my lord, but I had hoped just to go home and see Madeleine,' Will responded. His eyes fell to the floor and he sounded terribly disappointed.

'What!' exclaimed Lord Porter. 'This is a great honour, man. Not only for yourselves but the organisation, too!' he boomed.

Hannah cleared her throat, catching everyone's attention. She then moved over to a side door and opened it. Immediately a young girl came hurrying in.

'Daddy, Daddy!' she squealed in excitement as she ran to Will, arms outstretched.

Will bent down as if poleaxed and gathered up his little bundle of joy. 'Rosie,' he was heard to say, burying his face in her neck as they cuddled.

Lord Porter sighed indignantly and stamped his walking cane off the deck in disgust. 'Do you think that for one minute I would have kept you from you family unnecessarily?'

Madeleine had by now quietly stepped into the room, unannounced. She stood to one side until Will noticed her; placing Rosie down on the floor, he rushed over to his betrothed and they embraced.

'As I said all these distractions… It simply is not on, is it, men?' he turned and asked both Sandy and Paddy.

Sandy stood and coughed in embarrassment, while Paddy looked at Lord Porter.

'I totally agree, my lord – terrible, isn't it?' He slapped the lord upon his left shoulder, almost knocking him to the ground.

The moment was not lost upon Hannah though. 'Charlotte… Sandy… does this mean…?' she asked excitedly.

Charlotte's face lit up in a great big smile; she nodded excitedly. 'It does,' was all she could say.

'Oh, congratulations to you, Charlotte – to the pair of you,' expressed Hannah as she embraced Charlotte once more.

'Oh Lord, does this mean what I think it means?' groaned Lord Porter.

'It sure does,' replied Paddy with a smile.

They all hurried from the ship for their train from Lime Street Station. The journey passed by in a blur as they all chatted excitedly. Will travelled down with his Rosie and Madeleine in one compartment while the others travelled down in another. They soon – or so it appeared – arrived in London. As they stepped off the train, Will took in a deep breath of air.

'Ah, smell that smog – welcome home to London,' he declared to the others, who sniggered.

'As I thought,' Lord Porter whispered to Hannah, 'all this stress affects the brain.'

Hannah smiled and glanced at him. 'Yes, my lord, so what is your excuse?' Again they all laughed. She then turned to Charlotte. 'As we are not due to meet Her Majesty until tomorrow morning, you may wish to purchase your dress this afternoon, Charlotte,' she suggested.

'Oh yes, most definitely,' agreed Charlotte, as she linked Hannah's arm.

'Not so quick, not so quick,' stalled Sandy. 'Have you not forgot our little date?' he questioned Charlotte.

'Oh yes.' She quickly turned to Hannah. 'May Sandy come, too?'

'Why of course, if he wishes,' replied Hannah, puzzled.

'Not to worry, Hannah; that shall not be necessary. I know exactly where I'm taking you, Charlotte. We shall only be gone some thirty minutes at the most; we shall then meet you all at the hotel,' Sandy announced as he led Charlotte away, leaving Paddy to carry their bags.

'Oh, great! This is how they intend to treat their friends – as packhorses!' he declared indignantly.

'Well, to be honest, Paddy, I can see the resemblance,' replied Will casually.

Sandy led Charlotte to a row of cabs, quickly helped her into the first, then they sped off.

'Sandy, where on earth are you taking me?' protested Charlotte. 'I really do require a new dress for tomorrow.'

'Yes, I know, my sweet, but first I must purchase and place upon your finger a ring that I first saw a year ago,' Sandy explained.

'A year ago!' Charlotte exclaimed.

'Yes, the first time we came here,' he said quickly. Soon the cab drew to a halt, and out leaped Sandy as if his life depended upon it. He helped Charlotte down to the pavement; she noticed they were stood outside a jeweller's.

She looked at him, an excited smile falling across her face. 'Sandy... my ring?' she said.

'Yes, my dearest. Come, let's see if it will fit.' He hurried her into the shop. There she was introduced to what appeared to be the *second* biggest diamond in the world. It was placed upon Charlotte's finger, and was a perfect fit. Sandy then led her back to the cab, which in turn began to whisked them back through the cobbled streets of London. She continually looked at her finger, admiring the glinting stone upon it.

'If we swap them, do you think Her Majesty would notice?' teased Sandy as he held her hand.

'I wouldn't want to swap them, my dearest; this is the perfect diamond for me,' she remarked; a tear formed in her eye.

'Oh, I'm sorry, Charlotte, I did not wish to upset you,' apologised Sandy.

'Oh, you big oaf, I'm not upset – this is so far the happiest day of my life. It is only a shame that my mother is not here to see it,' Charlotte said sadly.

'She'll be here, Charlie. She'll be here for her little girl,' assured Sandy as they sat back in each other's arms.

On their arrival at the hotel, they were ushered into a side room, where their friends all stood.

'I took the liberty of ordering some champagne to mark the occasion,' declared Lord Porter, as he held up a glass. 'A toast to Charlotte and Sandy – may they be happy, healthy and wealthy,' he announced.

The others all followed before Hannah and Madeleine hurried about Charlotte to view her ring.

'Yer do realise that yer will have to remove that ring when we go operational, don't yer?' announced Paddy.

'Yes, of course I do,' Charlotte replied.

'Good, because we don't want the enemy seeing us when we are still miles away,' he chuckled.

Charlotte did not reply but she narrowed her eyes and looked at him threateningly.

'Right, Charlotte. Madeleine and I are taking you shopping – come on,' announced Hannah, as she led Charlotte back out through the foyer.

The men quickly filled Lord Porter in on a few minor details about the operation before the report was handed in.

'Oh, and Murdoch McLeod sends his regards, my lord,' added Sandy as an afterthought.

'Oh yes, Mad Dog McLeod – a real firebrand he was too,' recalled Lord Porter, as he thought of his one-time sergeant. 'A very brave man, a good man to have in a tight squeeze.'

The others smiled.

Next morning, they all met downstairs in the reception area. Lord Porter was a little nervous as he checked everybody off.

'Everyone all right, are we?' he asked anxiously.

'Yes, my lord, everyone is fine,' assured Hannah.

'Do we all know the protocol for such an occasion, and where to stand?' he fussed.

'Yes, my lord, we went through this last night,' replied Hannah.

'Will, you still have the diamond, don't you?' he then asked.

Will smiled and nodded. 'Yes, my lord, it is still here in this velvet pouch,' he said as he held it up for all to see.

Satisfied, Lord Porter then led them out into the street, where they clambered into two carriages that had been waiting for them. Lord Porter was to travel in the first with Will, Madeleine and Rosie, while Hannah would travel with Paddy, Charlotte and Sandy. The journey to Buckingham Palace did not take long, and soon they were deposited outside the grand building, within the courtyard. Here Hannah, Madeleine and Rosie were taken to a side room, while the others were led into a large, very elegant room. The footman announced them and then they were led in to face Her Majesty Queen Victoria. She elegantly held out her hand for Lord Porter to take.

'My dear Lord Porter, how nice to see you once again.' She turned her attention to the four members of the team stood behind Lord Porter in a line, as if for inspection.

'Your Majesty, may we present you with an item that is yours by right, but which we found lost.' Will bowed and stepped forward; he held out his hand in which the velvet pouch sat.

Lord Porter took it from Will's hand and give it to Her Majesty, who took it gently. Without opening the pouch she turned once more to face the members of Storm Force Alpha.

'My dear friends, I have but only recently heard of your exploits, which in view of what dangers you face on my behalf I feel is a great shame. You may never receive the just recognition or rewards that your exploits deserve – and probably more so than those less deserving as yourselves in your defence of the realm. So please never forget my unrelenting admiration and appreciation of your services, given and still to give on both my and my subjects' behalf.' She smiled majestically at them as they stood to attention.

'Now, Lord Porter, please introduce me to your gallant members,' she asked.

Lord Porter bowed, as best he could. 'Certainly, ma'am.' He then stood up and with his right hand gestured to Will, who bowed as his name was declared. 'This is the team leader, William Price, ma'am,' he began. Then he took one step and introduced Charlotte, who curtsied and bowed her head. 'Miss Charlotte Nicholson; Mr Sean O'Brien.' He bowed in his turn. 'And finally but not least, Mr Alexander McBride, ma'am.' He followed the others and bowed in his turn. Lord Porter then stood to attention himself and joined the line as he finished the introductions; turning to their left they all began to walk out, dignified, following their very proud leader. As the door was closed behind them he turned to face them all.

'Well, done all of you. There was a time during the operation when I did fear for you all. But I did not inform Madeleine – nor did anyone else, for that matter,' he added for Will's benefit.

'Thank you, my lord,' responded Will.

'Now then, let us return to Drumloch, where you have an important appointment I believe.' He patted Will upon the shoulder then turned and limped away to the courtyard. There, Hannah, Madeleine and Rosie were all stood waiting for them to return.

Again the journey north towards Glasgow was not as long as any of them cared to remember. They chatted freely about everything, laughing and joking like a bunch of excited schoolchildren. Even Lord Porter became infected as he gave anecdote after anecdote about his old army days, especially those that he could remember about Murdoch and the Sudan.

Paddy too was able to add his best Irish humour to the scene, until Hannah asked, 'Can everyone present play similes?'

'Why yes, we can,' Will replied.

'Right then, we shall all play similes, I shall be host and we shall begin with you, my lord.'

'Oh dear, must we?' he groaned, to the amusement of the others.

'Yes, now listen. As black as…?' Hannah then asked him.

'Oh,' he raised a finger in acknowledgement. 'That's coal,' he answered.

'Good,' replied Hannah. 'Now, Sandy. As pure as…?' she asked.

'The driven snow,' replied Sandy.

'Good. Charlotte, as bright as…?'

Charlotte held a finger to her mouth. 'Oh dear, as bright as…' She glanced at Sandy. 'As the north star.' She laughed at her own folly.

'No, you're quite wrong; it's "as bright as a button",' declared Hannah, as she too smiled. 'Your out, I'm afraid, Charlotte. Now Paddy, as proud as…?' Hannah asked.

'A peacock?' Paddy replied without hesitation.

Hannah smiled. 'Yes, now Will: as quick as…?'

'Oh heck,' he struggled, the others laughed. 'I haven't a clue,' he admitted.

'As quick as a wink,' Hannah smiled. 'Now then, Madeleine, as keen as…?'

'Will trying to get home,' joked Sandy.

Everyone laughed. The game took up the rest of the journey and they entered Glasgow in next to no time.

As the bells rang out at the small church within the village of Glenmuir, the nearest village to Drumloch, and a handsomely polished black carriage arrived at the gates. Lord Porter stepped down from the carriage; turning, he assisted a beautiful Madeleine down to the pavement. She was dressed in white with a beautiful floral tiara worn in her hair. Once Hannah and Charlotte had helped sort out her train, he offered her his arm. This she took with a smile; since her arrival the year previous they had all become firm friends.

Lord Porter proudly and elegantly led the bride into the church, followed by Hannah, Charlotte, and of course Rosie as bridesmaids. They waited passively at the back of the church as the congregation all stood. Paddy, as best man, pushed and prodded Will into place, and Sandy stood to one side at the end of the aisle as usher. He winked at Charlotte and smiled as she gracefully glided past him to the strains of the wedding march played out upon the church organ. The vicar then led them through the ceremony, and at the end, Will turned to give Madeleine a loving kiss.

'Come on, Mrs Price, now that we have all of the love in the world, what we require is time,' smiled Will as he led his new bride back down towards the church doorway.

Outside in the glorious sunshine, Madeleine turned her back to the waiting ladies and threw her bouquet over her head. It was caught by Elizabeth, who leapt up and down excitedly.

'Never mind, old chap,' smiled Sandy as he patted Charles upon his back. 'It could be worse.'

'How on earth is that?' asked Charles indignantly.

'Paddy could have caught it.' Sandy smiled as he walked off.

Paddy stood next to Hannah as they cheered and waved the newlyweds off.

'I did not see you put up much of a struggle to catch that, Hannah,' he said in passing.

Hannah glanced at him and smiled. 'I'm afraid my time is too busy being taken up with all of this,' she explained, raising her hands.

'You should get out more; all work an' no play makes Jack a dull boy,' smiled Paddy.

'Maybe, but where would I go? There is only my father's,' Hannah stated.

'Well, that's a start. Have none of the single fellows offered to show you about the country?' he asked.

'No, most certainly not, Sean! What kind of lady do you take me for?'

'A little lonely perhaps,' he answered perceptively.

'What do you mean, sir?' she declared sharply.

Paddy turned to face her and smiled. 'If you wish, the next time I go, I shall take you to Ireland. How's that?' he offered.

She smiled back. 'I'm sorry, Sean – that would be most delightful; yes, I would like that very much.' She watched him as he nodded and then stepped away.

Charlotte stepped up to her. 'Are you all right?'

'Yes, Charlotte, and you?' Hannah replied.

'I'm fine – and very excited,' Charlotte went on.

'Of course… forgive me, Charlotte.' She turned and smiled at her young friend. 'When are you going?' Hannah then asked.

'As soon as the reception is over. We're heading to Newcastle first, then on to Paris,' Charlotte explained excitedly.

Hannah smiled. 'I'm very happy for you, Charlotte. But are you not a little nervous – of meeting his family, I mean?'

'Yes, very. But as Sandy said, I must meet them one day.' She shrugged her shoulders.

'I'm sure they will be fine,' assured Hannah.

'Yes, I'm sure they will,' she replied. Her eyes fell upon Sandy as he helped Madeleine into the carriage before it pulled away.

Printed in the United Kingdom by
Lightning Source UK Ltd., Milton Keynes
138396UK00001B/8/P

9 781847 484628